D1351466

Constructing Crime

Also by Christiana Gregoriou

DEVIANCE IN CONTEMPORARY CRIME FICTION

ENGLISH LITERARY STYLISTICS

LANGUAGE, IDEOLOGY AND IDENTITY IN SERIAL KILLER NARRATIVES

Constructing Crime

Discourse and Cultural Representations of Crime and 'Deviance'

Edited by

Christiana Gregoriou
Lecturer in English Language, School of English,
University of Leeds, UK

First published 2012 by
PALGRAVE MACMILLAN

Palgrave Macmillan in the UK is an imprint of Macmillan Publishers Limited,
registered in England, company number 785998, of Houndmills, Basingstoke,
Hampshire RG21 6XS.

Palgrave Macmillan in the US is a division of St Martin's Press LLC,
175 Fifth Avenue, New York, NY 10010.

Palgrave Macmillan is the global academic imprint of the above companies
and has companies and representatives throughout the world.

Palgrave® and Macmillan® are registered trademarks in the United States,
the United Kingdom, Europe and other countries.

ISBN 978–0–230–29977–1

This book is printed on paper suitable for recycling and made from fully
managed and sustained forest sources. Logging, pulping and manufacturing
processes are expected to conform to the environmental regulations of the
country of origin.

A catalogue record for this book is available from the British Library.

A catalog record for this book is available from the Library of Congress.

10   9   8   7   6   5   4   3   2   1
21 20 19 18 17 16 15 14 13 12

Printed and bound in Great Britain by
CPI Antony Rowe, Chippenham and Eastbourne

Contents

Tables, Figures and Illustrations

Tables

Figures

Illustrations

The images in Illustrations 3.2.1–3.2.3 are reproduced by kind permission of the Syndics of Cambridge University Library

Preface

Crime and criminals are a pervasive theme in all areas of our culture, including media and journalism, film and literary fiction. But how is crime constructed and culturally represented, and how would scholars working in different disciplines contribute to a better understanding of crime's construction? Crime studies has become increasingly crucial across a variety of academic disciplines – from classics to forensics, from health and safety studies to English literature and film, from cultural studies to criminology and sociology – while crime fiction continues to be the top-selling form of genre fiction, not only in Britain but also elsewhere.

As a response to the study of crime fiction and culture undergoing a considerable expansion, the Crime Studies Network was inaugurated in 2008, an association to foster cross-institutional and interdisciplinary collaboration on all topics pertaining to the study and representations of crime. With an aim to facilitate and support research between an international group of scholars of crime in cultural studies, criminology, law and the humanities, we originally established a JISC mailing list and have since organised conferences in Leeds and Newcastle, not to mention set up a charter, blog and website.[1] Via this network, which I am currently chairing, scholars working in crime studies were invited to submit abstracts exploring critical approaches to the construction of crime and deviance, cross-institution and cross-discipline. Colleagues were drawn from disciplines including literary studies, linguistics and other humanities and social sciences, while possible topics for discussion included 'popular discourses of deviance', 'representation of mass and serial killers', 'crime and mental illness', 'social justice and detective fiction', 'crime literature, drama and film', 'linguistic approaches to crime and punishment', 'the courtroom in fact and fiction' and 'crime and narrative structure'.

I settled on 15 chapters for the *Constructing Crime* collection, organised into four overarching sections:

1. **Constructing Criminal Facts** (four chapters, from criminology, English, linguistics-communication studies, and law).
2. **Constructing Criminal Fictions** (four chapters, from critical and cultural studies, Victorian and contemporary literature, and music).

3. **Constructing Social Identities and Wrongdoings** (four chapters, from linguistics, Spanish, postcolonial literature and disability studies)
4. **Constructing Gendered Crime** (three chapters, from English and women's studies)

This collection offers a mixture of chapters from leading figures, other established academics and several up-and-coming voices (see the Notes on contributors and also the section introductions), all of whom agree that the construction of crime is a fascinating field and one that concerns a whole *range* of not only academic subjects, but indeed areas of life. On a personal note, it is also a field that never fails to amaze me. I only hope that this collection has the same effect on you.

Christiana Gregoriou
Leeds, UK
September 2011

Note

1. For the Crime Studies Network, a grouping that aims to foster interdisciplinary collaboration on all aspects of crime and its representation in literature and the media, see www.crimestudies.net.

Notes on Contributors

Charlotte Beyer is Senior Lecturer in English Literature at the University of Gloucestershire. Beyer has published articles on Margaret Atwood, recent book chapters on Willa Cather's journalism (Routledge, 2007) and 'the boy detective' (McFarland, 2010), and has recent and forthcoming articles on contemporary women's writing and on crime fiction.

Richard Brown is Reader in Modern Literature at the University of Leeds. His *Companion to James Joyce* (Wiley-Blackwell) is now in paperback. Recent essays on crime include 'A wilderness of mirrors: The mediated Berlin backgrounds for Ian McEwan's *The Innocent*' in *Anglistik* (Heidelberg), 21(2), February 2010.

Martyn Colebrook is in the final stages of a PhD focusing on the works of Iain Banks. He has published chapters on 'Don DeLillo and terorrism', 'J. G. Ballard', 'Gothic fiction and mental disorder' and 'Paul Auster, the music of chance and alienation'.

Malcah Effron (PhD, Newcastle University) is currently Adjunct Faculty at the Community College of Baltimore County. Effron has presented papers on detective fiction internationally. Her publications include articles in the *Journal of Narrative Theory* and *Narrative*, and she is the editor of *The Millennial Detective: Essays in Crime Fiction 1990–2010*.

Lucy Evans is Lecturer in Postcolonial Literature at the University of Leicester, UK. She has published articles in the *Journal of Commonwealth Literature*, *Moving Worlds*, the *Caribbean Quarterly* and *Atlantic Studies*. She has also co-edited a collection of essays, *The Caribbean Short Story: Critical Perspectives* (Peepal Tree Press, 2011).

Christiana Gregoriou is a stylistician and an English Language lecturer at Leeds University's School of English. Her recent publications include a 'Crime Files' series monograph on *Deviance in Contemporary Crime Fiction* (Palgrave, 2007) and a critical stylistics monograph on *Language, Ideology and Identity in Serial Killer Narratives* (Routledge, 2011).

David Ireland is a film music psychologist currently completing a PhD at the School of Music, University of Leeds, supervised by Dr Luke Windsor and Professor David Cooper. Ireland's doctoral research, which seeks to theorise incongruent film music, is funded by a Leeds University Research Scholarship.

Michelle E. Iwen recently completed her PhD in Critical and Cultural Theory at Cardiff University. She currently manages the Creative Writing programme at Arizona State University and teaches English at Mesa Community College. Her work has appeared in the journals *Gender Forum* (2009) and *Assuming Gender* (2010).

Mandy Koolen is a Lecturer in English and Women's Studies at Laurentian University. Her recent publications include a paper entitled 'Historical fiction and the revaluing of historical continuity in Sarah Waters's *Tipping the Velvet*' (*Contemporary Literature*, 2010) and 'Masculine trans-formations in Jackie Kay's *Trumpet*' (*Atlantis*, 2010).

Stuart Murray is Professor of Contemporary Literatures and Film, and Director of Medical Humanities Research, in the School of English at the University of Leeds. He is the author of *Representing Autism: Culture, Narrative, Fascination* (Liverpool University Press, 2008) and *Autism* (Routledge, 2011), as well as numerous articles on disability representation.

Alison Sinclair is Professor of Modern Spanish Literature and Intellectual History at the University of Cambridge, and has worked most recently on the history of sexuality in Spain and on her 2009 monograph, *Trafficking Knowledge in Twentieth-Century Spain* (Boydell and Brewer). Her current research relates to her AHRC-funded project, 'Wrongdoing in Spain 1808–1936: Realities, representations, reactions'.

Ulrike Tabbert is a part-time PhD student of English Language at the University of Huddersfield. She holds a German law degree and works for a prosecution office in Germany. Her research focuses on the linguistic construction of offenders, victims and crimes in the British and German press.

Pinelopi Troullinou is a Research Assistant for the EU fp7 project ICT ethics, and PhD candidate at the University of Leeds. She holds two MAs: one in Bioethics and one in Communications Studies. Her research interests focus on biometrics, surveillance studies and resistance to digital surveillance.

David S. Wall is Professor of Criminology at Durham University, where he researches and teaches cybercrime, policing and intellectual property crime. He has published a wide range of articles and books on these subjects, which include among others *Cybercrime: The Transformation of Crime in the Information Age* (Polity, 2007).

Tony Ward is a legal scholar and criminologist with research interests in issues relating to expert evidence, and in the criminal behaviour of governments and their officials. He is a Reader in Law at the University of Hull, and his recent publications include *Law and Crime* (with Gerry Johnstone, Sage, 2010).

Kate Watson received her PhD in English Literature from Cardiff University in 2010. She would like to thank the Arts and Humanities Research Council for their research support and PhD scholarship. Her recent publications include 'The hounds of fortune: Dog detection in the nineteenth century' (*Clues*, 2011) and a forthcoming monograph with McFarland & Co. (2012).

1
Constructing Criminal Facts

1.0
Introduction and Rationale

Crime is a phenomenon observable all around us, but to what extent are narratives surrounding real crime constructing possible worlds that are in fact far from the real one? This section explores the way in which criminal discourses are indeed needlessly constructing myths, generating fear and panic, even allowing a hindering of our personal freedoms and rights. David Wall addresses this very issue in relation to the cultural construction of cybercrime, a term whose current meaning he examines, before observing that cybercrime-related narratives have a certain assuredness. Besides, despite cybercrime originating in narratives of fiction, our understanding of it, Wall claims, shapes how we all societally react to online deviance in real life. Christiana Gregoriou and Pinelopi Troullinou scrutinise another contemporary crime-related phenomenon, the fear of terrorist air attacks, itself employed to create justification for the imposing of extreme security measures on flying passengers in some UK airports. By linguistically and philosophically investigating the ways in which the media reacted to the use of full-body scanning in given UK airports, the authors question whether such measures in fact harvest a surveillance society, paranoia, poor health and even xenophobia. In a related chapter, Tony Ward interrogates the difficulty of exploring the truth in delayed civil actions for child abuse. Can the construction of past crimes be anything more than an 'account', and how do these narratives provide structure for events from the far past that can never be fully knowable? Finally, Martyn Colebrook investigates Burn's true crime work, observing different discourses at work, similarly questioning the linkage between fact and fiction, memory and allusion.

1.1
The Devil Drives a Lada: The Social Construction of Hackers as Cybercriminals[1]

David S. Wall

A senior police officer recently described to me a serious dilemma that he had just faced. The officer had received reliable intelligence that a serious financial crime had been committed by an East European Mafia group using a computer located within his police force area. Early one morning, anticipating stiff resistance, he sent an armed unit to the house containing the computer. After breaking down the door, his officers were shocked to find a sleepy breakfasting family, rather than the violent mafia gang they had expected to meet. On this occasion, the police had chosen the wrong course of action, because the family's computer had been infected by malicious software and used remotely by fraudsters as part of a botnet (robot network).

This simple vignette graphically illustrates how new forms of understanding are required about crimes relating to the internet (cybercrimes) that fall outside routine police activities. It also indicates how the senior officer's actions were influenced by the cultural constructions of cybercrime and cybercriminals that shape the relationships between the technical and the social. Furthermore, in the above case, the 'culture of fear' around cybercrime, which heightens public fear and anxiety (explained in detail below), had created a situation where the senior officer was criticised for overreacting, but, had he not acted in the way that he did, would have been equally criticised for not protecting his officers and the public.

It will be argued in this chapter that the roots of cybercrime are cultural rather than scientific, and that they shape the way in which we view and react societally to online deviance. It is important to understand this relationship, because it also frames legal and policy responses to cybercrime. The first part of this chapter will emphasise the normative nature of the term 'cybercrime'. The second part will explore the role of cyberpunk literature in developing the basic cultural conceptualisation

4

of cybercrime. The third part will look at the way in which those concepts have been strengthened in hacker-related movies and media. The fourth part will show how the hacker narrative has been strengthened by dystopic fiction and then perpetuated by the culture of fear and flaws in the news-production process.

Cybercrime and the cybercriminal

'Cybercrime' is a normatively laden concept, and simple mention of it invokes dramatic images of planes falling from the skies, nuclear power stations in various states of meltdown, bank accounts haemorrhaging, evil paedophiles grooming innocents and so on. Similarly, the very mention of the word 'cybercriminal' equally conjures up stereotypical and dramatic mental images of legions of young hackers: introverted and unshaven Russian males glued to their computer hacking into the bank accounts of innocent westerners at the behest of some bejewelled Russian crime baron whose other interests include drugs, prostitution, people trafficking and child pornography. Indeed, the etymology of the term 'hacker' is also normatively laden, as it initially described those who illicitly explored (hacked) forbidden spaces such as roofs and tunnels and was then adopted by MIT computer scientists (Harvey 1985). Until early 2010, when the paper on which this chapter is based was first delivered to the Constructing Crime workshop in Leeds, the reader only had to type the words 'hackers attack' into a search engine and the first page of results would be populated by stories about Chinese hackers attacking Google, Russian hackers attacking Estonia, Iranian hackers attacking China, Romanian hackers attacking the *Daily Telegraph*, not to mention the ongoing saga of (alleged) Israeli hackers attacking Iran using the sophisticated Stuxnet worm. Since mid-2010, the highly publicised exploits of the political hacker (hacktivist) groups Anonymous and LulzSec, working in support of Wikileaks and other causes, have overshadowed such headlines following their successful reprisal attacks on the websites of key institutions.[2] At the time of writing in 2011, it is too early to tell whether their publicity-seeking activities are changing the hacker stereotype in ways other than simply to strengthen it (Mansfield-Devine 2011:5). What is certain is that the hard mental images conjured up by the emotive terminology that is used contrast with the rather sad pictures of lone, dejected, young hackers being led to jail handcuffed to law enforcement officers, images that are usually accompanied by inconclusive descriptions of their actions that never seem to match the drama of the initial media reporting of their exploits.

The most striking observation from the contrast between imagery and reality is not that hacking is a fiction, for it certainly does take place and has some serious, damaging consequences for society and its infrastructure. Nor is it the predictable post-glasnost reconstruction of the cold-war bogeymen attacking the cherished icons of the West. Rather, what is prominent is the unquestioning assuredness of commentators, policy makers, law enforcement officers and all other actors involved in cybersecurity about who the hackers are and the seriousness of what they have done, even though the dogmatic headlines and some of the available evidence often place speculation above the facts.[3] Why, then, do these expectations as to who the hackers are exist, and why do we 'naturally' expect cybercrime to be dramatic, when both are not necessarily evidenced by fact? Indeed, it almost feels wrong to think otherwise, which begs the question: Does the (folk) devil actually drive a Lada or do we just think he does, and why do we assume that he is a he?

Questioning these assumptions is very important, because they obfuscate some very important distinctions between cybercriminals. Hackers, for example, fall into three different groups (Wall 2007:55, 61). The first are the ethical or 'white hat' hackers, who are driven by ethical motivations, usually relating to improving computing security. The second are the unethical or 'black hat' hackers, who are mainly driven by the prospect of financial gain. The third are the hacktivists (such as Anonymous and LulzSec), who are driven by political motivation or revenge. While the first and third categories tend to seek public recognition as a group and in some cases as individuals, the second does not. Furthermore, whatever gender, ethnic origin, age and so on they may be, the unethical hackers will try to keep as low a profile as possible; if they do have to be visible for some reason or another, then they are likely to present themselves as close to the prevailing cybercriminal stereotype as they can, in order to put pursuers off the trail. How, then, has the fixation with the hacker criminal stereotype arisen?

Although 'cybercrime' (and de facto the term 'cybercriminal') was originally a social science fictional construction without an original reference point in law, science or social action, it has come to symbolise online insecurity and risk. It is widely used today to describe the crimes or harms that are committed using networked technologies. It is also often used metaphorically and emotively, rather than rationally, to express ambivalent and general concerns about hacking. Yet 'cybercrime', a fictional construction, is gradually entering formal legal terminology to describe computer misuse, no doubt partly due to the use of the term in naming the 2001 Council of Europe Cybercrime Convention

(ETS No. 185); see also Australia (Cybercrime Act 2001), Nigeria (Draft Cybercrime Act) and the United States (proposed Cybercrime Act 2007). Even the United Kingdom has introduced a Cyber Crime Strategy (Home Office 2010). The irony here is that many of the so-called cybercrimes covered by media reportage are not necessarily crimes in criminal law, nor are they variations of traditional forms of offending (Wall 2007:10). So why does the term cybercrime carry so much baggage? This 'baggage' exists because cybercrime is the product of a security discourse that has been shaped by a process of cultural construction rooted in social science fiction and other relevant genres.

Social science fiction and cyberpunk

The cultural baggage of cybercrime can be traced back to the cyberpunk social science fiction literature of the 1970s and 1980s. Cyberpunk authors combined cybernetics with the culture of the contemporary punk movement to form a genre of science fiction that thematically joined ideas about dystopic advances in science and information technology with their potential capability to break down the social order. As Person (1998:1) observed, the '[c]lassic cyberpunk characters were marginalized, alienated loners who lived on the edge of society in futures where daily life was impacted by rapid technological change, an ubiquitous datasphere of computerized information and invasive modification of the human body'. The cyberpunk leitmotif was essentially a 'high-tech but low-life' aesthetic, and the 'classic cyberpunk characters' described by Person became a social blueprint for the hacker stereotype.

The origins of the term 'cyberspace' appear to lie in Gibson's 1982 highly influential short story 'Burning Chrome' about the hacker group Cyberspace Seven.[4] The story was published in *Omni Magazine* (1978–98), a science-fiction-meets-hard-science forum that promoted explorations into cyberpunk. Along with other science fiction forums, novels and films during the 1980s, *Omni* contributed to the progressive definition of 'cyberspace' as a contrast to real space, the physical environment (see Gibson 1984). The linkage between cyberspace and crime was just another short step. Having said this, the linkage has been somewhat confused by the evolution of two quite different visions of cyberspace that are usefully delineated by Jordan (1999:23–58). Gibson's original symbolic vision of cyberspace sees individuals leaving their physical bodies behind and shifting their consciousness from their 'meat-space' into 'cyberspace', as, for example, in the movie *The Matrix* (1999,

Wachowski and Wachowski). John Perry Barlow's hybrid (Barlovian) vision, on the other hand, joined the virtual with the real and combined Gibson's concept with real-world experience (Jordan 1999:56; Bell 2001:21). The product was an environment that could be constitutionalised, and one over which order could prevail (Barlow 1996). Albeit ambitious, this alternative vision of cyberspace is, after Sterling (1994: xi), a place that is neither inside the computer, nor inside the technology of communication, but in the imaginations of those individuals who are being connected. Although imaginary, it is nevertheless real in the sense that the things that happen in that space have real consequences for those who are participating in it.

The origin of the term 'cybercrime', in contrast to cyberspace, is unclear. It seems to have emerged in the late 1980s or even early 1990s in the later cyberpunk print and audiovisual media. All the same, the linkage between cyberspace and crime was implicit in the early cyberpunk short stories by William Gibson, Bruce Sterling, Bruce Bethke[5] and many others. The cyberspace crime theme was subsequently taken to a wider audience in popular contemporary novels such as Gibson's 'Sprawl' trilogy of *Neuromancer* (1984), *Count Zero* (1986a) and *Mona Lisa Overdrive* (1988), and also Stephenson's *Snowcrash* (1992). Cyberpunk effectively defined cybercrime as a harmful activity that takes place in virtual environments and made the 'high-tech low-life' hacker narrative a norm in the entertainment industry. It is interesting to note at this point that while social theorists were adopting the Barlovian model of cyberspace, it was the Gibsonian model that shaped the public imagination through the visual media.

Hacker movies

Cyberpunk was very popular within the social science fiction community during the 1980s, but its audience was nevertheless relatively small. The cultural fusion of cyberspace and crime into mainstream popular culture was largely due to the second and third of four generations of hacker movies into which some of the cyberpunk ideas dripped. The first generation was defined by original mainframe computer technology and committed within discrete computing systems (Wall 2007:44). It conceptually predated cyberpunk but demonstrated to a wider audience the power of the computer 'hack'. Central to the four generations of hacker movies is the concept of 'haxploitation',[6] the deliberate exploitation of the public fear of hackers for entertainment purposes (my definition). The dramatic exploitation of this fear can, in situations where there is little counter-factual information, have the effect of increasing levels of public fear.

The first generation of movies included the *Billion Dollar Brain* (1967, Russell), *Hot Millions* (1968, Till), *The* (original) *Italian Job* (1969, Collinson), *Superman III* (1983, Lester) and *Bellman and True* (1988, Loncraine). In these movies, the 'hackers' tended to be portrayed as male, fairly old and usually somewhat comically eccentric. See, for example, Benny Hill as Professor Peach in *The Italian Job*; Richard Pryor as Gus Gorman in *Superman III*; Peter Ustinov as Marcus Pendleton in *Hot Millions*.

The second generation of hacker movies were defined by early network technology (typically using dial-up modems) (Wall 2007:45). They were clearly influenced by cyberpunk ideas, in contrast to the first generation, and focused on the hacker rather than the hack. The earlier second-generation films romanticised the guile of the hacker as a penetrator of interconnected computer systems. These early movies consolidated the 'hacker' stereotype that endures to this day of a disenfranchised, misunderstood genius teenage male who uses technology to put wrongs right while having a 'coming-of-age' experience and possibly some fun in the process. Such films included *War Games* (1983, Badham), *Electric Dreams* (1984, Barron), *Real Genius* (1985, Coolidge), *Weird Science* (1985, Hughes) and *Ferris Bueller's Day Off* (1986, Hughes). The later second-generation films were a little more sophisticated, because the narrative shifted from portraying hacks across (dial-in) communication networks to hacks using the broadband internet, or an imaginative sci-fi equivalent. The later second-generation films include *Die Hard* (1988, McTiernan), *Sneakers* (1992, Robinson), *Goldeneye* (1995, Campbell), *Hackers* (1995, Softley), *The Net* (1995, Winkler), *Johnny Mnemonic* (1995, Longo), *Independence Day* (1996, Emmerich), *Enemy of the State* (1998, Scott), *Takedown* (2000, Chappelle), *AntiTrust* (2001, Howitt), *Swordfish* (2001, Sena) and *The* (new) *Italian Job* (2003, Gray). In this later, second generation, hackers were still young(ish), but not predominantly male. Female characters include Sandra Bullock's part in *The Net* (1995, Winkler), Trinity in *The Matrix* trilogy (1999, 2003, 2003, Wachowski brothers) and the Lisbeth Salander character in Stieg Larsson's trilogy *The Girl With the Dragon Tattoo* (2009, Oplev); *The Girl Who Played with Fire* (2009, Alfredson); and *The Girl Who Kicked the Hornets' Nest* (2009, Alfredson). Gordon (2010) found that only 7 of the 60 film hackers studied in his analysis were female. Hackers were also less likely to adopt the moral high ground as in earlier films; and, ethically, the ends tended to justify the 'technological' means in their modus operandi.

The third generation of hacker movies depict both hacker and the hack within a virtual environment (Wall 2007:47). They are epitomised by *The Matrix* (1999, Wachowski and Wachowski) and its later derivatives, but also *TRON* (1982, Lisberger) and *TRON: Legacy* (2010, Kosinski). Underlying the narrative of *The Matrix*, and to some extent also *TRON*, is an articulation of the Gibsonian linkage between cyberspace and meatspace via the avatar, set within the conceptual framework of French social philosophy. Jean Baudrillard's (1994) ideas about 'hyper-reality' – the inability to differentiate fantasy from reality – greatly inspired the Wachowski brothers who wrote and produced *The Matrix*. Indeed, so strongly did the idea of hyper-reality shape the construction of the film's narrative that Baudrillard's *Simulacra and Simulation* (Baudrillard 1994) was allegedly set as required reading for the film's principal cast and crew (McLemee 2007). However, true to Baudrillard's critical personality, when asked for his view on this application of his work, he is reported to have bluntly retorted that he thought the producers and writers had misunderstood it (Longworth 2007). An interesting micro-detail related to *The Matrix* is that observant viewers of the 'follow the white rabbit' scene will notice that Neo stores his computer disks in a hollowed-out hardback copy of Baudrillard's *Simulacra and Simulation*. As the World Wide Web has become more and more embedded in our everyday lives and virtual reality becomes our 'reality', then the third generation of hacker movies is giving way to a new, fourth generation.

The fourth generation is emerging to exploit the potentially dystopic relationships experienced by today's 'digital natives' between online and real-world environments, and derives its (usually crime-based) drama from the ways in which online relationships can have real-world effects. In the fourth generation movies there is a noticeable shift away from the traditional hack narrative, which emphasised the hacker's (often humiliating) power over the state and society, towards exploitation of the fears and risks associated with the technologies of today, especially interoperable converged networked technologies and social networking sites; see for example *Hard Candy* (2005, Slade). It is anticipated that the new fourth-generation haxploitation narrative will continue to erode the now traditional relationship between the outlawed individual hacker and the state in order to re-express the latter's dominant norms. Moreover, in the new narrative, there is often a clear reversal of the roles so that (in some cases) the state, or the victim corporate organisation, develops strategic alliances with hackers in order to protect itself or further its own goals. In movies such as *Die Hard 4.0* (2007, Wiseman), for example, the state hits back against a rogue element within it with help from a previously outlawed hacker. Alternatively, in *Enemy of the State* (1998, Scott), rogue elements in the state apparatus hack the individual.

Where the fourth generation differs from its predecessors is that the battle lines are not so clearly drawn as before in the never-ending cyber arms race. As a consequence, today's 'hacker' equivalent is not the reclusive male seen in the second-generation movies. The hacker may still be as active online as the early hackers were, but the information exchanged now largely relates to social activities. Curiously, the term hacker is now used colloquially to describe someone who invades a friend or enemy's social network account and changes it to poke fun at or humiliate the victim in front of their friends. Consequently, a new social network hacker is evolving as a much more social individual, though the old ethical and unethical hacker types remain on the sidelines.

The cultural impact of hacker movies is significant. Factional[7] hacker narratives skilfully combine fact with fiction to crystallise the 'super-hacker' offender stereotype as the archetypal 'cybercriminal' (Wall 2007:16). The combination of the image of the independent 'outsider' with an expression of the power that they can yield against individuals, corporations and the state configures the hacker as a potential folk devil, which is precisely what the image of the hacker has become (Nissenbaum 2004). What makes these various hack-related sources of visual and textual imagery significant is that 'contemporary movie and media imagery subconsciously orders the line between fact and fiction' (Furedi 2006, cited in Wall 2007:16). So much so that Burrows (1997) argued that not only has the Gibsonian concept of cyberspace transmuted into a tangible reality, but Gibson's technological vision has also fed back into the theory and design of computer and information systems. Furthermore, despite the contradictions between the different visions of cyberspace, Gibson's fictional perspectives on cultural, economic and social phenomena have also begun to find their way into social and cultural analyses as viable characterisations of our contemporary world (Burrows 1997). Yet, as outlined earlier, it was the hybrid Barlovian model of cyberspace, rather than the pure Gibsonian vision, that has actually found greater purchase with social theorists, especially in thinking about cybercrime. This is because if cyberspace is also a space in which criminal intent can be expressed as action, then the extent to which harmful acts are mediated by networked technologies therefore becomes a useful measure of whether or not an act is a true cybercrime or not.

Before moving on, it must be noted that the science fiction hacker narrative is not entirely original. In fact, it has echoes in a character type that originated in Victorian science fiction, a person who constructs or appropriates technological inventions in order to give him or her extra-human power to wield control over others. It is as popular now as a core theme of science fiction as it was a century or so ago in the novels of H. G. Wells[8] and his contemporaries. These are novels that were written during a time of great social upheaval caused by technological innovation, and that described worlds that had been transformed, but also threatened by new and potentially oppressive technologies. This tradition continued throughout the twentieth century to the cyberpunk of the present day via the works of Brian Aldiss, Aldous Huxley and many others. At the centre of many of the earlier works was the 'savant', a learned person of profound knowledge who could utilise technology to his or her (usually his) advantage for good or bad. It is the power that savants can independently wield by using technology (for good or evil) that makes them so much more interesting as science fictional characters. The savant was, in many ways, a Victorian prototype of the hacker.

Risk society, the culture of fear and the news process

The different science fiction genres have, over time, not only strength-ened the modern 'hacker' narrative by emphasising the technological power binary (powerful versus non-powerful), but more generally they have also helped to interpret and strengthen postwar cultural reactions to techno-social change. Interleaved with science fiction, for example, was the dystopic social science fiction novel, of which the best-known example was probably Orwell's now classic work *Nineteen Eighty-Four*, first published in 1949 (Orwell 1990). Orwell and contemporaries captured the postwar zeitgeist by combining ideas about technological change with contemporary political events and social theory in order to describe a dark future in which state power was augmented by techno-logical innovation in surveillance. *Nineteen Eighty-Four*, and the literary offspring it inspired, served to heighten cold-war anxieties about the potentially oppressive power of technological invention and also fed these ideas back into social theory.

Toffler's *Futureshock* (1970) is one example of a theory that draws on dystopia to describe how fear of the future tends to rear its head whenever there is a significant period of technological transformation. The fear of the future easily becomes articulated as a fear of technology, because technology symbolically and literally reflects the future. Fear of technology is both symptom and cause of what Beck (1992), Giddens (1999) and others have called the 'risk society' – a contemporary post-modern society preoccupied with the future and safety (Giddens 1999:3). One of the knock-on effects of the growing societal concern over risk has been a proliferation of fears about the future and the development of a 'culture of fear' about everyday issues such as technology and also crime. Taipale (2006:153) has argued that the fear of technology, or what he calls 'Franken-Tech', now exists because the 'public debate on complex policy issues is often dominated by information entrepreneurs (including activists and the media) who attempt to engender informa-tion cascades to further their own particular agenda'. Furedi (2002) and others (such as Glassner 2009) have more broadly described a prevailing culture of fear as a sort of ideological fear of fear that leads to exagger-ated public expectations of, among other things, crime and danger, which is felt regardless of whether any actually exist. Such a process is not far from Garland's (2001) 'crime complex', whereby public anxiety about crime has become the norm and now frames our everyday lives, so that we expect crime to exist regardless of whether it actually does, and we are shocked, and even panic, when we do not find it. Garland (2001) and Simon (2007) have further suggested that governments and policymakers tactically use prevailing fears of crime to control a broad range of risks. That this tactic should also be used with cybercrime is of no surprise.

For the various reasons articulated earlier, cybercrime has become 'over-problematised' (Wall 2011[2008]), which has meant that any resolution of the apparent problems that arise tends to take place 'in situations where the manageable risks are inflated or misunderstood' (Taipale 2006:153). Consequently, unnecessary levels of public anxiety can result in resource managers being pressurised into misallocating (usually public) resources. Moreover, they may simply not be able to deliver what is demanded and a gap inevitably emerges between what security the public expect and the provision of security that can only be filled by providing reassurance. In the policing literature this gap is referred to as a *reassurance gap* (Innes 2004). With cybercrime, the need for security reassurance typically becomes expressed in the form of public demands for more law and police action, which, of course, the police and governments find hard to provide, because not only is the factual basis of the demands flawed, police funding models are usually determined by responsive routine activities based on the 170-year-old Peeilian[9] (after Robert Peel's police reforms) model of policing dangerousness (Wall 2007:161). This Peelian model remains similar in principle to its original form in the late 1820s, even though it now exists in more complex late modern societies.

The distortions described above are largely reflections of, and also reflect on, the ways in which incidents of cybercrime are reported in the news, which has the knock-on effect of reinforcing and amplifying existing (cyber) fears. In his 2008 research into changes in the news process, Davies found that only 12 per cent of newspaper stories are the product of journalists' own initiative and are thoroughly checked for integrity. Most stories simply reprocessed press releases (HOC 2009:Ev126, Q402; Davies 2010). Yet the quality of news reportage is important because of its dynamic rather than causal relationship with the public: it simultaneously feeds the public's lust for 'shocking' information, but also feeds off it. The endless demand for sensationalism sustains the confusion of rhetoric with reality to create what Baudrillard (1998:34) described as 'le vertige de la réalité' or 'dizzying whirl of reality'. By blurring predictions about 'what could happen' with 'what is actually happening', the message is given by various media that unusual events are far more prevalent than they really are. Once a 'signal event', such as a novel form of cybercrime, captures media attention and heightens existing public anxiety, then other news sources will feed off the original news story and spread virally across cyberspace. In such a manner, relatively minor events can have significant impacts on public beliefs compared with their actual consequences, especially when they result in moral panics (Garland 2008). Furthermore, although signal events may not necessarily constitute a major infraction of criminal law, their outcome is that they 'nonetheless disrupt the sense of social order' (Innes 2004:151). By capturing the public and media's attention, they exert 'a disproportionate impact upon beliefs and attitudes when compared with their "objective" consequences' (Innes 2005:5), raising levels of (cyber) fear and sustaining the hacker cybercriminal stereotype.

Conclusion

Popular cultures have been very influential in shaping our understandings of cybercrime. Rightly or wrongly, the social science fiction-driven hacker narrative has become uncritically coupled with ambiguous scientific conceptualisations of networked virtual space. Cyberpunk and associated popular cultures filled an information gap at a time when 'cybercrime' possessed very high news value, but was not very well defined or for that matter established enough for there to be any meaningful common experience. It is not being argued here that cybercrime was purposefully constructed, because many of the ideas on which the cyberpunk and contributing literature were based were located in scientific discovery or technological developments. Rather, the argument is that this cultural background did frame thinking by creating plausible expectations of cybercrime, as 'proof-of-concept', often before they actually began to occur. From 1990 until the mid-2000s the cybercrime threat was soberly anticipated in many cautionary tales, but it is arguable that during the early years of the World Wide Web, cybercrime was largely a 'significant nuisance'. During the mid-2000s, the cyber-threat landscape changed as technological power increased with faster computers and broadband, and the emergence of powerful botnets around 2004/05 (Wall 2007:150). The change in the threat landscape was also encouraged by the increase in monetary value found on the internet, and the deeper involvement of users in cyberspace-produced social networks. Such changes have become the bedrock of the new digital economy and have changed the face of advertising and also politics. These developments have led to more criminal activity in trying to appropriate information with value. In addition, the step change in the quality and ambition of virus writers (and also frauds through social engineering) has increased the impact potential of cybercrimes enough to force us to think afresh about security and policing. It has required those involved with cybersecurity to think outside the Peelian view of the dangerous criminal and an absolute concept of security, towards a holistic enterprise model of security that is designed to enable trust and may comprise different levels of security. Doing otherwise is to risk perpetuating stereotypes of cybercriminals that, according to Gordon (2010), are corrosive because they pervade popular culture and blind 'policy makers as to the genuine threats to computer and communications security'. Lastly, the stereotypes lower 'comfort levels with computer use at work and at play' for many users (ScienceDaily 2010).

Notes

1. For the uninitiated, the title of this chapter is a pun on David Frankel's film *The Devil Wears Prada* (2006). For those too young to remember, a Lada is the colloquial term for a car based on a box-like Fiat 124 design that was manufactured by the Russian Lada Car Company in the 1970s and 1980s. This chapter develops the discussion found in the first section of Wall (2011[2008]).
2. An important aspect of the drama of Anonymous and LulzSec is that they deliberately play to the media (Mick 2011; Mackenzie 2011). A web search for Anonymous and LulzSec reveals the most recent coverage.

3. In Wall (2011[2008]), I challenge some of the myths that result from the stereotypes.
4. Not to be confused with Gibson's 1986 book of short stories called *Burning Chrome*, though the short story is reproduced on p. 176.
5. Writer Bruce Bethke is credited with coining the word 'Cyberpunk' in his 1980 story 'Cyberpunk'. See Bethke (1997).
6. The term was initially coined by John Leyden (2001).
7. I use the word 'factional' because there is some science behind the ideas used.
8. H. G. Wells's better-known science fiction novels are *The Time Machine* (1895), *The Island of Dr Moreau* (1896), *The Invisible Man* (1897), *The War of the Worlds* (1898) and *The First Men in the Moon* (1901).
9. The concept is named after Sir Robert Peel, the founder of the British Police. The structure and principles of the British Police were subsequently adopted by many countries around the world.

References

Barlow, John Perry. (1996). A declaration of the independence of cyberspace. John Perry Barlow Library. Available at https://projects.eff.org/~barlow/Declaration-Final.html [accessed June 2011].

Baudrillard, Jean. (1994). *Simulacra and Simulation*. Ann Arbor: University of Michigan Press.

Baudrillard, Jean. (1998). *The Consumer Society: Myths and Structures*. London: Sage.

Beck, Ulrich. (1992). *Risk Society: Towards a New Modernity*. New Delhi: Sage.

Bell, Daniel. (2001). *An Introduction to Cybercultures*. London: Routledge.

Bethke, Bruce. (1997). The etymology of 'cyberpunk'. Available at http://www.brucebethke.com/articles/re_cp.html [accessed June 2011].

Burrows, Roger. (1997). Cyberpunk as social theory. In Sallie Westwood and John Williams (eds). *Imagining Cities: Scripts, Signs and Memories*. London: Routledge, 235–48.

Davies, Nick. (2010). *Flat Earth News*. London: Chatto.

Furedi, Frank. (1997). *Culture of Fear: Risk Taking and the Morality of Low Expectation*. London: Continuum.

Furedi, Frank. (2002). *Culture of Fear*. London: Continuum.

Furedi, Frank. (2006). What is distinct about our rules of fear? Leeds Social Sciences Institute Public Guest Lecture, Leeds, 23 October.

Garland, David. (2001). *The Culture of Control*. Oxford: Oxford University Press.

Garland, David. (2008). On the concept of moral panic. *Crime Media Culture*, 4(1), 9–30.

Gibson, William. (1982). Burning chrome. *Omni Magazine*, July. [Reproduced in William Gibson. (1986b). *Burning Chrome*. New York: Arbor House, 169–91.]

Gibson, William. (1984). *Neuromancer*. London: Grafton.

Gibson, William. (1986a). *Count Zero*. London: Grafton.

Gibson, William. (1988). *Mona Lisa Overdrive*. London: Grafton.

Giddens, Anthony. (1999). *Runaway World: How Globalization Is Reshaping Our Lives*. London: Profile Books.

Glassner, Barry. (2009). *Culture of Fear: Why Americans Are Afraid of the Wrong Things*. New York: Basic Books.

Gordon, Damian. (2010). Forty years of movie hacking: Considering the potential implications of the popular media representation of computer hackers from 1968 to 2008. *International Journal of Internet Technology and Secured Transactions* 2(1/2), 59–87.

Harvey, Brian. (1985). Computer hacking and ethics, *ACM Select Panel on Hacking*. Available at http://www.cs.berkeley.edu/~bh/hacker.html [accessed September 2011].

HOC. (2009). Press standards, privacy and libel, Second report of session 2009–10, Volume 2. Unprinted Evidence, House of Commons: Culture, Media and Sport Committee, HC 362-II, April. [Nick Davies' evidence on Tuesday 21 April 2009, Q402–Q495, 125–49.] Available at http://www.publications.parliament.uk/pa/cm200910/cmselect/cmcumeds/362/362ii.pdf [accessed June 2011].

Home Office. (2010). *Cyber Crime Strategy*, Cm 7842, London: Office of Public Sector Information, March. Available at http://www.official-documents.gov.uk/document/cm78/7842/7842.pdf [accessed June 2011].

Innes, M. (2004). Reinventing tradition? Reassurance, neighbourhood security and policing. *Criminology and Criminal Justice* 4(2), 151–71.

Innes, M. (2005). Why disorder matters? Antisocial behaviour and incivility as signals of risk. Paper given to the *Social Contexts and Responses to Risk (SCARR) Conference*, Kent, UK, 28–30 January. Available at http://www.kent.ac.uk/scarr/events/finalpapers/Innes.pdf [accessed June 2011].

Jordan, Tim. (1999). *Cyberpower: The Culture and Politics of Cyberspace and the Internet*. London: Routledge.

Leyden, John. (2001). Haxploitation: the complete Reg guide to hackers in film. *The Register*, 3 August. Available at http://www.theregister.co.uk/2001/08/03/haxploitation_the_complete_reg_guide/ [accessed June 2011].

Leyden, John. (2007). Tiger team brings haxploitation to TV: Penetration testing telly show up against the Queen. *The Register*, 19 December. Available at http://www.theregister.co.uk/2007/12/19/tiger_team/ [accessed June 2011].

Longworth, Karina. (2007). Jean Baudrillard and American popular culture, *International Journal of Baudrillard Studies*, 4(3). Available at http://www.ubishops.ca/baudrillardstudies/vol4_3/v4-3-article58-longworth.html [accessed June 2011].

Mackenzie, Iain. (2011). Who loves the hacktivists? BBC News Online, 22 June. Available at http://www.bbc.co.uk/news/technology-13872755 [accessed June 2011].

Mansfield-Devine, Steve. (2011). Hacktivism: Assessing the damage. *Network Security*, 2011(8), 5–13.

McLemee, S. (2007) Remember Baudrillard, *Inside Higher Ed*, 14 March. Available at http://www.insidehighered.com/views/mclemee/mclemee135 [accessed June 2011].

Mick, Jason. (2011). LulzSec, Anonymous declare 'war' on U.S., international gov'ts, banks. *Daily Tech*. Available at http://www.dailytech.com/LulzSec+Anonymous+Declare+War+on+US+International+Govts+Banks/article21952.htm [accessed June 2011].

Nissenbaum, Helen. (2004). Hackers and the contested ontology of cyberspace. *New Media & Society* 6(2), 195–217.

Orwell, George. (1990[1949]). *1984 Nineteen Eighty-Four*. London: Penguin.

Person, Lawrence. (1998). Notes toward a postcyberpunk manifesto. *Nova Express* 16. Available at http://project.cyberpunk.ru/idb/notes_toward_a_postcyberpunk_manifesto.html [accessed June 2011].

ScienceDaily. (2010). Hackers at the Movies. *ScienceDaily*. 8 February. Available at http://www.sciencedaily.com/releases/2010/02/100205120215.htm [accessed June 2011].

Simon, Jonathan. (2007). *Governing through Crime: How the War on Crime Transformed American Democracy and Created a Culture of Fear*. New York: Oxford University Press.

Stephenson, Neal. (1992). *Snowcrash*. London: ROC/Penguin.

Sterling, Bruce. (1994). *The Hacker Crackdown: Law and Disorder on the Electronic Frontier*. London: Penguin.

Taipale, Kim. (2006). Why can't we all get along? How technology, security, and privacy can coexist in the digital age. In Jack Balkin, James Grimmelmann, Ethan Katz, Nimrod Kozlovski, Shlomit Wagman and Tal Zarsky (eds). *Cybercrime: Digital Cops in a Networked Environment*. New York: New York University Press, 151–83.

Toffler, Alvin. (1970). *Future Shock*. New York: Bantam Books.

Wall, David. (2007). *Cybercrimes: The Transformation of Crime in the Information Age*. Cambridge: Polity.

Wall, David. (2008) [revised 2011]. Cybercrime and the culture of fear: Social science fiction(s) and the production of knowledge about cybercrime. *Information, Communication & Society* 11(6), 861–84. Available at http://papers.ssrn.com/sol3/papers.cfm?abstract_id=1155155 [accessed June 2011].

1.2
Scanning Bodies, Stripping Rights? How Do UK Media Discourses Portray Airport Security Measures?

Christiana Gregoriou and Pinelopi Troullinou

In light of the tenth anniversary of the 9/11 terrorist attacks, body scanning as an airport security measure has been much featured in the press. Political parties, non-governmental organisations and civil liberties groups have raised concerns over the use of such equipment, underlining potential health risks and abuse of human rights. In response to such concerns, this chapter employs discourse and content analysis to investigate how British broadsheet media texts in particular report, question and/or justify airport security measures, and full body scanning to be exact. Analysing media texts is particularly important where terrorism is concerned, not least because such coverage itself 'helps define the meaning of terrorist acts' (Papacharissi and Oliveira 2008:55), also revealing such acts' underlying reasoning.

It was in the aftermath of terrorist attempts that individual states, including those forming part of the European Union, have found themselves increasingly concerned with security measures in aviation. Following the 'shoe-bomber' attempt on a US aircraft in December 2001, several countries boosted the screening of shoes, while after the terrorist attempt in 2006 to blow up a number of aircraft over the Atlantic using liquid explosives, airport security banned the carrying of all liquids on board commercial aircraft (European Commission 2010a). Similarly, following the failed 2009 Christmas Day bombing attempt on a flight from Amsterdam to Detroit, scanners producing a near-naked image were employed as a complementary screening measure for flying passengers from several airports around the globe. The body scanners were introduced particularly because the air terrorist in question (the Nigerian Umar Farouk Abdulmutallab) had carried the explosives onto the flight in his underwear. As of June 2011, these scanners are located and in use at Britain's major international airport terminals – London Heathrow and Manchester – and also airports in Finland, the Netherlands, France and Italy (see European Commission 2010a, 2010b). Security scanners had, nevertheless, already been trialled at London Heathrow airport, Amsterdam Schiphol airport and Helsinki Vantaa airport some years prior to the 2009 terrorist attempt (European Commission 2008).

Rather than an actual psychological outcome related to people's direct experiences, Furedi (2002, 2007) argues that today's *fear* is instead a social and cultural construct, central to which is 'the belief that humanity is confronted by powerful destructive forces that threaten our everyday existence' (Furedi, 2002:vii). Following Furedi's reasoning, not only are we all encouraged to fear regardless of the actual nature of such specific threats as terrorism, but we essentially become assessors of a negatively connoted risk (for contemporary understandings of 'risk', see Lupton 1999), indeed pessimists, expecting the worst possible scenarios and ultimately compromising our personal freedoms in response to such potentialities in real life (for more on the 'culture of fear' but also the issue of responsibilisation, vulnerability and risk consciousness, see also Mythen and Walklate 2006; Furedi 2007). 'Through risk management, fear is institutionalised' and 'fear response is further encouraged and culturally affirmed' (Furedi, 2007), while ultimately such fear of crime can prove 'a more widespread problem than crime itself' (Bannister and Fyfe 2001:808). Risk management can harvest a surveillance society, paranoia, poor health and even xenophobia; through igniting western cultures' fear of the non-white, non-Anglo-American, terroristic other, such texts could well be generating racist ideologies and even related hate crime. It is this *culture of fear* concept that we interrogate in this chapter through discourse and content analysis of media texts about airport scanners in Britain. Do such media texts indeed promote fear of terrorism, and how does language contribute to this impression? To take a linguistically relativistic view (see Sapir 1921, 1929; Whorf 1956), language very much shapes how we see and experience the world around us, how we categorise entities and view notions; and language 'can (unconsciously) influence thought and determine or reinforce particular, non-neutral, world views' (Wales 2001:103).

To start with, this chapter explores the way in which selected newspapers portray body scanners through framing theory, a premise describing the way in which the public, driven by the media, shapes particular correlations between a given topic and specific concepts (Chong and Druckman 2007:104). Framing is encountered in sociology, media studies and psychology. From a psychological perspective, Tversky and Kahneman (1981) and Kahneman and Tversky (1984) examined the effects of framing in decision-making procedures, exploring how individuals can make different choices given the same scenarios portrayed in different ways. Scheufele and Tewksbury (2007:11) argue that framing follows the assumption that the way in which news reports portray a topic can influence the way in which an audience perceives it. Even more so, it is not the content of the message as such that influences public opinion, but rather 'the modes of the presentation' of the message, which give more salience to selected aspects of an issue (Scheufele and Tewksbury 2007:9, 14). Headlines in news coverage seem to be particularly important in the process of public opinion formation; the public depends on headlines to provide necessary details around a given topic, therefore saving both time and energy (Dor 2003:719). Additionally, Fiske and Taylor (1991) contributed the term 'cognitive misers', describing the idea that human beings perceive little information when making decisions and depend on cognitive shortcuts when evaluating this information. In this sense, framing is very important; it can have an effect over the way in which the audience perceives the topics presented.

To return to the current topic of newspapers and our methodology, framing can help us establish whether the public is invited to shape the opinion that body scanners are increasing security or preventing future terrorist attacks, or whether body scanners are instead portrayed as a threat to privacy and civil liberties. Utilising quantitative framing content analysis and methodology, we measure the frequency of the security body scanners' presentation and the repeated framework within which this security measure is covered in representative national press (for content analysis, see Neuendorf 2002:10). The computerised quantitative (media studies-based) method of content analysis will be supplemented with a qualitative (linguistic) critical discourse analytic approach (for CDA see, for instance, Fairclough 1992; for critical linguistics and the news, see Fowler 1991). Here, we use linguistic expertise to explore such issues as the naming and describing of the main stakeholders (see Jeffries 2007, 2010), grammatical transitivity and modality, metaphoricity and semantic presuppositions. This part of the approach enables us to explore the social implications embedded in the linguistic choices. More specifically, we investigate how security policies surrounding terrorism are portrayed, reasoned and communicated to the public. This is in response to the 'need to guard against the introduction of legislation that falls below the standard of the liberties and freedoms that formally elected democratic governments purport to protect' (Mythen and Walklate 2006:130). According to the same source, it is worth ensuring that 'the price we pay for our security is not our liberty in every sense of the word' (Mythen and Walklate 2006:137).

Two British, up-market national daily newspapers were specifically chosen for analysis – the traditionally centre-right *The Times*, and the centre-left *The Guardian* – therefore covering two different sides of the British political spectrum's reaction to the measures. Aspects of readership and financing are also worth considering. Both *The Times* and *The Guardian* are upmarket, quality papers meant to observe high standards of news reporting (Jucker 1992:47), this also referring to the socioeconomic classes of the people who read them, but also the way in which the papers are themselves financed. To elaborate, Jucker (1992:58) explains that downmarket papers earn their money mainly though copy sales, whereas upmarket papers draw the greatest part of their revenue from selling advertising space. Restricting a LexisNexis computational search to the given broadsheets, and using 'Body scanner' as keywords for the period from 13 December 2009 to 13 December 2010, elicited 60 articles. Having eliminated those articles that were repeats or bore no relevance to airport body scanning left us with 42 articles altogether, 15 of which came from *The Times* and 27 from *The Guardian*. As it is oriented towards a consideration of human rights, it is perhaps unsurprising that *The Guardian* devoted more space to discussing this issue and raising concerns. Despite this imbalance, all the articles were qualitatively and quantitatively analysed. The articles ranged from those on News and Features pages to Opinion Columns, Editorials and Comment and Debate pages.

Following the articles' selection, content analysis variables were set up for the coding of both the newspaper headlines and their main text. Based on the claims of official documents about aviation security measures on the one hand, and the concerns posed by actors opposing the use of body scanners at airports on the other, we hypothesise that the main discourses around body scanners as security means are either the enhancement of security or the abuse of privacy and civil liberties, not to mention health risks. Criticism was also directed to body scanners being technically inadequate to deal with a terroristic threat. For this reason, value labels were set to examine whether body scanners were portrayed in one of three frames:

- Boosting security, such as in *The Times*'s '"No-fly" lists, scanners and Yemeni ban to tighten air security after Christmas plot'.
- Abuse of human and individual rights (including health risks), such as in *The Guardian*'s 'Airport worker accused of ogling woman in body scanner'.
- Mostly technical inadequacy in relation to security, such as in *The Guardian*'s 'We can't rely solely on airport body scanners'.

Finally, there is the category of text with no frame but factual information, such as in the *Guardian*'s 'Brown gives go-ahead for full-body scanners'.

The evaluation of the news articles was additionally explored in order to examine whether, individually, each selected headline and each main article was positive (in other words, in favour of), negative (against) or neutral (straightforwardly informative) towards body scanners, while critical linguistic analysis further interrogated the articles qualitatively. The findings of our cross-disciplinary approach are outlined in the rest of this chapter.

Salience of security measures

Even from the stage of news article collection, this survey's findings seem significant. As mentioned above, 15 out of the 42 articles here included for analysis originated from *The Times*, whereas almost twice as many – that is, 27 – came from *The Guardian*. Even more so, within each article, *The Guardian* devoted more column inches to a discussion of the body scanning security measure at UK airports. We divided all the articles into three length-related categories – less than 400, 400–800 and more than 800 words – and found that the vast majority of articles fell into the middle category. The findings showed that 63% of *Guardian* articles were sized between 400 and 800 words, in contrast with *The Times* that devoted such length only to 33.3% of articles. Out of the remaining *Guardian* texts, 18.5% of articles were shorter than 400 words (including those falling within the Editorial and Comment sections) and 18.5% of articles were longer than 800 words. On the other hand, out of the remaining articles from *The Times*, 40% were shorter than 400 words and 26.7% over 800 words. In other words, not only did *The Guardian* dedicate more articles to this issue but, on average, it gave each article more column space as well.

Evaluation of security measures

Interestingly, the majority of *The Guardian* articles negatively evaluate body scanners, both when headlining and in the main text of the articles themselves (see Table 1.2.1). The articles coded as holding a negative evaluation show that the reader would perceive a negative opinion of body scanners. In particular, 48.1% of the total of *Guardian* articles examined had negatively evaluating headlines regarding body scanners whereas, in terms of the main body of the articles, 66.7% negatively evaluated this measure. No *Guardian* headline positively evaluated body scanners. In other words, the reader would not perceive body scanners in a positive way based on the *Guardian* headlines, and only 7.4% of the

Table 1.2.1   Comparison of articles from *The Guardian* and *The Times*: Evaluation of headline(Hd)/content(Cnt)

	Negative – against body scanners		Positive – in favour of body scanners		Neutral – informative		Non-applicable		Total
	Hd	Cnt	Hd	Cnt	Hd	Cnt	Hd	Cnt	
The Times	40%	53.3%	20%	46.7%	26.7%	0%	13.3%	–	100%
The Guardian	48.1%	66.7%	0%	7.4%	25.9%	25.9%	25.9%	–	100%

articles' main body text evaluated the measure positively. There was a neutral evaluation in 25.9% of the articles where both the content and the headlines are concerned. 25.9% of articles referred to body scanners in the main body of the text, though the headline was not directly related to them.[1]

Regarding *The Times* headlines, 40% negatively evaluated the measure, 20% positively evaluated the measure and 26.7% were neutral towards it. There were headlines not referring to body scanners in 13.3% of articles, so these were deemed non-applicable. Based on the main body of the articles, 53.3% negatively evaluated the measure and 46.7% positively evaluated it.

The results of the evaluation of the headline and the main body of the articles are remarkable. The data derived from the left-oriented *Guardian* proved the assumed sensitivity on measures that raise concerns on human rights; the majority of these articles, both in the headlines and the main body, evaluated body scanners negatively. That means that the readers would perceive body scanners in a negative way, the extent of this of course depending on the information they obtain from the relevant articles. The majority of the right-oriented *Times* articles also present negative evaluations in the headlines regarding body scanners although, based on the main body of the articles themselves, *The Times* proved more balanced, with almost half of the articles negatively evaluating this security measure, while the rest evaluate it positively.

Framing of security measures

The findings regarding both sets of articles' main body and headlines showed that *The Guardian* portrayed body scanners in the majority of the articles in terms of abuse of human and individual rights, including health risks (48.1% content, 40.7% headline; see Table 1.2.2). Only 11.1% of

Table 1.2.2   Comparison of articles from *The Guardian* and *The Times*: Framing of headline/content

	Body scanners boost security		Body scanners abuse human/ individual rights (including health risks)		Body scanners are inadequate security measure (including technical problems)		Informative regarding body scanners		Non-applicable		Total
	Headline	Content	Headline	Content	Headline	Content	Headline	Content	Headline	Content	
The Times	13.3%	40%	20%	40%	6.7%	13.3%	33.3%	6.7%	26.7%	–	100%
The Guardian	3.7%	11.1%	40.7%	48.1%	3.7%	22.2%	18.5%	18.5%	33.3%	–	100%

Guardian articles presented body scanners as a tool for boosting security in the main article, while just 3.7% adopted this frame within the headline. An 18.5% of *Guardian* articles presented body scanners informatively both in terms of the main text and the headline itself. *The Guardian* portrayed body scanners in 22.2% of articles as an inadequate tool for safeguarding security, referring also to technical problems in the main body, and only 3.7% had this frame for the headline. Finally, 33.3% of *Guardian* headlines did not refer to body scanners specifically.

Returning to the articles derived from *The Times*, the findings showed that the headlines were mostly informative (33.3%); 13.3% of the articles were framed under headlines referring to body scanners as a measure to boost security, while 20% of the headlines correlated body scanners to abuse of human and individual rights (a frame that included health risks for the coding). Only 6.7% of the headlines referred to body scanners as an inadequate security measure, and 26.7% of the headlines did not refer to body scanners directly (Table 1.2.2). In terms of the main body of the articles derived from *The Times*, the analysis showed that 40% of articles framed body scanners as a measure to boost security, and the same number of articles (40%) correlated body scanners with abuse of human and individual rights (including health risks). While 13.3% of the articles presented body scanners as an inadequate security measure, only 6.7% of articles were coded as informative, meaning that they just gave information on the use of body scanners at airports, choosing not to assess the measure in any of the given frames.

The content analysis results indeed confirmed the hypothesis that the left-oriented *Guardian* would portray body scanners as a measure abusing human rights such as privacy, and that body scanners are seen as proven inadequate to safeguard security. On the other hand, since *The Times* is a right-oriented newspaper, we hypothesised that it would favour body scanners as a tool for boosting security and keeping potential threats at bay. A right-oriented newspaper was not expected to show sensitivity to human rights issues; security is considered more salient. Conversely, the findings showed that *The Times* presented body scanners in a more balanced manner than expected. We next turn to engaging qualitatively with the data, this time from a critical linguistic point of view.

Qualitative discourse analysis: *The Guardian*

The Guardian objects to, and indeed exaggerates, the invasiveness of airport security measures, with one writer, for instance, ironically and humorously saying that, to remember a holiday experience, one can take metaphorically unfortunate 'souvenirs' generated by the Transportation Security Administration (TSA) in the form of pat-downs and scanned naked images: 'they will feel you up, or take naked photos of you', he says. Elsewhere, holidaying in the United States is explicitly amusingly likened to 'a really bad relationship, played in reverse', in that '[y]ou get yelled at when you arrive, and felt up when you leave', security measures also 'springing up' like unwanted plants coming out of nowhere. The body scanning measure is also explicitly said to have already been in place two months before the given bombing attempt, at which point 'Rapiscan won a $25m deal to supply 150 imaging machines to the US transportation security', thus highlighting the huge financial gain that certain companies would have via the introduction of the technology. One writer even explains that, rather than being concerned with the clashing of agendas to do with security and privacy, we should concern ourselves with a third agenda of technology, which is often used in the destruction of privacy (see, for instance, the use of biometric passports) and to make the unacceptable (in this case being asked to strip) acceptable.

Terroristic action is also here said to be interpreted by TSA officials as a metaphorical series of fashion trends or daily changing servings with which they seemingly mindlessly need to keep up: 'explosive underwear – sooooo autumn/winter 2009'; 'the latest boom for security firms [...]'; 'The terrorist threat du jour is no longer ink cartridges' (the latter being a reference to the October 2010 air cargo bomb plot). The suggestion here is that body scanners are merely hastily showcased (see also reference to 'window dressing' searches) to reassure nervous passengers. These can only potentially protect us against a single type of suicide bomber ('there was only a 50% to 60% chance that a full body scanner would have detected the explosives moulded to Abdulmutallab's body') and hence cannot be relied on exclusively ('A scanner on its own is not enough'). Those who come up with the measures are here implied to be far less than able ('the fact that some dude in Colorado has already found a way to block the scanners might raise certain questions about the efficacy of these security measures'), reactionary rather than truly preventative ('Surely they should be anticipating the event, not reacting to it') and deliberately intrusive ('here are some methods to [...] continue the TSA's sterling efforts in making flying as degrading and unpleasant as possible'). To drive the point home, the measures are clearly sexualised, with method number 3 here mockingly reading 'Every passenger about to fly must have sex with a TSA staff member', while the searches are elsewhere said to 'include a firm pressing of a security guard's hand on genitalia and breasts', the machines all the while 'offer[ing] security guards an all but naked view of passengers'. The nakedness of the produced images is taken as a 'given', almost pornographic offering meant to intimately amuse the unquestionably voyeuristic guards, who also get to engage tactilely with flying passengers at their sexual whim. As another *Guardian* writer notes, 'Privacy campaigners have claimed the images created by the machines are so graphic that they amount to virtual strip-teasing', the reference to strip-teasing again alluding to the image of an audience to be voyeuristically entertained by the images produced by the screening. The Pope himself is quoted as saying that '[i]t is essential never to lose sight of respect for the primacy of the person', suggesting that the measures are possibly disrespectful, while references to our rights being 'suspended' once we are inside an airport clearly imply a needless but seemingly acceptable violation of them.

Officials, such as the British Home Secretary, distinguish 'people who pose a terrorist threat' from 'people here in the UK', suggesting that the two groups do not overlap. Though claiming that racial and religious profiling is explicitly banned, certain races ('It's a Lebanese Danny Zuko', 'a Nigerian terrorist', 'a prominent pro-Iranian US activist', 'men of Yemeni origin') get to be explicitly mentioned, suggesting that it is people of (at least) non-British origin or residence of whom we should be fearful. The supposed randomness with which people are meant to be selected for scanning is also challenged and indeed mocked as 'celebrity scanning' of 'certain individuals' whom security staff 'single out' 'at their discretion', clearly implying that particular races' human freedoms and civil liberties are here violated not only through the measures themselves in general, but also through the way in which they are implemented on these people alone. A *Guardian* writer even says that '[a]fter being "randomly selected" six times in a row, I was sick of being treated as a threat', the quotation marks along with the 'six times in a row' reference clearly contrasting with, and therefore negating, the supposed 'randomness' of the body scanning selection process. As the head of the Equalities and Human Rights Commission is quoted as saying categorically, 'serious concerns existed about invasion of privacy and there was an apparent lack of safeguards to ensure scanners were operated fairly and without discrimination'. The suggestion here is that scanners could well be operated unfairly and in a discriminating manner. Elsewhere, behavioural profiling is promoted and contrasted to random and religious or ethnic profiling, the behavioural kind explained as that meant to spot passengers who act suspiciously (such as those who pay cash, travel with little luggage, behave erratically and so on). Not only does ethnic and religious profiling homogenise people into stereotypes, it here gets metaphorically constructed as a 'breeding ground for militant jihadism', spreading a 'mental virus' and therefore igniting those very attacks it is there to prevent. To encourage the Muslim community to accept profiling, a Labour MP even says that 'people would rather be profiled than blown up', the contrastive pairing suggesting that these are firmly the only options available to the community in question. Notice here also the nominalisation of all kinds of profiling, which interestingly disguises the agency and stereotyping action on behalf of certain unnamed individuals.

Qualitative discourse analysis: *The Times*

While *The Times* quotes security officials admitting the invasiveness of body scanning as a security measure, what the officials also highlight is the realness of the nominalised and therefore unquestioned terroristic threat ('the threat is real', an FBI veteran says) against which these body scanners will prove a metaphorical defensive weapon. 'Scanners are just one useful tool in our security armoury', a spokesman for the Department for Transport is quoted as saying. It is 'the safety of the travelling public [being their] highest priority' that indeed justifies these measures' implementation. Elsewhere, it is the terrorists themselves, and not the TSA officials who are assigned the responsibility for forcing these measures on the public: 'The full body scanner [...] owes its roll-out nationwide to the Christmas Day bomber.' Another such official draws the image of a folk narrative to attack the media who are opposing these measures: 'The fact that some in the media would hail the traveller as some kind of folk hero is shameful.' *The Times* says that John Tyner, a traveller who was one of the first to object to such security measures, features in such 'shameful' narrativised accounts of this type as a 'hero' for the travelling public to supposedly imitate. *The Times* is referring to such assertions as the *Guardian*'s 'It all started with a man [Tyner] who said no one was going to touch his "junk"'.

The body scanning measure is described as 'welcome' by one *Times* editorial writer, while also noting that this 'new kit' is 'dependent' on deficient, 'imperfect humans'. The human factor in this supposed fight against terrorism is here contrasted with the (new) technological factor, the latter being found unquestionably superior and certainly more useful than humans. People to be screened are also diminished to elements or particles for security to sift through ('this more precise sifting should raise the game of security staff', 'his name cropped up as "a trace", indicating that at some point he had associated with extremist elements'), while racial and ethnic profiling is hailed to be 'politically controversial' but also 'necessary', and certainly 'a more sensible, honest' approach to what security officers are currently doing. What the writer here suggests is that 'we' should not succumb to the fear of generating controversy via profiling, controversy itself being a mere hindrance to 'our' (in other words, inclusive of all readers) battle. As he explicitly concludes, 'it's not a surprise that terrorists are likely to be young Asian males', after all. A linking between 'young Asian males' and 'terrorism' is established, despite the use of the epistemically modalised adverb 'likely' that could well go unnoticed here. Illegal immigrants are also linked to potential terrorists in quotes from officials. In saying that '[i]t seems terrible that someone [...] put on an immigration watchlist is not included on a security watchlist', the Chairman of the Conservative Party suggests that the two categories need to be merged. Other officials are quoted describing terrorists as 'inventive and determined', the attributive adjectival use suggesting that terrorists are unquestionably so. It is for this reason that an *Aviation Security* magazine editor is quoted calling for 'streetwise and trained professionals' for us to rely on in determining what technological means are to be used to detect terrorists. The naming is interesting here, the attributive adjectival use again suggesting that all security officers are to be comfortingly professional enough, well trained and streetwise.

The Times reduces passengers' legitimate reactions to the body scanning measure to mere 'moaning' ('new restrictions are being moaned about'), while when reporting on the airport scanner campaign in the United States, the grouping is hailed as 'protesters' and as 'a loose coalition of online campaigners' potentially posing 'chaos' and 'largescale confrontation' at US airports. Elsewhere, the paper even creates an image of an enraged mob, their 'outrage', 'anger' and 'fury' 'mounting', their metaphorically constructed fire 'fuelled by thousands of complaints' posing a physical 'threat', to the extent that it is aligned with the actions of a dangerous army indeed triggering a metaphorical 'battle': 'The first shot in the battle against the body scanners was fired by Brian Sodergren', National Opt-Out Day's online organiser. In other words, while body scanners are metaphorically said to be a defensive weapon against the army of terrorism, campaigning action is reduced to a battle against such a defence and therefore, by implication, a battle on the side of terrorism. Protesting action is here presented as somehow illegitimate. Such descriptions clearly negatively predispose readers to this grouping's actions and underlying intentions, not to mention generate the impression that the campaigners' actions were indeed to have an impact on other travellers unhelpfully rather than helpfully on what indeed 'was one of the busiest travel days of the year', the Thanksgiving holiday. As the TSA head is quoted as saying, campaigners' actions would ultimately 'prevent many Americans from getting home "to see their loved ones"', appealing to passengers' emotional needs to get them to 'desist from a boycott'. Sentences such as '[t]heir action would have ensured that [passengers] received an equally controversial "pat down" by security officials' suggest that campaigners' action would have needlessly (notice the qualifying 'equally controversial') inconvenienced passengers, even though the statement is epistemically modalised, seeing that no chaos or inconvenience actually ensued. Evident here, also, is the reference to this campaigning grouping functioning as a grammatical agent, as the grouping that deontically and actively ('would have ensured') generates action on the flying passengers, in contrast to the truly acting officials being backgrounded in the prepositional phrase that follows ('by security officials'). Similarly, in references to travellers seeking to 'sabotage the entire [security] process' and 'undermine the new regime', not only are travellers again functioning as irresponsibly acting agents, they are also aligned with disobedient, anarchic behaviour against the nominalised and, therefore, unquestioned 'new [security] regime'. The newspaper further highlights that security officials are subjected to verbal abuse by the public that they here portray as merely uninformed. The scanners are said to have been proven not to pose a risk ('Some opponents of the scanners claimed that they posed a health risk, despite checks carried out by the Food and Drug Administration and Johns Hopkins University'), while their images are, at least no longer, sexualising or undignified: 'images obtained by the scanners were no longer "titillating" and the whole process would proceed with dignity'.

Conclusion

Overall, *The Guardian* devoted more and lengthier articles in response to the body scanning security measure than did *The Times* within the period in question. *The Guardian* opted for a majority of articles negatively evaluating this measure, as did *The Times* headlines in particular. In comparison, the main *Times* article body text proved more balanced in its view. *The Guardian* focused mostly on scanners' abuse of human rights, and less on the measure's inadequacy as a security measure, whereas *The Times* texts proved more informative in fact, and focused on the abuse of human rights a little less. In this sense at least, the papers seem to agree that scanning bodies indeed abuses people's rights.

It was the closer, qualitative analysis that highlighted more bias on behalf of *The Times*, though. It portrayed the scanners as a weapon to be employed in the war against 'terrorism', with technology deemed superior to humans, themselves being reduced merely to particles for security staff to handle. Young Asian males are unquestionably linked to the terroristic threat, as are illegal immigrants for some reason, a grouping that is used almost interchangeably with that of 'Asians'. To undermine the passengers' reactionary behaviour to the body scanning measure, they are reduced to a moaning, but also dangerous mob, irresponsibly causing chaos and delays for other, more obedient passengers. *The Guardian* instead perhaps exaggerates the invasiveness and sexualisation of the new security body scanning measure, and warns against the power assigned to the government's 'technology agenda' over and beyond people's rights and liberties. The measures are said to have been hastily introduced, and merely showcased to comfort those who fly in fear. *The Guardian* is also not afraid to highlight issues relating to the measure's discriminating implementation, suggesting here multiple ways in which body scanners can be deemed problematic for everyone.

All in all, the controversial body scanning airport security measure was one that proved instrumental for different papers to promote their own agendas. There is power in the number of articles devoted to this issue, power in the length of these texts and power in their framing. Having said that, however the articles are framed, and by whichever political stance they are framed, it is worth exploring them closely and qualitatively for their true underlying ideologies to come to light so that they are opened for real criticism from readers and analysis not only by academics but hopefully policymakers as well.

The increasing imposition of aviation security measures has proven controversial. One question in particular remains: Are we paying too high a price in the name of security?

Note

1. We need to mention here that these articles that did not directly refer in their headlines to body scanners were coded as *non-applicable* with respect to the headline evaluation and headline framing. When processing these specific articles, readers would not expect to read texts about body scanners, but ones that dealt with airport security in general. These articles were included in the present study in terms of content evaluation and content framing, however, as it was their main article text that explored body scanners in particular.

References

Bannister, Jon and Nick Fyfe. (2001). Introduction: Fear and the city. *Urban Studies* 38(5/6), 801–13.

Chong, Dennis and James N. Druckman. (2007). Framing theory. *Annual Review of Political Science* 10, 103–26.

Dor, Daniel. (2003). On newspaper headlines as relevance optimizers. *Journal of Pragmatics* 35(5), 695–721.

European Commission. (2008). *Aviation Security: Workshop on Body Scanners.* European EC Rapid Press Release MEMO/08/684.

European Commission. (2010a). *Communication from the Commission to the European Parliament and the Council on the Use of Security Scanners at EU airports.* Brussels, 15.6.2010 COM (2010) 311 final, 1–20.

European Commission. (2010b). *Commission Examines the Use of Security Scanners at EU Airports.* Press Release Brussels, 15 June 2010 (IP/10/740).

Fairclough, Norman. (1992). *Discourse and Social Change.* Cambridge: Polity Press.

Fiske, Susan T. and Shelley E. Taylor. (1991). *Social Cognition* (2nd edn). New York: McGraw-Hill.

Fowler, Roger. (1991). *Language in the News: Discourse Ideology in the Press.* London: Routledge.

Furedi, Frank. (2002). *Culture of Fear: Risk Taking and the Morality of Low Expectation.* London: Continuum.

Furedi, Frank. (2007). The only thing we have to fear is the 'culture of fear' itself. *Spike.* Available at http://www.spiked-online.com/index.php?/site/article/3053/ [accessed June 2010].

Jeffries, Lesley. (2007). *Textual Construction of the Female Body: A Critical Discourse Approach.* Basingstoke: Palgrave.

Jeffries, Lesley. (2010). *Critical Stylistics: The Power of English.* Basingstoke: Palgrave.

Jucker, Andreas H. (1992). *Social Stylistics: Syntactic Variation in British Newspapers.* Berlin: Mouton de Gruyter.

Kahneman, Daniel and Amos Tversky. (1984). Choices, values and frames. *American Psychologist* 39(4), 341–50.

Lupton, Deborah. (1999). *Risk.* New York: Routledge.

Mythen, Gabe and Sandra Walklate. (2006). Communicating the terrorist risk: Harnessing a culture of fear? *Crime, Media, Culture* 2(2), 123–42.

Neuendorf, Kimberly A. (2002). *The Content Analysis Guidebook.* London: Sage.

Papacharissi, Zizi and Maria de Fatima Oliveira. (2008). New frames terrorism: A comparative analysis of frames employed in terrorism coverage in U.S. and U.K. newspapers. *International Journal of Press/Politics* 13(1), 52–74.

Sapir, Edward. (1921). *Language.* New York: Harcourt, Brace.

Sapir, Edward. (1929). The status of linguistics as a science. *Language* 5, 207–14.

Scheufele, Dietram A. and David Tewksbury. (2007). Framing, agenda setting, and priming: The evolution of three media effects models. *Journal of Communication* 57(1), 9–20.

Tversky, Amos and Daniel Kahneman. (1981). The framing of decisions and the psychology of choice. *Science,* new series, 211(4481), 453–58.

Wales, Katie. (2001). *A Dictionary of Stylistics* (2nd edn). London: Longman.

Whorf, Benjamin Lee. (1956). Science and linguistics. In J. B. Carroll (ed.) *Language, Thought and Reality: Selected Writings of Benjamin Lee Whorf.* Cambridge, MA: MIT Press.

1.3

Narrative and Historical Truth in Delayed Civil Actions for Child Abuse

Tony Ward

Most crimes are also civil wrongs, so allegations of criminal wrongdoing are sometimes tested by civil judges who sit without juries, give reasons for their findings of fact, and reach those findings on the balance of probabilities rather than claiming that they are 'beyond reasonable doubt'. A finding reached by the narrowest margin of probability is as much a 'fact' for legal purposes as one that is beyond dispute. As Lord Hoffman put it in one case of alleged child sexual abuse:

> If a legal rule requires a fact to be proved [...] a judge or jury must decide whether or not it happened. There is no room for a finding that it might have happened. The law operates a binary system in which the only values are zero and one. (*Re B* 2008:2)[1]

As Ricoeur (2006:320) remarks, the need to 'set at an appropriate distance the guilty party and the victim, in accordance with an imperiously binary topology' is what distinguishes the judge from the historian (which is not to say that historians never make such distinctions, only that they are under no obligation to do so in every case).

There is, however, an exception to this imperious code in cases where a complainant seeks leave (the permission of the court) to bring an action for personal injury outside the normal limitation period (the period after an alleged event within which an action must be brought – three years for most personal injuries). Leave to bring the action may be granted where the judge considers it 'equitable' to do so, taking account of a number of factors, including 'the extent to which, having regard to the delay, the evidence adduced or likely to be adduced by the plaintiff or the defendant is or is likely to be less cogent than if the action had been brought within' the normal limitation period (Limitation Act

1980, s. 33(3)). In *A* v. *Hoare* (2008), the House of Lords decided that actions for rape and child abuse fell within this section, giving judges a discretion to extend the limitation period beyond the statutory limit of three years (calculated from the claimant's 18th birthday or the date when she or he became aware of having suffered significant injury attributable to the defendant). By overruling its previous interpretation of the Limitation Act in *Stubbings* v. *Webb* (1993), the House of Lords opened the door to actions for so-called historic sexual abuse, in cases where the alleged abuse occurred many years before the proceedings commenced.

Section 33(3) requires the court to assess the cogency of the evidence 'adduced, or likely to be adduced'. As the Court of Appeal explained in *AB* v. *Nugent Care Society* (2009), this means that while in some cases the likely cogency of the evidence can be assessed from the written pleadings, in other cases the judge will need to hear all the witnesses before deciding how cogent the evidence is. If the result is a decision to disapply the limitation period, then the judge may proceed directly to a decision on the substantive issue. Thus rather than a simple binary choice – the complainant was abused or not – the judge has a third option: to decide that whether the abuse occurred or not, the complainant's claim should not be allowed to proceed (see, for example, *Albonetti* v. *Wirral MBC*, 2008). Consequently, defendants in such cases need not counter the claimant's claims with a coherent alternative account of events: it suffices to produce a 'shadow story' (Abbott 2008:182); that is, a story such as 'an unidentified intruder committed the murder', which fails to specify many elements of a complete narrative (such as who the intruder was and why he murdered the victim), but provides an alternative to a competing story. The very shadowiness of the story can support the argument that it would be unfair to allow the litigation to continue.

This chapter will examine two judgments delivered in 2009 by Mrs Justice Swift, in both of which she disapplied the limitation period and, in the main, upheld the complainant's allegations. Drawing on both legal and literary theory, I shall then consider to what extent and in what sense these judgments can be said to have 'constructed' the facts about past sexual assaults.

Raggett v. *Society of Jesus Trust 1929 for Roman Catholic Purposes*

In this case, the claimant (who waived anonymity) sued the proprietors of a Roman Catholic boys' school for sexual abuse by one of the teachers,

Father Spencer, between 1971 and 1974. Father Spencer was dead by the time the case was brought. The action was ordered to be heard in two stages: the first dealing with the limitation issue and, if leave to bring the action out of time was granted, the issue of liability; and the second – still pending at the time of writing – dealing with what losses the claimant had suffered as a result of the abuse and the amount of damages.

Although the claimant said he had 'retained no conscious memory of much of the sexual abuse' (*Raggett* 2009:para. 48), it was clear that he remembered many of the acts that he now interpreted as abuse, such as Father Spencer's filming him naked in the showers and rubbing his groin after a football injury. What he had not done, he now maintained, was to remember them as serious acts of abuse. For example, in pursuit of his literary ambitions, he published a memoir about his childhood relationship with a football-obsessed priest (clearly Father Spencer), in which he wrote that when the priest filmed him doing press-ups in his 'birthday suit', he had 'sensed something sad, not sinister, underlying his voyeurism' (Raggett 1999:207).

The legal issue was not whether Mr Raggett knew that he had been 'abused' (a term that has no legal definition in this context), but whether he had suffered a 'significant injury'; that is, an injury for which it would be reasonable to institute legal proceedings (Limitation Act 1980, ss. 11(3) and 14; *Raggett* 2009:86). In his evidence, he described how his perception suddenly changed during an argument with another priest, Father Dunkling, in 2005. 'A kind of flash flood' came over him as he remembered the intense fear and humiliation induced by the incidents and for the first time, with great distress, saw himself as a victim of abuse (*Raggett* 2009:54). In this respect, his account was typical of the 'sexual stories' analysed by Ken Plummer (1995), in which a period of suffering culminates in an 'epiphany', a breaking of silence about the past, and a transformation of the protagonist into someone who recognises and begins to surpass the source of his suffering. Counsel for the defendants did not accept this account, arguing that Mr Raggett 'had been aware of those facts all along and had deliberately deployed them during a drunken debate' with Father Dunkling (*Raggett* 2009:62). The judge accepted that he had experienced a significant 'awakening' of memories and emotions in 2005, but that for the purposes of the Limitation Act, he had 'known' all along about many of the acts of abuse, and therefore he was some 28 years outside the normal three-year period (which commenced on his 18th birthday) for bringing an action. Nevertheless, she found it 'equitable' in the circumstances to allow the action to be brought out of time (*Raggett* 2009:106, 108, 129).

The defendants made little headway in challenging Mr Raggett's central allegations, which were corroborated by 11 of his former fellow pupils. In order to persuade the judge that their case would have been more cogent had the action been brought earlier, they had to point to a plausible 'shadow story' that, had Father Spencer been alive to tell it, might have explained away the facts relied on by the complainant. The construction of clerical sexual abuse as a problem particularly associated with the Catholic Church, beginning in the United States in the mid-1980s and spreading to other countries, including the United Kingdom (Jenkins 2001:iv, 34–49), has made the construction of such alternative narratives difficult.

In 2009, to ascribe Father Spencer's actions to anything other than abuse was as inconceivable as 'the possibility of a priest abusing a boy in his care' had been for Mr Raggett's mother in the early 1970s (*Raggett* 2009:para. 32). Mrs Justice Swift found it

> difficult to envisage circumstances in which a denial of the abuse by Father Spencer (assuming he had denied it) would have prevailed over the evidence of the claimant and his witnesses. In particular, he could have had no plausible innocent explanation for the contents of his letter of 28 June 2000. (*Raggett* 2009:124)

Six months before his death, after Mr Raggett renewed contact with him, Father Spencer wrote him a letter in which he referred to the nude photographs as 'the super-specials – *never* seen by *anyone*', which 'unfortunately, had to be "eliminated" years later' (quoted at *Raggett* 2009:para. 47, emphasis in original). It is not hard to imagine that Father Spencer might have offered some such 'innocent' interpretation as: 'sadly, my finest studies of the male nude – which, out of respect for your privacy, I never showed anyone else – would nowadays be considered indecent, so I destroyed them lest they fall into the hands of Philistines'. The judge's comments imply that such a story would have stood little chance of being believed.

This part of the judgment shows how hard it is to disentangle the issue of whether it is equitable to allow the action to proceed outside the limitation period from the substantive question of liability. The defendants' case depended on producing a 'shadow story' for which there might have been cogent evidence had the key witness still been alive. The more firmly the judge believed the claimant's evidence, the less likely she was to accept that there could have been cogent evidence that would cast doubt on it. Mrs Justice Swift's decision to extend the limitation period was challenged on appeal on the ground that she had 'put the cart before the horse', by finding first that the abuse had occurred and then that there could be no cogent evidence that it had not occurred (*Raggett* 2010:5). The Court of Appeal, however, ruled that this was merely a matter of the order in which findings were presented in the judgment. In other words, the appellants were confusing the ordering of events in the narrative discourse of the judgment with the order of events in the story of how the judge reached her decision. The case will now proceed (unless it is settled) to a second stage concerned with the quantum of damages. Whether Mr Raggett can win anything approaching the £4.3 million that he claims (*Raggett* 2010:4) will depend on the construction of a convincing 'forking path narrative' (Abbott 2008:167–9) of his successful career in a parallel world where the abuse did not take place, in contrast to his marital and professional failures in real life. This very large sum, reflecting a moderately successful lawyer's claims about the greater earning power of which he has been deprived, can be contrasted with the much smaller awards in other cases (including the *NXS* case, discussed below). For example, one claimant who was found to have suffered post-traumatic stress disorder as a result of abuse received only £5000 on the grounds that he was already suffering a personality disorder and other problems when he entered the defendants' care, so his life would have turned out badly in any event (Case 2007:238).

Raggett is a relatively simple case, but it has a degree of narrative complexity resulting from the need to consider the limitation issue and the substantive issue simultaneously. In the following case, a combination of missing evidence and delayed revelations poses a greater challenge to the judge's ability to formulate a definitive account of past events.

NXS v. Camden Borough Council

In this case, the anonymous complainant, NXS, sued the local council for negligence in leaving her in the care of her mother, referred to in the judgment as 'Miss P', and thereby allowing Miss P to subject her to prolonged physical and sexual abuse between NXS's birth in 1975 and the Council's eventual decision to take her into care in 1989. In contrast to *Raggett*, where the judge's account of events is built around the complainant's testimony, in *NXS* the judgment is heavily reliant on material from the defendant Council's file, which provides only fragmentary, episodic glimpses of the complainant's childhood. One reason for its fragmentary character is that in addition to the general file on Miss P and her family, the Council appeared to have kept another file relating specifically to NXS that it subsequently lost. The way in which the incomplete documents hint at a now lost narrative is reminiscent of some pieces of 'historiographic metafiction' (Hutcheon 1998); that is, works of historical fiction that self-consciously draw attention to their own construction and in so doing raise questions about the construction of history. For example, the chapter entitled 'Deposition' in Adam Thorpe's novel *Ulverton* (1992) also tells its story through fragments of legal records and letters, thereby calling attention to the many voices that are absent from the historical record.

The judgment in *NXS* runs to over 35 000 words and displays a narrative structure that would do credit to the most ingenious novelist. After a very brief summary of the facts, the judge introduces the legal issues. These include the 'shadow story' of the missing file, which the Council claims makes it impossible to assess the quality of their monitoring of NXS's upbringing (*NXS* 2009:para. 9), and the issue of 'factual causation', which depends on the 'forking path' that would have been taken by social workers who were reasonably competent by the standards of the late 1970s. They would, the complainant contended, have removed her from Miss P's care in or about 1976, sparing her years of abuse (*NXS* 2009:9–11). There then follow 105 paragraphs headed 'The History', which draw all their material from the defendant's documents, despite the fact that 'very few [documents] survive' from the period 1977–89 (*NXS* 2009:9). What emerges quite vividly from this fragmentary record is the characterisation of Miss P as manipulative, verbally aggressive and sometimes violent. That at least is how she appears in reports of her clearly tense and difficult encounters with social workers. For example, an entry in 1976 records Miss P saying 'archly': 'I'm a baby batterer – that's what you are all thinking aren't you?' When the social worker 'asked her if she thought that she was in danger of harming the claimant,' – NXS is always 'the claimant', even as a baby – 'Miss P replied, "I slap her but I couldn't hurt her badly or I shouldn't have said that about being a baby batterer"'. The entry then records Miss P's demands for a place in a particular nursery and a flat in a particular location. This self-recanting confession can be read in a number of ways: as a form of resistance against state intrusion (cf. Ferguson 2004), as a way of raising the social worker's concern so that she will give Miss P what she wants, or as a qualified admission that she is, in fact, 'hurting' her child.

In entries for the period shortly before NXS was taken into care, there are a number of hints of possible sexual abuse: when NXS is 14, Miss P says that she 'finds it easy to be affectionate when [the claimant] is sleeping with her' but not otherwise (*NXS* 2009:110, square brackets in original). In a subsequent case conference, '[Mr AM] reported that [Miss P] and [the claimant] had been sharing a bed and he feels that something may have gone on. [Mrs PE] had also sensed that there was a secret that [the claimant] must not talk about' (*NXS* 2009:115, square brackets in original). 'Lots of innuendoes about possible sexual abuse but nothing definite', reported a social worker who spoke with NXS later in the same year (*NXS* 2009:117).

The long section of the judgment drawn from the defendant's files is followed by two different accounts provided by NXS herself. The first is drawn from her video-recorded interview with the police, to whom she complained in 2004 about Miss P's physical abuse of her as child. NXS describes how Miss P

> used violence virtually on a daily basis. She would slap, punch and kick the claimant, and strike her with shoes and other objects. She burned her with an iron and made marks on the palm of her hand with a knife. She threw hot tea and buckets of urine over her. (*NXS* 2009:122)

In this account, the only mention of sexual abuse is a denial that it occurred – NXS told the police: 'If I was abused sexually it would be easier' (*NXS* 2009:124). The first allegation of abuse, without any details, emerged in the particulars of NXS's claim against the council. Only a few days before the hearing did she provide a supplemental witness statement giving details of her abuse by Miss P and by Miss P's brother G:

> She described how Miss P had forced her to share a bed with her and, three or four times a week, would compel the claimant to masturbate her and to perform oral sex on her. She would also request the claimant to perform sexual acts on G and to masturbate her while G watched. She said that, at times, Miss P and G (who were of course siblings) had a sexual relationship and she was forced to watch them having intercourse. She said that the sexual abuse by her mother took place from as long as she could remember until she was removed into care. The abuse by G ended when he died some time in the 1980s. (*NXS* 2009:134)

It might be thought that 'framing' this dramatic revelation with an account of its late emergence in response to the pressure of litigation, coupled with the description of NXS as suffering from 'an emotionally unstable personality disorder and dependence on drugs' (*NXS* 2009:12), would make her seem a thoroughly unreliable narrator. The judgment, however, casts a more sympathetic light on this framing narrative by setting it in the context of a larger narrative of NXS's quest to find the truth about her childhood and the reason she was left in Miss P's care. Repeatedly frustrated in her attempts to gain access to the Council's files, NXS eventually purloined a Council document from her GP's file showing that the Council was aware of her being abused as a baby. Still unable to obtain further information from the Council, she 'felt compelled to initiate criminal proceedings' against her mother. These led to her applying to the Criminal Injuries Compensation Scheme at the suggestion of the police and then, at the suggestion of her solicitor, suing the Council for negligence.

The judge does not say at this stage whether she believes the allegation of sexual abuse, but instead returns to the Council files and the 'shadow story' of the missing file. The experts on child protection called on behalf of both parties agreed that if the social workers had done no more than was recorded in the available file, they would have been incompetent even by the standards of the time, with their relatively high threshold of what constituted serious abuse. They also agreed that another file (which it was accepted the Council had done all it reasonably could to find) had probably existed, but they disagreed about what could be inferred about the likely contents of the file, about what judgment of the social workers' conduct could be made in its absence, and about how differently things might have turned out had they done a better job.

As is usual in civil litigation, the two experts had met and drawn up a statement of areas of agreement and disagreement. This included a statement that 'we are of the opinion that no opinion can be formed about the quality of monitoring in this period [after February 1977] given the absence of records' (quoted at *NXS* 2009:178). In the witness box, the complainant's expert was quite willing to express opinions about this period, giving rise to the accusation that she had resiled from her agreement and was an unreliable witness. As Edmond (2000) has noted, however, such inconsistencies can be portrayed either as undermining an expert's evidence or as normal reactions to the process of argument in a complex case.

All the pieces of the complex structure of interlocking narratives are now in place. The story of the experts' agreement and its breakdown frames two alternative interpretations of the stories told or implied in the surviving and the missing files, as well as constructing and questioning a 'forking path narrative' set in a parallel world with more competent social workers. NXS's account of her quest for the same files frames her two mutually inconsistent accounts of events, culminating in the detailed account of sexual abuse.

The key to the judge's resolution of the puzzle is her finding that there was already enough evidence in the relatively complete records from 1975–77 to give rise to serious concern about Miss P as a parent. Not only was she known to use violence against her daughter (albeit to a degree that might not have been considered very serious by the standards of the time), but there was reason to doubt her ability to protect NXS from others – particularly Miss P's brother, G – and to suspect that she did not really care for NXS but was using her as way to obtain a home of her own. Given this finding, it was relatively easy for the judge to resolve the dispute between the experts: she preferred the complainant's expert's evidence because the defendant's expert had failed to appreciate the significance of matters other than Miss P's physical violence towards her baby. In accepting (apart from one detail) NXS's oral evidence of the physical, emotional and sexual abuse that she had suffered, the judge declared her to be 'a compelling witness' (*NXS* 2009:211), whose previous reticence about the sexual abuse was convincingly explained by her obvious distress in recalling it. Rather than displaying the 'extreme discomfort, shock and disbelief' that reports of mother–daughter incest often elicit (Ogilvie 2004:5), the judge accepted that the 'catalogue of physical, emotional – and even sexual – abuse' alleged by NXS was 'not exceptional' (*NXS* 2009:222). What was unusual, and should have alerted the social workers, was Miss P's frankness about her feelings towards NXS and her violence towards NXS on a number of occasions when witnesses were present. Finally, the judge confidently endorsed the claimant's 'forking path' narrative:

> I am entirely satisfied on a balance of probabilities that, had it not been for the defendant's breach of duty, the claimant would have been removed from Miss P's care and that removal would have taken place no later than the end of 1978, as a result of which the claimant would have been spared the years of abuse that followed and the resultant injuries. (*NXS* 2009:279)

NXS was awarded damages that had been agreed at £60 000 – the relatively modest sum reflecting the fact that damages based mainly on lost earnings bear little relation to the moral gravity of the wrong that the complainant has suffered.

By attaching decisive significance to the complainant's oral testimony (supported by that of her aunt), Mrs Justice Swift made her judgment in favour of NXS very hard to challenge on appeal. As the Court of Appeal recently confirmed, 'it is very well established that findings of primary fact, particularly if founded upon an assessment of the credibility of witnesses, are virtually unassailable' (*Southall* v. *General Medical Council* 2010:47).

Realism and historical truth

As I remarked above, the fragmented and contradictory narratives in *NXS*, and the way in which they call into question the recoverability of historical truth, can be compared to techniques of 'historiographic metafiction'. Just as metafictions draw attention to their own fictionality, the judgment draws attention to its own construction from incomplete and contested evidence. To call into question the possibility of knowing the past in this way is exactly what the defendant was seeking to do. The complainant's case, however, was more akin to a realist narrative in which 'to delay truth is to constitute it' (Barthes 1990:267). NXS's long quest to resolve the enigma of her childhood culminates in a final dramatic revelation of a truth that she has known all along but been unable to reveal. And narrative realism prevails in the judge's ruling that the past can be known well enough for justice to be done.

That judges have a preference for narrative realism over postmodernist uncertainty should come as no surprise (Twining 2006). Courts have to be able to claim to know the past with sufficient certainty for the sanctions they impose to be generally related to actual past events. Otherwise citizens would be unable to predict how their present actions would be narrated in the law's future constructions of the past. In such a Kafkaesque (or Carrollesque) world, the law could provide no guidance as to how to avoid its sanctions. 'All rights and obligations are meaningless without accurate fact finding' (Allen 2008:321). It is only in cases where the courts are required to look further back into the past than they normally do that the option of finding that the past is unknowable is open to them. In several cases since *A* v. *Hoare* (2008) the courts have taken this option, justifying their conclusions not by constructing elaborately nested narratives, but rather by a simple emphasis on the length of the delay and the resulting difficulties for the defendant. For example, the judge in *TCD* v. *Harrow LBC* (2008) dismissed another claim that a council negligently exposed a child to sexual abuse, with a comparable chronology to *NXS*, in a judgment that is less than a fifth of the length of *NXS* and gives little detail of the evidence. *NXS* and *Raggett* are richer and more complex texts because they have to persuade the reader that their reconstructions of the past can reasonably be accepted as true.

Both the narratives examined in this chapter are ones that I find quite persuasive; I am certainly not suggesting that the acts of abuse they relate did not take place. That judges and juries arrive at conclusions about the past by assessing the coherence and plausibility of competing narratives is widely accepted in legal scholarship (see, for example, Bennett and Feldman 1981; Jackson 1995). To accept this, however, is emphatically not to endorse a radically sceptical view that the facts of cases are nothing but narratives or that there is no important difference between fact and fiction. While a few legal scholars have embraced 'radical constructivism' and epistemological scepticism (Teubner 1989:737), others maintain – correctly in my view – that 'narrative coherence [...] provides a test as to the truth or probable truth of propositions about unperceived things and events' (MacCormick 2005:226). One account of how it does so is that inferring the probable truth of a narrative from its coherence exemplifies the non-deductive but rational form of argument known as inference to the best explanation (Pardo and Allen 2008; Amaya 2009). This degree of rationalism is, however, compatible with the claim that, in significant senses, judges 'construct' rather than simply 'find' facts.

One way in which judges clearly do 'construct facts' is that in the act of giving judgment, a probabilistic inference about past events is constituted as a 'fact' that is to be taken as true for legal purposes. In the words of the legal philosopher Hans Kelsen:

> [o]nly by being first ascertained through a legal procedure are facts brought into the sphere of law or do they, so to speak, come into existence within this sphere. Formulating this in a somewhat paradoxically pointed way, we could say that the competent organ ascertaining the conditioning facts legally 'creates' those facts. (Kelsen 1949:136)

What Kelsen calls the 'conditioning facts' – those that are the condition for the application of a legal norm – are typically not 'brute facts' but rather 'actions under a description', such as intentional actions (Anscombe 2000). As we have seen, Mr Raggett always knew that Father Spencer took nude photographs of him, but the significance of those acts depended greatly on whether they were described as artistic, voyeuristic or abusive. It is in this limited respect that Hacking (1998:234) argues that there is a certain 'indeterminacy in the past'. Events that the participants would not at the time have described as 'child abuse' may be appropriately described in that way when viewed from a later period. Historians and judges 'construct' the past by their choice of descriptions of human actions.

A related form of construction to which Hacking (1998:239; 1999: 103–105) draws attention is that of 'human kinds'. Unlike classificatory schemes in, for example, geology and botany, classifications of human beings directly affect their objects, because humans, unlike rocks or plants, can apply those classifications to themselves. As the effects of Mr Raggett's sudden realisation that he could define himself as a victim of abuse vividly illustrate, '[e]xperiences are not only redescribed; they are re-felt' (Hacking 1999:130). In the *NXS* case, we see Miss P using a category that was prominent in the media in the mid-1970s (Parton 1985) to play on the possibility that she was a 'baby batterer'.

There is clearly a danger inherent in the construction of legal and bureaucratic facts about human behaviour that is particularly salient in relation to child abuse. Once a particular kind of human behaviour is 'discovered' and named, there will often be a proliferation of mutually reinforcing narratives about it. Each story about, for example, satanic abuse seems plausible because it fits into an already constructed category of such stories and, adding one more story to the existing category, makes future stories still more plausible (La Fontaine 1998).

The reader may have noticed that the last sentence itself tells a meta-story about how stories of satanic abuse get constructed. Such sceptical meta-stories have a tendency to emerge in child abuse cases, not least because defendants in litigation have an interest in constructing them. In *Raggett* (*Raggett* 2009:para. 72), the judge explicitly takes account of one stock sceptical narrative, that of the memory 'recovered' in the course of therapy, and discounts the specific allegations that relied on memories of this type, which were only a small part of the complaint's case. Implicitly, she also counters another sceptical story, that of apparently corroborative testimony discovered by 'trawling' for witnesses (see Webster 2009). She notes that six of the eleven witnesses who testified for Mr Raggett came forward 'spontaneously' and that their evidence was 'not challenged' by the defendants. From what she relates of their evidence, it does not appear that they were themselves claiming to have been victimised in ways for which they were likely to seek compensation. From a (cautiously) rationalist point of view, the fact that these sceptical narratives are incorporated within the judgment and themselves subjected to sceptical scrutiny makes it more likely that the judge has arrived at the right conclusion.

The most difficult problem confronting the reader of judicial narratives is that the evidence they explain is only the evidence that the judge chooses to mention. In a complex case the judge is bound to be selective, and the choice of explanation may itself shape the selection of evidence. Webster (2009) provides disturbing evidence of judicial selectivity in some cases of alleged institutional child abuse, which have themselves contributed to the plausibility of other narratives of institutional abuse. Unless the reader has access to all the evidence, considerable caution is required in treating even the most persuasive judicial narratives as records of historical truth.

Note

1. In references to judgments, the numbers refer to paragraphs, not pages. All judgments cited, except *Stubbings* v. *Webb* (1993), are available at www.bailii.org.

References

A v. *Hoare* [2008] UKHL 6, [2008] 2 All ER 1.

AB v. *Nugent Care Society; GR* v. *Wirral MBC* [2009] EWCA Civ 827.

Abbott, H. Porter. (2008). *The Cambridge Introduction to Narrative* (2nd edn). Cambridge: Cambridge University Press.

Albonetti v. *Wirral MBC* [2008] EWHC 3523 (QB).

Allen, Ronald J. (2008). Explanationism all the way down. *Episteme* 5, 320–28.

Amaya, Amalia. (2009). Inference to the best legal explanation. In H. Kaptein, H. Prakken and B. Verheij (eds), *Legal Evidence and Proof: Statistics, Stories, Logic*. Farnham: Ashgate.

Anscombe, G. E. M. (2000). *Intention*. Cambridge, MA: Harvard University Press.

Barthes, Roland. (1990). *S/Z*, trans. R. Miller. Oxford: Blackwell.

Bennett, W. L. and M. S. Feldman. (1981). *Reconstructing Reality in the Courtroom*. London: Tavistock.

Case, Paula. (2007). *Compensating Child Abuse in England and Wales*. Cambridge: Cambridge University Press.

Edmond, Gary. (2000). Judicial representations of scientific evidence. *Modern Law Review* 73, 216–51.

Ferguson, H. (2004). *Protecting Children in Time: Child Abuse, Child Protection and the Consequences of Modernity*. Basingstoke: Palgrave Macmillan.

Hacking, Ian. (1998). *Rewriting the Soul: Multiple Personality and the Sciences of Memory*. Princeton: Princeton University Press.

Hacking, Ian. (1999). *The Social Construction of What?* Cambridge, MA: Harvard University Press.

Hutcheon, Linda. (1988). *A Poetics of Postmodernism*. New York: Routledge.

Jackson, Bernard. (1995). *Making Sense in Law*. Liverpool: Deborah Charles.

Jenkins, Philip. (2001). *Pedophiles and Priests: Anatomy of a Contemporary Crisis* (new edn). Oxford: Oxford University Press.

Kelsen, Hans. (1949). *General Theory of Law and State.* Cambridge, MA: Harvard University Press.

La Fontaine, Jean. (1998). *Speak of the Devil: Tales of Satanic Abuse in Contemporary England.* Cambridge: Cambridge University Press.

MacCormick, Neil. (2005). *Rhetoric and the Rule of Law: A Theory of Legal Reasoning.* Oxford: Oxford University Press.

NXS v. *Camden London Borough Council* [2009] EWHC 1786 (QB); [2009] 3 FCR 157.

Ogilvie, Beverley. (2004). *Mother-Daughter Incest: A Guide for Helping Professionals.* London: Routledge.

Pardo, M. S. and R. J. Allen. (2008). Juridical proof and the best explanation. *Law and Philosophy* 27, 223–68.

Parton, Nigel. (1985). *The Politics of Child Abuse.* Basingstoke: Macmillan.

Plummer, Ken. (1995). *Telling Sexual Stories.* London: Routledge.

Raggett, Patrick. (1999). Bells, smells and Georgie Best. In Simon Kuper and Marcela Mora y Araujo (eds), *Perfect Pitch 4: Dirt.* London: Headline.

Raggett v. *Society of Jesus 1929 Trust for Roman Catholic Purposes and Another* [2009] EWHC 909 (QB), (2009) BMLR 147.

Raggett v. *Society of Jesus 1929 Trust for Roman Catholic Purposes, Governors of Preston Catholic College* [2010] EWCA Civ 1002.

Re B (Children) [2008] UKHL 35, [2009] 1 AC 11.

Ricoeur, Paul. (2006). *Memory, History, Forgetting.* Chicago: Chicago University Press.

Southall v. *General Medical Council* [2010] EWCA Civ 407, [2010] 2 FLR 1550.

Stubbings v. *Webb* [1993] AC 498.

TCD v. *Harrow London Borough Council* [2008] EWHC 3048 (QB), [2009] 2 FCR 297.

Teubner, Gunther. (1989). How the law thinks: Toward a constructivist epistemology of law. *Law and Society Review* 23, 727–57.

Thorpe, Adam. (1992). *Ulverton.* London: Viking.

Twining, William. (2006). *Rethinking Evidence* (2nd edn). Cambridge: Cambridge University Press.

Webster, Richard. (2009). *The Secret of Bryn Estyn: The Making of a Modern Witch Hunt* (rev. edn). Oxford: Orwell Press.

1.4

The Edgier Waters of the Era: Gordon Burn's *Somebody's Husband, Somebody's Son*

Martyn Colebrook

> With the West case, I had everything: I had access to their belongings, to the police interviews – everything, basically, that you could possibly wish to get – and you spend three years writing a book, and you still don't know what made these two people do the kind of things they did. (Lea 2009)

In an article written for *The Guardian* concerning Norman Mailer's *The Executioner's Song*, a novel about the state of Utah's execution of Gary Gilmore, Gordon Burn describes the origins of his own novel about crime, *Somebody's Husband, Somebody's Son* (2004[1984]), which focuses on the Yorkshire Ripper:

> Instead of being repelled by it, as I should have been, I found, instead, that I wanted to draw closer. On January 2 1981 I was on the final pages of *The Executioner's Song*, which I had read at a gallop. Around tea-time it came on the television that they had arrested a man in Sheffield in connection with the Yorkshire Ripper murders. Forty-eight hours later I was in the bar of the Norfolk Gardens Hotel in Bradford listening to claim and counter-claim about who had 'got his chequebook out' for Peter Sutcliffe's father or 'locked up' the brother, making notes towards *Somebody's Husband, Somebody's Son*, a book for which Norman Mailer would generously volunteer a quote when it was published in America. (Burn 2004)

During his writing life, Gordon Burn carved out a reputation for working on fiction relating to crime, deviance, celebrity and serial killers. A celebrated traverser of the boundaries between fact and fiction, his award-winning oeuvre also features *Alma Colgan* (2004[1991]), which overlapped the case of Myra Hindley with that of an imaginary post-celebrity popular singer who died in 1966, an ambitious and provocative 'meditation on artifice and obscurity'. *Fullalove* (2004[1995]) features the seedy London tabloids and Norman Miller, a journalist reporting on a series of brutal sex crimes who comes to wonder whether he is a witness or a deeper part of the cause and effect of these crimes. *Happy Like Murderers* (2001[1998]) focuses on Frederick and Rosemary West and is a book about criminals, as opposed to their crimes. His final novel, *Born Yesterday* (2008), is a blended mosaic that highlights the impact of and manipulation of cultural discourses such as the media on and by Gerry and Kate McCann (among others).

A journalist by profession, Burn worked for *The Guardian* and *Rolling Stone*, which gave him an insider's perspective on the major cultural events of the 1970s and drove him to recount them for people on the outside. This in itself gives his work a formidable cross-cultural foundation and the capacity to bridge and integrate a variety of different literary forms into his writing. Hailed as being 'far ahead of the rest of the literary world' and 'one of the great literary innovators of these times' (Lea 2009), his novels respond to an ongoing feeling of social, cultural and political fragmentation by using a fragmentary style of writing; there is the collage of sources, the historicised fiction, the Ripper myth. Burn's subjects appeal to a number of the underpinning themes in contemporary crime writing: trauma, spectacle and serial killing. Burn was fascinated by the dark side of celebrity, and his writing and impulse represent attempts to find understanding and meaning in the most disturbing of contemporary events.

After the sentencing of Peter Sutcliffe to life imprisonment in 1981, it seemed as though the case would finally be closed. However, in 1984 Burn published *Somebody's Husband, Somebody's Son* after living for three years in Sutcliffe's home town of Bingley and researching his life, friends and family, spending night after night listening to stories of the murderer's early life. Burn's novel was an attempt to follow in the footsteps of Truman Capote's *In Cold Blood* (1966) and Norman Mailer's *The Executioner's Song* (1980), telling the story from the inside out. Further to this, Burn depicted the society of Bingley in the cultural context of the 1980s, and particularly the latent aggression towards women that was present and prevalent during this time.

Written using a combination of discourses including memoir and realism with cross-cuttings to newspaper clippings, television interviews and familial recollection, this text draws on a wide range of sources to craft a narrative account of the family in which Sutcliffe was brought up, as well as tracing the different worlds in which he lived, observing, identifying and documenting. Burn's style is atmospheric and falls into the cadence of David Peace and Robert Meadley – it is an idiomatically constructed Yorkshire of memory, allusion and semi-quotation.

Burn's editor, David Robson, offered these observations about Burn's journalistic and authorial technique: Burn, like David Peace (who acknowledges a debt to Burn), possesses a ferocious eye for detail and an intimate knowledge and connection with the landscape about which he is writing:

> He had a phenomenal eye for telling detail, an acute ear and an unusual ability to get to the truth of a situation. From the start he was clear to the point of truculence about what he was and was not interested in, and over the years he showed such constancy of vision and fixity of purpose that his became a strong and unique voice. He was never middle-of-the-road, and spotted many truths about modern life that others missed. (Robson, cited in Wainwright 2009)

This blend of journalistic eye and creative talent ensures that Burn's novels, and *Somebody's Husband, Somebody's Son* particularly, succeed through the deployment of narrative techniques and writing strategies used in pulp crime fiction – Bloom (1996:3) explains that 'Pulp fiction' is where 'the violent, erotic, and sentimental excesses of contemporary life signify different facets of the modern experience played out in the gaudy pages of sensational and kitsch literature: novels, comic books, tabloid newspapers'. The title of Burn's novel is taken from one of the many nationwide appeals for information about the identity of the Yorkshire Ripper. The quotation 'this individual could be somebody's husband, somebody's son' establishes the normality of the life Sutcliffe led among his community, family and friends, a life that was in contrast with the extremities of his crimes.

The cultural context for Sutcliffe's upbringing has been seized on by commentators, such as Nicole Ward Jouve, as informing and influencing his crimes, the attitudes he displayed, as well as the violence and atrocities he committed against his victims. My reading of these environmental conditions draws together familial, regional, historical and biographical information and uses Jouve's (1986) critical work *The Street Cleaner: The Yorkshire Ripper Case on Trial*, which adopts a feminist/poststructuralist analysis of the Sutcliffe murder case, as a foundational text.

Burn's novel begins by invoking Elizabeth Gaskell and Emily Brontë's assessment of the West Yorkshire landscape, emphasising how Bradford and the surrounding area were congruent with the social conditions of a dependency on industry as the main source of employment, as well as the social and economic strata of the people who lived there. The area in which Sutcliffe grew up is 'a conservative community, tolerant of mild eccentricity but more given to "shamming gaumless" [behaviour suggesting 'high jinks' or 'larks'], than to acts of flamboyance or outward display' (Burn 2004[1984]:3). This was a community of interiority, where conflicts and domestic problems were dealt with behind closed doors and no 'dirty laundry' was to be aired in public, lest the outward perception of a family was to be tarnished. These are the tenets of a classic working-class community, with great pride placed on the high standards of the domestic and the endurance of the labouring males. While someone who is a little out of the ordinary is seen as relatively acceptable or expected, 'because every street's got one', the extreme or the outlandishly different will be punished and shunned by their peers and made to suffer the physical consequences of their difference. Burn (2004[1984]:4) goes onto describe how

> the blackened stone on the semi-detached villas and Victorian terraces on the gentler slopes is overpowered by the paler brick of the post-war estates which provide the physical link between the heart of the old town and the scattered hamlets and villages high up on the moor's edge.

The contrasts and markers here are dominated by generational change and different social strata coming to occupy separate areas of the community. These 'post-war estates' are the symbol of overspill and an inability to contain an expanding populace. Differing signs of wealth come into collision with the higher economic bracket living independently on the 'moor's edge' while the estate 'overpowered' these terraces, suggesting that physical strength and resistance form a dominant force. Indeed, physical strength is the force that is applied to correct or punish people who are different or who transgress their expected social roles – openly outspoken women, people of colour, rebellious children, men who are openly homosexual, all of whom are notably absent from this community. On experiencing this community and the areas of Bradford where Sutcliffe carried out the crimes, Jouve (1986:18) comments: 'You couldn't help wondering what connections there were between the socio-economic dereliction which much of the geography expressed, and the type of violence which was at work in the nooks and crannies of those landscapes.' The 'dereliction' Jouve identifies is symptomatic of an underlying crisis in identity, where man is rapidly replaced by a more efficient machine, undermining his role as a dominant force in the workplace. As Zaretsky (1976:28) argues, '[i]n this form, male supremacy, which long antedated Capitalism, became an institutionalized part of the capitalist system of production', and this mastery in the workplace must also continue at home. There is something intensely Gothic about the landscape in which Sutcliffe was brought up, with its tenets of industry and (eventually) postindustrial legacy. Williams (2007:13) reminds us that modernity and the Gothic are mutual conditions for the emergence of the serial killer, 'this sobriquet having been handed down to us from the populist presses and penny dreadfuls'. A pattern emerges from such socioeconomic conditions where violence against an individual becomes the outward expression of internalised fears and frustrations. Jouve (1986:21) describes further the 'Ugly high-rise. Ugly council houses. The beautiful architecture is that of the Victorian temples to industry, the town halls and factories and warehouses, crenellated tops, gothic arches, gloomy grandeur'. The textile industry and other harbingers of Victorian industrial development were the dominant force behind provision of employment in the area in which Sutcliffe was brought up. Despite this, previous generations of his family had successfully found better-paid work that betrayed distinct markers of socioeconomic advancement. Such advancement was at odds with the community in which they grew up. As Newman (1993:20) points out, '"The Ripper" is a type of *given* of a certain landscape – a required designation or focus for a number of traits'.

Bloom (1996:177) continues Newman's discussion, highlighting why the Ripper narrative emerges from the Gothic so powerfully: 'The Ripper's script has violence, eroticism, sentimentality and the supernatural: a text to live out the sensationalism of the modern.' Peter was the third generation of Sutcliffes to be born in Bingley after his imposing great-grandfather John 'Willie' Sutcliffe moved there from Bradford, but Peter bucked this trend by moving away to Bradford after his marriage. John Sutcliffe, in an indication of the culture in which his son was brought up, recounted both the fear that 'Willie' would instil in his workers, and his appetites for butcher's shop offcuts (offal, tripe, chitterlings), which John rapidly identified as 'man's food' (Burn 2004[1984]:7). It was these same entrails and internal organs that would be openly displayed on the bodies of Sutcliffe's victims when his attacks reached their most frenzied point, with deliberate violations of the stomach and lower body areas using pieces of wood or screwdrivers. Vera Millward, murdered on 16 May 1978, was found in Manchester Royal Infirmary car park: 'When her coat was removed, it could be seen that her stomach had been mutilated so badly that her intestines had spilled onto the ground' (Burn 2004[1984]:201). The weekly display of eating such volumes of this food was an image with which Sutcliffe grew up, and it is an image mirrored in the reduction of his victims' status to that of animals, through the use of the victims' bodies for consumption, both physically and sexually. The attitudes displayed towards women – they're 'for frying bacon and screwin' (Burn 2004[1984]:68) – highlight a culture wherein violence and oppression were expected and certainly accepted. Jouve (1986:24) shrewdly observes: 'perhaps when you're surrounded by dereliction, you feel like inflicting it too?'

The movement away from industry and into accounts and other lower-middle-class professions, along with a father whose own abilities ensured that he was forever receiving acclaim in the local newspaper for his prowess on the sports field (as a cricketer) or performing in local amateur dramatic events, demonstrate an aspirational side to the Sutcliffes, a desire to 'better themselves'. Parallels can be drawn here with the novel by John Braine, *Room at the Top* (1957), set in the familiar fictional West Yorkshire location of 'Warnley' where the figure of Joe Lampton, socially aspirational but ultimately prepared to sacrifice others as he continues his relentless quest for success, determines to reach his peak and causes the death of a woman in the process; Jouve expands on these parallels, but it is the presence of an intimate connection between the desire to escape and the demise of the women around you that haunts the Ripper's cultural context. Burn examines further parallels here when he considers John Sutcliffe's other sons, Mick and Carl:

> The people up Gilstead and Eldwick really looked down on the people from 'the estate' as they called it. [...] John Sutcliffe, however, not only chose to ignore the social barriers that had been erected but was pleased to call the bank managers and schoolteachers [...] in other words, the very people singled out by Braine as the embodiment of small-town bourgeois values in his book – his friends. (Burn 2004[1984]:158)

That this sense of class dislocation or confusion would have underpinned Sutcliffe's upbringing is telling when considering the lack of stability in his own working life and the distinctly unconventional traits that he will come to display. Not seemingly aspirational in a professional context, Sutcliffe does, however, come to embody these middle-class traits through his financial conservatism, his dutiful attitude to his family and his eventual success in a stable, secure job.

When recounting his understanding of the different attitudes displayed by men and women in relation to the birth of their first child, John Sutcliffe commented that '[t]hey pretend to be delighted when it's a girl, but they'd have been much more delighted if it had been a boy, the first one. It's the sort of thing that fellers do' (Burn 2004[1984]:13). This further reinforces the fierce sense of tradition, inheritance and atavism that characterised the environment into which Peter Sutcliffe was born, where the clearly defined roles for men and women stood firm and were reinforced by each generation. There also remained an underlying suspicion of overambition beyond one's social status and a pervasive mistrust of those who were different. The privileging of males as patriarchs within the family structure evidences their assumed superiority and the weight of expectation that was placed on them. Earlier references to the domineering Ivy Sutcliffe, who marshalled her husband and son behind closed doors, further stigmatise the women within this community. As Burn (2004[1984]:19) describes, 'John Sutcliffe was always a great advocate of the "old-fashioned" virtues of family life' and, in communities such as these, the male was seen the locus of the family. The male's role demanded repeated outward shows of unity from the family irrespective of domestic difficulties, and the expectation was that the male offspring would follow in their father's footsteps and continue the family line. When he was at work, the responsibility for nurturing the children lay with John Sutcliffe's wife, but this ended the moment John returned to the domestic sphere: 'When he was in the house, however, his children were left in no doubt at all who was master: he brooked no contradiction, and his word was law' (Burn 2004[1984]:28).

Born as weak as a sapling and displaying distinct developmental difficulties with regard to walking and speech, as well as an aversion to social interaction and engagement with his peers, Peter Sutcliffe was at odds with the expectations of his gender in Bingley from an early age. Even at 5 years old, 'Peter still hadn't got out of the habit of clinging limpet-like to his mother's hems' (Burn 2004[1984]:23). His schooling took him to Cottingley Manor where, after repeated episodes of bullying, Sutcliffe eventually absconded until being discovered by his parents. After a visit to the school by his father, Peter was sent back and, despite the suspicion of problems, never complained or returned home. This, for his father, marked 'the beginnings of "character" that his wife's "cossetting" and over-protective attitude had always denied' (Burn 2004[1984]:35).

As Comer (1974:13) claims, 'while a girl may for a while, "emulate acceptable masculine behaviour", no such toleration is extended to the boy. The traffic is only one way ... a boy may not join ranks with his inferiors.'

Sutcliffe's working life commenced in August 1961, aged 15, as an apprentice fitter at the engineering works of Fairbank and Brearley in Church Street, Bingley, but, as became a hallmark of his stints in employment with Bingley Cemetery and the Water Board, timekeeping was a problem. Colleagues remember that '[h]e seemed to be looking at the world from a distance, as if it were just so many images, flickering on a screen' (Burn 2004[1984]:39) and, in addition to this, Sutcliffe displayed a sense of detachment and complete comfort in his own company as well as a lack of needing people around him. Personal qualities for which Sutcliffe was noted were an inability to control certain aspects of his voice, laughing with a sense of inappropriateness, and repeated incidents of drifting into dazes where his 're-entry' would be swift and often violent – in one incident smashing a glass against a table in a pub. The difficulties with timekeeping, the developmental problems, his introspection and isolation from the world around him, not to mention his extreme discomfort with his own body, would lead to a possible contemporary rereading of Sutcliffe as being positioned somewhere on the spectrum for autistic disorder.

Sutcliffe's reluctance to or inability to join the 'men' overtly lasted until he was 18, and it was this 'character' that was to be reinforced by a conscious decision to 'bulk up' and devote himself to the use of a Bullring for weight training and body building, which expanded him physically in a rapid amount of time. His change of career to being a grave digger in Bingley provided the necessary manual labour to support this development.

The Bullring that Peter acquired when he was 18 led to his physical improvement and was inspired by adverts featuring the icons of Charles Atlas and other 'men' who had come from being 'half a man'. Being anything less than 'a man' in Bingley and the surrounding areas was deemed unacceptable, hence Sutcliffe's father's repeated insistence that Peter was never 'a shirt-lifter' (a derogatory term meaning homosexual). Body building is a notoriously solitary pursuit, predicated on narcissism and driven by a desire for perfection and self-improvement. It requires displaying dominance in response to physical challenges, regular and structured adherence to routine, and subservience to the Bullring, which provides the facility for this.

The affinity with solitary pursuits led to Sutcliffe finding work in the profession with which he was seemingly most happy, as a long-distance lorry driver for T. and W. H. Clark, a small engineering firm based in the industrial estate between Bradford and Shipley. Having 'graduated' to one of two Ford Transcontinental lorries ('big rigs') that the firm owned, his brother, Mick, found that the truck's 'height, combined with the sense of mass and speed, seemed to invigorate Peter and fill him with the confidence he normally lacked' (Burn 2004[1984]:157). By Sutcliffe surrendering himself to machines, of the mechanical and bodybuilding kind, Jouve argues, 'the industrial tools or engines stand as a substitute for powerful manhood' (Jouve 1986:72). Sutcliffe finally achieves being more than 'half a man' as he gains total control of the vehicle and 'masters' the Bullring.

Sutcliffe's first attack comes after a prostitute takes his money and disappears, leaving her male friends to intimidate him into leaving the area. He returns later with a friend, Trevor, and attacks a woman who resembles her, with a large stone in a sock. Following the first incident with the prostitute, Sutcliffe came to describe how 'his mind was "in a turmoil"' and 'he developed "a general loathing for any prostitute"'. He felt himself being pushed "over the brink"' (Burn 2004[1984]:98). Coupling this with a revelation over his wife's infidelity and a religious education that had taught him about the 'unclean ways' of the activities engaged in by prostitutes, Sutcliffe took on his self-designated role as 'The Street-Cleaner', an individual who was set to rid the streets of prostitutes and their trade. Jouve (1986:93) comments that 'what the "code" expresses is not just aggression between males, it's the permissibility of aggression between males, it's the permissibility of aggression against females, provided consensus (that they're somehow sub-human).'

Sutcliffe advised Trevor about always keeping a rock handy because of its use as a weapon. This echoes the pervasive cultural conditions that legitimised the use of violence as a corrective tool towards women and as a method for asserting one's masculinity. Further evidence of how widely accepted such attitudes to women were can be found in the police terminology for Sutcliffe's first murder:

> Far from being what is known as a 'fish-and-chips job' – the one-off murder of a prostitute after closing time – the murder of Wilma McCann turned out to be the first of an appalling series of killings and attacks by a man the media called the Yorkshire Ripper. (Jouve 1986:1)

The term 'fish-and-chips job' highlights the status afforded to prostitutes, cheap and low-grade goods that can be purchased, consumed quickly and disposed of easily. Jouve (1986:32) argues further that 'Nowhere in the whole Ripper case do women figure as people. They figure as bodies, on which violence has left an "obscene" inscription, which is in turn deciphered by the police and the media.' Ava Reivers, who was arrested with Sutcliffe when he tried to murder her, was told: 'We're not interested in you, we're interested in *him*' (Jouve 1986:32). The deciphering is extended to Sutcliffe's wife, who becomes a figurative 'talking head' when she is placed 'on trial' after his appeal, albeit in a role more complicit than she would imagine. For the majority of Burn's account, Sonia lives her life either locked away in the house or cast out from social situations because of her ongoing illnesses. Plain (2001:13) supports Jouve's claims, arguing that, in crime fiction

> [m]urder is literally 'written on the body' and bodies are never neutral. They inevitably bear the inscriptions of their cultural production – socially determined markers of gender, race, sexuality and class that profoundly influence the ways in which they are read by witnesses, police, detectives and readers.

What is significant about these markers and their interpretation is that Sutcliffe only targeted prostitutes. Having begun with this approach and varied the ethnicity of his targets – among them a Jamaican woman, who had her claims dismissed because she was thought to be a victim of domestic violence, and an Eastern European – Sutcliffe then murdered Josephine Whittaker at Easter 1979. The next morning it was revealed that she was not a prostitute, but a 19-year-old clerk at Halifax Building Society. This, along with the murder of Jayne MacDonald (a shop worker from Leeds), gave the police's investigation a different dimension, because the socioeconomic status of his victims had been elevated through their employment in more 'respectable' professions. As Jouve (1986:181) argues,

> [h]is murders also *look like* social exploitation. He kills prostitutes, office-cleaners, shop-assistants, clerks, secretaries, students, the social level rises as his own ascent makes him more confident, he aims 'higher'. But none of the victims is rich, none of them a 'professional' woman in that other sense of the word. Students? Yes. Lecturers like myself? No.

The sense of ascent reflects Sutcliffe's vision of himself as a higher being through this 'cleaning', adopting a moral standpoint superior to those men who accepted or used prostitutes. There is also the idea of a social mobility as he aspires from the depths of the grave digging to the top of the lorry, a master of his own machinery.

On 4 January 1981, Peter Sutcliffe's questioning by Inspector John Boyle regarding his soliciting for prostitution in the Bradford area came to a dramatic conclusion with the following exchange:

(S)   I think you have been leading up to it.
(B)   Leading up to what?
(S)   The Yorkshire Ripper.
(B)   What about the Yorkshire Ripper?
(S)   Well, it's me. (Burn 2004[1984]:275)

With such an understated acknowledgement that they had secured their killer, Peter Sutcliffe brought to a conclusion the terrifying reign of Britain's most notorious serial killer (at the time). Following a 16-hour written documentation of his crimes, Sutcliffe had only one request: that he was to be the person to tell his wife, Sonia. As further evidence of the masculine culture that surrounded this case, what happened in the wake of his admission is described by Burn (2004[1984]:277): 'The scene was suddenly like the victors' dressing room in the minutes following the FA Cup Final at Wembley, with the all-male company playfully punching each other and hugging each other and pumping each other's hands'. The sporting register, saturated with homosocial bonding and congratulations, notably excludes women and, as Jouve notes, they remain the dead, the wounded and the socially invisible, slipping back into the red light districts of Bradford to ply their unspoken, anonymous trade.

Continuing the sporting register, which demonstrates just how strongly the Ripper story had permeated popular culture, police had already been taunted by supporters on the terraces chanting 'Ripper 10, Police Nil' and 'There's only one Yorkshire Ripper', but the tone now changed. David Yallop's 1981 account *Deliver Us from Evil* (the title itself imitating Sutcliffe's self-proclaimed Messianic status) describes the scene in the witness box when Peter Sutcliffe came to stand trial: 'The Yorkshireman in the witness box is reminiscent of Boycott in top form, batting against Lilley and Thomson bowling at half pace' (Yallop 1981:354–5). The Yorkshireman in question was all too willing to dismiss the 'half volleys' and 'full tosses' thrown at him by a Queen's Counsel determined to secure the conviction, finding his array of verbal shots to be impervious to the latter's own slovenly pace of delivery. The dynamic of the case rested on whether Sutcliffe could secure a reduced conviction on the grounds of diminished responsibility due to his diagnosis of paranoid schizophrenia. It is telling that when Sutcliffe's wife, Sonia, was brought to the trial as a witness, she changed from the wife of the Ripper into a far more tainted individual:

> In a way, Sonia was in the dock, too. For soon her enigmatic façade had been stripped away, revealing her as a domineering woman who henpecked her husband. She, too, heard voices. She, too, was schizophrenic [...] Dr Milne told the courts that Sutcliffe's version of his wife's behaviour 'accounts for his aggressive behaviour towards many women' [...] So suddenly Sonia, not God, was to blame. (Beattie 1981:152–3)

The stigmatising of his violent behaviour towards women is reduced during Sonia's 'trial' because such violence was seen as acceptable when a woman is threatening to dominate the male. Effectively, the argument was that the Ripper's victims are a consequence of another woman's violence – a woman who is further stigmatised by a diagnosis of mental health problems. Such displaced actions effectively represented attempts at continued absolution, in the social and the religious sense. It is telling that Bloom (1996:162) assesses the Ripper (as a post-nineteenth-century construct) in similar terms:

> Jack becomes the focus for the bizarre in the ordinary misery of everyday life in the metropolitan slums. Jack the murderer becomes Jack the *missionary* who focused on problems other investigators were unable to bring to such a wide audience. From the nineteenth century to the present day, the cultural context of the Ripper, whether Jack or Peter, seems strikingly similar, and still dominated by the same pretexts and concepts.

Burn's novel fits into a trajectory of Ripperana (material that engages with the Ripper myth) spanning the twentieth and twenty-first centuries. Commemoration of Sutcliffe does exist, as Burn highlights at the conclusion of *Somebody's Husband, Somebody's Son*. Sutcliffe's brother, Carl, visited the House of Horrors wax museum in Blackpool (a place by which Peter Sutcliffe became fascinated) with his girlfriend and was confronted, as he walked in, by a museum of his brother surrounded by extracts from the popular press. The taunting letters sent to George Oldfield by the individual we suspect to be 'Wearside Jack' are part of another strategy that Burn uses to great effect. Bloom (1996:163) explains that:

> [t]he Ripper letters are a form of *true life confession* heightened to the level of a fiction which embraces a 'cockney' persona, a sense of black humour, a melodramatic villain ('them curses of coppers') and a ghoul ('sending innerds') and mixes it with a sense of the dramatic and a feeling for rhetorical climax. In these letters, life and popular theatre come together to act upon the popular imagination.

By embracing the strategies used in pulp fiction, Burn succeeds with a novel where the cultural context would have made it easy to fail or to produce a text insufficient to cover the scope and the vista needed for such a subject. The popular imagination that this captures does not place Burn in the genre of popular fiction, but does explain why Ripperana has continued to permeate many different genres that are connected with crime and detective fiction. Bloom (1996:165) continues:

> Jack the Ripper is a name for both a necessary fiction and a fact missing its history […] Separable from his origins, the Ripper is a strange historicized fiction, a designation for a type of murderer and his scenario (for the game is to give 'Jack' his real name and collapse fiction into biography) whilst also being a structural necessity for a type of fictional genre: the author of the 'Dear Boss' letter, etc.

Bloom seems to be arguing that the 'designation' is a template, hence the 'game' is to give 'Jack' his real name. Burn succeeds in the naming process, producing a fiction that collapses into biography and, arguably, a biography that collapses into fiction.

References

Beattie, John. (1981). *The Yorkshire Ripper Story*. London: Quartet/Daily Star.
Bloom, Clive. (1996). *Cult Fiction: Popular Reading and Cult Theory*. Basingstoke: Macmillan.
Braine, John. (1989). *Room at the Top*. London: Arrow.
Burn, Gordon. (2004[1984]). *Somebody's Husband, Somebody's Son*. Kent: Faber and Faber.
Burn, Gordon. (2004[1991]). *Alma Colgan*. Kent: Faber and Faber.
Burn, Gordon. (2004[1995]). *Fullalove*. Kent: Faber and Faber.
Burn, Gordon. (2001[1998]). *Happy Like Murderers*. Kent: Faber and Faber.
Burn, Gordon. (2004). Dead calm. *The Guardian*, 5 June 2004. Available at http://www.guardian.co.uk/books/2004/jun/05/featuresreviews.guardianreview37 [accessed March 2011].

Burn, Gordon. (2008). *Born Yesterday.* Kent: Faber and Faber.

Capote, Truman. (1967). *In Cold Blood.* London: Penguin.

Comer, Lee. (1974). *Wedlocked Women.* New York: Feminist Press.

Jouve, Nicole Ward. (1986). *The Street Cleaner: The Yorkshire Ripper Case on Trial.* London: Marion Boyars.

Lea, Richard. (2009). Groundbreaking author Gordon Burn dies aged 61. *The Guardian*, 20 July 2009. Available at http://www.guardian.co.uk/books/2009/jul/20/gordon-burn-dies-aged-61 [accessed March 2011].

Mailer, Norman. (1979). *The Executioner's Song.* London: Hutchinson.

Newman, Kim. (1993). Forever on the prowl. *Million: The Magazine about Popular Fiction*, 14, 19–21.

Plain, Gill. (2001). *Twentieth Century Crime Fiction: Gender, Sexuality and the Body.* Edinburgh: Edinburgh University Press.

Wainwright, Martin. (2009). Gordon Burn: Obituary. *The Guardian*, 20 July 2009. Available at http://www.guardian.co.uk/books/2009/jul/20/gordon-burn-obituary [accessed March 2011].

Williams, Mark. (2007). Out of mind: Fictions about conflict. Unpublished paper presented at *Globalisation and Writing*, Bath Spa University, 31 March–3 April.

Yallop, David. (1981). *Deliver Us from Evil.* London: Macdonald Futura.

Zaretsky, Eli. (1976). *Capitalism, the Family and Personal Life.* London: Pluto Press.

2
Constructing Criminal Fictions

2.0
Introduction and Rationale

The fictionalisation of crime has not only become a much-loved pursuit, but also a means of analysing society, even an excuse to do so. This chapter's contributors are drawn to popular crime fiction, through the analysis of which they also scrutinise culture. Michelle Iwen's analysis of the *Shutter Island* novel and its filmic incarnation explores the subjects of insanity, violence and murder, and their relation to medical, philosophical and authority-related discourses. Richard Brown's work investigates the concept of the 'millennial' in relation to Peace and Larsson's popular crime fiction, to talk about politics, moral crises and terminality. Dave Ireland is also interested in criminal construction in fiction, and in the use of music to portray the cinematic criminal in particular. Through this insight from the area of music psychology, we notice the phenomenon of incongruent music soundtracking violent action, making such moments not only memorable and iconic, but also interpretable in particular ways that relate to identity and space construction, not to mention viewer identification. Staying with the theme of fictionality in crime narratives, Malcah Effron explains how particular novelists set their work apart from reality, justifying its existence and demanding that readers suspend their disbeliefs, while maintaining a firm grasp on legal, readerly reality also.

2.1
Cogito ergo sum: Criminal Logic and Mad Discourse in *Shutter Island*

Michelle E. Iwen

> Better a tale with a barbed moral and a tragic ending
> than no story at all. (Porter 2006)

The philosophical discussion of reason and the boundary between sanity and madness has been a contentious topic since long before the Enlightenment. This problematic boundary is discussed at length in Dennis Lehane's thriller *Shutter Island* (2003) and in the Martin Scorsese film adaptation of the same name (2009). The protagonist of *Shutter Island*, US Marshal Teddy Daniels, visits a psychiatric prison complex for the criminally insane to search for a missing patient while operating under his own agenda of finding Andrew Laeddis, his wife's killer. The book and the surprisingly faithful film adaptation follow Daniels as his investigation on the island forces him to confront his own fractured psyche: that Daniels *is* Laeddis and has created an elaborate fantasy world to avoid confronting the guilt he feels over neglecting his wife's obvious mental illness, leading her to drown their three children, and his own fatal act in her murder. Lehane constructs *Shutter Island* as a conscious meditation on the blurred boundary between the animalistic violence of the madman, highlighted in seventeenth-and eighteenth-century confinement discourses and Descartes's best-known contribution to philosophy, *cogito ergo sum*, also known as the cogito. The syllogistic logic of the well-known maxim *I think, therefore I am* is examined throughout the novel in Daniels's conversations with both partner Chuck Aule and island psychiatrist Dr Cawley about missing patient and convicted murderer Rachel Solando, whose disappearance serves as the inciting incidence in Daniels's visit to the island. The logic of the cogito is also mused on during the climax at the island's lighthouse, when Daniels is confronted with overwhelming evidence of his insanity through his own cryptic clues. Lehane uses Daniels's intelligence and self-awareness to problematise the effect of Enlightenment philosophy, medical discourses of confinement and psychiatric moral therapy. Lehane also uses Daniels's philosophical inquiry to illustrate modern man's negotiations within the transitioning state of scientific and moral epistemes.[1]

Written shortly after the critically acclaimed 2001 novel *Mystic River*, Lehane's *Shutter Island* marks a conspicuous departure from his more formulaic crime novels, with an intentional eye towards *noir* and Gothic literature. Written from the third-person, omniscient point of view, the novel is set entirely on the fictional Shutter Island, a small island in Boston Harbour, accessible only by ferry. Lehane spends much of the novel emphasising the isolation and melancholic mood of the island, reflecting his stated intent of blending the evocative Gothic writing of the Brontë sisters with the pulpy noir of the film *Invasion of the Body Snatchers* (Weich 2003). This melancholic tension is recreated in the film version through mood lighting and an oppressive minor-key score (Scorsese 2009), in a clear homage to the groundbreaking German Expressionist silent film *The Cabinet of Dr. Caligari*, directed by Robert Wiene (1921).[2] As mentioned, Shutter Island is home to Ashecliffe Hospital for the Criminally Insane and it is under the guise of searching for escaped patient Rachel Solando that we find US Marshall Teddy Daniels investigating her disappearance, in addition to his own personal search for Andrew Laeddis. It is after Teddy and his partner, US Marshal Chuck Aule/psychiatrist Dr. Lester Sheehan, become temporarily trapped on the island due to a hurricane that the real investigation begins. Daniels becomes increasingly convinced that the physicians of the hospital are continuing psychiatric experiments begun by the Nazis, adding an additional level of tension with his paranoid delusions of a government-sponsored psychosurgical and psychotropic drug-induced army to fight the 1950s 'Red Scare' of communism. Throughout his physical journey on the island, Daniels suffers from increasingly graphic dreams and hallucinations, both accompanied by migraine headaches, illuminating a familiar philosophical question: can one truly tell a dream from reality? It is the climactic scene at the lighthouse where Daniels is confronted with concrete evidence of his identity as Laeddis and his own role in the death of his wife and children that serves as the figurative and physical symbol for psychiatry's attempt to enlighten unreasonable patients through psycho-surgery and drug therapy. It is in the lighthouse that Laeddis recognises the error of his own carefully constructed identity as Daniels and is informed that his search of the island was condoned by the entire hospital as a therapeutic process, rather than utilising psycho-surgery as a solution to Daniels/Laeddis's violent reactions.[3] The final scene finds Daniels/Laeddis reverting to the Daniels persona, with a pending lobotomy implied as orderlies approach him with a straitjacket.

While Lehane's text provides a wealth of potential analysis focused on patient rights and the concept of liberatory madness, it is his clever manipulation of philosophical syllogisms and its embodied discussion of the problems with Cartesian dualism that make it an effective text for examination. *Shutter Island* is rife with rhetorical philosophical questions. Especially interesting is Daniels and psychiatrist Dr. Cawley's discussion of the schizophrenic structure of escaped patient Rachel Solando's delusions (Solando herself being an imagined character of Daniels), in which her husband was alive and she had yet to drown her children. After Daniels receives Solando's first cryptic mathematical clue, Dr. Cawley explains that 'Rachel is quite brilliant in her games. Her delusions [...] are conceived on a very delicate architecture. To sustain the structure, she employs an elaborate narrative thread to her life that is completely fictitious' (Lehane 2003:50). The idea of a carefully constructed yet structurally unsound architecture of Solando's damaged pysche is what allows her to exist in a maximum security psychiatric hospital while cognisant only of her home and maternal and wifely duties. After Daniels questions the logic behind her scribbled numbers, Dr. Cawley confirms that indeed nothing is random or purposeless with Solando, for 'she had to keep the structure in her head from collapsing, and to do that, she had to be *thinking* always' (Lehane 2003:51). This constant yet unconscious production of thoughts sophisticated enough to challenge the obvious sensory experience of hospital life is a frequent theme throughout the book and film. It is this very act of thinking that defines both Solando and Daniels as Laeddis's projected personalities – this act of thinking is also what creates their existence in the Cartesian sense. Arguably the best-known philosophical maxim, Rene Descartes's *cogito ergo sum*, I think, therefore I am, allows for the metaphysical 'life' of these projected personalities to exist within the logically ordered and finely structured narrative thread of Laeddis's mind. Solando and Daniels exist for Laeddis alone, just as Descartes demonstrated to 'himself his own existence by performing an act of thinking' (Hintikka 1990:133).

The cogito positions Descartes's work as the symbolic culmination of philosophical developments in relation to subjectivity and cognition: specifically, what it means to be a thinking human. Descartes published

Meditations on First Philosophy (1641), which contained six proofs or meditations that defend the use of doubt as a baseline for philosophical and scientific inquiry in order ultimately to prove the existence of God. Detailed in the Second Meditation, the cogito involves a destructive[4] approach to philosophical inquiry and, by association, scientific inquiry, for to be able to prove something without a doubt one must reduce it to its most base element. For Descartes, this reduction disproves the bodily senses, which can be faulty, in dreaming or in madness, and gives primacy to the irreducible immortal soul or thinking mind. Descartes concludes that while bodily and sensory perceptions are susceptible to division and misapprehension, the soul/mind is the basis for existence: 'I am therefore, speaking precisely, only a thinking thing, that is, a mind, or a soul, or an intellect, or a reason' (Descartes 2008:19). Descartes hierarchically separates the fallible and reducible body and the irreducible and immaterial mind, citing the cognitive process of thinking as the strongest proof of existence. Thinking as a proof for existence is not without problems, though, as the signs of thinking are themselves problematised in any discussion of the cogito. Descartes (2008:23) states that 'although I am considering all this in myself silently and without speech, yet I am still ensnared by words themselves, and all but deceived by the very ways in which we usually put things'. It is here that he expresses the common struggle inherent in using narrative language to build philosophical proofs, the very struggle described by Dr. Cawley in relation to Daniels/Solando's constant reconstruction of their delusional narrative structure.

The layers of narrative architecture built by Laeddis to avoid his own feelings of guilt over the death of his wife and children are formed from two distinct understandings of the thinking subject, as explained in Hintikka's categories of identification. Hintikka (1990:135) defines perspectival identification as subject centred, or the internalised 'I', and public identification as object centred, or the environmentally located 'I', in the two categories of cognitive identification. As a distanced and criminalised projection of Laeddis's psyche, Solando is formed solely from the public identification. Acted out by a role-playing nurse, Solando exists only through her public interactions with Daniels, first as the murderous and deluded homemaker, and second as a potential victim of the hospital administration's experiments – in the novel she has no inner dialogue and exists only as seen through Daniels's cognitive lens. Though the physical character of Solando is portrayed by a nurse, the character of Solando is an imaginative creation of Daniels/Laeddis, created in order to distance himself from his own feelings of guilt over his wife's murder. Daniels encounters a second physical version of Solando in a cave on the island – it is this Solando who confirms the existence of unethical, government-sponsored experiments on patients. Solando, the public identification of Daniels's guilt, discusses syllogisms as a way of proving her sanity in the face of Daniels's own perspectival identification: 'if you are deemed insane, then all actions that would otherwise prove you are not do, in actuality, fall into the framework of an insane person's actions' (Lehane 2003:270). Here Solando presents the crux of the problem in Daniels/Laeddis's logic, that no matter how reasonably Daniels acts, the structurally unsound construction of his perspectival identification will act out in violence. It is the perspectival identification that allows Daniels to build the narrative structure of his delusions, sophisticated enough to allow him to maintain not just one but three distinct personalities.

As mentioned, even though *Shutter Island* is written from the third-person, omniscient point of view, the entire novel is told through the interpretive, subjective lens of Daniels. Interestingly, Lehane maintains Daniels as the protagonist throughout the novel, even after he has his climactic breakthrough and recognises his true subjective state, that of murderer and patient Andrew Laeddis. Though Dr. Cawley and Chuck Aule/Dr. Sheehan call Daniels by his public persona of Andrew Laeddis, and Daniels confirms this identity verbally, Lehane judiciously uses the more vague pronoun 'he' rather than shifting the speaker tags and perspectival identity of the protagonist from Daniels to Laeddis (Lehane 2003:364). Likewise, though Daniels publicly confirms that he is indeed Andrew Laeddis and that he was incarcerated for murdering his wife because she killed their three children, the speaking protagonist remains defined as Daniels, so that it is Daniels who recognises that he created the projection of Rachel Solando because he could not 'take knowing that [he] let [his] wife kill [his] babies' (Lehane 2003:365). Though Laeddis recognises that both Solando and Daniels are invented projections of his own guilt, the conceit of Daniels as protagonist is maintained. Despite there being three distinct characters, he is the only one who thinks himself into consciousness and, therefore, existence.

Another interesting issue of subjectivity and cognition examined throughout the novel is the most fundamental question of where this subject-creating thought takes place. The brain serves as a trope for both the mechanistic organ, reminiscent of Enlightenment ideas of a *machina carnis* or 'machine of the flesh' (Porter 2003:51), and the metaphysical seat of the consciousness. The idea of the *machina carnis* is witnessed by Daniels when he and Chuck Aule question Peter Breene, a violent patient who was confined for disfiguring his father's nurse. Ironically, it is Peter who describes the mind and brain as a faulty mechanism:

> It's an engine essentially. It is what it is. A very delicate, intricate motor. And it's got all of these pieces, all these gears and bolts and hinges. And we don't even know what half of them do. But if just one gear slips, just one [...] Have you thought about that? (Lehane 2003:109)

Peter goes on to say '[t]hat it's all trapped in here and you can't get to it, and you don't really control it. But it controls you, doesn't it?' (Lehane 2003:109). This idea of the mind as a delicate yet inaccessible machine is further developed in the form of Daniels's frequent and increasingly debilitating migraines. Each time Daniels experiences a migraine headache, the boundary of his delusional narrative structure frays, allowing the liminal space between the created reality of his identity as US Marshal Teddy Daniels and the true reality of his existence as confined murderer Andrew Laeddis to blur through dreams and hallucinations. It is after a particularly bad migraine that finds Daniels collapsing in front of Dr. Cawley and Aule that his projected perspectival and public identities conflate. Daniels dreams of his wife, confusing Rachel with Dolores, and assures the dream version of Dr. Cawley that he indeed can love a woman who killed her children because 'she didn't mean to [...] she was just scared' (Lehane 2003:184). It is only when dreaming that Daniels can confront the truth of his complicity in the death of his children and wife. While the migraine was a simple mechanical failure in the blood vessels of Daniels's brain, on waking he separates the brain-as-organ from the brain-as-consciousness: 'he felt he'd wrenched himself awake, tore his brain into consciousness just to get out of that dream' (Lehane 2003:187).

The brain as machine is also reflected in the frequent and ominous references to the transorbital lobotomy found throughout the novel and film. The idea of psycho-surgery is described by Daniels as a punishment for unruly patients:

> They zap you with electroshock and then they go in through your eye with, get this, an ice pick. I'm not kidding. No anaesthesia. They poke around here and there and take a few nerve fibres out of your brain, and then that's it, it's over. Piece of cake. (Lehane 2003:153)

Though described rather callously by Daniels, the idea of stimulating or removing various portions of the brain in order to alter behaviour was a popular tactic during the novel's mid-twentieth-century setting. The crude surgery of the transorbital lobotomy concentrated on disturbing the front regions of the brain near the thalamus, 'the seat of emotion', with the goal of interrupting the connection between emotion and associated behaviour (Morgan and Denney 1955:59). While it is true that the lobotomised patient was likely to find it difficult to engage in the same level of emotional intensity as before surgery, postsurgery patients are described by Morgan and Denny as childlike and helpless, requiring significant care to relearn day-to-day activities. Postlobotomy patients frequently exhibited 'apathy, indifference, somnolence, dullness, laxness, perseveration, euphoria, playfulness, facetiousness, irritability, negativism, and immodesty' (Morgan and Denney 1955:60). The concept of the faulty mechanical brain is clear in the description of psycho-surgery side effects after the surgical attempt to create a more malleable and complacent patient. This child-like range of emotions contrasts sharply with Daniels's obvious intelligence, helping to illuminate the extent of the threat at the novel's end. It is during the climactic lighthouse scene that Dr. Cawley and Dr. Sheehan confirm for Daniels that the series of events on Shutter Island was an elaborate ruse designed to help him face his unresolved guilt and thereby cease his violence. It is only through Daniels's recognition of his own identity and evidence of calm behaviour that he can avoid the lobotomy demanded by other hospital psychiatrists (Lehane 2003:346).

Using philosophical discourse, specifically Descartes's cogito, to speak of the science behind the brain is appropriate on multiple levels. At the most basic level, Descartes's intention was to 'achieve certainty in the sciences' (Moriarty 2008:xxv). In doubting every presupposition to the level of existence, Descartes provides the founding method of scientific inquiry. It is this very doubt that gives rise to medical experimentation during the Enlightenment, and that in turn led to the crude experiments in psycho-surgery during the mid-twentieth century. The foundation of scientific inquiry is based on experiential and replicable data, and Descartes's contributions to eighteenth-century thought can be found not only in the popular understanding of the mind(soul)/body dualism, but in mathematical and scientific theory. In the novel, the web of this descendant scientific knowledge is examined when immediately after the hurricane Daniels searches the ominous Ward C for Andrew Laeddis. Daniels and Aule encounter an escaped paranoid patient who babbles about the threat of hydrogen bombs:

> A hydrogen bomb, it implodes. It falls in on itself and goes through a series of internal breakdowns, collapsing and collapsing. But all

that collapsing? It creates mass and density. See, the fury of its own self-destruction creates an entirely new monster. You get it? Do you? The bigger the breakdown, then the bigger the destruction of self, then the more potent it becomes. And then, okay, okay? Fucking blammo! [...] In its absence of self, it spreads. (Lehane 2003:223)

This passage is notable for multiple layers of mimetic representation. In one layer, the description of the bomb reflects a very real concern for the period in question – the development and use of atomic weaponry in 1945 and the subsequent Cold War. The development of atomic weaponry denoted an epistemic rupture, marking the twentieth century as a turning point in the Nuclear Age. In his 1984 essay 'No apocalypse, not now', Jacques Derrida muses on the hyperspeed with which information and weaponry have been amassed since the dawning of the nuclear age. He states that nuclear bombs are in themselves 'fabulously textual' in their dependence on multiple structural layers of information, language, both vocalised and not, and codes (Derrida 1984:23). This structural layering of instantaneous information and language exchange provides a textual marker in the boundary of pre- and postnuclear age, much like the notable demarcation that Descartes provides in pre- and post-Enlightenment thought and scientific inquiry. The idea of the scientifically groundbreaking bomb as a marker for the Nuclear Age reflects a similar liminal space that Descartes inhabits as the symbolic boundary between two epistemes. Just as Descartes serves as a symbolic liminal boundary between epistemes, so do his ideas work on multiple levels layered on the character of Daniels. It was Descartes's development of the idea of philosophical and scientific inquiry as an 'individual search, conducted along the correct methodological lines' rather than an external search focused on hierarchical texts that forms the basis of Daniels's own investigation (Moriarty 2008: xvii). Daniels's actions on Shutter Island are the enactment of Descartes's ideas of reliance on individual search and inquiry, while avoiding the authoritative texts that form the methodological background of Daniels's academically trained counterpart Chuck Aule/Dr. Sheehan. Daniels conducts his own individual search, externally, as he uses his body to interpret the physical clues in his search of the island, in addition to the internal cognitive and psychic search that Laeddis experiences in the personality of Daniels.

The more obvious mimetic feature of the hydrogen bomb passage is the collapsing structure of Daniels's own psyche. Much like Daniels's creation of Rachel, whose constant thinking allows her to maintain the narrative structure of her delusions, Daniels himself is the continually thinking persona built from Laeddis's fractured psyche. Both the image of the hurricane with its calm central eye and the hydrogen bomb that implodes in on itself rather than outwardly mimic Daniels's inner turmoil. Thus when the escaped patient from Ward C speaks of the bomb's potency, 'the bigger the breakdown, then the bigger the destruction of self' (Lehane 2003:223), the reader is immediately pointed towards Daniels's own destruction of self. More telling, however, is the subtle closing statement 'in [the bomb's] absence of self, it spreads' (Lehane 2003:223). This idea of absence or lack as inadvertent creative force is a trope seen throughout the novel. A similar symbolic boundary is most clearly evidenced in Descartes's dualistic vision of the mind(soul)/body hierarchy. As Descartes states in the synopsis to *Meditations on First Philosophy*, as 'we understand no body except as divisible, but on the other hand no mind except as indivisible: for we cannot conceive a half of any mind, as we can with any body' (Descartes 2008:10–11). Therefore for Descartes, the mind and divine soul, inextricably intertwined as they are, form a distinct and indivisible entity, unlike the body, which is subject to decay and corruptibility. He goes on to parse the materiality of the mind/soul as being of an immortal and divine 'pure substance', whereas the body is itself a collection of parts, easily divisible and, ultimately, perishable (Descartes 2008:11). Thus the physical, bodily interpreted information that Daniels receives during his investigation on the island is of secondary importance to the internal struggle in which he engages to solve the mystery of his relationship to Laeddis.

It is here that Lehane's construction of the dualistic self differs widely from Descartes's earlier construction. Descartes asks in the second meditation 'Am I so bound up with my body and senses that I cannot exist without them?' as a form of a priori acknowledgement that the immortal and immaterial soul is hierarchically greater than the material and fallible body (Descartes 2008:18). His very definition of the body as 'everything capable of being bounded by some shape, of existing in a definite place, of filling a space in such a way as to exclude the presence of any other body within it' specifically defines the body as an experienceable object with discrete boundaries (Descartes 2008:19). However, the persona of Daniels problematises the logic of this idea of the measurable body as a mere casing for the immaterial soul. Daniels, as the primary conscious persona of Laeddis and protagonist of the novel, exists both within the boundaries of the physical body and also as an extension of the conscious state, moving between relative lucidity and outright hallucination. Daniels is a body *within* Laeddis's body, experiencing the full gamut of bodily senses to synthesise information about Solando, Laeddis, Ashecliffe Hospital and the hurricane-ravaged island itself. Daniels's body is immaterial, however, disproving the need for the physical presence that Descartes requires for humanity's earthly existence. The delicate structure of Daniels's immaterial body exists only within the absence of Laeddis's consciousness, reflecting yet again the idea of the hydrogen bomb exploding in on itself – Laeddis has room to create Daniels and Solando in order to fill the absence, setting the stage for the inevitable destructive explosion at the lighthouse.

Lehane also develops beyond the hierarchical dualism inherent in Descartes's cogito in his use and manipulation of the body. The material body, denigrated and corruptible in the cogito, earns a place of importance in the world of *Shutter Island*. Taking the idea of mechanistic bodily functions and applying it to the mind as previously mentioned in character Peter Breene, the brain is a physical and material artefact. It is what the island's psychiatrists and psycho-surgeons view as a malfunction in the mechanics of the brain, which allows them to discipline patients through surgeries such as the transorbital lobotomy. In the final scene when Laeddis regresses to the Daniels persona and the straitjacket is ominously brought forth by the orderlies, the operation of psychiatric power, about which Michel Foucault writes so eloquently, can be seen enacted on his physical body. As Foucault reminds us:

> Disciplinary power refers [...] to a final or optimum state. It looks forward to the future, towards the moment when it will keep going by itself and only a virtual supervision will be required, when discipline, consequently, will have become habit. (Foucault 2003:47)

Thus by 'fixing' Daniels's malfunctioning brain through psycho-surgery, he becomes a more physically pliable subject, capable of easy monitoring through retraining and reintegration into the psychiatric community.

This bodily retraining, which focuses on both the moral imposition of authority in the patient's internalisation of the physician authority figure and the physical modification in behaviour, does not provide a therapeutic function, merely a disciplinary one. Daniels is allowed to lead his elaborate investigation throughout the island because during his frequent violent bouts he injured ten guards, five orderlies and four patients (Lehane 2003:350). Dr. Cawley hoped to trigger his memory in order to modify his violent behaviour, with a secondary aim of healing his fractured psyche. Interestingly, Dr. Cawley provides one of the only voices of moderation in *Shutter Island*, preferring talk therapy to psycho-surgery or drug-induced behaviour modification. In Scorsese's film adaptation, Dr. Cawley is played by veteran actor Ben Kingsley, imbuing the role with subtle gentleness and compassion, a clear foil to Daniels's own reckless, undisciplined violence (Scorsese 2009). Dr. Cawley expresses concern over psycho-surgical limitations; namely, that behavioural modification as a result of surgery does nothing to repair the neural damage found in the memory-processing area of Daniels's brain, which causes his violent outbursts. Explicit memories imprint themselves onto the hippocampus through chemical signatures, causing permanent changes. Neuropsychiatrist and Nobel prize winner Eric Kandel goes so far as to suggest that the hippocampus serves as a 'cognitive map of space', as a 'cellular representation of extrapersonal space' (Kandel 2005:360). When proteins are synthesised during heightened emotional states, they imprint more significantly onto the cognitive map, creating permanent memories and muscle memory (Kandel 2005:259), helping to explain why Daniels spends so much of his non-lucid flashbacks physically interacting with Dolores, the wife whom he shot in an act of mercy. Daniels expresses his longing for Dolores in both emotional and physical terms; 'I miss her like you [...] If I was underwater, I wouldn't miss oxygen that much' (Lehane 2003:189). He later goes on to say that he could feel

> her in him, pressed at the base of his throat. He could see her sitting in the early July haze, in that dark orange light a city gets on summer nights just after sundown, looking up as he pulled to the curb. (Lehane 2003:242)

This physical and emotional recollection of Dolores is centred in the hippocampus, just as Daniels's violent behaviour towards the hospital staff is a learned behaviour from his years as a battalion sergeant during the Second World War (Lehane 2003:213). The transorbital lobotomy described in *Shutter Island* was a procedure that altered the thalamus, the emotional core of the brain (Morgan and Denney 1955:59), but, notably, a procedure that in no way changes the base memories that serve to recall the trauma. The lobotomy itself eases emotion and the related antisocial behaviours, but does not act as a therapeutic method to ease traumatic memories. As such, a postlobotomy Daniels would be likely to be a calmer and more manageable patient, but importantly not a cured patient.

Daniels's legal responsibility comes into question when one considers the penal rather than therapeutic aspect of his scheduled lobotomy.

The most basic tenets of the legal insanity defence state that 'a person utterly unconscious of the distinction between good and evil, justice and injustice, right and wrong, at the time of committing the offense, by the common consent and judgment of mankind, is not responsible for his act' (Elwell *et al.* 1882:2), an elaboration of the McNaughtan Rules, which place the basis for punishment on the criminal's state of reason (Loughnan 2007:379). In his essay 'My body, this paper, this fire', written as a response to Jacques Derrida's critique of his reading of the cogito, Foucault discusses Descartes's interpretation of this legal imperative to sanity:

> To be *insanus* (to be insane) is to take oneself for what one is not, it is to believe in chimeras, to be the victim of delusions; these at least are the signs [...] *Insanus* is not a term of characterization, *amens* and *demens* (to be out of one's mind) are disqualifying terms. The first refers to signs; the other two to capability. (Foucault 2009:559)

According to Foucault, Descartes uses madmen as a referent to preface the cogito in order to locate doubt as the basic premise of reason – the inverse of which suggests that to be legally insane is to enact or perform the signs of unreason. Using this logic, it is clear that Daniels's behaviour exhibits the signs of insanity as he builds the elaborate yet delusional narrative structures to sustain his madness.

This is not to say that Daniels's designation as legally insane and therefore incapable of standing trial for his murderous actions means that he is incapable of reason. Descartes himself bases his cogito on the premise that we must doubt everything in a destructive manner, for fear of falling victim to madness, like one of 'those madmen, whose little brains have been so befuddled by pestilential vapour arising from the black bile' of humoural imbalance (Descartes 2008:14). For Descartes madness is folly and lack of reasonable logic, but Daniels provides an alternative reading of madness – that of carefully constructed reason. Throughout the novel, the personas of Solando and Daniels repeatedly form intricate narrative structures to maintain their lies. The idea of right reasoning as anathema to delirium is rooted in the idea of an inherent morality and, for Descartes, a morality based on a presupposition of Christianity. In a telling statement from Nurse Marino during an interrogation with Daniels, and in response to a question about whether Solando complained about the hospital with good reason, 'one could argue the reason was understandable possibly. We don't colour reasons or motives in terms of good or bad moral suppositions' (Lehane 2003:60). This careful denial of moral imposition on the part of a minor psychiatric authority figure contrasts with the moral imposition to right reason based on Christianity. Indeed, in Descartes's introductory letter to the Faculty of Theology at the University of Paris, found in *Meditations on First Philosophy*, he states that he writes to reason out the existence of God and the soul (Descartes 2008:3), which implies a divinely based morality.

During the Enlightenment, the idea of a secular morality formed an important project – Foucault suggests that the development of secular reasoning into scientific inquiry was bordered by the 'precipice of madness', delineated by a conscious ethical decision to search for the truth, not the discrete and dualistic idea of madness *versus* reason as suggested by Descartes. Nurse Marino's quote reflects the outcome of the Enlightenment project of secular reasoning. It is this ability to separate reason and moral behaviour that allows modern readers to engage and empathise with Daniels, an unreliable protagonist and admitted alcoholic, murderer and man prone to violent outbursts. In the novel especially, with its close insight into Daniels's point of view, the reader is asked to empathise with him. After his lighthouse epiphany, the reader understands Daniels's actions in murdering his wife and why he is unable truly to hate her for drowning their three children; 'if he could sacrifice his own mind to save hers, he would' (Lehane 2003:360). The reader is sympathetic towards Daniels and understands the logic behind his subsequent actions. Dolores begs Daniels 'I need you to love me [...] I need you to free me', to which he shoots her, freeing her from her tortured existence (Lehane 2003:362). Daniels's murderous act is an act of mercy, and not an unreasonable act of violence.

In the novel and film *Shutter Island*, the reader is asked to set aside his or her preconceived ideas of moral responsibility and understanding of subjectivity in order to empathise with Teddy Daniels, an imagined character, a violent and unreliable one at that, as he journeys through the delusional narrative structure of his own damaged psyche. As examined in this chapter, Dennis Lehane makes careful references to philosophical and scientific discourse throughout the novel, both utilising and problematising Descartes's cogito as one of the foundational maxims in modern philosophy. By focusing on the liminal space between the functional mechanics of the brain, the construction of subjectivity and the animalistic violence of madmen, Lehane requires readers to be sophisticated in their readings of the seemingly distinct realms of sanity versus reason and madness versus mercy.

Notes

1. An episteme in the Foucauldian sense refers to the collective discursive practices of a given time period. Epistemes rupture when a measurable change occurs within discursive practices.
2. *The Cabinet of Dr. Caligari* mirrors the plot of *Shutter Island* in both the overall structure of a frame narrative and in the use of an unreliable narrator, Francis, not to mention a twist ending. As in *Shutter Island*, the protagonist of *The Cabinet of Dr. Caligari* is an unwilling patient in a mental hospital who suffers from paranoid delusions that the asylum director is a murderer. Interestingly, as influential as *The Cabinet of Dr. Caligari* is for contemporary filmmakers, Dennis Lehane was unaware of its plot conventions and theme when he wrote the novel *Shutter Island* (Kung 2010).
3. The idea of physician-sponsored play acting as a means of therapy has long-standing traditions in psychiatry. From the classical age onwards, in order to lead the mad person out of his delusion towards reason, physicians participated in and embraced the patient's delirium (Foucault 2009:333).
4. The term 'destructive' is used in reference to Russell's (1972:567) description of Descartes's theory of knowledge as destructive, meaning that Descartes's theory helps strip away presuppositions in order to find the most basic, irreducible kernel of logic.

References

Derrida, Jacques. (1984). No apocalypse, not now (full speed ahead, seven missiles, seven missives). *Diacritics*, 14(2), 20–31.

Descartes, Rene. (2008). *Meditations on First Philosophy with Selections from the Objections and Replies*. Oxford: Oxford University Press.

Elwell, J., E.C. Seguin, George Beard, J. Jewell and Charles Folsum. (1882). The moral responsibility of the insane. *The North American Review*, 134(302), 1–39.

Foucault, Michel. (2003). *Psychiatric Power: Lectures at the College de France, 1973–1974*. New York: Picador.

Foucault, Michel. (2009). My body, this fire, this paper. In Michel Foucault, *The History of Madness*. New York: Routledge.

Hintikka, Jaakko. (1990). The Cartesian cogito, epistemic logic and neuroscience: Some surprising interrelations. *Synthese*, 83(1), 133–56.

Kandel, Eric. (2005). The molecular biology of memory storage. In Eric Kandel (ed.), *Psychiatry, Psychoanalysis, and the New Biology of Mind*. London: American Psychiatric Publishing.

Kung, Michelle. (2010). The author who aced Hollywood. *The Wall Street Journal*. Available at http://online.wsj.com/article/SB100014240527487048209045750 55330609042848.html [accessed September 2011].

Lehane, Dennis. (2001). *Mystic River*. New York: Harper Paperbacks.

Lehane, Dennis. (2003). *Shutter Island*. New York: Harper Perennial.

Loughnan, Arlie. (2007). 'Manifest madness': Towards a new understanding of the insanity defense. *Modern Law Review*, 70(3), 379–401.

Morgan, Moiveline and Mary Denney. (1955). Retraining after a prefrontal lobotomy. *American Journal of Nursing*, 55(1), 59–62.

Moriarty, Michael. (2008). Introduction. In Michael Moriarty, *Meditations on First Philosophy with Selections from the Objections and Replies.* Oxford: Oxford University Press.

Porter, Roy. (2003). *Flesh in the Age of Reason: How the Enlightenment Transformed the Way We See Our Bodies and Souls.* London: Penguin.

Porter, Roy. (2006). *The Cambridge History of Medicine.* Cambridge: Cambridge University Press.

Russell, Bertrand. (1972). *The History of Western Philosophy.* New York: Simon & Schuster.

Scorsese, Martin (dir.). (2009). *Shutter Island.* Paramount.

Weich, Dave. (2003). Dennis Lehane meets the Bronte sisters. PowellsBooks.Blog. Available at http://www.powells.com/authors.lehane.html [accessed December 2010].

Wiene, Robert (dir.). (1921). *The Cabinet of Dr. Caligari.* Image Entertainment.

2.2
'Armageddon Was Yesterday – Today We Have a Serious Problem': Pre- and Postmillennial Tropes for Crime and Criminality in Fiction by David Peace and Stieg Larsson

Richard Brown

Crime writing is a genre of popular narrative ideally placed to draw on the social, political and intellectual aspirations and anxieties of the turn of the last millennium, and to exploit certain characteristic narrative fictional tropes that might be associated with them. These aspirations and anxieties surfaced widely in popular literature and political discourses and in cultural theory before, during and after the year 2000. Prominent examples include the building of millennial-themed civic monuments throughout the United Kingdom, including the London Millennium Dome (now O_2 Arena) in Greenwich, the work of writers in science fiction such as Arthur C. Clark, Philip K. Dick and J.G. Ballard, and films based on their work. Other examples include works of narrative and cultural theory, from Frank Kermode's *The Sense of an Ending*, which first appeared in 1967, to the work of Jean Baudrillard, who wrote much about the millennial in his book *The Illusions of the End* (1994), and, more recently, Slavoj Žižek, who takes up the theme in his book *Living in the End Times* (2010).

Such work draws on the more or less unconscious structures of prophetic religious thought, on the nature of temporality and narrative discourse, and on ideas of judgement, including judgements of social justice. It draws on a range of uncanny experiences and anxieties associated with rapid advances in technology, social change, environmental and social crisis, the culture of postmodernity and the so-called virtualisation of reality. Countless examples from the fiction of the last half-century might be invoked to demonstrate the pervasiveness of such 'millennial' tropes and anxieties. As I began by suggesting, crime

81

writing, with its strong emphasis on narrative endings, its promise of some kind of 'revelation' and its exploration of judgements of right and wrong, is a genre well suited to reflect these anxieties.

This chapter considers two examples drawn from the popular crime fiction of the turn of the millennium in which the idea of the millennial is specifically named and used: one 'pre-' and one 'postmillennial' novel sequence. These are the Red Riding Quartet of Yorkshire crime writer David Peace (Peace 1999–2004) and the Millennium Trilogy of the Swedish writer Stieg Larsson (Larsson 2005–07; translated 2008–09). Both of these appeared successfully as novel sequences and have been turned into popular films.

As was the case with the Greenwich Dome project, the millennial can function as an empty space, a symbolic container for any number of symptomatic elements of the contemporary zeitgeist, and it does so in these works. In what follows, I want to argue that these two writers, though different in certain ways, both draw on millennial tropes to mark their contemporary moment, to stigmatise the extreme pathological conditions of certain of their criminal characters. They use ideas of the millennial to expand their sense of criminality. In so doing, they offer a broad social critique, exploring themes of social unease and employing a sense of the postmodern to highlight structures of narrative temporality, stimulating and still withholding readerly desire for narrative closure and control.

Millennial chaos in David Peace's Red Riding Quartet

Written over the turn of the millennium, though set in the 1970s and 1980s, David Peace's Red Riding novel sequence provides an extremely dark and violent vision of northern provincial Britain in the grip of a social and cultural crisis. The period is marked by reference to more or less fictionalised historical crimes, and reinforced by the narrative strategy of starkly naming dates in the titles of the volumes of the sequence: *1974* (Peace 1999), *1977* (Peace 2000), *1980* (Peace 2001) and *1983* (Peace 2002). I would suggest that the novel sequence might be described as 'millennial' in several ways, which include Peace's picture of his criminals and of a criminality that deeply implicates the corrupted and compromised police officers and journalists who animate his fictional world. He creates an atmosphere of apocalyptic social and moral crisis that can be contextualised in the traumatic postindustrial economic transitions of the West Riding of Yorkshire during this period, especially the political unrest associated with the miners' strike in 1984.

The importance of this context for him became more explicitly apparent in his next novel, *GB84* (Peace 2004), which brought him wider recognition, partly through its inclusion in *Granta*'s highly influential decadal anthology *Best of Young British Novelists* (Jack 2003). But the event may equally suggest a political context for the divided and crisis-ridden social atmosphere that inflects the other novels.

What I am calling the millennial flavour of the Quartet is in part created by Peace's use of temporal markers and the sense they generate that the time is one of crisis. This remained evident in the first volume of his subsequent Tokyo trilogy *Tokyo Year Zero* (Peace 2007), a crime novel set in a resonantly postapocalyptic, postnuclear 1946. But Year Zero images and other such temporal markers are already present in the Quartet, reinforcing the novels' extreme vision of the end of a century, the end of a moral epoch. As I shall argue, the sense of crisis comes along with a fantastical and delusional atmosphere, reinforced by biblical quotation. Furthermore, the structuring of the novels deploys several broadly apocalyptic narrative tropes, which include a hyperconsciousness of temporality itself and such features as a disturbing overlapping of material within and between volumes as part of the investigative processes they describe. Throughout the Quartet, Peace is as much concerned with the personal traumas and crises of those conducting the investigation as with the crimes themselves.

Such features were noted when the 2009 Channel 4 TV film version of the Red Riding Trilogy appeared, with writer Toni Grisoni adapting the four volumes to three (omitting *1977*) and Channel 4 using the interesting and unsettling trope of employing different directors for each section (James and Grisoni 2009). Reviewers were struck by the strangeness of the experience, and the power of its evocation of a world of criminal insanity and corruption in which a doomed contemporaneity is imagined. As David Thomson wrote (2010:33), '[it] is not just hard to follow – it believes in a culture and a narrative where things no longer click together'.

The novels thus gained urgency and relevance from the turn of the millennium moment when they appeared, though they had looked back to the highly publicised real-life sex crimes of the previous decades, including the murder of children by the Moors murderers Ian Brady and Myra Hindley, which took place in the 1960s and featured in *1974*. In *1977* and *1980*, the thread that stood out for most readers centred on the case of Peter Sutcliffe, the so-called Yorkshire Ripper, who committed a series of 13 murders of women between 1975 and 1980. Sutcliffe had become associated with the 1890s Whitechapel murderer Jack the Ripper through certain lurid aspects of the crimes themselves (which Peace retains in his books) and through a much-publicised hoax perpetrated during the investigation by a man called John Humble, who sent a number of letters and audio cassettes in 1978 and 1979 to George Oldfield, the relevant police investigator at the time. The Jack the Ripper connection encouraged various associations between the end of the twentieth century and the moral decadence often associated with the end of the nineteenth. Moreover, the 'Ripper' hoax, which delayed and distracted the investigation, provides an atmosphere of distraction that Peace's novels exploit and develop in the more fictional parts of their plots. These gradually implicate the police themselves in criminal complicity with prostitution, the sex trade and even, in *1980*, in their own hoax Ripper murder, committed in an attempt to conceal their involvement in sex crime. By 1983, Sutcliffe had been captured and imprisoned, and Peace's novel about that year concentrated on a fictionalised version of a different real-life crime: the case of Stefan Kiszko, who had been wrongly sentenced to 16 years' imprisonment for the murder of Lesley Molseed, an 11-year-old schoolgirl from Rochdale in 1975. Here too, then, the miscarriage of justice as much as crime itself defines Peace's sense of the moral crisis of the contemporary world.

As well as these uncannily half-fictionalised historical references, in Peace's Red Riding Quartet one finds certain self-conscious narrative tropes and devices that include real-life locations and, as I have said, a concern with temporality itself conditioning the disturbing reading experience. Thus, in *1974* we have a narrative that is deliberately presented in the first-person present tense of the character of a young journalist, Eddie Dunford, who seems initially one of the more promising characters in the Quartet (for readers who might want the reassurance of identifying with the relatively stable consciousness of a central character). The chapters are pointedly dated one by one in a kind of journal style on single days from 13 December 1974 to the Christmas Eve killing in a Wakefield town-centre pub of the main villain of the piece, Derek Box, who is a gangster property developer and paedophile. The plot depends at least residually on the conflict between the investigative reporter and the gangster, and at this level concerns the gradual revelation of Box's involvement in the attempt to develop a new shopping mall and to terrorise the gypsies previously resident on the site. The plot also depends on Box's implication in the horrendous sex crime of the murder and horrifying disfigurement of a girl victim, an even more disturbing theme. Such elements clearly work both to reinforce a sense of the horrendousness of the crimes and to create a broadened sense of criminality. Meanwhile, Dunford's own increasingly traumatised attempts to hold the threads of his investigation and his own consciousness together produce a sense of a still more widely traumatised and crisis-ridden cultural and political environment.

In *1977*, Peace's narrative strategies are further complicated, since the narration is here divided between police Sergeant Bob Fraser and the older, more cynical hack journalist Jack Whitehead. Both constantly refer to themselves as 'I', and their repeated attempts at self-identification create an uncanny effect in which their individual consciousnesses and even perhaps the concept of identity itself are increasingly troubled and in question. The narrative is further punctuated by Peace's use of chapter head pieces in the form of a dialogue between an extremely alienated taxi-driver caller to a radio chat show and the equally intolerant and cynical chat-show host. The two keep up a bitter commentary on the progress of the police investigation.

In this, the second volume of the Quartet, the main crime is the murder of Marie Watts, a fictionalised version of real-life Sutcliffe victim Irene Richardson. The novel invokes the atmosphere of the Leeds and Bradford black and Asian communities where the early Sutcliffe crimes and investigations were focused, and where prostitution was rife at the time. Any initial sympathy with Fraser and Whitehead, policeman and journalist, is rapidly eroded as both are terribly compromised figures who are driven to the limits of sanity through their involvement in this criminal world. Fraser is himself in love with a Chapeltown prostitute, and is haunted by images of his wife Louise and son Bobby as their marriage falls apart and she, too, conducts an affair. Whitehead is haunted by his wife Carol and by memories of an earlier '*Exorcist*' murder case, which seems to have involved both her and mysterious maverick priest Reverend Martin Laws, with whom he has a series of increasingly bizarre encounters in Leeds's Griffin Hotel.

The figure of Laws, who is a kind of priest, and Whitehead's repeated references to Leeds's Roman Catholic St Anne's Cathedral introduce into the novel a series of prophetic and apocalyptic biblical references. These include prophetic clues about the 'just man [...] turning from the path of righteousness' in the epigraphic quotation from Ezekiel 18:26–7, the extended quotation of Psalm 88 and the quotation from the apocalyptic prophecies of the 'last days' in the Old Testament book of the prophet Joel 2:18, which is requoted in the New Testament in Acts 2:17 (Peace 2000:110). This prophetic element is further underscored by the radio caller, who quotes Revelation 9:20–21 (Peace 2000:334).

Specific dates relating to the weeks from 29 May to 17 June 1977 are prominently given in this volume too, and these dates produce a mesmeric magical or delusional resonance in the minds of the characters and in the narration itself from the start. These are indented for typographical emphasis. The first chapter begins:

> Leeds.
> Sunday 29 May 1977.
> It's happening again.
> *When the two sevens clash...*

The year in question is that of Queen Elizabeth II's Silver Jubilee, which was marked by official celebrations but also, in subcultural history, as the year of the subversive anarchist 'jubilee' of the Sex Pistols, of punk rock and of Derek Jarman's 1977 punk-styled film *Jubilee*. Peace's 'Jack' thus undercuts the Union Jack.

Especially suggestive in the context of the black Leeds setting of Peace's *1977* is the idea that there might be some foreboding power in a fateful symbolic date when 'two sevens clash'. This has a powerful cross-cultural symbolic resonance, since it is apparently based on the millennial predictions of Jamaican black power leader Marcus Garvey, who prophesied chaos on 7 July 1977, when the 'sevens' met (Jacques-Garvey 1986). Jamaican Rastafarian culture became widely popular in the multicultural Britain of the 1970s, partly through the popularity of reggae music. Bob Marley and the Wailers released their 1973 breakthrough album *Burnin'*, through which many Rastafarian ideas became widely known. Garvey's prediction itself was prominently used in 1977 in a reggae recording by a performer called Joseph Hill and his band Culture. 'Two Sevens Clash' was the title track of their best-known album, whose apocalyptic message echoes through Peace's novel's obtrusive numerology. This culminates in the noting of the time, 7.07, the date 17 June and the events that take place in a room numbered 77 in the Griffin Hotel, where Jack Whitehead has his odd climactic encounter with Martin Laws at the end. The material gives a sense of the social and cultural changes associated with immigration at the time as well as a note of extreme foreboding for the future. Indeed, the novel concludes with the iconic two-word punk rock mantra from the Sex Pistols' famous song 'God Save the Queen': '*No future!*' (Peace 2000:341).

There is, nevertheless, a kind of future produced in the third novel in the sequence, in which things in Peace's fictional world deteriorate still further into apocalyptic chaos. Several crimes and criminal characters return, including Martin Laws, who becomes a significant figure in following up darker trails of the investigation. In *1980*, the real Sutcliffe crime to which Peace provides a fictional equivalent at the start is the murder of Leeds student Jacqueline Hill, who is here fictionalised as Lauren Bell. By the end of the volume, the police have their man in custody, as they finally did in reality in January 1981 after picking him up in a car with false number plates. The main plot of this novel focuses on the investigation by Manchester policeman Peter Hunter, who has been brought in to sort out the failing local force. Those policemen are not only involved in prostitution but in a murder of their own, that of Clare Strachan, which they hope to pass off as one of the Ripper's. Narration is in Hunter's voice as he comes anew to the jumbled lists and accumulations of crime and evidence. Since he is such an unpopular figure, and one from whom the others are determined to withhold information, his point of view is an unsettling and alienating one for the reader to occupy. Parallel to the 'radio call show' device used in *1977* is the use here of chapter-heading passages, perhaps a 'citizens' band broadcast'. These are written in an asyntactic prose style somewhat reminiscent of Samuel Beckett or William Burroughs, and are apparently the product of a more extreme disconnected consciousness giving a flavour to the whole (Peace 2001:2, 14 etc.).

The marking of specific dates remains a crucial feature of Peace's incantatory prose style. The dates here mark a progress from 11 December 1980 to New Year's Eve. The sense of an aborted Christmas and of the coming end of the year and decade overlap with concern at the wider political context. There is alarm at the potential local impact of Thatcherism (Margaret Thatcher's first Conservative government had been elected in 1979). Such images combine to invoke traumatic images of the end of the world. Peace (2001:363) begins his final chapter in typical style:

New Year's Eve, 1980.
Dawn or dusk it's all fucked up –
The End of the World –

In *1983*, the fourth and final volume of the sequence, the 'end of the world' still has not yet happened or is maybe still in the process of happening in the various ways that the intensely dark narrative subject and technique evoke. In 'real-crime' terms, the Ripper murders have now ended, but the discovery of a new missing-child case brings into question the conviction of the Stefan Kiszko-based character Michael Mishkin from the first volume, *1974*. In this last volume, the resources of Peace's narrative syntax have been further extended. We now get alternating chapters from each of three narrators: the first-person narration of the veteran policeman Maurice Jobson, who is deeply implicated in what has gone before; the second-person 'you' narration of solicitor John Piggott, who investigates the Mishkin case; and the third-person 'BJ' narration of the rent boy BJ, whose witnessing of events from all the previous volumes throws many of them into a new light.

However, conventional images of clarification and enlightenment are not as prominent as their opposite. It is rather an experience of 'Disintegrating –/ Disappearing –/ Deceasing –/ Declining –/ Decaying –/ Dying –/ Dead –/ Circles, circles of hell; local hells' (Peace 2002:185) that Peace's narrative pursues. The return to the Mishkin investigation from the 1970s creates an atmosphere that is at least partly regressive. Moreover, the strategy of dating in this volume has a double time scheme. One sequence numbers the days of the police investigation of the missing girl, starting with Day 2 on 13 May 1983 in the Jobson chapters. The second is a countdown to 'D-Day' from an initially mysterious 'D –26' in the Piggott narration of Chapter 2. This suggests a broad millennial countdown. More specifically, it refers to the contemporary political context of the re-election of Margaret Thatcher with an increased majority for a second term on 9 June 1983, which was a trigger for the miners' strike of 1984. Peace's narrative strategies work to generate a paradoxical apocalyptic drive and to place crime itself in the context of a wider concept of criminality, which includes the political.

The crisis-torn millennial atmosphere of Peace's Quartet is produced, then, by the obsession with temporal structures, disorientating strategies of narration, the insistent repetitive mesmeric style, the monosyllabic snatches of dialogue and brief narrative impressions interrupted by voices and written discourses of journalism and investigation. During the four volumes we have first one, then two, then three central characters struggling to hold things together, while they are themselves falling apart under the pressures of the investigation. It is not so much the tension between investigator and crime, more that there is not anything else but crime in this world, and that one crime slips into another, and fact into fantasy, with little prospect of resolution or of an alleviation of the brutality that this implies. There are uncanny mixtures of real crime and adapted or imagined events. Fictionalised scenes occur in real locations from the centre of Leeds, the Griffin Hotel and Millgarth Police Station, to the badlands of south central Wakefield and such surrounding areas as Osset, Castleford, ex-mining community Fitzwilliam and the Redbeck Café and Motel. The reader has an uneasy sense of crossing borderlines between the voices inside the characters' heads and those of the community outside, suggesting a world as it might seem to a mind thoroughly disturbed by the traumatic exaggerations and disaster rhetoric of mass-media journalism, let alone the events that it attempts to report.

Into this world, the repeated use of specifically biblical apocalyptic discourse adds a further dimension: a use of the millennial not so much to reinforce meaning as to inscribe meaninglessness. Millennial prophecy speeds and fuels the horrendous, hellish atmosphere of darkly obsessive criminality and misplaced vengeful fantasy – a postmodern apocalypse where the only certainties seem to be the recurrence of criminality, and in which neither reason nor justice seems likely to prevail.

Stieg Larsson's Millennium Trilogy

Stieg Larsson's Millennium Trilogy has become one of the most successful international publishing, film and television successes of recent years, with a number of biographical studies already having appeared since the author's premature death at the age of 50 in 2004. Like Peace, Larsson offers readers an expansive novel sequence creating a sustained, partly factual, partly fictional world. Whereas the Red Riding Quartet offers a retrospect over the run-up to the end of the century, the Millennium Trilogy fictionalises a more recent past moment, albeit one with roots in the last century.

Larsson's Trilogy shares with Peace's Quartet a fascination with temporality, which is evident in the meticulous reconstruction of the criminal back-history of the industrialist Henrik Vanger family that makes up much of its first volume (Larsson 2008:78, 105). Larsson's narrative also employs a strategy of precisely dating its events. The days and months of the investigation are noted at the head of each chapter throughout the three volumes. This encourages the reader to ground the events narrated in a real time (and space) that is the time of the reader and also the symbolically unreal time of the turn of the last millennium. These dates indicate that the action of the three volumes takes place during the years 2002–03, 2004–05 and 2005 respectively, extending, in other words, into the future beyond what turned out to be the extent of the writer's own life.

Larsson boldly names the 'millennial' in the title of his Trilogy and that makes us want to ask what it is that is millennial about it. The reader is invited to explore the ways in which the work draws on and defines a sense of the more or less specifically millennial among the distinctive zeitgeist markers that characterise the work as being up to date and contemporary. Much of what is millennial about Larsson's Trilogy can be understood by way of its presentation of itself as contemporary. Its picture of the contemporary world is as dark as Peace's in its expanded sense of a criminality that pervades wider aspects of contemporary society and is as much the focus of the fiction as crime itself. However, it appeared after the turn of the century, and perhaps as a consequence its version of the millennial appears less purely disintegrative, pessimistic and crisis ridden than Peace's. Though it is far from uncritically or naively optimistic in its vision of the present and the future, its larger narrative movement implies some progression from past exploitation to future trust, from concealment to revelation. It reassuringly underscores such values as companionship (including sexual companionship), knowledge and investigation. Many of these positive values are achieved through the experiences of social alienation of his hero and heroine, and their ultimate vindication through study and research against the worst misrepresentations and most nightmarishly malicious powers that they confront.

This is nowhere more evident than in the primary ostensible referent of the 'Millennium' of the title: the investigative magazine *Millennium* for which the principal protagonist Mikael Blomkvist writes. Blomkvist's character and role as researcher and writer is as crucial to the Trilogy as that of Larson's celebrated creation Lisbeth Salander, the spectacular tattooed, bisexual, computer-hacking, gender-revenging, action superheroine who has been widely admired. Both Blomkvist and Salander are successful creations whose characters can be read as 'millennial' in various ways, not least in Lisbeth's involvement in and remarkable skills with the 'techno-digital' world of computing, her absorption of gender-positive contemporary cultural prototypes such as Lara Croft, and the suitably apocalyptic dragon image of her tattoo. Yet readers of the Trilogy may be surprised to find how much of it is given over to the more routine description of the journalistic, editorial and even business and administrative life of the magazine itself, and how persistent the magazine plot is throughout the three volumes.

In *The Girl with the Dragon Tattoo* (Larsson 2008), Blomkvist is introduced as journalist and publisher of the magazine, convicted of libel at the start as a result of its exposure of the business corruption of the Wennerström empire. His forced resignation leads to his investigations into the rival Vanger family that make up the body of the plot of that volume. The extreme sexual violence of the Vanger family history (which involves the grotesque serial sex torture and murder nightmare of Gottfried and Martin Vanger), the growing importance to the investigation of Salander's computer world and background, and the very violent, action-filled denouement might all threaten to distract from the magazine plot, but they do not in fact do so. Indeed, Henrik Vanger, and ultimately also his rediscovered missing granddaughter Harriet Vanger, become involved with the support of the magazine and its investigative project.

In the second book, *The Girl Who Played with Fire* (2009a), the prominence of the magazine plot element is sustained, despite the more lurid developments in the crime and sexual-violence plots, which are announced in the Prologue and are developed in the characters of Zalaschenko and Niederman, super-villains from Lisbeth's family past. It is the murder of two of the magazine's investigative reporters that sets off this phase of the plot. In *The Girl That Kicked the Hornet's Nest* (2009b), the slow building of Lisbeth's medical recovery and legal defence involves a parallel exploration of the professional worlds of medicine and law. Journalism remains a significant part of the story, prominent not least since Lisbeth herself spends some 500 of the 1800 pages of the trilogy confined to bed. The move of Blomkvist's colleague Erika Berger to Stockholm's leading daily newspaper as editor and subsequent conflicts associated with that become a vital plot mover. In the second and third volumes, the story draws in the Swedish Secret Service and the Swedish government right up to Prime Minister level, perhaps inevitably including reference to the 1986 shooting of Olof Palme that is often regarded as Sweden's 9/11 (2009a:194). Spheres of connectedness expand throughout social and political worlds to give a fully contemporary concept of criminality.

Some readers of the Trilogy may well be surprised to find the opening of the first volume less like crime fiction and more like a piece of business, legal or investigative reporting than they had expected. The frequent presence of such discursive material is confirmed in the book titles that draw from contemporary business management jargon: 'Incentive', 'Consequence Analyses', 'Mergers', 'Hostile Takeover' and 'Final Audit' (Larsson 2008:7, 113, 245, 399, 513), and in Salander's full account of the contents of the book Blomkvist has written about the sorry state of business reporting (Larsson 2008:90–93). Following the characters in their labour of careful investigation, of the gathering of information and paperwork, are a substantial part of the experience of reading the Trilogy. Certainly, investigation is less traumatising for the investigators than it is, for instance, in the David Peace Quartet. The business meetings of *Millennium* magazine can be almost as interesting to its narrative gaze as the more sensational plot elements, not least in terms of the alliance of economic values and prosperity with the ethical and political values with which Harriet Vanger wants to be involved (Larsson 2009a:94–7, 99).

This balance of interests in the Trilogy can partly be explained through biography since, as is explained on various websites and articles and in the biography *Stieg* by Jan-Erik Pettersson, Larsson himself worked from the 1970s as a journalist, author and lecturer writing articles on Swedish business, politics and right-wing extremism. He became correspondent for the British magazine *Searchlight* and then, in 1995, one of the founders of investigative anti-racist *Expo* magazine (Pettersson 2011). That magazine, issued four times a year, contains investigative journalism focused on nationalist, racist, anti-democratic, anti-semitic and far-right movements and organisations. Clearly, Larsson connects the spheres of family crime and the business world in such a way as to support the widely expanded concept of criminality, which I have suggested is characteristic of the millennial moment. More subtly, the references to the magazine *Millennium* maintain a consistent meta-fictional level of self-reference to the progress of the Millennium Trilogy novel sequence itself.

Such meta-fictional resonances apparently reveal Larsson to be engaged in an attempt to sophisticate and extend the range of the crime-writing genre into more or less explicit social and political commentary. It is arguably a significant postmodern or millennial feature of the narrative strategy to subvert and transgress generic boundaries, self-consciously to incorporate and move between several narrative and non-fiction discourses. In the first volume, the ageing industrialist Vanger's real interest in the mystery of the supposed murder of his granddaughter Harriet in 1966 is given as his pretext for inviting Blomkvist to write the investigative history of his family company, its rise and fall and its intrigues, including secret links with fascism in the Second World War. Blomkvist realises that Vanger wants to tell him 'a meticulously rehearsed story' but, in a witty, meta-fictional moment, he describes himself as being wary of the potential longueurs of the 'sort of locked room mystery in island format' of writers like Dorothy M. Sayers that this would seem to involve (Larsson 2008:85). Larsson mixes genres to give readers much more violent action than the Sayers murder mystery could but, by the time we get to the violent denouement, he has also cleverly slipped enough economic and political history under the net to show his confidence that these other discourses (as well as gender politics and computing modernity) can vie with the more sensational crime genre excitements to keep his readers' attention. In the second volume, as the history unfolds of Lisbeth Salander's violent sexual abuse by her corrupt guardian Advokat Bjurman (anticipated in the graphic Prologue), we are given an extended explanation of the law relating to guardianship, almost appropriate for a civil rights magazine or a citizen's rights bureau. Explanations of anti-colonial rebellion in Grenada accompany the journey that Lisbeth undertakes there. Her mathematical studies into equations and Pierre de Fermat's absurd theorem provide a discursive point of reference for the head pieces of the books. They help to construct the impression of Salander's abstract intelligence, and also contribute a hint of the postmodern mathematics of the absurd.

At one point, there is an explicit trace of Christian apocalypticism in the narrative. As in Peace's *1977*, this appears in the context of a fragmented and delusional reading of the Bible, which is here particularly associated with vengeful criminality against women. Blomkvist's daughter Pernille is interested in religion (somewhat to his disapproval) and a chance visit from her helps him to piece together a code. This reveals that the young Harriet Vanger, back in 1949, has apparently connected local killings of women with quotations of passages from Leviticus in which strange punishments are prescribed for women guilty of sexual crimes (Larsson 2008:283–6). These have apparently been used as some kind of insane justification for their murders. This gives Blomkvist an investigative lead and the novel an interesting point of reference, even if the lead itself turns out to be a distraction.

According to Blomkvist, his daughter's kind of Christian millennialism is something that the secular investigative *Millennium* magazine would tend to '[l]ambast' (Larsson 2008:283). Yet somehow, ghosted behind this trace of a perverted and criminal kind of punishment, which may or may not explain the sex crimes of the Vanger family past, is the novel's own more secular project of social and gendered self-justification and revenge that Salander herself so strongly represents. At times, she is presented as symbol of a kind of punk chaotic force for revenge. Her lesbian lover Mimmi, for instance, describes her at one point as an 'entropic chaos factor' (Larsson 2009a:107). At other times, though an outlaw, she can represent a force of justice, moral integrity and legitimacy that is beyond the conventional boundaries of the law. Her previous guardian Palmgren 'trusted her enough still to know that whatever she was up to might be dubious in the eyes of the law, but not a crime against God's laws. [He...] was sure that Salander was a genuinely moral person' (Larsson 2009a:134).

Much of the focus of the Larsson Trilogy can be seen as a debate about the legitimacy of Lisbeth Salander: her criminality or otherwise, her sanity or otherwise, her ability to show proper human feelings or otherwise. She is angry, difficult, embodying the memorable words printed on the t-shirt she wears to her trial: 'I am annoyed' (2009b:611). However, her awkwardness and refusal to cooperate or communicate are clearly of a different order from the 'congenital analgesia' of her brother, which represents a posthuman dystopia of a more disturbing kind.

The exposure of criminality in the Trilogy is contextualised in relation to the expansion of the power of digital information and the possibilities for eavesdropping on digital information that the millennium represents. The mixture of revelation and computing makes for timely references to, at one point, the 'Millennium bomb' (Larsson 2008:527). One millennial aspect of the novel sequence is certainly its response to the anxieties of the digital age, among which were widespread rumours around the so-called Millennium bug or Millennium bomb that was frequently discussed at the time.

In the event, I think that Larsson's Millennium Trilogy reassures as much as it disturbs with the techno-digital parts of its vision, which offer less of a posthuman doomsday scenario and more of a sense that human agency (even quasi-criminal agency) can indeed control the digital information archive and, given the right motivations, can do so to good effect. The 'Hacker Republic', of which Salander is a member, is a strange community of socially alienated, marginal and, to some extent, inadequate beings. They nevertheless represent one of the most powerful agencies in the novel's world and, for long periods, Salander's most supportive group of friends.

Likewise, the Trilogy, though parts of it are quite as fully immersed in the contemporary popular cultural sensation of criminal sexual violence as is Peace's Quartet, has many other parts that offer a more sane and non-traumatised representation of the possibility of a range of contemporary sexual experiences that are both adventurous and non-destructive. Blomkvist has a cheerfully complex sex life, which consists in an ex-marriage and 'occasional lovers', including Erika Berger (with her husband's knowledge and tolerance), Celia and subsequently Harriet Vanger, Lisbeth Salander and, in the third volume, the 'exceptionally fit' policewoman Figuerola (2009b:295). Lisbeth's occasional need for recreational sex and her relationship with Mimmi all testify to a world that, if not quite a millennial utopia, is nevertheless one of relatively unconstrained and relatively normal sexual relationships. Not all the ground rules of this world are easy to agree, nor is the affective fallout easy to manage, but nevertheless sexual relationships can happen without the violence and exploitation against which much of the novels' anger is directed. The world of Blomkvist and Salander is one in which differences can be acknowledged and respected for what they are.

In Larsson's novel sequence, then, the prospect of a disastrous apocalyptic futurity is replaced or at least partly mitigated by the 'postmillennial' sentiment suggested in the quotation that I use in the title to this essay: that after the 'Armageddon' of the turn of the century, we return to sorting out the 'serious problems' of personal and political life that remain. Such optimistic touches are not infrequent in the Millennium Trilogy, from the repeated invocation of premillennial myths of childhood to the simpler ideas of character, gender and nation that are suggested in the novels' references to the famous child heroes of the author Astrid Lindgren. Lisbeth is nicknamed Pippi Longstocking and Blomkvist is, from the start, nicknamed by her and others after Lindgren's boy detective 'Kalle' Blomkvist, despite his dislike of that.

In popular crime writing, with its frequent recourse to the sensational, extreme images of the millennial and apocalyptic as well as subtler traces of it can, no doubt, often be found. David Peace's Red Riding Quartet and Stieg Larsson's Millennium Trilogy offer two intriguing examples. In both we see explicitly Christian forms of millennialism in a marginalised and pathological form but, more interestingly, a variety of features that might themselves be thought millennial. These include obsessions with forms of temporality, play with narrative strategy and an ambition to widen the range of the crime fiction genre to introduce a wider concept of criminality across the social and political sphere. They deal with a range of contemporary concerns from racial and gender politics to new technology. In them, defining the millennial seems as elusive as ever, but alongside extreme images of disorientation and disaster we can find millennial tropes that have much positive as well as negative resonance for the new century.

References

Baudrillard, Jean. (1994). *The Illusion of the End*. London: Polity Press.
Forshaw, Barry. (2010). *The Man Who Left too Soon: The Biography of Stieg Larsson*. London: John Blake.
Jack, Ian (ed.). (2003). *Best of Young British Novelists*. Cambridge: Granta.
Jacques-Garvey, Amy (ed.). (1986). *The Philosophy and Opinions of Marcus Garvey or Africa for the Africans*. Dover, MA: Majority Press.

James, Nick and Tony Grisoni. (2009). Bloody Yorkshire. *Sight and Sound*, March, 31–3.

Kermode, Frank. (1967). *The Sense of an Ending*. Oxford: Oxford University Press.

Larsson, Stieg. (2008). *The Girl with the Dragon Tattoo, Millennium I*, trans. Reg Keeland. London: Quercus. Swedish publication 2005.

Larsson,Stieg. (2009a). *The Girl Who Played with Fire, Millennium II*, trans. Reg Keeland. London: Quercus. Swedish publication 2006.

Larsson, Stieg. (2009b). *The Girl That Kicked the Hornet's Nest, Millennium III*, trans. Reg Keeland. London: Quercus. Swedish publication 2007.

Peace, David. (1999). *1974*. London: Serpent's Tail.

Peace, David. (2000). *1977*. London: Serpent's Tail.

Peace, David. (2001). *1980*. London: Serpent's Tail.

Peace, David. (2002). *1984*. London: Serpent's Tail.

Peace, David. (2004). *GB 1984*. London: Faber and Faber.

Peace, David. (2007). *Tokyo Year Zero*. London: Faber and Faber.

Pettersson, Jan-Erik. (2011). *Stieg*, trans. Tom Geddes. London: Quercus.

Thomson, David. (2010). Murder in the north. *New York Review of Books*, 14 January, 32–4.

Žižek, Slavoj. (2010). *Living in the End Times*. London: Polity Press.

2.3

'It's a sin [...] using Ludwig van like that. He did no harm to anyone, Beethoven just wrote music': The Role of the Incongruent Soundtrack in the Representation of the Cinematic Criminal

David Ireland

The musicologist Kalinak (2010:xiii) chooses a telling case study to open her recent *Film Music: A Very Short Introduction*, a text aiming 'to provide a lucid, accessible, and engaging overview of film music'. The sequence, from *Reservoir Dogs* (Tarantino 1992), depicts gangster Mr. Blonde torturing a policeman and severing his ear, while Stealers Wheel's lively pop song 'Stuck in the Middle with You' plays on the radio. Kalinak (2010:8, 7) suggests that this example 'demonstrates so many of the key properties of film music', including creating mood and unity across the sequence, and potentially 'fashion[ing] a complicated emotional response for the audience'. Similarly, Coulthard (2009:1) suggests that the scene is 'a defining moment for [...] the role of the song in cinema', as its juxtaposition with the graphic imagery 'struck viewers and critics alike as provocative, innovative, and indicative of a new, potentially troubling approach to film violence in contemporary American cinema'. Both views demonstrate the level of discussion generated by this and stylistically similar filmic moments.

Yet 'Tarantino is certainly not the first nor the last director to pair brutal images with frothy music' (Kalinak 2010:2). As Link (2004:1) observes, films can use 'unexpectedly trivial, light or even beautiful classical and popular music as an accompaniment to their moments of most intense threat and violence'. Thus, a related technique to the juxtaposition of lively popular music with violent imagery is the frequent association of high art music with criminality. Examples of this include

Alex from *A Clockwork Orange* (Kubrick 1971), 'whose principal interests are rape, ultra-violence and Beethoven' according to a promotional tagline for the film, and the cannibal Hannibal Lecter, who listens to Bach while savagely attacking his prison guards in *The Silence of the Lambs* (Demme 1991).

Both scoring techniques pair seemingly mismatched music with depictions of crime, violence and its perpetrators. Extending terminology from film music psychology, these audio-visual relationships could be labelled aesthetically incongruent: the values and ideologies associated with the music do not always appear to correspond with the visuals or narrative, creating a philosophical mismatch. This appropriation of the label 'aesthetic' draws on Beard and Gloag's (2005:4) definition of aesthetics as 'a general term [...] to describe philosophical reflection on the arts'. The breadth offered by this definition is beneficial, as the scoring techniques discussed presently not only challenge views about the music's perceived cultural connotations and values, but also how these relate to its use within film. Indeed, such incongruities are seemingly even apparent to the cinematic criminals, as Alex from *A Clockwork Orange* demonstrates while undergoing aversion therapy during his rehabilitation. He is given drugs to enforce revulsion and forced to watch ultra-violent films, one of which is coincidentally accompanied by Beethoven's Fifth Symphony. This prompts him to cry out, in Burgess's (1972:90) novel and its filmic adaptation: 'It's a sin [...] a filthy unforgivable sin [...] Using Ludwig van like that. He did no harm to anyone. Beethoven just wrote music.' Like the average cinema goer, Alex finds his assumptions about, and responses to, familiar music challenged by its complex relationship with film.

The current chapter considers how these scoring techniques help to construct the cinematic criminal. Link (2004:15) suggests that such uses of music, in contrast to more traditional approaches, individualise the characters and the 'personality *disorders*' that may explain their deviant behaviour. These characters largely engage in extreme criminal activity, notably brutal violence. Rather than using problematic diagnostic labels such as 'psychopath' or 'sociopath', which are often misapplied interchangeably, the present discussion considers these characters within the broader context of the collective label 'criminal'. This provides interesting perspectives, as similar scoring techniques have also been used within filmic representations of more commonplace deviance. Examples of this include scenes from *Trainspotting* (Boyle 1996) and *Fear and Loathing in Las Vegas* (Gilliam 1998), in which lively popular music occurs during moments depicting recreational drug use and anti-social behaviour. Considering the characters discussed here within this wider context can highlight implicit attitudes towards different types of art and deviance that may have an impact on judgements of how appropriate the film music is. Accordingly, existing analyses of filmic moments depicting extreme criminality are compared and contextualised with additional examples and research from music psychology. These examples are considered in the context of incongruence as a perspective that accounts for both the analytical concerns of film music studies and the perceptual concerns of film music psychology. However, to appreciate these theoretical benefits, a brief conceptual (re)definition is initially required.

The incongruent perspective

Empirical evidence within film music psychology suggests that perceived congruence, or fit, between film and music can result in joint encoding of auditory and visual information. This may subsequently direct attention to specific aspects of the scene (see Cohen 2009 for a recent overview of such research). Correspondingly, perceived incongruence can result in independent encoding, and draw attention to a scene's component parts rather than the unified whole (Boltz 2004). This can enable consideration of the nature of their combination and the potential contribution of each part, supporting wider ideas in film music studies suggesting that meaning emerges through the juxtaposition of these elements. As Cook (2000:270) observes, in multimedia contexts, '[m]eaning lies not in musical sound, then, nor in the media with which it is aligned, but in the encounter between them'. Recognising incongruence as a factor that can influence perception, allowing for greater consideration of a scene's parts, helps to explain the identification of seemingly mismatched audio-visual combinations and the subsequent range of interpretations that they may evoke.

However, the language used to analyse film music does not always satisfactorily account for such complex moments. Traditional terminology has described music as working in either parallel or counterpoint to a film's images and narrative. Stilwell (1997:552) suggests that '[t]he theoretical weakness of this duality is in some respects a result of the modernist, *auteur*-based approach of film studies [...which] focuses on the point of creation rather than reception'. Yet a similar dichotomy appears evident within film music psychology, despite its emphasis on perception and response. Within this discipline, congruence and incongruence are often treated as opposing judgements of fit on either structural or semantic levels, as determined by specific experimental designs. Subsequently, more complicated, subtle or abstract mismatches are not always adequately explained. The aforementioned *Reservoir Dogs* sequence provides an effective illustration of these difficulties. Romney and Wootton (1995:5) assert that the scene 'works on the principle of radical incongruity', while Link (2004:19) argues that in some ways the song 'already *is* "congruent"' with Mr. Blonde. Meanwhile, Powrie (2005:102) asserts that the scene can be interpreted as either a moment of 'congruent incongruence' or one of 'incongruous congruence'. He suggests that these interpretations are dependent on whether the audience are disaffected and can reconcile the audio-visual differences as an instance of pure cinema, or conversely if they cannot reconcile these differences and instead identify with the violence, viewing the moment as one of pure horror. Such terminological discrepancies highlight that there are various ways in which music can contribute towards, and influence interpretations of, perceived meaning in film. These different readings also emphasise the various levels on which audio-visual fit can be judged. Descriptive precursors that identify specific types of incongruence, such as 'aesthetic' in this chapter, provide some clarity. A similar perceptual idea can be found in the psychologists Kim and Iwamiya's (2008:430) label 'subjective congruency', which emphasises that evaluations of congruence comprise judgements of fit on both formal and semantic levels.

Such ideas begin to reflect the multidimensional nature of perceived meaning and fit. However, consideration of what exactly constitutes congruence, incongruence and the boundaries between them is also necessary. Boltz (2004:1202) refers to a 'lack of shared dimensions' between incongruent film and music, while Sheinberg (2000:14) suggests that 'each component of an incongruous correlation bears more responsibility for providing information than any otherwise parallel component in a congruous one'. These approaches display an objective quality that ensures that incongruence does not always connote a negative state requiring resolution or become synonymous for the ironic use of music in film. Instead, these ideas account for the active contribution that perceived audio-visual differences can make towards meaning. Redefined in this manner, and given its perceptual implications, incongruence provides a perspective with which to approach apparently mismatched film music and the range of responses it can provoke. This perspective provides an effective conceptual context in which to discuss aesthetically incongruent music and the filmic depiction of criminality.

The film text

An initial factor to consider when analysing these cinematic representations of violent criminality is the nature of their construction. While mediated by an external agent, such as a composer, director or author, often the characters appear to be involved in the selection of music in certain situations. Information can be gleaned from whether the characters are permitted to make these choices or, conversely, if the music features on the non-diegetic soundtrack. To use the increasingly contested traditional terminology (see Stilwell 2007 for an example of contemporary scholarship critiquing the diegetic/non-diegetic dichotomy), non-diegetic music is part of 'the cinematic apparatus that represents' a film's story world (Stilwell 2007:184), and is presumably inaudible within that narrative world. Subsequently, non-diegetic music can be more beneficial to the audience and may influence their aesthetic experience or interpretation. However, when the violent criminals are permitted to select music diegetically, it individualises their characters (Link 2004) and provides an everyday counterpoint to their deviant behaviour: they are shown choosing and using music with broadly similar motivations to the audience, such as listening for pleasure (Garner 2001). As Link (2004:5) observes, this can enable them to 'sustain narrative interest beyond the repulsive spectacle of their actions' and, as Kalinak (2010:4) notes, can 'provide insight into character psychology'.

The music that an individual chooses often reveals information about their personal preferences. Hargreaves *et al.* (2002:1) suggest that 'music can be used increasingly as a means by which we formulate and express our individual identities'. However, the role of music in identity construction is to some extent dependent on the validity of the associations ascribed to particular styles. The psychologists Rentfrow and Gosling (2007) identified and empirically tested the validity of such stereotypes. Their results suggested 'that there are robust and clearly defined music-stereotypes' that often 'possess grains of truth [...] indicat[ing] that music-preference information communicates accurate information about the psychological characteristics of individuals' (Rentfrow and Gosling 2007:323). Yet such generalisations cannot account for every individual who likes a particular style of music. Rentfrow and Gosling (2007:322) note that their methodology was conducted in one geographical location and that their participants were undergraduate students with an average age of 18.9 years. These observations raise questions about the influence of demographic factors on specific stereotype details. However, the very existence of such discussion emphasises that society does make assumptions that can influence the perception of certain musical genres and those who choose to identify with them.

Music also has numerous functional qualities, and recent technological developments have enabled greater access to it either through personal choice or more passively in public contexts. The music psychologists Sloboda *et al.* (2009:431) identify a 'growing prevalence of "musical consumers"' who use music to accompany everyday situations and to 'enhance that activity in some way by affecting a psychological state which impacts on desired outcomes'. Garner (2001:189) observes that in Tarantino's films the character's selection of music is foregrounded and celebrated, noting that '[i]t is the choice of this-music or that-music in these particular circumstances, its switching on and off [...] which is made indicative of character or situation'. He suggests that this 'situational use' (Garner 2001:190) of music reflects the audience's experiences (2001:201) and that music psychology can explain such moments further. Incongruence, highlighting the lack of shared properties between the music and film, emphasises the social and psychological principles, such as identity construction or mood management, that may underlie such listening choices.

A frequently cited example is found in *The Silence of the Lambs* when Hannibal Lecter mutilates his prison guards while listening to a recording of the pianist Glenn Gould performing Bach's *Goldberg Variations*. Genre stereotypes suggest that those who like classical music can often be more introverted and higher in agreeableness, conscientiousness and emotional stability (Rentfrow and Gosling 2007:315). These descriptions reflect the image that Hannibal presents to subdue his guards, but do not necessarily correspond with his actions or underlying motivations. However, they do match traditional hegemonic ideologies surrounding such works, which are often ascribed to the canon of Western art music, acquiring a longevity that implies their value as objects of study and models of compositional structure and aesthetic beauty. These views are reflected in Harris's (1999:225) original novel, which describes Bach's music as 'beautiful beyond plight and time'. Stereotypically, such opinions also imply the refined taste and intellect of those who appreciate classical music, something that has historically often been linked to social class. Duncan (2003:137) suggests that classical music in cinema can be 'offhandedly and shorthandedly used to evoke class, culture, accomplishment, and a multitude of relations to them'. Yet, as Link (2004:8) argues, '[w]hether classical music is actually connected to intelligence [or class] is secondary to our *belief* that it is and our willingness to bring that belief to bear on characterizations in film'.

Fahy (2003:30) observes Hannibal's '[c]ivility and propriety, as evident in his educated tastes, manicured dress, and refined speech'. He also likens the intricate structure of the *Goldberg Variations* to the cunning and measure of Hannibal's crimes (Fahy 2003:32). This point is also suggested in Harris's (1999:225) novel, which states that the piece 'interested [Hannibal] structurally'. All of these factors 'play [...] on social assumptions that high culture reflects civility as well as an elevated personal and moral character' (Fahy 2003:30). Thus, Hannibal's preference for Bach is appropriate on some levels, and perhaps it is his violent behaviour with which the music is judged as incongruent rather than his personality or character. Harris (1999:229) describes Hannibal stopping the cassette and listening, presumably to see if anyone has heard the commotion of his attack. However, when his victims are later discovered, the music is again playing (1999:232), implying that he has restarted it, perhaps to convey a sense of normality or to mask the sound of his escape. Thus, Hannibal uses this music on several levels: he clearly enjoys it and the associations and status that it can convey, but he also uses it for practical reasons to facilitate his escape.

A similar example is found in the James Bond film *The Spy Who Loved Me* (Gilbert 1977), when the antagonist Stromberg listens to the Air from Bach's Third Orchestral Suite while feeding an associate he suspects of betrayal to a shark. The source of this music is harder to locate than Hannibal's cassette player. It begins as Stromberg presses a button on a control panel that lifts the paintings on his dining room wall, revealing the shark tank. The music then fades as these paintings descend into place after the victim has been eaten, implying that the music is connected to the panel and is under Stromberg's control. Koldau (2010:106) supports this interpretation and describes how listening to classical music while watching the shark attack is 'one of Stromberg's little pleasures'. Similar placement of the slow movement from Mozart's Twenty-first Piano Concerto in a scene in which his underwater hideout rises, also instigated by the control panel, again suggests that these musical choices are directly attributable to Stromberg.

This association with classical music corresponds to the self-image that Stromberg may wish to convey. Speaking on the 'Designing Bond' featurette of the film's 2006 DVD release, production designer Ken Adam comments: 'they [Bond villains] were megalomaniacs but why shouldn't they have a Picasso or a Rembrandt or whatever?' [00:12:57]. Presumably such views also apply to Stromberg's musical tastes. Adam's use of the label 'megalomaniac' also has interesting implications, corresponding to Stromberg's scheme for global annihilation and his interactions with music. The death he has orchestrated for the shark victim and his method of viewing this all convey something of the theatrical, and reflect his wealth and power. Stromberg's apparent absorption in the tranquil musical accompaniment conveys this control to his uneasy companions, whom he makes watch these events. However, this spectacle is clearly for his own pleasure, as he later kills these men, suggesting that he does not require their approval or respect, although this may provide temporary satisfaction. Again, Stromberg's choice of music is functional while also suggesting character information.

Similar points can be raised about the *Reservoir Dogs* torture sequence, despite the radically different musical genre and its accompanying connotations. In this instance, the Stealers Wheel song is not directly chosen by Mr. Blonde, leading Link (2004:10) to suggest that it is not his music, as it does not reflect his 'personal taste as directly as Lecter's tape of Bach'. However, Blonde describes the radio programme, K-Billy's *Super Sounds of the Seventies*, as his 'personal favourite': he names the genre-specific broadcast, verbally identifying with it and indicating some preference for this style, even though, as Link notes, the specific song is K-Billy's choice. Link (2004:11, 10) argues that this scene presents Blonde as 'an "average guy" whose musical tastes are neither elevated nor elevating', and that he exploits this 'uncontrolled, coincidental accompaniment', feeding from the music's energy and being more of an improviser than a planner. For Blonde, the music becomes a tool for torture; he taunts the policeman, discussing the song with him, dancing and singing along while wielding a knife and dousing him in petrol. Garner (2001:202) draws on music psychology to suggest that Blonde uses the song consciously to maintain his level of arousal, which contributes towards making 'his conduct [...] so disturbing'. This interpretation corresponds with Sloboda *et al.*'s (2009:431) observations that lively music that energises 'is a means of maintaining arousal and task attention' and is a 'recurring function [...] of self-chosen music use'.

Music can be employed in a similar way without character involvement. A café scene from *L4yer Cake* (Vaughn 2004) provides an interesting contrast; in some ways it is stylistically similar to the *Reservoir Dogs* example, but, unlike the previous examples, the music, Duran Duran's 'Ordinary World', has no direct link to any of the characters. However, the song's lyrics and upbeat character contrast with the visual and narrative content, which may influence interpretation of the character and events. The sequence depicts Morty, the minder to a drugs dealer, being reunited with Freddy, an old acquaintance whose ineptitude resulted in Morty spending ten years in prison for a crime he did not commit.

Freddy's indifference and increasingly demanding attitude eventually cause Morty to snap, viciously assaulting Freddy using his breakfast cutlery and a pot of steaming tea from the café counter. Some parallels can be drawn with Link's reading of Mr. Blonde as improviser, as reflected by Morty's use of weapons that are merely to hand. However, the music plays no role in supporting this interpretation: while Blonde uses it as part of his torture, here music has little involvement in the attack. Music, perhaps from a jukebox or radio, quietly accompanies the scene and later becomes prominent on the non-diegetic soundtrack, which is external to the story world. Regardless of the source, the music's rise in volume is presumably not audible in the café; thus, it cannot be suggested that Morty directly uses it, but it could be interpreted as facilitating identification with the general situation. Initially, the music functions like a jukebox, reflecting the space of the café and the public nature of this location, especially when considered in contrast with the secluded warehouse where Blonde tortures his victim. The non-diegetic foregrounding could be seen as reflecting how this everyday space and situation alter so suddenly and could provide empathy with Morty, mirroring his loss of temper, and the unpremeditated nature of the attack. The energetic music could be interpreted as representing Morty's arousal levels, and arguably those of the audience, as the dramatic intensity increases. However, such assertions must be made with the clear awareness that he is not controlling or choosing to identify directly with this music.

The association of the 'Ode to Joy', the final movement from Beethoven's Ninth Symphony, with Hans Gruber from *Die Hard* (McTiernan 1988) draws together these ideas: it is used by the character, director and composer, and can be interpreted as commenting on the character, location and their relationship. The non-diegetic connection of this theme with Hans, a compositional strategy influenced by the soundtrack to *A Clockwork Orange*, is established through its first fragmentary quotation on the initial sighting of his van. This pre-established association 'wrests control' (Stilwell 1997:563) of the music from the string quartet that later plays it at the party taking place as Hans's team storms the Nakatomi building. Hans later hums this melody and, as Stilwell (1997:562) notes, such character actions can 'stamp [...] their ownership on a song-theme'. Hans's humming seems opportunistic, inspired by the string quartet, much like Mr. Blonde taking control of Stealers Wheel from the radio. Functionally, this may relieve the boredom of the elevator ride during which he hums, but it simultaneously conveys arrogance and disregard for his hostage. Stilwell (1997:562, 564) suggests that this theme gives Hans presence in the soundtrack, particularly in contrast to the hero John McClane, who has 'few musical associations [...] of very low musical distinctiveness': this musical dominance reflects Hans's control of the building, and the film's plot, which is driven by his robbery plan. Stilwell (1997:574) argues that this narrative and musical power helps to subvert traditional narrative hierarchies, giving Hans the status of anti-hero rather than villain, by allowing him 'the active role and assigning the reactive role to the nominal hero'. This strategy provides greater opportunity to emphasise his charismatic traits and potentially win the audience's sympathy.

The audience

Awareness of who is controlling the music furthers understanding about how it can provide information and influence interpretation. As the preceding examples demonstrate, it can be judged as appropriate on certain levels but not others, which can challenge the audience members' perspectives. The perceptual implications of incongruence help to explain how these differences are identified and influence perceived meaning and response. Studying the psychological principles that influence such judgements can also prove informative, and the idea of violated expectations and sociologically motivated assumptions is of particular relevance. This corresponds with influential research in music psychology, notably Meyer's (1956) theory relating emotional response to the realisation or violation of expectations, particularly at points of structural significance. Meyer draws on ideas from Gestalt psychology, acknowledging the importance of perceptual processes such as grouping and closure, which help to make sense of stimuli. Such organisational principles help to explain the joint encoding that congruent soundtracks enable and that incongruence challenges due to the lack of shared properties between the scene's component parts.

The preceding examples demonstrate that violations of expectations can occur in response to the music itself and the way it is used within the film. Link (2004:6) suggests that the fact of the *Goldberg Variations* accompanying Hannibal's attack is 'surprising in light of our traditional expectation that music should somehow react to, or comment on, the scene'. Such comments demonstrate that music can thwart expectations by appearing neither to foreshadow nor to accompany events appropriately. The aforementioned examples also highlight that pre-existing music, rather than music specifically composed for the film, is often employed in such scenes. Familiarity with these pre-existing works can influence an audience member's attitudes about what this music may signify and can subsequently influence their expectations and interpretation. However, genre conventions may equally influence response and highlight seemingly inappropriate aspects of the music, as can the emotional incongruence often also created by such moments.

Violations of expectation can also challenge the audience's interpretation by altering their point of identification or with what their attention and sympathy are allied. The cinematic criminal's interactions with music often present a more three-dimensional character that can create further points of identification. If Hannibal's preference for Bach corresponds with certain aspects of his character, could the audience identify with him on some level because they too might appreciate classical music? Similarly, several analyses (including Garner 2001:202 and Link 2004:10) agree that Mr. Blonde's detachment is emphasised by his interaction with Stealers Wheel, again challenging the viewer's attitudes. Kalinak (2010:5, 8) quotes Tarantino suggesting that the audience is essentially complicit in the torture as they are drawn into the situation and may focus attention on Blonde and his dancing: the song's lively and accessible properties can lead to them being absorbed 'into the spectacle of the film'. However, Coulthard (2009:2) suggests that such uses of music, in conjunction with other aspects of Tarantino's directorial style, 'are precisely structured to stress their cinematic substance, form, and materiality', reminding the viewer 'of their spectatorial position [...] (even when they are being encouraged to enter into, and fully enjoy, the [film])'. She draws on Žižek's notion of interpassivity, suggesting that the pleasurable qualities of the song enable it to 'control, reduce, and delimit [affective response] – in short, to force it into a realm of pure and passive enjoyment' (Coulthard 2009:5). Accordingly, the text influences interpretation through self-reflexive participation in the perceptual process. It enjoys the moment for the viewer, allowing awareness of the artifice of the cinematic experience rather than detailed reflection on the action, making the moment pleasurable 'regardless of our own personal response' (Coulthard 2009:4).

This emphasises the levels on which response may occur. Coulthard (2009:2) highlights the 'mode of reception' that Tarantino's juxtapositions of lively music with graphic violence can create, which combines 'emotional disengagement, superficial participation, and spectatorial comfort'. Similarly, while discussing Hannibal's use of Bach, Stilwell (2007:192) identifies the fluidity of identification, questioning whether it necessarily matters 'at which position exactly the audience perceives itself at any one instant during this scene'. Such analyses raise interesting questions about the nature of response. Does absorption imply more active engagement? Does awareness of the artificial nature of cinema necessarily result in a lack of involvement or create distance? What constitutes distance, and does this necessarily imply apathy? As Link (2004:19) observes, '[d]istance is also a "feeling"'. These analyses and hypothetical questions emphasise the personal dimensions of response. Incongruence, providing perceptual space to consider the levels on which meaning is constructed, can account for the subjectivity inherent in the answers to these questions.

Regardless of how incongruence influences response and identification, as this music often relates to the criminal, it generally defers attention away from his or her victims. Subsequently, these moments are often labelled anempathetic, using Chion's (1994:8) notion that such music presents a 'conspicuous indifference' to the scene. This interpretation is applicable on many levels, given the disregard that many of these characters show for their victims, actions and, when self-chosen, their music. Link (2004) argues that musical anempathy individualises the characters and Powrie (2005:100) observes that the 'received notion' of the *Reservoir Dogs* torture scene is that the song is anempathetic, given that the upbeat music does not reflect the brutality of the torture. However, Powrie (2005:105) acknowledges that the music's use 'goes much deeper than a superficial anempathetic relationship', relating this to the issues of spectatorship that the song raises. This demonstrates that empathy and anempathy share similar difficulties with other labels used to describe film music.

The term anempathy carries problematic connotations, as the idea of indifference can imply an apathy and impartiality that are not necessarily present. This is somewhat misleading given that the music can actively influence the narrative or interpretation of it. None of the analyses cited infer that anempathy is simplistic or innocent, and indeed actively suggest the opposite by discussing the music's contribution to characterisation and influencing response. As Link (2004:18) observes, the effects of anempathy 'are paradoxically far from insincere'. Link (2004:7, 18) suggests that anempathy 'diffracts the scene into its component elements', 'opens spaces for description' and 'has the power to create radically different and unexpected affective states'. This approach towards anempathy has many similarities to the present conceptualisation of incongruence. However, the perceptual implications of incongruence also offer psychological explanations for the subjectivity of response that can inform analytical approaches that consider the levels on which music contributes towards meaning. Accordingly, incongruence can enable anempathy to participate, as appropriate, as part of a more holistic strategy for understanding these ambiguous moments.

Ideas of anempathy and the violation of expectations re-emphasise questions about societal attitudes towards the value and functions of music – or, to quote Link (2004:9): 'should music care?' The association of music with cinematic crime and violence raises such questions, as it is the values implicit in our answers that contribute towards assumptions or expectations that can be violated and challenged. Link (2004:7, 20) observes that 'an uncomfortable fit makes us very aware of having anticipated something else' and questions why the audience often assumes that music should provide empathy with the victim rather than the criminal. An implication of these ideas, which incongruence highlights by acknowledging the multidimensional nature of perceived meaning, is that perhaps the most pertinent level on which fit is assessed is that of our own subjectivity, influenced by preconceived ideas and attitudes, rather than properties of the film or music itself.

Aesthetic incongruence allows reinterpretation of familiar musical works or genres and the assumptions surrounding them. Fahy (2003:35) argues that Hannibal's artistic tastes 'recast [...] classic art in a modern framework'. Similarly, Stilwell (1997:569) refers to the postmodern notion of the text as 'a nexus of cultural processes only loosely bracketed by the boundaries of the "work"'. She suggests that '[i]f the original material is a potential for interpretation [...] then its use in an unfamiliar and unexpected context is merely another interpretation' (1997:569). Referring to the 'accrual of meaning' (Stilwell 1997:569) and challenging notions of autonomy, she argues that this can provide opportunity for interpretation on many levels. This relates preexisting music and its filmic context to wider sociological and aesthetic judgements, again supporting the notion that it is our values and opinions that are being challenged. However, it is important also to recall the subjectivity of perception, acknowledging that while aesthetic incongruence may challenge some very directly, others may be affected subconsciously or not at all, perhaps viewing such moments as emotionally incongruent or not even noticing the soundtrack.

Conclusions

The incongruent soundtrack can contribute to the construction of the cinematic criminal in many ways. It can be employed by character, director or composer for reasons including the construction of identity, or more abstract concerns surrounding narrative development or hierarchy. Incongruent music draws attention to itself by obstructing joint perceptual encoding and encouraging analysis of a scene's component parts and their relationships, enabling space for deeper questions and responses from viewers if they choose. By altering their point of identification, such musical constructions can challenge viewers to assess where their sympathies lie: with the criminal, the victim or indeed themselves as they try to understand the situation depicted. Similarly, by challenging wider cultural and traditional ideas about the role of music, and implications about certain styles and those who identify with them, incongruent music can violate expectations and provoke an emotional response. These factors highlight the complex ways in which music contributes to film and the two will interact differently with each other depending on the context. An awareness of such factors, facilitated by the analytical and perceptual perspective that a redefined approach to incongruence enables, goes some way in helping to appreciate why such film–music combinations can be so memorable and effective.

References

Beard, David and Kenneth Gloag. (2005). *Musicology: The Key Concepts*. London: Routledge.

Boltz, Marilyn G. (2004). The cognitive processing of film and musical soundtracks. *Memory and Cognition* 32(7), 1194–205.

Burgess, Anthony. (1972). *A Clockwork Orange*. London: Penguin.

Chion, Michel. (1994). *Audio-Vision: Sound on Screen*, ed. and trans. Claudia Gorbman. New York: Columbia University Press.

Cohen, Annabel J. (2009). Music in performance arts: Film, theatre and dance. In Susan Hallam, Ian Cross and Michael Thaut (eds), *The Oxford Handbook of Music Psychology*. Oxford: Oxford University Press.

Cook, Nicholas. (2000). *Analysing Musical Multimedia*. Oxford: Oxford University Press.

Coulthard, Lisa. (2009). Torture tunes: Tarantino, popular music and new Hollywood ultraviolence. *Music and the Moving Image* 2(2), 1–6.

Duncan, Dean. (2003). *Charms That Soothe: Classical Music and the Narrative Film*. New York: Fordham University Press.

Fahy, Thomas. (2003). Killer culture: Classical music and the art of killing in *Silence of the Lambs* and *Se7en*. *Journal of Popular Culture* 37(1), 28–42.

Garner, Ken. (2001). 'Would you like to hear some music?' Music in-and-out-of-control in the films of Quentin Tarantino. In Kevin J. Donnelly (ed.), *Film Music: Critical Approaches*. Edinburgh: Edinburgh University Press.

Hargreaves, David J., Dorothy Miell and Raymond A.R. MacDonald. (2002). What are musical identities, and why are they important? In Raymond A.R. MacDonald, David J. Hargreaves and Dorothy Miell (eds), *Musical Identities*. Oxford: Oxford University Press.

Harris, Thomas. (1999). *The Silence of the Lambs*. London: Arrow Books.

Kalinak, Kathryn. (2010). *Film Music: A Very Short Introduction*. New York: Oxford University Press.

Kim, Ki-Hong and Shin-Ichiro Iwamiya. (2008). Formal congruency between telop patterns and sound effects. *Music Perception* 25(5), 429–48.

Koldau, Linda M. (2010). Of submarines and sharks: Musical settings of a silent menace. *Horror Studies* 1(1), 89–110.

Link, Stan. (2004). Sympathy with the devil? Music of the psycho post-*Psycho*. *Screen* 45(1), 1–20.

Meyer, Leonard B. (1956). *Emotion and Meaning in Music*. Chicago: University of Chicago Press.

Powrie, Phil. (2005). Blonde abjection: Spectatorship and the abject anal space in-between. In Steve Lannin and Matthew Caley (eds), *Pop Fiction: The Song in Cinema*. Bristol: Intellect Books.

Rentfrow, Peter J. and Samuel D. Gosling. (2007). The content and validity of music-genre stereotypes among college students. *Psychology of Music* 35(2), 306–26.

Romney, Jonathan and Adrian Wootton. (1995). Introduction. In Jonathan Romney and Adrian Wootton (eds), *Celluloid Jukebox: Popular Music and the Movies since the 50s*. London: British Film Institute.

Sheinberg, Esti. (2000). *Irony, Satire, Parody and the Grotesque in the Music of Shostakovich: A Theory of Musical Incongruities*. Aldershot: Ashgate.

Sloboda, John, Alexandra Lamont and Alinka Greasley. (2009). Choosing to hear music: Motivation, process and effect. In Susan Hallam, Ian Cross and Michael Thaut (eds), *The Oxford Handbook of Music Psychology*. Oxford: Oxford University Press.

Stilwell, Robynn J. (1997). 'I just put a drone under him ...': Collage and subversion in the score of 'Die Hard'. *Music and Letters* 78(4), 551–80.

Stilwell, Robynn, J. (2007). The fantastical gap between diegetic and nondiegetic. In Daniel Goldmark, Lawrence Kramer and Richard Leppert (eds), *Beyond the Soundtrack: Representing Music in Cinema*. Berkeley: University of California Press.

The Spy Who Loved Me. (2006[1977]). Lewis Gilbert (dir.). *The Spy Who Loved Me: Ultimate Edition 2-disc DVD set*. [DVD] Metro-Goldwyn-Mayer Studios.

2.4
Criminal Publication and Victorian Prefaces: Suspending Disbelief in Sensation Fiction

Malcah Effron

In fiction, and particularly in crime fiction, introductory material has taken on an important role in legally establishing novels as fictional, defensively demanding the suspension of readerly disbelief. This even appears in crime fiction's nineteenth-century precursors, as seen, for example, in the Prefaces to Charles Dickens's (1853) *Bleak House* and Wilkie Collins's (1861) *The Woman in White*. Dickens's *Bleak House* interweaves different narratives of intrigue, including subplots addressing a variety of social concerns in industrialised London. These subplots unite in a critique of the Victorian legal system and its ability to provide justice for its citizens, as the novel opens and is driven by the plot of Jarndyce and Jarndyce, a fictional inheritance case that has been before the Court of Chancery for generations. Unlike *Bleak House*'s court setting, Collins's *The Woman in White* argues a fictional case that cannot be tried in a Victorian court, the kidnap of and fraud perpetrated against Laura Fairlie by her husband, Sir Percivale Glyde, and his friend, Count Fosco. Through the organising narrator of Laura's second husband, Walter Hartright, the novel explores the legal system from the perspective of those excluded from its mechanisms of justice. By focusing on elements of the legal system, both these novels construct systems of crime and punishment within a literary frame that is meant to represent and to critique the Victorian legal system.

Because realistic representation and persuasive critique are important to both these novels, their Prefaces insist on the accuracy of the details used to describe the legal system that structures the novels' plots. This legal component is key to the principal construction of criminality; that which is criminal is defined and produced by the legal system, and it is the legal system that defines what actions constitute criminal acts. Both book Prefaces respond to external criticism by insisting that they have provided valid accounts of the unjust behaviour that corrupts the Victorian legal system. Even more so, they provide evidence such as might be used in a legal trial to support their claims of realism. Nevertheless, both Prefaces conclude by referring to the narratives' statuses as inventions. While these claims to realism and to fictionality seem to contradict each other, they seemingly arise from the same motivation, as they both defend the narrative project against readerly criticism. In proclaiming their fictional statuses, the narratives free themselves from the legal ramifications of libel and other criticism. Yet this proclamation does not seem to free the author from the responsibility of depicting society realistically, bringing issues of legal responsibility into conversation with representations of reality. As such, Dickens's and Collins's Prefaces instruct their readers on how to interpret the cases they present before them, focusing the readers' attention on the crimes constructed by the plots rather than on any criminal misrepresentation within the novels.

Defending the law

Since the early twentieth century, both popular and academic criticism of the crime genre has focused on the use of realistic investigative procedure within detective fiction, highlighting readerly insistence on 'fair play', or the ability for the reader to solve the mystery like the detective protagonist.[1] Unlike their twentieth-century descendants, the Prefaces of these Victorian precursors to detective fiction indicate that Dickens's and Collins's nineteenth-century readers do not respond to questions about the investigative procedure. Rather than fault the investigation, these readers focused on the accurate representation of the law within the novels' plots. While archival searches of both contemporary reviews and readers' letters to the authors can validate this interest in the legal accuracy of storytelling, the authors' defensiveness on this point directly indicates the impact such criticism had on the process of crafting and revising the novels. As such, the Prefaces indicate how the authors prioritise their accuracy in representing the Victorian legal and criminal systems as a means of authenticating the novels' realistic representations.

In responding to challenges to the accuracy of his portrayal of the legal system represented in *Bleak House*, Dickens (1992[1853]:xxvi) does not refer to reviews or letters but to a public statement on the part of a Chancery judge, 'at which point I [Dickens] thought the Judge's eye had cast in my direction'. Taking this starting point, Dickens suggests that he responds to a challenge that indirectly implicates his critique of the Court of Chancery. He also indicates that, despite the covert nature of the criticism, the counter-argument is a direct attack on the accuracy of his novelistic representation. Responding to critics' attacks on his realistic accuracy, Dickens (1992[1853]:xxvi) lambasts his attackers as he defends not only his novel but also his authorial integrity:

> But as it is wholesome that the parsimonious public should know what has been doing, and still is doing, in this connexion, I mention here that everything set forth in these pages concerning the Court of Chancery is substantially true and within the truth.

The repetition of 'true' and 'truth' argues the veracity of both Dickens's representations and his critiques. Furthermore, as Julius (1998:53, original emphasis) suggests, by insisting that he does not exceed the realities of Chancery, 'Dickens is also insisting that the work is not to be read as a *satire*, that is to say, as a deliberately overdrawn account of Chancery, exaggerated for the purposes of indictment and to prompt reform'. Julius highlights here that the strength of Dickens's criticism stems not from his ability to mock the general practices of the court, but from his ability to capture its injustices precisely. The qualifiers 'substantially' and 'within' validate Dickens's claims within the fictional context, as he is no longer required to report cases but can reinvent them to suit the purposes of his narrative. Furthermore, this caveat protects against claims of libel, both from those named in the suits he uses as his sources and from the court that he suggests is in need of reform. This defensive manoeuvre, however, mitigates the full authority of the claims to accuracy that he makes.

Whereas Dickens addressed his refutations to oral claims implicitly made against his novel, Collins (1993[1861]:3) responds to written challenges in his Preface to the three-volume edition of the novel. According to Sutherland (cited in 1999[1996]:669, ellipsis in original), he refers to a critical review of the novel in the *Saturday Review* on 25 August 1860, in which the reviewer disparages Collins's knowledge of wills and the legal system surrounding them, proposing that:

> Mr. Wilkie Collins ... on the subject of life estates, is either more obscure in his expressions, or else less sound in his law, than we could wish. As the case at present stands, we cannot help thinking that half the crime and folly in the tale has been committed in consequence of a misconception.

This critic proposes that Collins does not understand certain inheritance laws, leading his criminals to commit murder unnecessarily (Sutherland 1999[1996]:669). In this regard, Collins's legal knowledge mitigates his ability to construct a realistic representation of crime, because misunderstanding undermines the plot's believability.

In addition to refuting the criticism launched in the *Saturday Review*, Collins needs to defend his legal accuracy to justify his plot strategy, with regard not only to the need for a murder but also to his ability to establish activities that are, in fact, criminal. These motives justify Collins's (1999[1861]:3) vigorous defence of his legal correctness, declaring 'I spared no pains – in this instance, as in all others – to preserve myself from unintentionally misleading my readers. A solicitor of great experience in his profession most kindly and carefully guided my steps.' In addition to providing literary precedent for the detective genre's interest in 'playing fair' with the reader, Collins here shows that, of all aspects of his work, authenticity remains at the top of his priorities. Thus, Collins rigorously defends the accuracy of his presentation of the legal system to authenticate both the events in and the structure of the narrative.

Dickens and Collins locate their defences of their legal representations differently in their Prefaces, suggesting a difference in the importance of the legal argument to the foundations of each of their novels. Dickens begins his Preface by responding to the challenges to his representation of Chancery, because the accuracy of his depiction is essential to his critique of the system. If viewed simply as a farcical exaggeration, the representation loses the weight of social critique. Collins, however, addresses the critique of his legal representation after he addresses a correction to the dating of events in the novel. The timeline in the serialised edition, Collins (1999[1861]:3) notes, is inaccurate, so he shows that he does make changes when the criticism is correct. Since he does not correct critiques of his legal representation, these other corrections reinforce the idea that he feels this aspect of his novel is accurate and does not need correcting. Furthermore, the positioning suggests that the problems proposed with the legal issues do not invalidate the plot to the point that the reviewer claims. Unlike Dickens, who needs people to believe in Chancery's injustices to convince them that the court does not serve the interests of justice, Collins does not need to follow proper inheritance law to allow the fraud and murder to serve as crimes. In his Preface, Dickens also chooses to defend himself against criticism he received for the inclusion of a subplot, the spontaneous combustion of Mr. Krooks, a shopkeeper. In the Preface, Dickens supports his realism by providing multiple examples verifying the real possibility of death by spontaneous combustion. Collins, however, does not counter with other issues of extratextual realistic representation, but instead defends his method of writing. While this highlights the difference in the types of comments each novel received, both types stress the believability of the characters and experiences in these narratives. The Prefaces thus indicate that these authors attempted to represent Victorian society realistically when establishing the backdrop for the construction of their fictions. Without showing the injustice of the legal system, Dickens cannot make his case for the criminal negligence of the court system, particularly as it is the system that he is condemning that has the authority to define that which is legal. Nevertheless, both Prefaces indicate the importance of accurate descriptions of the Victorian legal system to enable readers to suspend disbelief for the novels' crime plots.

By prioritising the validity of their representations of the legal system, both Dickens and Collins denote that, for their novels that centre on crime and its investigation, the legal system establishes the criminality of the events that follow. The Prefaces emphasise that they have accurately interpreted the Victorian legal system, defending the plots' narrative and reformist goals. As such, their responses to public criticism of their novels indicate the importance they place on certain comments over others; specifically, they prioritise the realistic accuracy of their legal systems. In this regard, they establish the legal system as the basis for the agendas of the novels.

The nature of evidence

Dickens and Collins do not anticipate that their readers will accept the prefatory assertion of accuracy without providing supporting evidence. As such, the types of support they provide in their Prefaces indicate assumptions about evidentiary proof in the Victorian period. In justifying their claims, they exemplify the type of proof needed to convince a Victorian audience. This is particularly the case for Collins's novel, which revolves around providing definitive proof to Laura Fairlie's identity and right to her inheritance. In this regard, the Prefaces serve to establish the nature of evidence for the novels.

In the Preface to *Bleak House*, Dickens bases his evidence on empirical data, using previous events as case studies for the validity of his claims. He mentions that there are specific cases on record that parallel the fictional occurrences in the novel. With regard to a secondary example that Dickens presents of the Chancery court system, the fictional Gridley case, the Preface claims: '[t]he case of Gridley is in no essential altered from one of actual occurrence, made public by a disinterested person who was professionally acquainted with the whole of the monstrous wrong from beginning to end' (Dickens 1992[1853]:xxiv). By claiming to have preserved the whole of the case from real events, Dickens generates credibility for his fictional portrayal of a court case. In his biography of Dickens, Forster (1874:50) identifies the case and the pamphlet that the novelist used as the basis for the Gridley case, thus verifying Dickens's claims of a real precedent. Dickens, however, does not identify the case, expecting the reader to accept his claim without concrete evidence of this true story, allowing the fact of an extratextual basis to do all the work of providing proof.

Dickens (1992[1853]:xxvi–ii, emphasis in original) similarly allows extratextual bases to validate his realism when he provides precedents for the central Chancery case, Jarndyce and Jarndyce:

> At the present moment there is a suit before the Court which was commenced nearly twenty years ago; in which from thirty to forty counsel have been known to appear at one time; in which costs have been incurred to the amount of seventy thousand pounds; which is a *friendly suit*; and which is (I am assured) no nearer to its termination now than when it was begun. There is another well-known suit in Chancery, not yet decided, which was commenced before the close of the last century, and in which more than double the amount of seventy thousand pounds has been swallowed up in costs. If I wanted other authorities for Jarndyce and Jarndyce, I could rain them on these pages.

In this explanation, Dickens claims to have real examples to support the validity of his fictional representations, arguing that the experiences described with Jarndyce and Jarndyce are not exaggerations of the extra-textual state of affairs. In particular, Dickens focuses on the cases' duration and expense, exposing these issues as the focus of his attack on the court system. Furthermore, by mentioning the quantity of attorneys for the real trials, Dickens emphasises that the circus element of the court system is not of his invention but part of his realistic representation. He underscores this absurdity when he claims that he could provide further examples. As such, these descriptions emphasise not only the validity of his invention, but also the focus of his rebuke.

In these instances, Dickens's proof again relies on the reader's faith that the anonymous descriptions are reported from actual trials and not invented by the novelist. With the Gridley trial precedent, Dickens (1992[1853]:xxvi) indicates that he was made aware of the case 'by a disinterested person who was professionally acquainted with the whole of the monstrous wrong from beginning to end'. By claiming to have received the information from another person, and particularly another person affiliated with the case, Dickens provides evidence, albeit still anonymous evidence, that the case exists outside his own invention. He does not offer similar evidence for the other cases mentioned in the Preface, nor does he provide sources for the myriad of other cases that he could 'rain [...] on these pages' (Dickens 1992[1853]:xxvi–ii). Scholars have discussed and discovered cases that could be the models for Jarndyce and Jarndyce. Dunstan (1997:24), echoed cautiously by Polden (2004:338), proposes that the early nineteenth-century inheritance suit of the Jennens family serves as the basis for Jarndyce and Jarndyce, and thus could be one of the suits to which Dickens refers in his introduction. In any case, such scholarship validates Dickens's claims of authenticity. Though these cases would perhaps have been familiar enough to readers in the 1850s so as not to need the cases to be identified specifically, Polden (2004:363) mentions that the Jennens case had not had any newsworthy action since the 1830s. While Polden doubts that Dickens would recall cases from the 1830s, Nabokov (2002[1980]:64) notes that as 'legal historians have shown, the bulk of our author's [Dickens] information on legal matters goes back to the 1820s and 1830s so that many of his targets had ceased to exist by the time *Bleak House* was written', indicating that Polden's rejection of the Jennens case might be based on erroneous assumptions. Nevertheless, since there were two decades of public silence on the Jennens case prior to the publication of *Bleak House*, this illustrates the faith that Dickens had that the reading public would accept his evidence of the truth when vocal members did not accept it in fiction.

Furthermore, Nabokov (2002[1980]:64) claims that because Dickens refers to cases that were over two decades old, 'many of his targets had ceased to exist by the time *Bleak House* was written'. However, in his Preface, Dickens (1992[1853]:xxiv) emphasises that the problems he discusses are still current. He describes one of the cases provided in support of the validity of Jarndyce and Jarndyce with the statement '[a]t the present moment there is a suit before the Court' and another with 'not yet decided'. Both these claims indicate that, at least in the instance of the cases to which Dickens refers in the Preface, the targets had not ceased to exist because of the reformation of the legal system in the 1830s (Julius 1998:57). If we accept the Jennens case as such an example, even if not *the* example, then Nabokov's proposal that Dickens's legal claims are outdated works only as support of his own reading of the novel. Nabokov (2002[1980]:64) reads *Bleak House* as outdated criticism – 'if the target is gone, let us enjoy the carved beauty of the weapon' – so that he does not have to pay attention to Dickens's authenticating goals in his Preface. Nabokov's reading proposes that the novel's importance lies in its aesthetics more than in its social agenda, as it launches obsolete critiques of the legal system.

Though Nabokov usefully distinguishes between the work of *Bleak House* and satire, he does so at the expense of the social implications, choosing to focus on word play rather than social consciousness. This approach to the novel seems at odds with Dickens's language in the Preface, where he clearly disparages the labyrinth of the legal system, referring to it as 'the monstrous wrong from beginning to end' (Dickens 1992[1853]:xxvi). Like Nabokov, Julius challenges the classification of *Bleak House* as a satire but, unlike Nabokov, he does so by reading the novel as a social critique rather than Nabokov's reading against it. Focusing instead on Dickens's prefatory claim that the novel *not* be read 'as a deliberately overdrawn account of Chancery', Julius (1998:53) argues that satire would undermine the authority of the portrayal of the legal system and thus weaken the claim against Chancery's injustices. In this regard, Julius's claims follow the language of the Preface in a manner that Nabokov's do not. Dickens writes his Preface in a manner that assures his readers that he presents an accurate portrait of the current state of the court systems so that he can propose that the legal system behaves criminally.

Dickens insists on his accurate portrait of the world, which he emphasises by spending the remainder of the Preface defending Krooks's death by spontaneous combustion. Unlike in his defence of the Chancery portrait, to prove spontaneous combustion Dickens (1992[1853]:xxvii) identifies his sources, naming not only the victims of spontaneous combustion but also the investigating authorities:

> There are about thirty cases on record, of which the most famous, that of the Countess Cornelia de Baudi Cesenate, was minutely investigated and described by Giuseppe Bianchini [...] otherwise distinguished in letters [...] The next most famous instance happened at Rheims, six years earlier; and the historian in that case is Le Cat, one of the most renowned surgeons produced by France. The subject was a woman [and] it was shown on evidence that she had died the death to which this name of Spontaneous Combustion is given.

In defending spontaneous combustion, which has subsequently been disproven (BMJ 1938:1106), Dickens provides detailed accounts of historical incidents, unlike the vague descriptions of legal cases. Furthermore, he invokes the testimony of expert witnesses about spontaneous combustion, but he rests on his own assertions when defending his portrait of the legal system. While the material is not wholly developed in the Preface, Dickens indicates that he gives a fuller, more precise summary of the events within the narrative (Dickens 1992[1853]: xxvii). This might seem repetitive but, by including generalities in the Preface, he ensures that his readers recognise the historical events in the fictions rather than assume that his evidence is part of his imaginative creations. As such, he reinforces that, as Ryan (1991:52) argues for all literature, the narrative 'project[s] upon these worlds everything we know about reality and we will make only the adjustments dictated by the text'. Dickens's Preface argues that neither details as large as the (dys)function of Chancery nor as small as spontaneous combustion require 'adjustments dictated by the text'.

Dickens's use of specific details for biological laws might indicate that the audience would have more trouble believing in spontaneous combustion than in a corrupted legal system. Furthermore, readers might have been more familiar with British court cases than with freak accidents in Italy, such as those he uses to support the reality of spontaneous combustion. Finally, by preserving the anonymity of the defendants, Dickens avoids prosecution for libel or defamation by the participants in the case. Nevertheless, by maintaining the anonymity of the examples, Dickens shows that he does not believe that his defence needs specific examples to support his point. Ultimately, the Preface indicates that, though the readership has not proven itself willing to accept his authority in fictional form, Dickens presumes on this authority in the non-fictional Preface.

Like Dickens, Collins also maintains the anonymity of his sources when he gives his evidence to support his realistic representation of the Victorian legal system. Unlike Dickens, Collins appeals to authority and meticulous research rather than to case studies to defend his claims. To convince his readers that he has accurately detailed the events according to the legal code, Collins (1999[1861]:3) responds:

A solicitor of great experience in his profession most kindly and carefully guided me into the labyrinth of the Law. Every doubtful question was submitted to this gentleman, before I ventured putting pen to paper; and all the proof-sheets which referred to legal matters were corrected by his hand before the story was published.

Collins emphasises that he had his ideas and his novel thoroughly verified by a legal expert before publishing his text, guaranteeing that there are no legal inaccuracies that would have any impact on the narrative or on the reading experience. Unlike contemporary writers, however, he does not add the clause that frequently concludes acknowledgements in twentieth- and twenty-first-century fiction that engages with the intricacies of the law, namely that 'any errors are [the author's] own'. In some sense, while asserting the correctness of his material, he also removes responsibility for any errors, projecting them instead onto his unnamed expert. In this regard, by preserving the anonymity of his expert, Collins protects him from criticism of his legal expertise at the hands of the reading public or, more specifically, *The Saturday Review*. Moreover, the anonymity focuses the attention to detail not on the calibre of the expert, but on the meticulousness of the procedure that Collins followed. Rather than advertising who his consultant is, the Preface emphasises the pains Collins took to ensure that he presented a legally correct document before his reading public, highlighting the care and attention put into crafting the novel. This attention to detail validates the author's authority over the case developed in the entire novel, and presents such attention as the means of establishing proof.

In this manner, the Preface supports the extra-judicial case that organises the narrative of *The Woman in White*, validating the middle-class protagonist Walter Hartright's meticulous investigation and documentation over the noble authority of Sir Percival Glyde and Count Fosco, the aristocratic villains. When establishing the basis for the novel, Collins (1999[1861]:5) engages a similar critique of the courts as Dickens – namely, that it is driven by profit rather than by justice:

> If the machinery of the Law could be depended on to fathom every case of suspicion, and to conduct every process of inquiry, with moderate assistance only from the lubricating influences of oil of gold, the events which fill these pages might have claimed their share of the public attention in a Court of Justice.
>
> But the Law is still, in certain inevitable cases, the pre-engaged servant of the long purse; and the story is left to be told, for the first time, in this place.

Hartright begins by condemning the court system for favouring the rich, as 'the pre-engaged servant of the long purse'. As such, he suggests that the corrupted legal system means that the narrative needs to construct the criminal acts for them to be recognised as crimes. The metaphorical language – for instance 'oil of gold' – reaffirms Dickens's issues, namely that the unjust act is neither perceived nor treated as criminal by the one system empowered to determine criminality: the Court of Justice. With this narrative, however, Hartright circumvents the legal system, literally trying the case in the popular press rather than in the courtroom. He thus produces a new means of constructing crime, one that does not rely on the courts.

Nevertheless, Hartright employs the language of the court system he eschews to produce his case:

> As the Judge might once have heard it, so the Reader shall hear it now. No circumstance of importance [...] shall be related on hearsay evidence [...] When [Walter Hartright's] experience fails, he will retire from the position of narrator; and his task will be continued [...] by other persons who can speak to the circumstances under notice from their own knowledge. (Collins 1999[1861]:5)

Though he disparages the biases of the courtroom, Hartright adopts its methods as a means of properly presenting evidence. As Luyster (2002:598) suggests, these methods indicate the novelist's 'appropriation of the authority of legal evocation to buttress realistic representation and enforce narrators' credibility claims'. This assessment emphasises that the legal format is a realist technique that allows the novelist to rely on the conventional assumption of truth telling associated with witness testimony to suspend readerly disbelief. In this sense, the format of the telling is integral to Hartright's ability to convince his audience: he needs the understood honesty of the courtroom to undermine the financial biases of the Victorian legal system.

As Hartright, the character, needs the code of behaviour associated with the courtroom to establish the believability of his narrative, Collins, the author, needs the minutiae of legal procedure to create the realistic representation that will establish Luyster's 'authority of legal evocation'. Collins's reliance on this dependability comes through not only his insistence on his correct procedure in producing the framework for the novel and in constructing its plot, but also his assurance of other experts' acceptance of the completed novel. Immediately after outlining his procedure for incorporating legal elements into his narrative, Collins (1999[1861]:3) assures future readers that his procedure has been reviewed and deemed successful:

> I can add, on high judicial authority, that these precautions [in the writing process] were not taken in vain. The 'law' in this book has

been discussed, since its publication, by more than one competent tribunal, and has been decided sound.

The author here again appeals to authority, emphasising that 'competent tribunal[s]' have tried and approved his novel. With the appeal to 'competent tribunal[s]', Collins also subtly disparages the legal authority of the author of the derogatory review. By assuring future readers that he has changed the errors of the serial publication and maintained the features that are, in fact, correct, he affirms the validity of the novel and thus the utility of its narrative experiment, which then becomes the focus of the remainder of the Preface. He uses authority to establish his correct representation of the law, establishing legal procedure as the means to authenticate the realism of the novel.

Despite their narrative critiques of the Victorian legal system, in their defences of their representations of the legal system both Dickens and Collins rely on the types of evidence often brought before a courtroom to make their case. Dickens appeals to the law of precedence, citing multiple examples of historical cases with the features that appear in his novels. Collins calls on expert witnesses as authority figures, a strategy that Dickens also uses to defend the idea of spontaneous combustion. The Prefaces, as well as the narratives, thus treat nineteenth-century readership as a nineteenth-century jury, demanding that they evaluate the case of realistic representation as they would assess any other legal violation.

Nothing but the... fiction

After having spent the majority of their Prefaces assuring their readerships that they have provided realistic images of the legal system, both Dickens and Collins conclude their Prefaces by stating that these novels are, in fact, works of fiction. Moments such as these seem to be early prototypes for the conventional disclaimer that now accompanies all works of fiction, namely that 'any resemblance to actual persons, living or dead, is entirely coincidental'. Neither Dickens nor Collins makes an absolute claim of this nature; however, the notion of distinguishing between a fictional invention and a factual representation remains at the core of these statements. In this regard, the conclusions seem to undermine the very reality that their Prefaces work to underscore, seemingly asking the readers to accept both the text's factuality and its fictionality simultaneously. Nevertheless, having assured the readers that it is safe for them to suspend their disbelief because the narrative universe they enter is the same as the one in which they live, these

Prefaces ask readers to enjoy the imaginative development of both novels, curtailing readerly criticism against any additional modifications made for the sake of the fiction. After authenticating both his invented legal cases and spontaneous combustion fatality, Dickens (1992[1853]:xxvii) concludes his Preface by insisting that '[i]n *Bleak House*, I have purposely dwelt on the romantic side of familiar things', officially stating that he has taken licence with the familiar components he has just enumerated and defended. Julius (1998:56–7, emphasis in original) reads this statement as a justification of Dickens's '*literary* lawbreaking which entails the violation of the criterion of plausibility. The "romance" permits characters and situations that exceed the constraints of what we might call [...] the classic realist text.' While Julius's diagnosis of generic experimentation fits both with Dickens's classification as a writer of sentimental fiction and *Bleak House*'s accepted place in the development of detective fiction, it seems to overturn completely the initial work in the Preface. If we read the opening gambit of the Preface as insisting on the realist basis of the text, then the reversal at the end can be read as allowing for narrative experimentation – as Julius suggests – without breaking the realist frame. Instead, it is an unhumbled declaration of rights to imagination and invention when creating characters in the realist setting. He thus allows for the entertaining fictional experiences to develop without being a slave to a realism. This might explain how Dickens (1992[1853]:xxvii) can conclude with his promotional sales pitch: 'I believe I never have had so many readers as in this book. May we meet again!'

Unlike Dickens, Collins (1999[1861]:4) does not suggest that he has intentionally created his work as a fiction, but he does address his philosophy of fiction writing: 'I have always held the old-fashioned opinion that the primary object of a work of fiction should be to tell a story.' Collins here extends his analysis of his writing process, as he began when referring to his legal construction, showing that the way he crafts fiction ties into his methods for realistic representation. While thus simultaneously asking for readerly suspension of disbelief and readerly approbation of his invention, he, too, asks readers to ignore the challenges to the accuracy of the portrayal in favour of the interest of the story. As such, once the accuracy of the legal portrait is assured, Collins (1999[1861]:4) assumes his own legal safety and his readerly popularity, concluding in a manner that echoes Dickens's Preface: 'I hope the time is not far distant when I may meet those friends again, and when I may try, through the medium of new characters, to awaken their interest in another story.'

Thus, in constructing their Prefaces, Dickens and Collins follow the legal forms that they explore in their fictions, providing non-fictional validation for the fictional formats. As such, they enable suspension of disbelief, working to safeguard their works from further criticism of inaccuracies, using both the defences that the texts are accurate and that they are fictions. On the one hand, there is nothing to reprove and, on the other, the novels are works of the imagination rather than slaves to reportage. These Prefaces redirect and reconstruct the crimes charged against their fictions. They charge their readers for misreading rather than allowing their novels to be charged with the crime of misrepresenting. They thus create the space for the modern era of introductory caveats defending works of fiction against charges of inaccuracy in realistic representation and of libellous accuracy in fictional incarnations.

Note

1. The correlation of realistic representation to critique overused devices appears clearly in the language of the rules for writing detective fiction that proliferated at the end of the 1920s. For instance, Knox (1943[1929]:xii–xiii, original emphasis) complains '*No Chinaman must figure in the story* [...] unless we can find a reason for it in our western habit of assuming that the Celestial is over-equipped in the matter of brains, and under-equipped in the matter of morals.'

References

BMJ. (1938). Spontaneous human combustion? *British Medical Journal*, *1*, 1106.

Collins, Wilkie. (1999[1861]). *The Woman in White*. Oxford: Oxford University Press.

Dickens, Charles. (1992[1853]). *Bleak House*. New York: Bantam Books.

Dunstan, William. (1997). The real Jarndyce and Jarndyce. *The Dickensian*, 93(1), 24–33.

Forster, John. (1874). *The Life of Charles Dickens, Vol. 3*. Philadelphia: J. B. Lippincott.

Julius, Anthony. (1998). Dickens the lawbreaker. *Critical Quarterly*, 40(3), 43–66.

Knox, Ronald. (1943[1929]). Introduction. In Ronald Knox and Henry Harrington (eds), *Best Detective Stories, First Series*. London: Faber and Faber.

Luyster, Deborah. (2002). English law courts and the novel. *Cardozo Studies in Law and Literature*, 14(3), 595–605.

Nabokov, Vladimir. (2002[1980]). *Lectures on Literature*. Boston: Houghton Mifflin Harcourt.

Polden, Patrick. (2004). Stranger than fiction? The Jennens inheritance in fact and fiction Part Two: The business of fortune hunting. *Common Law World Review*, 32(4), 338–67.

Ryan, Marie-Laure. (1991). *Possible Worlds, Artificial Intelligence, and Narrative Theory*. Bloomington: Indiana University Press.

Sutherland, Jonathan. (1999[1996]). Introduction. In Wilkie Collins, *The Woman in White*. Oxford: Oxford University Press.

3
Constructing Social Identities and Wrongdoings

3.0
Introduction and Rationale

'Crime hardly exists outside of narrative', Peach (2006:viii) says in *Masquerade, Crime and Fiction: Criminal Deceptions*, and narrative hardly exists without characters, social identities, much defined by means of doing good and wrong. This chapter directly explores the ways in which identities are constructed in narratives of 'crime' from across different ages and cultural contexts. Ulrike Tabbert's critical linguistic and computational corpus approach focuses on the ways in which victims and offenders are named and described in the UK press, manipulating the audience's sympathies in accordance with the relevant papers' stance. Alison Sinclair's chapter, though focusing on the related but also different genre of eighteenth- and nineteenth-century Spanish chapbooks, is also focused on identities surrounding popular narratives of crime. Looking at the *pictorial* portrayal of criminals this time, Sinclair, like Tabbert, aims to discover the complexities of public reaction being aimed at. In an equally international context, Lucy Evans takes us into Jamaican literature and film, and finds uncomfortable influences of the gangster/badman and 'cowboy', heroic-outlaw-like figure in character action, while also looking at the stereotype of the black male youth as deterministically criminal. Finally, Stuart Murray considers disabled detectives in contemporary crime fiction, and questions the linkage between such characters' neurological exceptionality and their exceptional detective skills. Taking the attention from the criminal and putting it onto the detective this time, Murray asks us to investigate the investigator, asking how effective 'normalising' the disabled identity actually is.

Reference

Peach, Linden. (2006). *Masquerade, Crime and Fiction: Criminal Deceptions*. London: Palgrave.

3.1

Crime through a Corpus: The Linguistic Construction of Offenders in the British Press

Ulrike Tabbert

Crime, especially when it includes violence against a person, has an enduring fascination (Jewkes 2004) and is presented in all sorts of media, ranging from crime fiction in novels to reports on crime that have taken place in reality. The media institutionalise the experience of crime and thus 'increase the salience of crime in everyday life' (Garland 2001:158). They provide a continuous flow of new crime reports for information and entertainment (Williams 1998) because consumers continually require new and spectacular stories about crime and criminals (Jewkes 2009).

The research presented in this chapter is part of a wider corpus-based project concerned with how victims, offenders and crimes are constructed in newspaper reports on crime in the British and German press (Tabbert in progress). This chapter focuses on the linguistic construction of offenders in British newspaper articles. The research questions on which this analysis is based are: (a) 'How are offenders constructed linguistically in news reports?' and (b) 'What linguistic tools are used to construct them?' Over a period of three months (February to April 2009) I collected all articles reporting on crime and criminal trials published in the online editions of the following newspapers: *Daily Mail, Daily Mirror, The Daily Telegraph, The Sun* as tabloids, *The Guardian, The Independent, The Times* as broadsheet newspapers and the *Yorkshire Post* as a regional newspaper. I extracted the articles from the online websites of these newspapers and adjusted them to the required format of the computer software used for this project. Although some articles contain pictures, I omitted them because it is beyond the scope of this analysis to include visual images. I limited the collection of articles (referred to as the 'corpus') concerning crimes that occurred in the United Kingdom to those committed in England and Wales, as these regions' legal system differs from those of Scotland and Northern Ireland. I also included reports on crime that occurred outside the United Kingdom. The resulting corpus consists of approximately 75 000 tokens (the total number of words in the corpus) and includes 143 articles. I approached the data by employing the tools of corpus linguistics (CL), combining them with critical discourse analysis (CDA). CL employs a statistical approach to texts by using frequency information about the occurrence of words or word phrases in texts and combines these statistical methods with functional interpretations (Biber *et al.* 1998). CDA interprets language in terms of its use in the creation and reproduction of ideologies (Wodak and Meyer 2009). By gaining the data for the CDA through using the objective approach of CL, it is possible to limit the CDA to the statistically most significant parts of the data and thus to reduce the researcher's bias in deciding what to focus on, thereby avoiding the subjectivity of which CDA is often accused (see Widdowson 1995, among others).

This chapter will start with an overview of other research that has been conducted on linguistic studies of crime and continue with a detailed outline of the method of analysis. This will be followed by a presentation of the 12 most significant linguistic tools that I detected, which are used to construct offenders in my research, each explained by drawing on an example from the corpus. I conclude with a brief summary of my findings.

I argue that offenders are not separated from their crimes but instead reduced to their criminal offending role and thus placed outside society. The negative associations of crime are transferred to the offender. In this way not only the criminal act but the entire person of the offender is constructed as being distant from society. It is language that constructs offenders and thereby transports ideologies. This is based on cultural stereotypes, societal discourse (that is, dynamic, communicative interaction between speakers and hearers in society, involving the generation and transfer of ideologies) and individual lexical priming. The latter means that vocabulary becomes loaded with meaning dependent on the context in which we repeatedly encounter it (Hoey 2005).

Linguistic studies of crime

Linguistic studies of crime, which are related to my work in terms of using qualitative analytical tools without employing CL, are the studies by Cotterill (2001, 2003), who worked on the transcript of the O.J. Simpson trial in the United States, and Ehrlich (1999; Ehrlich and King 1996), with her analysis of the transcript of a tribunal at a US university where a male student was accused of raping two female students. The first study shows the differing language used by the prosecution and the defence attorneys when referring to the crime, while the second study deals with the use of language to mitigate the offender's guilt. Clark (1992) pointed out the importance of 'naming' in her study of the representation of women in reports on sexual violence and Mayr (2008) analysed prison discourse as a means of control and resistance (see also Tabbert 2010 for a review). Barnett (2006) looked at newspaper articles about women who killed their children and the dichotomous way in which these women are constructed (as 'superior nurturers driven to insanity' or 'inferior caretakers who [...] cared so little' [Barnett 2006:411]). Teo (2000) analysed the Australian newspaper coverage of crimes committed by the 5T, 'a gang of young Vietnamese drug-dealers' (Teo 2000:10). Timor and Weiss (2008) showed how a linguistic analysis of a prisoner's text about his crime can uncover his worldview and contribute to his therapy. Ruigrok and van Atteveldt (2007) analysed the US, British and Dutch press coverage of global and local terrorist attacks. Henley *et al.* (1995) analysed the use of the passive voice when reporting on violence against women and, in another study (2002), the use of nominalisation and passivisation in reports on anti-gay attacks. Finally, Rasinger (2010) comes closest to my approach by analysing a corpus of newspaper articles in the *Cambridge Evening News* reporting on Lithuanian migrants and their supposed contribution to the increase of the regional crime figures using a combined approach of CDA and CL.

Methodology

I approached the data by executing a corpus linguistic analysis using the software package WordSmith Tools (Scott 2004). I created a wordlist, which lists all the words in the corpus sorted according to their frequency, examined the list manually and extracted all those nouns that could possibly refer to offenders, because these themselves transport ideologies already. I excluded all personal and possessive pronouns as well as all proper nouns, because these relate to aboutness and structure, while the articles in the corpus report on many different criminal cases, not just one particular offender.

   In order to keep the analysis manageable, I chose to set the cut-off point at word number 901 in the wordlist, which has a frequency of 11 occurrences in the corpus. Next, I created concordance lines of every word extracted as above and examined these lists manually. A concordance line shows the word under examination in its context and therefore highlights whether the word names an offender. This allows the analyst to delete all those words referring to persons other than offenders, such as the victims, lawyers and judges. Through this procedure, I extracted the 49 most frequent words that name offenders in the corpus. To reduce the number of words further and keep the size of the analysis manageable and focused on the statistically most significant words, I chose three more cut-off points. I counted the number of sentences in which each of the 49 offender-referring words occurred and set the cut-off point at seven, which means that each of the resulting words occurred in at least seven sentences. Another cut-off point was the percentage of occurrences of the offender-referring words in relation to their total occurrence in my corpus, which I set at 15%. This means that, of all occurrences of a word in my corpus, the word has to refer to offenders in 15% of its occurrences. The final cut-off point was the log-likelihood of each of the 49 words, which I set at 30. This test relates the number of occurrences of the lemmas (the rootform of a word – for example *go* is the lemma of *going, went, goes* etc.) of each target word (node) in my corpus to the number of occurrences in a reference corpus. In CL a reference corpus is used to establish whether the findings in the target corpus are significant in comparison to a different sample of texts. The reference corpus I used is FLOB (the Freiburg-Lancaster-Oslo-Bergen Corpus of British English), which consists of written British English (texts from newspapers, books and periodicals) used in 1991, and contains approximately one million words. It thereby represents a broader language variety than the newspaper articles in my corpus and allowed me to establish whether the 49 most frequent words in my corpus are used comparably often in the reference corpus as well, or whether these words are overrepresented in my corpus and thereby significant.

Through defining these cut-off points, I reduced the 49 words naming offenders to the following 23 nouns, although *year-old* is used as a noun as well as an adjective. The words are listed in order of frequency, the number in brackets indicating the number of sentences in which the 'offender-naming' word is used: *man* (87), *gang* (85), *year-old* (46), *boy* (43), *brother* (43), *killer* (38), *driver* (36), *defendant* (34), *father* (30), *member* (29), *mother* (27), *suspect* (25), *officer* (23), *attacker* (22), *rapist* (22), *husband* (21), *girl* (19), *couple* (16), *cab* (14), *offender* (13), *teenager* (13), *chef* (9), *student* (7).

Eliminating all repetitions of the same sentence, I derived 607 sentences, which I finally analysed using the tools offered by critical stylistics (Jeffries 2010a). I looked at the noun phrases in which the 23 remaining words (nodes) listed above occur, the verb choices (active/passive voice, transitivity), presuppositions, implicatures, speech and thought presentation and opposition. I focused on counting sentences as opposed to occurrences and phrases, because the figure in which I was interested was the percentage, which will not change when counting occurrences. The following section presents the major findings in terms of statistical significance and explains their use in context.

Constructing offenders

Naming and equating

The way offenders are referred to in terms of noun choices is one aspect of how they are viewed (Erwin-Tripp 1969; Richardson 2007:49). The major constructive tool when naming offenders in noun phrases is the nominal reference, sometimes combined with a pre- or postmodifier.

The 23 nominal references listed above can be grouped as shown in Figure 3.1.1.

The majority of references to offenders relate to their gender or their social role. Offenders are also named by addressing their role in the criminal proceedings, as well as by equalising them with their crime through defining them by what they did. Each naming noun reduces the person to one role out of many. The choice of nominalising a criminal offence and thereby backgrounding the process to its product constructs the offender as the personified crime using the negative associations intrinsic to the criminal offence, for example to rape – *rapist*. I will return to some of these as they occur in the examples.

In 405 sentences (out of 607 in total, 66.72%) the node occurs in a subject position, and in 171 sentences (28.17%) in an object position. In 61 sentences (10.04%) a subject complement is used that equalises the subject with its complement and thereby assigns characteristics to the subject. An example of using *suspect* as a subject complement can be found in the following sentence:

> (1) He says he did this believing he would be a suspect because he was black.
>
> (*The Times*, 04.04.09)

In this sentence, the four subjects *he*, which all refer to the offender, are in two cases followed by a subject complement – *a suspect* and *black* – which describe and thereby construct the offender as if he was assuming that he was under suspicion of a criminal offence because of his black skin colour.

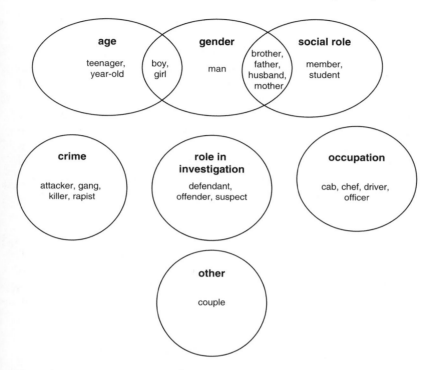

Figure 3.1.1 Grouping the 23 offender-referring words into categories

In 159 sentences (out of 607, 26.19%), the node occurs together with other premodifying nouns.

(2) Black cab rapist John Worboys: Profile of 'Jekyll and Hyde' character

(The Daily Telegraph, 13.03.09)

This headline contains two nodes, *cab* and *rapist*. The extended noun phrase *Black cab rapist John Worboys* allows the writer to 'package up' (Jeffries 2010a:19) the information that John Worboys is a *rapist* as well as a *black cab* driver, which the reader is unlikely to question and rather takes for granted. The combination of the subject position of the nodes *cab* and *rapist*, the packaged-up noun phrase and the use of the extended noun phrase *Profile of 'Jekyll and Hyde'*, inclusive of the postmodifying prepositional phrase *of 'Jekyll and Hyde'*, equalises the offender with the fictional and psychopathic character of Dr Jekyll and Mr Hyde.

Another example of 'packaging up' is where writers employ adjectives as premodifiers in a noun phrase. The adjective is 'the most typical vehicle for characterizing in English' (Jeffries 2007:64). The analysis of the 23 nodes shows that adjectives occur in 162 sentences (out of 607, 26.68%) as part of a noun phrase. The adjective *black* in example (2) premodifies the noun *cab* in the extended noun phrase *Black cab rapist John Worboys* by objectively describing the colour of the cab. These kinds of adjectives are descriptive. In my corpus I found 116 descriptive and 52 evaluative adjectives. An evaluative adjective, which provides an opinion or a judgement, can assign negative characteristics to the offender, as the following example shows:

(3) Notorious Gooch Gang smashed as leaders jailed
(*The Times*, 07.04.09)

This subjective assessment (*notorious*) constructs the gang as being infamous and ill-reputed and thereby arouses interest in the offenders, here seen as celebrities, people to be watched and be interested in (Gregoriou 2011).

The following example of a descriptive adjective (*alleged*) premodifying the noun and node *attackers* in the subject phrase (*None of the alleged attackers*) shows another effect of premodifying:

(4) None of the alleged attackers was more than 18 at the time.
(*Daily Mail*, 21.04.09; also in *The Times*, 21.04.09)

In this case, the offenders are under suspicion, though only further investigation and a court trial can determine whether their guilt can be proven. The adjectival use of *alleged* is rather negligible for the reader, because in the subject phrase (*None of the alleged attackers*) the information is hidden as a premodifier of the noun *attackers* and hence remains unquestioned by the reader. This information is backgrounded against the foregrounded attackers' age in the subject complement phrase *more than 18*, which takes the focus away from the fact that the offenders have not been sentenced yet and are therefore still to be regarded as innocent.

Looking at postmodifiers of the 23 nodes, the analysis shows that, in 150 sentences (out of 607, 24.71%), a subordinate clause is used compared to the other possibility of postmodifying by a prepositional phrase, employed in 57 sentences (9.39%).

(5) Colin Joyce, 29, the self-styled General, and Lee Amos, 32, who led the Gooch Gang that terrorised South Manchester over two decades, and nine of their henchmen face long jail sentences after a five-month trial.

(The Times, 07.04.09)

This sentence contains an extended noun phrase that functions as the subject (from *Colin Joyce* to *henchmen).* If we focus on the middle part, from *Lee Amos* to *decades,* we find a subordinate clause postmodifying *Lee Amos,* starting with *who* and containing the object *Gooch Gang* (the node), which itself is postmodified by the subordinate clause *that terrorised South Manchester over two decades.* It is this subordinate clause that I chose to demonstrate the effect of postmodifying the node. This clause describes the Gooch Gang's activities rather vaguely through the verb *terrorised,* which evokes the picture of terrorists and terrorist attacks. By giving a time frame of *over two decades,* also called time deixis, the gang is constructed as persistent and comparable to terrorists, the sentencing of its leaders being a relief for the community.

As mentioned, a subject complement equalises the subject with its complement and is separated from it by an intensive verb, in example (1) a form of the verb *to be,* which opens the relevant descriptor for debate. Another means of equalising is apposition, 'the clearest example of a frame which creates equivalence', which puts the word into the 'same syntactic role' as the node to which it refers (Jeffries 2007:104) and therefore is less open to debate. An example of apposition can be found in the beginning of example (5): *Colin Joyce, 29, the self-styled General* uses *Colin Joyce* as (part of) the subject and *the self-styled General* as the apposition identifying Colin Joyce. In my corpus an apposition occurs in 41 sentences (out of 607, 6.75%) and is therefore less often used compared to a subject complement (61 sentences, 10.04%). An example of an apposition is found in the following sentence:

(6) Dougal, a qualified advanced driver, was travelling so fast he had effectively become a passenger in his own car, and had surrendered 'to physics', an expert witness told the jury.

(The Times, 08.04.09; also in *The Independent,* 08.04.09)

PC John Dougal, a police officer who ran over and fatally injured a schoolgirl by speeding with his patrol car in pursuit of a suspect, is constructed by the employment of an apposition as *a qualified advanced driver.* This description, even if it is objective, remains unquestioned although it is opposed to the fact that he was no longer in control of his car due to the speed at which he drove. This implies that, because of his driving abilities, he should have been able to judge the situation correctly and thereby prevent the accident.

Another finding concerning noun phrases is nominalisation, the transformation of a process into a state. I found nominalisation at least once in 299 sentences (out of 607, 49.25%). The effect of nominalisation is that the information is presented as a given fact or status instead of a process. This reduces the amount of information available to the reader (Henley *et al.* 2002), while a fact is less likely to be questioned by the reader than a process. The impact of nominalisation can be found when looking at the node *rapist*, which occurs 22 times in the corpus and is the nominalisation of the process *to rape*. The following example illustrates the impact of nominalisation:

> (7) The full harrowing ordeal suffered by incest rapist Josef Fritzl's daughter was spelled out in hours of her video evidence to his trial yesterday.
>
> (*Yorkshire Post*, 18.03.09)

In this case, the offender Josef Fritzl is equalised with his crime and is thereby reduced to it. This naming option does not focus on his role in the criminal trial (for example *defendant*) or his gender (for example *man*), but instead merely on the crime he committed. This negative impact gets enhanced by the premodifying noun *incest*, which makes him even more abominable. The impact of this naming choice is further enhanced by the connotations of the words *harrowing ordeal suffered*, each of which is used when referring to extreme crime.

Contrasting

Another means of constructing offenders is through the employment of contrasts, either by creating opposition or by a negation, a subcategory of opposition besides antonymous sense relation, syntactic trigger and so on (Jeffries 2010a). Opposition puts two events, states or existences into contrast to each other; negation opposes non-events against events, non-states against states or non-existence against existence and thereby constructs 'unrealized worlds' (Nahajec 2009:109). 'Opposites are [...] one of the most important of the linguistic-cognitive structures by which we characterize and organize our world, and thus also our world-view' (Jeffries 2010b:26). The analysis of the corpus shows that

93 sentences (out of 607, 15.32%) contain opposition and 62 sentences (10.21%) negation.

> (8) She said: 'The man who attacked me avoided paying for his crime for all these years, whilst the effect of what happened that night has stayed with me.'
>
> *(Yorkshire Post,* 16.03.09)

This sentence refers to a rape that happened in 1997. Because the offender fled after his first arrest and disappeared for many years, he was only convicted in 2009. The sentence contrasts the offender's refusal to 'pay for his crime' in the past against the enduring effect of the crime for the victim. The syntactic trigger for opposition in this sentence is the conjunction *whilst*. The choice of verb tense (past tense in the first clause [*avoided*] and present perfect in the second [*has stayed*]) under-lines the oppositional meaning: the offender's one-time avoidance to pay for the crime versus the enduring effect of the crime for the victim. Out of the context in the article it becomes clear that paying for his crime means a court conducting a criminal trial with a guilty verdict and a sentence in the end. This implies that the offender must take respon-sibility for his crime and his avoiding being brought to justice is not tolerated. This constructs the offender as being cowardly and too weak to take responsibility for his offence, in contrast to the victim who could not avoid the crime and its consequences and is still affected by them.

> (9) Despite having been narrowed down to one of three suspects early in the investigation, Reid, whose brother is a policeman, was never interviewed and did not have his DNA taken.
>
> *(The Times,* 27.03.09)

This sentence shows a combination of contrastive opposition, triggered by the preposition *despite*, and negation, triggered by *never* and *not*. It opposes the 'unrealized world' (Nahajec 2009:109) of being interviewed and having a DNA sample taken with the realisation of those activities. It thereby constructs a police failure by presupposing that these things should have been done. It further opposes these mistakes with the fact that Reid, the offender, was one of just three suspects, implying that it would have been possible for the police to take a DNA sample. Reid prof-ited from this failure and was able to continue his *'string of sex attacks'* *(The Times,* 27.03.09). Another opposition is hidden in the subordinate clause *whose brother is a policeman.* It contrasts the offending Reid to his policeman brother, which implies that the latter is law-abiding and reliable, character features that Reid does not have.

Constructing processes and states

In the majority of sentences, I found active-voice verbs (444 sentences out of 607, 73.14%), whereas in just 196 sentences the passive voice is used (32.28%). The overlap of 33 sentences is due to sentences that contain active- and passive-voice verbs in their different clauses. I also analysed transitivity, using the model developed by Simpson (1993) from Halliday's work (1985), and the findings thereof completed the picture of verb choices in my corpus. In the majority of sentences, material action intention (456 sentences out of 607, 75.12%) is employed, with the node as the actor in 231 sentences or the node as the goal in 229 sentences. Material action intention (MAI) can be defined as an animate actor actively 'doing' an action to a goal (Simpson 1993:89). In 129 sentences the actor is omitted. Even though the majority of sentences contain the active voice, the shares of the node being the actor or the goal are nearly equal in size. The majority of sentences describe either the offender's intentional actions, mainly the crime or his or her behaviour in court, or what happened to the offender during the investigation or the criminal trial. Henley *et al.* (1995:60) found that 'news media often report violence against women [...] in passive-verb format', meaning that the women are the subjects of clauses about the crime done to them and thereby the goal of the crime. This foregrounds the women and not the agents acting on them and influences the 'perceptions of violence and its effects' as well as hiding agency (Henley *et al.* 1995:65).

> (10) A TEENAGE girl who stabbed a woman in a jealous rage was jailed for nine years yesterday.
>
> *(The Sun, 20.02.09)*

This subheadline shows a combination of active and passive voice. The subject *A TEENAGE girl* is the actor of an MAI (*stabbed*) in the subordinate clause and, at the same time, the goal of the action *was jailed* in the main clause with the actor (a judge) being omitted. The MAI of sentencing the girl is foregrounded through the main clause, whereas the crime the girl committed is presented in a subordinate clause that functions as a postmodifier to the head noun *girl*. This contrasts the offender as an actor intentionally committing the crime versus her being the goal by passively getting sentenced. It also shows the reason as well as the necessity of bringing the offender to justice and emphasises that justice has been done.

Presenting opinions

One way to present opinions is to quote other people's utterances. There are different ways to present their verbiage according to the model introduced by Leech and Short (1981). The two most frequently used options are direct speech (DS), which occurs in 103 sentences (out of 607, 16.96%), and indirect speech (IS), which contains the verbiage 'as a version of the supposed verbatim speech' (Jeffries 2010a:134). The latter occurs in 108 sentences (17.79%). An example of DS can be found in the following sentence uttered by a prosecutor:

> (11) Ieuan Morris, prosecuting, said: 'The defendant is a predatory paedophile and sexual pervert who secretly engaged in two known acts of sexual penetration with a pre-pubescent girl who was either asleep or for some reason not conscious, at night, in the isolation of his static caravan in Mid Wales.'
>
> (*The Independent*, 17.04.09)

This sentence constructs the offender as being evil and taking advantage of an underaged and unconscious girl in a remote area. He is equalised with his crime by being named as a *predatory paedophile and sexual pervert* and thereby ostracised from society. This judgement is given weight by being officially uttered by a prosecutor, an authoritative person who has a vested interest in creating such a construction. This is a very manipulative way of implanting other people's views in the reader, because in this context the reader assumes that the prosecutor has insight and knows all the facts, and his statement is therefore not to be questioned. Whether or not the prosecutor's utterance is quoted correctly and comprehensively will not be validated by most readers; it would take some effort to obtain the transcript of the trial.

The following example shows the combined use of DS and IS, which is even more manipulative because it blends verbatim quotations with a reworded version of the original verbiage:

> (12) Judge Langstaff said that Joyce possessed 'considerable personal charm', organisational ability and business skills, but also had 'murderous intent' and was a 'deeply controlling man ... I accept undoubtedly you are a leader of men'.
>
> (*The Times*, 08.04.09)

In this example, DS, marked by inverted commas and embedded in the IS, both present the judge's opinion of the offender. Here again an authoritative person, a judge, is quoted, which assigns the judgement a high value. The reader is unable to assess if this blend of the judge's words and their reformulation still contain the original illocutionary force, which is the underlying intention of the speaker. The offender Joyce is constructed as possessing certain positive character features (*considerable personal charm, organisational ability, business skills*), but these, combined with his negative character features *murderous intent* and him being a *deeply controlling man*, turn him into a calculating and dangerous perpetrator able to lead a gang of criminals whom he uses for his criminal purposes. His being a negative leading figure is underpinned by the final phrase *I accept undoubtedly you are a leader of men*, which implies that a *leader of men* with a *murderous intent* and the need to control others cannot be positively associated.

Conclusion

The 'central fact about deviance' is that it 'is created by society' and being labelled as deviant becomes a master status trait that sticks to the offender throughout his or her life (Becker 1966:8). People mainly become labelled as deviant through a criminal conviction, but also through the way society views them. The latter largely depends on crime reports in the news, because not many people get first-hand information on crime and criminals and they therefore depend on media reports for information surrounding this issue. This study names and illustrates the statistically most significant linguistic tools used to construct the offenders in my corpus. Adjectives and combinations of nouns in noun phrases 'package up' (Jeffries 2010a:19) information about the offender that remains unquestioned. The same effect is achieved by nominalisation and apposition. DS and IS are used to transport subjective assessments about the offender, mainly quoting authoritative persons who sometimes make those subjective assessments. The offenders are also constructed by contrasting them against the victim, which arouses a dichotomous picture of the innocent and pitiable victim versus an evil and despicable offender. The linguistic tools work together and construct an image of the offender that places him or her outside society and labels him or her (and not only the offence) as deviant. I found verification through this analysis that offenders are equalised with their crimes. This contributes to the current societal tendency of turning away from the notion of rehabilitating offenders, improving their self-esteem and developing 'insight' into their behaviour patterns, as opposed to imposing 'restrictions' on them (Garland 2001:176). Being aware of 'the power of English' (Jeffries 2010a) helps us uncover these ideologies and take a different view of offenders – as the human beings they still are.

References

Barnett, Barbara. (2006). Medea in the media: Narrative and myth in newspaper coverage of women who kill their children. *Journalism, 7*(4), 411–32.

Becker, Howard S. (1966). *Outsiders: Studies in the Sociology of Deviance*. New York: Free Press.

Biber, Douglas, Susan Conrad and Radi Reppen. (1998). *Corpus Linguistics: Investigating Language Structure and Use*. Cambridge: Cambridge University Press.

Clark, Kate. (1992). The linguistics of blame: Representations of women in *The Sun's* reporting of crimes of sexual violence. In M. Toolan (ed.), *Language, Text and Context: Essays in Stylistics*. London: Routledge.

Cotterill, Janet. (2001). Domestic discord, rocky relationships: Semantic prosodies in representations of marital violence in the O.J. Simpson trial. *Discourse and Society*, 12(3), 291–312.

Cotterill, Janet. (2003). *Language and Power in Court: A Linguistic Analysis of the O.J. Simpson Trial*. Basingstoke: Palgrave Macmillan.

Ehrlich, Susan. (1999). Communities of practice, gender and the representation of sexual assault. *Language in Society*, 28(2), 239–56.

Ehrlich, Susan and Ruth King. (1996). Consensual sex or sexual harassment: Negotiating meaning. In V. L. Bergvall, J. M. Bing and A. F. Freed (eds), *Rethinking Language and Gender Research: Theory and Practice*. Harlow: Addison Wesley Longman.

Erwin-Tripp, S.M. (1969). Sociolinguistic rules of address. In J. B. Pride and J. Holmes (eds), *Sociolinguistics*. Harmondsworth: Penguin.

Garland, David. (2001). *The Culture of Control: Crime and Social Order in Contemporary Society*. Oxford: Oxford University Press.

Gregoriou, Christiana. (2011). *Language, Ideology and Identity in Serial Killer Narratives*. London: Routledge.

Halliday, M.A.K. (1985). *An Introduction to Functional Grammar*. London: Edward Arnold.

Henley, Nancy M., Michelle Miller and Jo Anne Beazley. (1995). Syntax, semantics and sexual violence: Agency and the passive voice. *Journal of Language and Social Psychology*, 14(1/2), 60–84.

Henley, Nancy M., Michelle D. Miller, Jo Ann Beazley, Diane N. Nguyen, Dana Kaminski and Robert Sanders. (2002). Frequency and specificity of referents to violence in news reports of anti-gay attacks. *Discourse and Society*, 13(1), 75–104.

Hoey, Michael. (2005). *Lexical Priming: A New Theory of Words and Language*. Abingdon: Routledge.

Jeffries, Lesley. (2007). *Textual Construction of the Female Body: A Critical Discourse Approach*. Basingstoke: Palgrave Macmillan.

Jeffries, Lesley. (2010a). *Critical Stylistics: The Power of English*. Basingstoke: Palgrave Macmillan.

Jeffries, Lesley. (2010b). *Opposition in Discourse: The Construction of Oppositional Meaning*. London: Continuum.

Jewkes, Yvonne. (2004). *Media and Crime*. London: Sage.

Jewkes, Yvonne (ed.). (2009). *Crime and Media, Vol. 2*. London: Sage.

Leech, Geoffrey N. and Michael H. Short. (1981). *Style in Fiction*. London: Longman.

Mayr, Andrea. (2008). *Language and Power: An Introduction to Institutional Discourse*. London: Continuum.

Nahajec, Lisa. (2009). Negation and the creation of implicit meaning in poetry. *Language and Literature*, 18(2), 109–27.

Rasinger, Sebastian M. (2010). 'Lithuanian migrants send crime rocketing': Representation of 'new' migrants in regional print media. *Media, Culture and Society*, 32(6), 1021–30.

Richardson, John E. (2007). *Analysing Newspapers: An Approach from Critical Discourse Analysis*. Basingstoke: Palgrave Macmillan.

Ruigrok, Nel and Wouter van Atteveldt. (2007). Global angling with a local angle: How U.S., British, and Dutch newspapers frame global and local terrorist attacks. *Harvard International Journal of Press/Politics*, 12(1), 68–90.

Scott, Mike. (2004). *WordSmith Tools Version 4*. Oxford: Oxford University Press.

Simpson, Paul. (1993). *Language, Ideology and Point of View*. London: Routledge.

Tabbert, Ulrike. (2010). Review of *Language and Power: An Introduction to Institutional Discourse*, Edited by Andrea Mayr, 2008. London: Continuum. *Language and Literature*, 19(2), 224–6.

Tabbert, Ulrike. (in progress). Crime through a corpus: The linguistic construction of victims and offenders in newspaper reports on crime in the British and German press. Unpublished PhD thesis, University of Huddersfield, Huddersfield.

Teo, Peter. (2000). Racism in the news: A critical discourse analysis of news reporting in two Australian newspapers. *Discourse and Society*, 11(1), 7–49.

Timor, Uri and Joshua M. Weiss. (2008). Sociolinguistic and psycholinguistic indications of behavior disorders: Analysis of a prisoner's discourse. *International Journal of Offender Therapy and Comparative Criminology*, 52(1), 112–26.

Widdowson, H.G. (1995). Discourse analysis: A critical view. *Language and Literature*, 4(3), 157–72.

Williams, Kevin. (1998). *Get Me a Murder a Day! A History of Mass Communication in Britain*. London: Arnold.

Wodak, Ruth and Michael Meyer. (2009). Critical discourse analysis: History, agenda, theory and methodology. In R. Wodak and M. Meyer (eds), *Methods of Critical Discourse Analysis*. London: Sage.

3.2
Popular Faces of Crime in Spain

Alison Sinclair

Spain has no equivalent of Dostoievsky's *Crime and Punishment* (1866) and yet, in the 1880s, it topped other countries in Europe for its record in *delitos de sangre* (homicide and violent crime) (Bernaldo de Quirós 1906). In this chapter, my interest lies in considering how crime and lesser wrongdoings were represented in texts of popular culture in Spain, and the modes of understanding of wrongdoers that were called up by their visual portrayals.[1]

Foucault (1969, cited in Ríos-Font 2005:336–8) leads us to expect that a subculture of literature on crime would exist in complement to canonical literature narratives. In the case of Spain, when we look at canonical literature, we find it strikingly bereft of representations of crime. Within written material, as Ríos-Font (2005:338–9) observes, there were *causas celebres* (celebrated cases) and newspaper accounts of crime. But there are riches to be found elsewhere. One of the better-known areas in textual terms is the tradition of *mala vida* (low-life)literature, prevalent from around 1870 (Cleminson and Fuentes Peris 2009).

Less well known, but possibly more significant and interesting because of its inclusion of visual material, is an earlier popular tradition of illustrated ephemeral popular literature in which we can find a broad spectrum of wrongdoings, ranging from publications of moral tales to the redaction of notorious murder cases. Some of the publications about famous wrongdoings begin in the eighteenth century, and their re-publications run through the nineteenth century. The specific medium of publication of popular literature on which I shall concentrate in this chapter is that of *pliegos sueltos* or chapbooks, but I shall also refer to the form of the *aleluya* or *auca* (the Catalan form of the *aleluya*). I shall argue that what we have is far from simple illustration in simple forms, and that there can be surprising suggestiveness and ambiguity in even the most basic popular forms. The point about the visual element is that it is immediate, but also that it is not straightforward in the reaction it elicits.

Pliegos sueltos, and more generally what was known as *literatura de cordel* ('string' literature, a reference to the way in which items were hung from strings on stalls in the street to display them), were widely available in Spain in the eighteenth and nineteenth centuries and, as Caro Baroja (1969:19) recollects, this type of literature was still being sold in the streets of Madrid around 1925. These ephemeral forms of literature, frequently in verse, provided the context for a framing of public excitement. Highly relevant to the impact of their visual element was the fact that they were offered to a public that was largely illiterate. A measure of this is that in 1860 the level of literacy nationally in Spain was 20%, much lower than that in rural areas (Vilanova and Moreno 1992:62; Sinclair 2009:140). The *pliegos sueltos* thus relied to a degree on two things for their power to communicate with their public: their form (the illustrations that accompanied them, and the long titles that promised drama and that were read aloud by their sellers) and their clear moral standpoint. The illustrations themselves, originally woodcuts and later engravings, are far from constituting fine art: in their crude form they aim to elicit simple responses of horror, condemnation and compliance with the justice to be meted out. But their crude form merits critical re-reading in order to discover the complexities of public reaction being aimed at in a context that was undeniably violent, and it is not always the case that the visual element was milked for its potential for horror.

My intention in this chapter is to focus on the *sueltos* as a prime example of ephemeral literature, with emphasis on their illustrations, and to look at the responses provoked by them. This is often at some variance with the accompanying narrative text. There is a complication to the assessment of these illustrations, namely the extent to which they were passed between printers (see Alvar 1974:12–38), sometimes being used with different text. This would undoubtedly have affected the combined impact of text and image in the *sueltos* in question, arguably one that was haphazard rather than intentional.

Moralities of wrongdoing

One genre, the *aleluya*, provides examples of publications on morality and bad behaviour as lesser forms of wrongdoing that could eventually lead to more serious crime. The *aleluya* was a type of broadside with illustrations (usually 48 or 36, accompanied by two-line captions, often in verse). Initially religious in content, the *aleluya* came to be used for examples of morality, generalised moral summaries of the lives of good and bad women, of the games of children or the *topos* of the world upside down (see Caro Baroja 1969:409–12; Grant 1964:307–08, 1972, 1973, 1979). It was later used for political caricature of a simple, even crude variety, as in the satires produced at the time of the 1868 revolution of Isabel II, and of some of the prominent politicians involved in the revolution and its aftermath (Sinclair 1977:27–87).

Not all *aleluyas* with moral import would be exemplary, but typically one could expect indications of the recognition of misdemeanour, no doubt so that there could at some stage be intervention, or retribution. An early example of wrongdoing in childhood appears in an undated Barcelona *aleluya*, *Travesuras de la infancia* (Mischiefs of childhood). Its illustrations correspond to what appears in cruder form in an *auca* without text, collected by Amades. This *auca* is assumed by Amades to be an earlier printing than the *Travesuras* and to be a simple representation of childhood games, rather than mischief (Amades *et al.* 1931 II, plate XXVII and I, 87 and XVII). The added text of the *Travesuras* offers an intention of moral focus, but the combination of text and image is ambiguous in impact.

The illustrations in this *aleluya* are relatively old and crude woodcuts (see Illustration 3.2.1(i). The podgy stylised figures could thus be argued to encourage a benign attitude to the subject matter; these are, after all, only children. Strikingly and somewhat disturbingly, however, many of the illustrations are ambiguous, complicating the moral message. The figures are unclothed and, while the activities in which they are engaged suggest that these are childhood pastimes, the actual figures are developed to a degree that is suggestive of an adult maturity of form. A possible explanation for this lack of fit between illustration and caption could derive from a gap of date in the sources, in that the typeface of the captions in this example suggests that it is of a significantly later date than the original illustrations. Number 6 looks more like play with whips than a whipping being carried out; the text introduces the idea of wilfulness on the part of the child involved:

Con el látigo en la mano
Da golpes al más cercano.
> (with whip in hand he hits whoever is nearest at hand)

In number 17, if we focus on the backward glance of the figure that is being pursued, the representation of what is supposedly a chase with

(i)   (ii)

6   Con el látigo en la mano
Dá golpes al mas cercano.

Mucha gente la visita
y alegre la felicita.

Bajo la losa mortuoria
vive eterna su memoria.

17   Y ya de fiero la echa
Y persigue con la flecha.

Cuando está en la casa sola
registra en una consola.

36   No pudiendo estarse quieto
Pone al prójimo en aprieto.

Al llegar su hora postrera
muere en un trozo de estera.

Illustration 3.2.1(i)   Anon. (n.d.). From *Travesuras de la infancia*. Barcelona. CUL Tab.b.724

(ii) From *Vida de la mujer buena y la mala*. Madrid. CUL Tab.b.721

a bow and arrow carries a suggestion of sexual flirtation, rather than a pursuit that is vengeful or ill-intentioned. In relation to this visual impression, however, the caption suggests an element of moral excess in the pursuer, rather than simple amorous breaking of bounds:

Y ya de fiero la echa
Y persigue con la flecha
> (and now he boasts and goes in pursuit with his arrow)

Number 36, about fighting, has a caption that refers to a child who is wilful and aggressive:

No pudiendo estarse quieto
Pone al prójimo en aprieto.
> (unable to stay still, he puts his companion into a tight spot)

However, the illustration could easily be confused with one from a pillow-book by the mixture of tenderness and directness of approach from the standing figure to the recumbent and submissive figure.

Taken as a whole, this odd marriage of illustrations and text presents an overall impression of waywardness that is adult in connotation, because of the visual indications that are related to sexual maturity. The images draw, even seduce the spectator (if not the reader) into a world of sexuality, while the text, by its style apparently a later addition, goes for a more straitlaced moral setting out of juvenile wrongs.

There is less ambiguity in a number of *aleluyas* clearly announced as moral examples. Some begin with a portrayal of virtuous behaviour that will be followed with a set of counter-examples. Thus the *Vida del hombre obrando bien* (Life of the man who acts well) is followed by the *Vida del hombre obrando mal* (Life of the man who acts badly) (Amades *et al.* 1931, I, Plate XXV and II, Plate LXVIII). Although the series of those who do badly is intended to impress their consumers with the evils of wrongdoing, there is a certain even-handedness of presentation in this laconic outlining of the actions of good and bad men respectively. There is arguably more starkness in the contrast of the good and bad women. The *Bida de la muger buena y consecuencias de la buena educación* (Life of the good woman and consequences of good upbringing) is followed by the *Bida de la muger mala o consecuencias de sus bicios* (Life of the good woman and consequences of her bad ways) and has simple captions written in capitals of two to three words indicating good or bad actions in the briefest of terms (Amades *et al.* 1931, I, Plate

XXV and II, Plate LXX). My last example from this genre is the *Vida de la mujer buena y la mala* (see Illustration 3.2.1(ii)). Its style of illustration and typeface suggest that it is later in date than the other examples discussed so far, and the text offers a more obviously novelistic frame. The idea of the split between the good woman and the bad woman is central to conduct manuals (see Aldaraca 1991; Jagoe 1994) and there is a nod towards the 'angel of the house' *topos* in the initial caption:

> *La mujer buena, en el suelo*
> *Es como un ángel del cielo.*
>   (The good woman is like an angel from heaven upon earth)

In this *aleluya* the drawing modes used for the two lives are chosen to guide the response of the reader or viewer. Thus for the life of the good woman, the sketches of a fundamentally happy life are harmonious and detailed. By contrast, the images of the life of the bad woman are more sparse and abstract. The life of the good woman contains images of union and happiness (as in number 17, with the visits of condolence after her father's death, where the 'good woman' is visibly supported by a framework of her friends). Even in death (number 24) there is a note of aesthetic pleasure: the image of her tomb, with lush plants, indicates how her memory will live on. Turn to the life of the bad woman and the images contain visual disruption. Her body is angular and distorted in posture, with twists of the body as she sneakily looks in the dresser of her employer (number 16). The visual impressions in the image of her wretched end in a prison cell (number 24), with their lack of aesthetic harmony, are clear in their moral import of criticism.

The heroism of bandits

A commonplace in relation to one form of wrongdoing in Spain is that of the heroism of bandits, predominantly because they were viewed as having a role in social protest (see Hobsbawm 1985[1969]). An example of a character within this framework is the tale of Don Juan de Serrallonga, executed on 8 January 1634 for his crimes, but celebrated for his role in Catalan nationalism. Lionised in the cultural accounts of his life, Serrallonga has given rise to cinematic representation, as in the 1910 film *Don Juan de Serrallonga* by Ricardo de Baños and Alberto Marro, and the 1949 film of the same name by Ricardo Gascón. Here I will concentrate on just four nineteenth-century visual representations. As far as the chronological sequence can be ascertained, we can see

Serrallonga shifting, at least in visual terms, from a mode that is heroic to one that lays some emphasis on retribution.

In the first three examples the texts include reference to his original misdeeds, including killings, but little weight is given to them. This is consistent with the observation in Zugasti's history of banditry in Andalusia, where he reports that when most famous bandits had become outlaws it was for *'la desdicha de haber dado muerte a uno en riña, por celos, o por otras pasiones'* (the misfortune of having killed someone in a fight provoked by jealousy or other strong feelings) (Zugasti 1876–80 I:30). The visual emphasis in these examples moves quite decidedly in the direction of portraying the wrongdoer in heroic or admirable terms.

The *auca* of Serrallonga's story, *Historia de Don Juan de Serrallonga*, is based on the play by Victor Balaguer first shown in Barcelona in 1858 (Amades *et al.* 1931 I:XL); it is thus a re-packaging already once placed in a fictional frame. Perhaps because this *auca* was based on the text of a play, there is a greater sense of coherence (and conceivably of civilised containment) about the treatment of the more shocking aspects. It is noteworthy, however, that there is some tension between the visual representation and the accompanying text. In the caption to Illustration 41, the shooting by Doña Juana, Serrallonga's beloved, of the traitor Roberto (not graced by any other name in Balaguer's work) is referred to as a *'muerte villana'* (villainous death), not referring to the quality of her action but giving a judgement on the wrongdoer. The visual emphasis is on the determined demeanour of Juana, her straight arm as she fires a pistol, and the undignified figure of Roberto as he falls. In the last illustration, number 48, showing the execution of Serrallonga, there is a mixture of uncomfortable graphic detail and a discourse of approbation. It illustrates his severed head being held aloft for public inspection, the shock of this offset by the fact that only two witnesses are shown. His body is stretched out at the feet of the executioner. The caption, however, indicates that our response to this end should be of awe, rather than simple horror. In the tradition of the tragic hero, Serrallonga is austere and stoical as he finally submits to the rule of justice and his consequent execution. In the text, his nobility and political progressiveness are equally noted: *'Por hidalgo y liberal/ sentenciado es Serrallonga/ à la pena capital'* (as a noble and a liberal, Serrallonga is sentenced to capital punishment).

Similar in style is the rather indulgently illustrated and novelesque prose version of 1865, printed in Barcelona by Llorens. The cover illustration shows the early incident where Serrallonga saves the life of Doña Juana de Torrellas by stabbing her bolting horse. This method of killing the horse is quite remarkable. Serrallonga, in true fencing manner, keeps his left hand behind his back as he reaches out for the horse's chest with his sword arm. The lack of realism here (he is surely too far away to be able to do the horse damage) is balanced with the hint of the daring of the bullfight in his demeanour, although he does not have the typical upright stance that would be expected in that context. The endangered and rather dishevelled lady, meanwhile, is quite improbably upright, seated side-saddle, with a look of surprised dismay on her face, rather than what might be a more realistic terror. The second illustration of this publication shows the moment just before Serrallonga's execution. Doña Juana has fainted at the arrival of the soldiers to escort her husband to the gallows, thus confirming her delicate victim status already indicated in the earlier illustration. Here the visual emphasis is on the 'between men' moment as Serrallonga hands his wife over to the future care of his friend Fadri. The latter, overcome with grief, covers his eyes with his left hand, while Serrallonga is contained enough to make a gesture indicating future care and guardianship. At no point in this publication is there any representation of the killings perpetrated by Serrallonga in his early bandit phase, confirming once again the view that bandits are out of the ring of condemnation.

An undated *suelto*, *D. Juan de Serrallonga*, printed in Barcelona (Imps. Hospital, 19, 'El Abanico'), possibly from the middle of the nineteenth century in view of other similar (dated) material by this printer, similarly emphasises the nobility of Serrallonga. He is shown seated with Juana in their encampment in the hills. Their bandit status is suggested by her holding a rifle (albeit by its butt) and his cradling of a sword in his left arm. In both cases these gestures suggest that, while they have dealings with violence, this is not really part of their fundamental nature. Even the hatchings of the engraving are calm and have a clear preponderance of straight lines (contrasting strongly with the rather unbridled lines of the prose version and its illustrations).

Finally there is the 1872 *Sentencia de Serrallonga, ó sea los bandos de Barcelona* (Sentencing of Serrallonga, or the edicts of Barcelona), printed in Barcelona by Ramírez. This has the illustration that comes closest to showing Serrallonga in criminal guise, and arguably reflects the increasing tradition of pathologisation of crime that accompanied the *mala vida* publications in this period. Although Serrallonga's end is as shown in the *auca*, in that he has been beheaded by an axe (an indication of his nobility), there are some crucial differences. His body is still seated, and additional horror is presumably intended by the way in which the head is visibly spattering blood (as it was in the *auca*), while blood is also dripping from the body. A far greater crowd of witnesses is shown in this representation. Most striking of all is the degree of resemblance between this execution and others showing death by garrotte. There is a clear tradition of pictorial conventions for this sort of execution, including the dais on which the condemned man is killed, and the presence of the church in the form of a shrouded crucifix held aloft in the crowd as a type of identificatory witnessing. This execution scene of Serrallonga has a combination of crudity and impassiveness that will be brought out as the prime qualities of popular literature by Valle-Inclán, via his character Don Estrafalario, in his 1921 play *Los cuernos de don Friolera* (The cuckolding of Mr Silly) (Valle-Inclán 1954:991–7), and thus sends out a markedly modern note.

Rebel or murderess?

The *relación* (account) of the terrible doings of Sebastiana del Castillo committed in the eighteenth century is one of a significant subset of the *sueltos* devoted to notorious crimes. Sebastiana's case is listed by Wilson in his landmark 1984 paper, where he talks engagingly about good bad men and bad bad men. She appears to have been real in origin but, as noted by Wilson (who courteously refers to her as Doña Sebastiana, and refrains from giving the full gory details of her crime), her life story continued to be printed not only through the nineteenth century but into the twentieth (Wilson and Kish 1984:150; Botrel 2001, note 45). She thus joins the ranks of bandits and other wrongdoers in becoming virtually a mythical figure (see Botrel 1986).

Sebastiana's behaviour clearly put her beyond the pale. Her story in the 1850 *Curioso romance* ... combines two recurrent motifs: that of the woman thwarted by family pressure in her sexual desires, and that of the outbreak of violence and bloodshed that such oppositions are liable to provoke, thus forming part of a literature of admonishment about the dangers contained in repressive parental attitudes, and about the fundamental dangerousness (and barbarity) of woman. Yet the illustrations emphasise Sebastiana's heroic stature, rather than her barbarity.

The text tells how Sebastiana, living in a small village in the Sierra Morena, is courted, her suitor securing her consent to his courtship, but not that of her parents. In an unpleasant bio-feedback of family discord, the family punishes Sebastiana, who just becomes all the more furious and extreme (tearing her clothing and her hair and well anticipating the sort of behaviour that will become associated with the hysteric in the late nineteenth century). They lock her in a room for a year and her brothers administer additional punishment there.

The enraged (and resourceful) Sebastiana manages to write to her lover, spurring him on in his persona as an *'hombre de bríos'* (man of spirit). He takes arms and goes to her house. His role is initially unclear, but it emerges that if he is not to be the perpetrator of a crime, he is to be the witness, and is warned by Sebastiana that, if he does not help, he will suffer the same fate as the parents. A momentary lack of clarity in the pronouns in the text allows the reader to imagine that it is the lover who is killing the parents, but it emerges that the murderer is in fact Sebastiana. More than this, having stabbed her parents to death, she then removes their hearts and fries them. The lover, not surprisingly, faints at this act and she kills him, dresses in her father's clothes and leaves, eventually taking refuge with two bandits (that is, she moves outside the law). When pursued by her brothers, she ambushes them, bandit-style, and shoots them dead, then cutting their heads off with a knife. She is reproached by her bandit companions for this and proceeds to treat them in like manner, taking the four heads to Ciudad Rodrigo to display them in the square as the sign of her vengeance.

The different versions of Sebastiana provide a wide range of visual images for this story. None is identifiably from the eighteenth century, although a possible example from this date can be seen in Alvar (1974). This version, *Sebastiana del Caslillo* [sic], is illustrated by two woodcuts (with possibly a third being incorporated in the illustration on the left). On the left, a man with a sword (dagger?) pointing downwards appears to stand above a sleeping pair, who look as if they are naked and as if their wrists are bound. This pair, representing Sebastiana's parents, is thus presented as a sort of Adam and Eve picture of primary innocence. This illustration appears to be a separate woodcut that has been included to show the initial victims of Sebastiana's crimes, but the positioning of the man with the sword (wrongly) suggests that he, and not Sebastiana, has perpetrated the killing. On the right, a separate woodcut shows a woman with a smoking pistol in her right hand. It is far from clear just who the elegant, slightly smiling Sebastiana is killing. Clearly this is a sort of patchwork illustration, but one that does not obviously condemn Sebastiana.

Mixed messages also emerge from other versions and the illustrations that accompany them. The Lérida 1850 version portrays Sebastiana, sword in hand, mounted on a lively horse. There is no sign of the crime to come or already accomplished, and the pose of horse and rider is a standard one associated with tales of valour. A yet more heroic (and archaic) image is the one heading the version printed by the Imprenta calle de Juanelo in Madrid. Here the mounted figure, sword in hand and on a prancing charger, wears a helmet (rather than the plumed hat of the Lérida version) and appears to be dressed in a crusader-style tunic, rather than the more domestic clothing of the Lérida version. There is no date on the Juanelo *suelto*, but it is bound in with others by the same printer, one of which, number 14, is dated 1828.

A different type of mixed message is conveyed by a Barcelona *suelto* of Sebastiana, from the Imprenta de los Herederos de la Viuda Pla, calle de Cotoners (see Illustration 3.2.2(i)). There is no date on this, but we could suggest a possible date in that it is bound in with another *suelto* by the same printer, number 37, which is dated 1853. In this we have a pair of woodcuts, better matched than some. Sebastiana stands on the right, her smoking gun (*carabina*) held to her shoulder, sending bullets towards two fleeing male figures on the right. At their feet is a further figure, presumably dead. The curious detail here is that Sebastiana is dressed as a woman, while in the text we are told that she took her father's clothes when she retreated to the hills, and presumably was still wearing them when she shot her brothers. A different dynamic and sense of motion in the plot are suggested in an 1847 version (Madrid: Imprenta de Marés), where Sebastiana, turned sideways in her saddle (and clearly dressed in men's clothing of civilian style), has just shot another mounted figure, while a third lies on the ground.

My final example of Sebastiana is of a version found in two different printings of what is termed a *relación* rather than a *romance*. For one the printer is given as 'Imps. Hospital, 19 "El Abanico"', a Barcelona printer. The other is also a Barcelona printing, this time being Llorens, of Palma de Sta Catalina n.° 6 (see Illustration 3.2.2(ii)) The framed illustration shows Sebastiana as a defiant quasi-revolutionary figure pointing to the four heads strung up in Ciudad Rodrigo, with at least six bodies on the ground. Dressed as a man (but with her tightened belt accentuating her womanly curves and a neckerchief denoting her recent association with bandits), and sword in hand, she looks decisive and energetic. Her attitude does not just suggest the display of her actions (a defiant making visible of her crime), but also recalls pictorial conventions of those leading troops into battle. Over the four heads is the banner '*Venganza*' (revenge). This is clearly an addition to the illustration, and indeed looks as if it has been super-imposed, together with the four heads.

Nowhere in all of this is a sense of the barbarities that Sebastiana has committed on her parents, although through this rich array of versions there is significant variety of styles of depiction. The text remains constant, while the titles and subtitles vary in length and in the degree to which they flag up in advance for the reader (or listener) what is

156

Illustration 3.2.2(i)   Anon. (n.d.). *Nuevo y famoso romance en que se refiere las atrocidades de Sebastiana del Castillo* [...] Barcelona. CUL S743:3.c.8.2 (38)

(ii) Anon. (n.d.). *Sebastiana del Castillo. Nueva y famosa relacion de las atrocidades de Sebastiana del Castillo* [...] Barcelona. CUL S743:3.c.8.8 (26)

to be expected. Most, but not all, specify that she killed her mother, father and brothers because they had kept her imprisoned for a year. The visual accompaniment renders this criminal sober, even brave and admirable, despite the atrocities referred to in the text.

Depicting victimhood: Women and abjection

If those who shed blood are dignified by certain illustrative traditions, the question is whether victimhood might similarly be divested of some of its shocking features. The tale of Rosaura from Trujillo, so frequently published as to suggest that she might have existed, is of a girl who commits the error of persuading her lover to elope. He comes, bringing a cousin, and the two of them take her to the woods, rape her and leave her naked and bound to a tree, where she is found by a huntsman. Chase of the villains takes place and retribution is finally meted out to them.

The majority of the versions focus on Rosaura as she is found by the huntsman. Typically she is naked from the waist upwards and the motif is exploited by seductive drawing. In the 1867 Barcelona *Historia de la infeliz Rosaura* (Story of the unhappy Rosaura; see Illustration 3.2.3(i)) she is shown at a three-quarters angle, breasts clearly visible, her left foot elegantly placed to save her modesty (otherwise protected by the bonds that unrealistically go down the line of her hip and are loosely attached to her left ankle). An execution scene is shown on the right, offering a sense of visual and moral balance. In an undated version printed by Llorens of Barcelona, *La desgraciada Rosaura* (The unfortunate Rosaura; see Illustration 3.2.3(ii)), modesty is further saved by Rosaura appearing in profile, with the huntsman approaching at an oblique angle (although his little dog has gone right up to her). Contrasting with these stylised and restrained images of victimhood, *La desgraciada Rosaura* produced by La Fleca of Reus (see Illustration 3.2.3(iii)), is far more novelistic in its style of illustration and verges on soft porn in its portrayal of Rosaura as victim. It includes a dramatic image of her abduction. To the right of this, instead of the habitual image that shows the hunter innocently coming upon her in the wood, here she is shown roped to the tree, with one man pointing a gun at her. It looks as if this is to force her, but the text says otherwise, as this is the cousin of the lover, who is the one who has told her to remove her clothes (this is after the rape), and the gun pointed at her is with the intention to kill. In this version, the response being suggested is not of the decorum of emotion that would be elicited by a certain decorum of representation.

Illustration 3.2.3(i) Anon. (1867). *Historia de la infeliz Rosaura. Puesta en trovos* [...] Barcelona. CUL F180.b.8.1 (68)

(ii) Anon. (n.d.). *La desgraciada Rosaura. Breve relación de sus infortunios* [...] Barcelona. CUL F180.b.8.1 (100)

(iii) Anon. (n.d.). *La desgraciada Rosaura. Breve relación de sus infortunios* [...] Reus. CUL 8743.b.13 (21)

Rather, here is the blow-by-blow detail that is intended to shock, but without the softening of feeling beyond that shock.

Conclusion

There is no simple tradition of depiction of wrongdoing in Spain. What the examples discussed above show, however, is that the relationship between text and illustration is often far from straightforward. The early examples suggest that in some ways 'less is more', while the detail of illustration that we find in the various examples of Rosaura and Sebastiana is such that it guides and limits the range of response. The more we are told, the less there is for the imagination. In the area of illustrations in popular literature reflecting wrongdoing in Spain, the move towards sophistication (which will arguably reach its climax in *mala vida* literature and in later 'real reporting' of crimes) does not necessarily entail a richer range of emotional impact.

Note

1. This chapter on popular illustrations of wrongdoing forms part of the AHRC-funded project 2011–14 on 'Wrongdoing in Spain 1800–1936: Realities, Representations, Reactions', based at the University of Cambridge.

References

Aldaraca, Bridget. (1991). *El Ángel del hogar: Galdós and the Ideology of Domesticity in Spain*. Chapel Hill: University of North Carolina.

Alvar, Manuel. (1974). *Romances en pliegos de cordel (siglo XVIII)*. Málaga: Delegación de cultura. Excmo. Ayuntamiento de Málaga.

Amades, Joan, Joan Colominas and P. Vila. (1931). *Imatgeria popular catalana: Les Auques*.2 vols. Barcelona: Editorial Orbis.

Anon. (n.d.) *Bida de la muger buena y consecuencias de la buena educación*, followed by *Bida de la muger mala o consecuencias de sus bicios*. In Amades, Joan, Joan Colominas and P. Vila (1931). *Imatgeria popular catalana: Les Auques*.2 vols. Barcelona: Editorial Orbis.I, Plate XXV and II, Plate LXX.

Anon. (n.d.). *D. Juan de Serrallonga (Historia escrita en trovos)*. [Barcelona]: Imps. Hospital, 19. 'El Abanico'. Universitat de Lleida, Fons Sol-Torres. Available at http://soltorres.udl.cat [accessed July 2010].

Anon. (n.d.). *Historia de Don Juan de Serrallonga*. Barcelona.

Anon. (1867). *Historia de la infeliz Rosaura. Puesta en trovos para cantar los aficionados con guitarra*. Barcelona: Imprenta de Juan Llorens.

Anon. (1865). *Historia de la vida y hechos de D. Juan de Serrallonga*. Barcelona: Imprenta de Juan Llorens.

Anon. (n.d.). *La desgraciada Rosaura. Breve relación de sus infortunios, modo como fué hallada, y castigo ejemplar de sus infames seductores*: Reus. Tip. La Fleca. Véndese en la Librería 'La Fleca' de Juan Grau.

Anon. (n.d.). *La desgraciada Rosaura. Breve relación de sus infortunios, modo como fué hallada, y castigo ejemplar de sus infames seductores.* Barcelona: Imprenta de Llorens.

Anon. (n.d.). *Nuevo y famoso romance en que se refiere las atrocidades de Sebastiana del Castillo; y como mató á su padre, á su madre y á dos hermanos suyos ...* Barcelona: Imprenta de los Herederos de la Viuda Pla.

Anon. (1850). *Sebastiana del Castillo. Curioso romance en que se declaran las atrocidades de Sebastiana del Castillo.* Lerida: Imp. de Corominas. Universitat de Lleida, Fons Sol-Torres. Available at http://soltorres.udl.cat [accessed July 2010].

Anon. (n.d.). *Sebastiana del Caslillo [sic]. Nuevo y curioso romance, en que se declaran las atrocidades de Sebastiana del Castillo: refierese, como matò à su padre, à su madre y à dos hermanos suyos ...* Málaga: En la Imprenta y Librería de D. Felix de Casas y Martinez. In Alvar, Manuel. (1974). *Romances en pliegos de cordel (siglo XVIII).* Málaga: Delegación de cultura. Excmo. Ayuntamiento de Málaga. 381–4.

Anon. (1847). *Sebastiana del Castillo. Nuevo y curioso romance en que se declara las atrocidades de Sebastiana del Castillo: refiérese como mató á sus padres y á dos hermanos ...* Madrid: Imprenta de Marés.

Anon. (n.d.). *Sebastiana del Castillo. Nuevo y curioso romance en que se declaran las atrocidades de Sebastiana del Castillo: refierese como mató á su padre y su madre, y á dos hermanos suyos ...* Madrid: Imprenta calle de Juanelo.

Anon. (n.d.). *Sebastiana del Castillo. Nueva y famosa relacion de las atrocidades de Sebastiana del Castillo y el trágico fin de su vida despues de haber muerto á su padre, madre y hermanos.* Barcelona: Imp. de Llorens.

Anon. (1872). *Sentencia de Serrallonga, ó sea los bandos de Barcelona.* Barcelona: Imp. de Ramirez y Ca.

Anon. (n.d.). *Travesuras de la infancia.* Barcelona: Se hallará de venta en casa los sucesores de Antonio Bosch.

Anon. (n.d.). *Vida del hombre obrando bien* followed by *Vida del hombre obrando mal.* Barcelona: Imprenta de Ignacio Estivill. In Amades, Joan, Joan Colominas and P. Vila. (1931). *Imatgeria popular catalana: Les Auques.* 2 vols. Barcelona: Editorial Orbis.I, Plate XXV and II, Plate LXVIII.

Anon. (n.d.). *Vida de la mujer buena y la mala.* Madrid: Despacho, Sucesores de Hernando.

Bernaldo de Quirós, Constancio. (1906). *Criminología de los delitos de sangre en España.* Madrid: Internacional.

Botrel, Jean-François. (1986). Diego Corrientes ou le bandit généreux: fonction et fonctionnement d'un mythe. In Yves-René Fonquerne and Alfonso Esteban (eds), *Culturas populares: Diferencias, divergencias, conflictos. Actas del Coloquio celebrado en la Casa de Velázquez, los días 30 de noviembre y 1-2 diciembre de 1983.* Madrid: Casa de Velázquez.

Botrel, Jean-François. (2001). El género de cordel. In Luis Díaz G. Viana (ed.), *Palabras para el pueblo. I. Aproximación general a la literatura de cordel.* Madrid: CSIC; and in Biblioteca Cervantes Virtual, www.cervantesvirtual.com.

Caro Baroja, Julio. (1969). *Ensayo sobre la literatura de cordel.* Madrid: Ediciones de la Revista de Occidente.

Cleminson, Richard and Teresa Fuentes Peris. (eds) (2009). *La mala vida.* Special issue of *Journal of Spanish Cultural Studies* 10(4).

Foucault, Michel. (1972[1969]) *The Archaeology of Knowledge and the Discourse on Language*, trans. A. M. Sheridan Smith. New York: Pantheon Books.

Grant, Helen. (1964). Una aleluya erótica de Federico García Lorca y las aleluyas populares del siglo XIX. *Actas del Primer Congreso de la Asociación Internacional de Hispanistas 1962*. Oxford: Dolphin. Available at http://cvc.cervantes.es/obref/aih/pdf/01/aih_01_1_029.pdf [accessed October 2011].

Grant, Helen. (1972). El mundo al revés. *Hispanic Studies in Honour of Joseph Manson*. Oxford: Dolphin.

Grant, Helen. (1973). The World Upside-Down. In Roy O. Jones (ed.), *Studies in Spanish Literature of the Golden Age Presented to Edward M. Wilson*. London: Tamesis.

Grant, Helen F. (1979). Images et gravures du monde à l'envers dans leurs relations avec la pensée et la littérature espagnoles. In J. Lafond and A. Redondo (eds), *L'Image du monde renversé et ses représentations littéraires et para-littéraires de la fin du XVIe siècle au milieu du XVIIe*. Paris: Vrin.

Hobsbawm, Eric J. (1985[1969]). *Bandits*. Harmondsworth: Penguin.

Jagoe, Catherine. (1994). *Ambiguous Angels: Gender in the Novels of Galdós*. Berkeley: University of California Press.

Ríos-Font, Wadda. (2005). El crimen de la calle de San Vicente: Crime Writing and Bourgeois Liberalism in Restoration Spain. *Modern Language Notes*, 120(2), 335–54.

Sinclair, Alison. (1977). *Valle-Inclán's 'Ruedo ibérico': A Popular View of Revolution*. London: Tamesis.

Sinclair, Alison. (2009). *Trafficking Knowledge in Early Twentieth-Century Spain: Centres of Exchange and Cultural Imaginaries*. Woodbridge: Tamesis.

Valle-Inclán, Ramón del. (1954). *Los cuernos de Don Friolera* [1921] in *Obras completas, Vol. I*. Madrid: Plenitud.

Vilanova, Mercedes and Xavier Moreno Juliá. (1992). *Atlas de la evolución de analfabetismo en España de 1887 a 1871*. Madrid: Centro de Publicaciones del Ministerio de Educación y Ciencia.

Wilson, Edward M. and Katherine Kish. (1984). Some Spanish Dick Turpins, or bad men in bad ballads. *Hispanic Review*, 52(2), 141–62.

Zugasti, Julián. (1876–80). *El bandolerismo: Estudio social y memorias históricas*. Madrid: Imprenta de Fortanet. 10 vols.

3.3
Reinventing the Badman in Jamaican Fiction and Film

Lucy Evans

The badman in the popular imagination

In June 2010, alleged drug lord Christopher Coke was extradited from Jamaica to the United States following an operation by police and military forces that resulted in the deaths of at least 76 local people in the Tivoli Gardens inner-city area of Western Kingston. Coke's public image became a subject of intrigue circulating locally and globally. While a reporter for the Jamaica *Gleaner* presents Coke's arrest as a significant achievement on the part of the authorities ('Coke's capture welcome, but ...' 2010), other newspaper reporters comment on how local people protested in support of Coke ('Jamaica security forces storm "drugs lord" stronghold' 2010; 'Toll from Jamaica violence climbs to 73' 2010) and emphasise his role as a 'community benefactor' ('This is not Somalia, we hope' 2009). Media coverage of the event indicates how the story of the elusive criminal leader had captured the popular imagination; an AOL News reporter observes that Coke became 'a larger-than-life figure in Jamaica' ('Is Jamaica's most wanted man like Robin Hood?' 2010). In this respect, Coke's story resembles that of a criminal from the 1940s, Ivanhoe Martin, nicknamed Rhygin. According to Thelwell (1992:182), Rhygin was a 'petty criminal and escaped convict' who was the subject of newspaper headlines over the course of a month and, as a result, 'became the first media created "superstar" in [Jamaican] cultural history'. Like Coke, Rhygin acquired legendary status in the minds of Jamaican people.

The echo of Rhygin's story in Coke's attests to the continuing significance of the badman image as a fiction circulating within Jamaican popular culture. In a study of contemporary criminal power structures in Kingston, Jaffe (forthcoming:1) draws attention to the 'aesthetic fashioning' of criminal leaders (known as 'dons') in twenty-first-century Jamaica. Giving Christopher Coke as an example, she examines the way in which popular culture has consolidated the power of criminal dons, elevating them as 'icons, underworld heroes, who at times achieve super-star status'. Examining a film released in 1972 directed by Perry Henzell and a novel by Garfield Ellis published in 2005 but set in the 1970s, this chapter considers the very different ways in which these two texts have mobilised the narrative of the badman. It situates Henzell's and Ellis's contrasting representations of the badman in the context of shifting relations between crime and politics in the decades following Jamaica's independence. Henzell's depiction of the badman as a revolutionary anti-hero is compared to Ellis's more critical portrayal of this figure as a divisive presence in a country torn apart by intercommunal violence.

The badman as anti-hero: Perry Henzell's *The Harder They Come*

Perry Henzell's classic film *The Harder They Come* (1972) was set and produced in Jamaica, and featured the Jamaican reggae star Jimmy Cliff alongside 'working class folk [...] without formal dramatic training' (Thelwell 1992:184). It is also about Jamaica; the protagonist, based on Ivanhoe 'Rhygin' Martin, arrives in Kingston from the country to make something of himself and, frustrated by the lack of opportunity available to young black men in a city that seemed to promise so much, achieves the stardom for which he longs by turning to crime and adopting the role of a wanted man. The film's release date coincided with the election of Michael Manley's PNP government, a hopeful moment in Jamaica's post-independence history in that Manley 'sought to end Jamaica's dependency on foreign companies and replace capitalism with democratic socialism' (Hope 2006: 2). As noted by Sives (2010:53), Jamaica's internal political dynamics in the decade preceding Manley's election were affected by two external movements: first 'the rise of Black Power and the radicalisation of the politics of race'; and second 'the hemispheric response to the consolidation of a Marxist regime in Cuba following the 1959 revolution'. The influence of these movements helped to build up an atmosphere of radical protest that came to a head with the 1968 Rodney Riots.

Produced in the wake of these developments, *The Harder They Come* has been hailed by some critics and reviewers as revolutionary in that it gives a voice to Kingston's economically underprivileged, socially marginalised and majority black inner-city communities. According to Warner (2000:81), the film 'was seen as a statement on the triumph of the people, and on their hope for the future'. In Rohlehr's (1973:6) view, the film 'measured the pressures of the sixties, and related them to the creative flowering of the people's music in Kingston's dry desert of stone'. The support of local people for the film can be seen in accounts of its 5 June premier, where 'over 6000 people had invaded the Carib cinema, with some 3000 more encamped outside' (Warner 2000:76). Reflecting on these events, Brathwaite (1984:41) considers how Henzell's film offered to local audiences for the first time 'a local face, a native ikon' as hero, and in the process generated a 'revolution as significant as emancipation'. These accounts can be compared to a range of less favourable responses. Gilroy (1992[1987]:169) considers the film's consumption by foreign white audiences, criticising the way in which the film circulated images of 'black life' as 'backward, violent, sexist and fratricidal'. Gaztambide-Fernández (2002:357) comments on the film's presentation of the black body 'as an object of desire for a white audience'. Taking a similar approach, Fulani (2005:paragraph 16) focuses on the 'fetishisation and commodification of the *ruud bwai*' figure, which, in her opinion, 'drains Ivan's rebellion of political significance'.[1]

This disparity in critical reception of *The Harder They Come* is largely due to the critics' tendency to focus exclusively on either a local audience, in the case of Warner, Rohlehr and Brathwaite, or a global audience, in the case of Gilroy, Gaztambide-Fernández and Fulani. As Gilroy (1992[1987]:170) explains, the commercial success of *The Harder They Come* in the 1970s coincided with the 'international mass-marketing of reggae', precipitated by Bob Marley's rise to fame. For Gilroy (1992[1987]:169), the 'gradual involvement of large corporations [...] in the selling of reggae' entailed 'a conscious attempt to separate the product from its producers and from its roots in black life'. However, Dawes (1999:68) claims that despite reggae's appeal to a global audience, it has kept its 'radical edge', and furthermore that its 'revolutionary rhetoric' (Dawes 1999:66) has prevented it from acquiring the status of rhythm and blues or soul and funk in mainstream US popular culture. In Dawes's (1999:68) view, Jamaican reggae has the 'capacity to be at once radical, highly localised, and internationally accessible (and commercially viable)'. In a similar way, I suggest, the international popularity of *The Harder They Come* did not divest it of its political edge, and its commercial success abroad did not come at the cost of its local significance.

The revolutionary potential of *The Harder They Come* manifests most prominently in the experiences and actions of its protagonist, Ivan, an embodiment of the badman image prevalent in Jamaican popular culture of the late 1960s and early 1970s. Roberts (1989:173) examines folk songs about Railroad Bill, who he describes as 'one of the many badman heroes to capture the black folk imagination during the 1890s'. He considers the relationship between badman heroes in the African American folk tradition and rebellious slaves in the plantation system, referred to by both enslaved Africans and white slave masters as 'bad niggers' (Roberts 1989:176). Discussions of the badman in the context of post-independence Jamaica suggest a similar association between this figure and the insubordinate slave. Collins (2003:57) considers the rude boy as an element of Jamaican urban youth culture and an emblem of 'potentially violent forces of social upheaval'. In a similar vein, Harriott (2008:18) reflects that 'some of the iconic figures in the history of violent crime in Jamaica are remembered as "social bandits" who adopted anti-system rhetorical postures', and Gray (2004:123) considers how the notion of 'badness' as 'a stylized outlawry' was respected within the slums 'for affirming a racially charged defiance'. Collins, Harriott and Gray all present the badman as a symbol of resistance against Jamaica's racially inflected class hierarchy, itself a product of colonialism and plantation slavery. With this in mind, Henzell's Ivan can be read as a voice of protest against a neocolonial social system that excludes and exploits young black men.

The film begins with a bus transporting Ivan, a naive country boy clutching a mango, into the heart of Kingston. This is accompanied by Jimmy Cliff's reggae hit 'You Can Get It If You Really Want', which hints at Ivan's investment in the myth of the city as a site of possibility and wish fulfilment. Although the song continues to play, this sentiment is swiftly undermined by the appearance of a billboard advertising Shell and featuring a white car; this detail indicates that the city's dreams are imported, for sale and the property of a light-skinned elite. As Ivan soon learns through his unsuccessful search for employment among crowds of other young black men, the glittering promise of this commercial centre is not freely available to everyone.

If the film's opening scene emphasises the impact of US consumer culture on Kingston's inhabitants, a later scene comments on the presence of an urban youth counter-culture. Dressed in a bright yellow beret and occupied in the workshop of a preacher who has taken him in, Ivan listens to The Slickers' reggae track 'Johnny Too Bad', which begins as follows:

> Walking down the road
> With your pistol in your waist,

Johnny you're too bad.
Walking down the road
With your ratchet in your waist,
Johnny you're too bad.

You're just robbing and you're stabbing and you're looting and
    you're shooting
Now you're too bad.
You're just robbing and you're stabbing and you're looting and
    you're shooting
Now you're too bad.[2]

While the second verse describes actions such as 'robbing', 'stabbing', 'looting' and 'shooting', the first verse, with its repetition of the clause 'walking down the road', focuses on the appearance of the badman striking a defiant pose on Kingston's streets. The badman's 'pistol' or 'ratchet' has a practical function, but the detail of its position at his waist suggests that it is part of a carefully conceived attire. The badman is less a reality here than a stylised image that imprints itself on the memory of listeners. This scene in *The Harder They Come* illustrates the prominence of the badman figure within Kingston's subculture, presenting the badman as a fiction circulating within a city where – as we see in later scenes – everyone is listening to the radio. Commenting sarcastically on Ivan's 'pretty hat', his co-worker Longa says 'You only need a gun now to look like Johnny', and as if on cue Ivan leaves the workshop to sit in a disused car, wearing reflective sunglasses and reading a comic, swept up in the fiction of what he might become. The preacher later discovers a toy gun in the car, which suggests that Ivan has attempted to complete the picture conjured up by the song.

With implicit reference to the way in which the historical fugitive Rhygin imitated the 'cowboy' character of US classic westerns (Thelwell 1992:183), *The Harder They Come* invites us to consider the influence of imported foreign films on the fictional Ivan's self-styling as a badman. Soon after Ivan's arrival in the city, we see him watching a film, Sergio Corbucci's *Django* (1966), at the Rialto cinema. The scene alternates between images from *Django* where the hero implausibly guns down a large number of opponents, and glimpses of the cinema audience of young black men cheering him on. Some critics have regarded this as a comment on the insidious influence of foreign cultural models that leads black male youths to inhabit a dangerous fantasy of themselves (Cooper 1993:98; Rohlehr 1973:9). However, others have interpreted the scene differently. Fumagalli (2008) and Younger (2005) comment on the significance of Henzell's choice of a spaghetti western rather than a classic Hollywood western as an intertext. In a study of this subgenre, Frayling (2006[1981]:xxv) describes how spaghetti westerns 'exploit the Hollywood Western, at the same time as "deconstructing" it – an act of demythologisation'. According to Fumagalli and Younger, *The Harder They Come* engages in a similar process. Both critics put forward the idea that Ellis's film appropriates the themes, motifs and techniques of the spaghetti western, resituating the genre's subversive power within the turbulent political climate of 1970s Jamaica.

Whether they consider Ivan as a passive consumer or a self-conscious manipulator of imported cultural forms, these critics' readings depend on an opposition between foreign cultural products and a local audience. For example, Fumagalli (2008:399) reminds us that 'Hollywood westerns and spaghetti (*anti-*) westerns are both "foreign paradigms" for Jamaicans'. I suggest that in its depiction of the badman figure, *The Harder They Come* complicates any neat division between local and foreign paradigms. In an anthropological study of late twentieth-century and early twenty-first-century Jamaica, Thomas (2005:250) develops a 'dialectical reading of the relationship between capitalist globalization and local cultural practices', noting that the Jamaican 'rude boy' phenomenon of the late 1960s and early 1970s was influenced by American westerns as well as the 'blaxploitation' film genre. She also comments on the way in which 'images of rudies and dancehall dons are circulated, canonized, and revised in [Jamaican] popular culture' (Thomas 2005:243). Thomas's observations illuminate how the badman figure has emerged out of an interchange between local and foreign cultural influences. It is at once transnational – absorbing foreign models and impacting on them in turn – and localised, acquiring specific historical and cultural significance in Jamaica. *The Harder They Come* both draws on and contributes to this complex imbrication of the local and the global. Ivan models himself on the foreign 'cowboy' figure of the spaghetti western, but this process is mediated through his awareness of localised 'badman' icons such as Johnny Too Bad.

The politicised nature of Ivan's performance as badman, and its basis in what Dawes describes as the 'radical edge' of Jamaican reggae, is clearly indicated in the lyrics of the title song 'The Harder They Come'.

> Well the oppressors are trying to keep me down
> Trying to drive me underground,
> And they think that they have got their battle won

I say: 'forgive them, Lord, they know not what they've done'
[...]
And I keep on fighting for the things I want
Though I know that when you're dead you can't
But I'd rather be a free man in my grave
Than living like a puppet or a slave (Cliff 1986:63)[3]

These two verses articulate a struggle against oppression that, in the context of the film, relates to the exploitative structures of a neocolonial society where both the music business and the ganja trade are controlled by a light-skinned elite. As Ivan finds out soon after recording the song, the wealthy entrepreneur Hilton monopolises the island's popular music industry, reaping the profits and controlling the public images of budding reggae stars. Disillusioned by this discovery, Ivan moves into drug dealing, only to encounter a similar situation: he is obliged to give a large proportion of his earnings to those he is working for and realises that most of the revenue is claimed by invisible powers at the top. The line 'I'd rather be a free man in my grave than living like a puppet or a slave' makes a direct link between these examples of the disempowerment of black youths within the commercial climate of post-independence Jamaica and the country's history of plantation slavery.

Ivan's conscious refusal to act as a 'puppet', expressed in this song, complicates readings of him as 'an empty fantasy-ridden character' (Rohlehr 1973:9) who uncritically imitates foreign models. Instead, Ivan's carefully crafted performance as a 'wanted man' eluding the authorities can be seen as an attack on the oppression and injustice referred to in his song. Refusing to be 'driven underground', he generates for himself a celebrity status. The story of Ivan as runaway ignites the public imagination and becomes a hit along with his song, as is illustrated in scenes of the song being repeatedly broadcast on local radio and listened to in various parts of the city. A later sequence, still accompanied by the same reggae track, presents us with graffiti on the city's corrugated iron fences, buildings and vehicles, with phrases such as 'I was here but I disappear', 'I was here', 'Here', 'See me here' and 'I am everywhere'. Ivan is absent from these scenes, but his public image remains and builds momentum as interest in his story grows. As an irreverent mode of expression that impinges on the city's public spaces, and a form of popular culture operating outside the control of Hilton's music industry, Ivan's graffiti could be seen as an act of defiance against the state's regulation of Kingston's inner-city areas. Through his self-styling as a badman, he inscribes his presence within a city that previously rendered him invisible.

Support for Ivan among Kingston's inner-city population, shown by the popularity of his song and glimpsed in the rabble of cheering children pursuing him during a gunfight with the drug dealer José, recalls the widespread public admiration for the historical badman Rhygin and his apparent invincibility. Although Ivan might appear to be dangerously caught up within the fantasy of his own badman image, his performance is in fact grounded in the lived experiences of Kingston's inner-city population. If he reduces himself to an icon, it is – importantly – a 'native ikon', to borrow Brathwaite's words. As can be seen from the film's carefully selected intertexts, the cowboy figure in the foreign films consumed by black youths such as Ivan coexists in their minds alongside and in tension with the indigenised badman icon celebrated in Jamaican popular culture. Ivan's 'stylized outlawry' is both drawn from and speaks to the urban subculture whose interests he represents.

Politicised violence in Garfield Ellis's *For Nothing at All*

Garfield Ellis's 2005 novel *For Nothing at All* consists of alternating episodes dealing with the childhood and adolescent experiences of the protagonist, Wesley, and three of his friends. Five untitled chapters offer the narrative of a single day in these characters' 11-year-old lives, but its flow is interrupted by five titled chapters, spanning several years, which chart their divergent paths. The bonds of friendship forming in the childhood episodes are similarly undercut in the adolescent episodes, where the group is split apart due to Stevie's emotional 'death', Skin's literal death, Colin's retreat into spirituality and Wesley's imprisonment. The childhood episodes are set in the early 1970s, around the time of the 1972 election of Michael Manley and the release of *The Harder They Come*. The adolescent episodes are set a few years later, dealing with the 1976 re-election of Manley's PNP government. Through this alternation between two distinct time frames, linked by the coming-of-age narratives of four fictional characters, Ellis reflects on the failure of Manley's vision of 'democratic socialism' to materialise in the years following his initial election. The personal blurs with the political as Wesley's shattered childhood dreams are identified with Manley's thwarted dream of freedom and equality.

Sives (2010:xiii) describes the rise in what she calls 'partisan political violence' in 1970s Kingston, as criminal gangs 'began to develop political identities and affiliations that tied them into a politicised, territorial space', leading to a situation where 'certain areas of the city became JLP and others PNP' (Sives 2010:76). Sives's account demonstrates how in the 1970s, the long-standing antagonism between Jamaica's two main political parties – the Jamaican Labour Party and the People's National Party – was played out in conflicts between rival gangs whose affiliation with one of these parties ensured not only financial gain and a heightened social status for criminal dons, but also welfare and employment opportunities for their communities. Alongside the growth in political clientelism came the development of garrison communities, described by Meeks (2007:69) as 'militarized inner-city communities that held allegiance to one or other of the dominant parties and ensured almost monolithic single-party voting on election day'. As Sives (2010:65, 68) explains, these politically homogenous communities were facilitated by the JLP government's inner-city housing scheme, built in the 1960s, which eradicated squatter settlements in Western Kingston and allocated housing on a partisan basis, 'deepening political divisions in the inner city communities'. With the creation of garrison communities, the city space was carved up into warring political factions.

Clarke (2006:208) compares the rude boy culture of the 1960s to the politicised violence of criminal gangs in the 1970s, and Hope (2006:91) considers how changing perceptions of the badman have been reflected in popular culture, as the idealised narrative of the 'rude bwoy' as a 'romantic', 'heroic' and 'anti-systemic' folk figure has given way to 'deviant heroes' whose public images are intertwined with 'political tribalism, narco-culture and gun culture'. As Clarke's and Hope's comments make clear, the figure of the badman as underdog, fighting corruption and voicing the grievances of an oppressed underclass, seen in *The Harder They Come*, jars with the altered dynamics of the late 1970s, where gang leaders have become key players within a corrupt political system.

Ellis's novel is set in Central Village, located between Spanish Town and Kingston. Writing in the same decade in which the book is set, Eyre (1979:97) describes how Central Village is bisected by the Kingston–Spanish Town highway, known locally as the 'Line of Demarcation', and separated into subunits with marked political allegiances. He comments on the debilitating 'fragmentation' of Central Village where social relations are 'fractious and difficult' (Eyre 1979:98). Opening with an action sequence on the Kingston–Spanish Town highway, *For Nothing at All* is concerned with the divisive effects of political tribalism, which have created long-lasting and irresolvable rivalries among Central Village inhabitants. Wesley and his friends inhabit a housing scheme that is separated from neighbouring areas by a ravine and 'very high concrete fences with barbed wire or bottles cemented into the concrete to make them hard to scale' (Ellis 2005:23). The teenage characters in the titled stories are being initiated into a system of patrol where they walk around the boundaries of their housing scheme after the 6 o'clock curfew, checking that no one is crossing the border.

The influential don Mr Johnson explains to Wesley: 'All country go through revolution. Is the seventies now. Look 'round the world. Grenada, Cuba, Angola, Mozambique.' He goes on to compare the role of gunmen protecting their local community to that of Che Guevara fighting for his country (Ellis 2005:128). With this reference to the Cuban revolution and its uncompromising hero, Ellis's novel alludes to Henzell's film, which ends with Ivan trying to escape on a boat bound for Cuba, assured by his friend Pedro that he will receive a warm welcome. However, unlike Henzell, Ellis stresses the hollowness of revolutionary rhetoric in a context where violence is primarily motivated by a power struggle between political parties and between criminal gangs. Sives (2010:xi) comments on the discrepancy between Jamaican politics and the political history of a country such as Cuba, observing that 'violence in Jamaican politics has occurred within the democratic framework between supporters of two main political parties [...] and has sought to influence electoral outcome rather than overthrow the state'. As we have seen, Ivan's badman performance in *The Harder They Come* is charged with a revolutionary energy that promises to endure even after his death. In contrast, Ellis's protagonist feels burdened by a culture of violence that, rather than liberating Jamaican people, locks them into a repetitive cycle of attack and reprisal. As Wesley finds out when he begins work on a construction site, criminal gang leaders collude with corrupt government officials rather than working against the state.

This comment on the Cuban revolution is one of several occasions where *For Nothing at All* refers back to *The Harder They Come*, inviting a comparative reading of the two texts. Like Henzell's film, Ellis's novel has a self-reflexive dimension regarding its form and style. Whereas *The Harder They Come* creatively manipulates the generic conventions of the spaghetti western, *For Nothing at All* at times replicates and at times departs from the format of the Hollywood western. 'Cowboy' movies are a continual point of reference for Ellis's characters, both as children and as adolescents. At the opening of the second episode, an adolescent Wesley excitedly discusses with his friend Skin a gunfight he has seen on the way home from school, proud of his role as a first-hand witness. His story merges with that of a classic Hollywood western: he tells Skin that it 'was like a scene from a cowboy movie, with two cowboys on a horse bearing down on another group bunkered down in a thicket', and describes the appearance of Spragga on his motorbike 'like a cowboy upright in his stirrups' (Ellis 2005:8). As can be seen in Wesley's sensationalised account, the boys respond to the gunfight less as a real event than as an entertaining spectacle. Wesley is '[n]ot afraid but mesmerised and fascinated' (Ellis 2005:9) and, although we hear in passing of damage to buildings and cars and the danger caused to other motorists, the focus is on the drama of the story rather than the repercussions of the gunfight. After hearing Wesley's story, Skin relates it to their friend Colin 'as if he had seen the shoot-out himself' (Ellis 2005:11), only to learn that Colin 'had heard about the whole thing' (Ellis 2005:11). The shoot-out becomes a fiction progressively embellished as it circulates within their small community, and as a result the gunmen – like Henzell's Ivan – become celebrities. In this way, Wesley and his friends resemble the unruly crowd of cheering children who trail behind Ivan during a shoot-out scene in *The Harder They Come*.

Despite the echoes of Henzell's film in Ellis's novel, there is a tension between the two texts' portrayal of the badman figure. While *The Harder They Come* positions the badman as a revolutionary anti-hero, *For Nothing at All* undercuts this glorification of the badman image, reflecting more critically on the role played by politicised criminal gangs in the shaping of post-independence Jamaica. Wesley comments on Mr Johnson's appearance:

> He wore a beautiful, grey Puma sweat suit and matching shoes. He seemed younger than I remembered and he wore the training gear in a fashionable way, with a gold chain resting on the netting of his exposed undershirt. He smelled of Old Spice and foreign shampoo and gave off an aura of raw, bullish power. (Ellis 2005:124)

This description focuses on Mr Johnson's immaculately colour-coordinated outfit, which calls to mind Ivan's wardrobe of deliberately ostentatious garments such as his yellow beret and his trademark sweatshirt featuring a large yellow star. It also resonates with The Slickers' depiction of the iconic Johnny Too Bad, pictured in a 'badman' pose with his 'ratchet in [his] waist'. An emphasis is placed not only on Mr Johnson's choice of clothing but on the self-consciously 'fashionable' way he wears it, calculated to generate in viewers an 'aura' distinctive to the badman.

However, whereas the excessively stylised aspect of Ivan's performance is part of its widespread appeal to audiences both within and beyond the fictional world of the film, Ellis critiques Mr Johnson's privileging of style over substance. Wesley's description of him draws attention to foreign influences: he wears clothes from the German multinational designer label Puma, and uses 'foreign shampoo' as well as the US brand of aftershave 'Old Spice'. In highlighting how Mr Johnson's badman 'aura' is acquired through his purchase of expensive foreign products, Ellis draws attention to his unsuitability as a spokesperson for Jamaica's impoverished underclass, or – to return to Loretta Collins's discussion of the 1960s rude boy – as a symbol of 'potentially violent forces of social upheaval'. Wesley compares Mr Johnson to a 'badman out of the movie, *The Harder They Come*, reciting words bigger than himself', and finds his costume and attitude 'comical' (Ellis 2005:129). In this scene, Ellis presents Mr Johnson as a hollow replica of Henzell's rebellious badman figure, emptied of counter-cultural energy.

Although the gunfight scene described above imitates the format of the classic Hollywood western, the novel's episodic form works against this, disrupting the swift pace of the action and obliging readers to pause and reflect on the relationship between the two parallel yet asymmetric narratives. Ellis's use of a different size and style of typeface for the titled stories invites us to read the childhood and adolescent experiences as discordantly juxtaposed. The lighthearted camaraderie of games such as 'chevy chase, hopscotch and marbles' (Ellis 2005:64) is overshadowed by the routine warfare of a politically divided community, and the idyllic setting of a sunlit river gives way to the strictly bounded spaces of the housing schemes. Just as the fonts of the two sets of stories are unmatching, Wesley's childhood memories '[do] not match' the altered surroundings of the later episodes: childhood friends become political enemies, and once whitewashed walls are covered with 'slogans and the faces of politicians' (Ellis 2005:63). The detail of graffitied public space also reinforces the discontinuity between Ellis's novel and Henzell's film; Ivan's self-affirming graffiti uncannily resurfaces in Ellis's depiction of a hill defaced by 'paintings and tags and threats of a new and ugly time' (Ellis 2005:63), an image that illustrates the scarring of Jamaica's landscape by politicised violence.

During Wesley's time on the construction site, the marking of a border between JLP and PNP territories results in the unearthing of a box of ammunition. With this image of buried weapons, Ellis portrays Jamaica's political culture of violence as deeply engrained, dating back to the beginning of the two-party system in the 1940s, and beyond it to times of slavery. To dig beneath the surface of 1970s Jamaica, he implies, is to encounter not solid ground but similarly explosive material. This scene illustrates how, as Meeks (2007:78) argues, Jamaica's present moment of 'heightened violence' cannot be explained simply as a 'result of inner-city poverty' or a 'short-term effect of drug cartel intervention', but has a 'longer genealogy, rooted in Jamaican social divisions and the failed attempts to transcend them'. Whereas *The Harder They Come* mobilises the badman image as a symbol of resistance against these deep-rooted social divisions, *For Nothing at All* offers a more ambivalent figuring of the badman as implicated within a corrupt political system that does little to reduce the gap between Jamaica's brown middle class and black urban underclass. Since its emergence in the 1940s, the figure of the badman has been repeatedly referenced within Jamaican literature, film, popular music and news media, acquiring mythic status. However, if Henzell's and Ellis's texts attest to the pervasive presence of the badman in the Jamaican popular imagination, they also document its changing iconography in the context of shifting structures of power.

Notes

1. According to the *Oxford English Dictionary*, the word 'rude boy' originates in Jamaica and refers to 'any of a class of unemployed black youths inhabiting the poorer areas of Jamaica and typically seen as indolent and apt to commit petty crimes', applying also to 'a member of the subculture associated with ska'.
2. Johnny Too Bad. Words & Music by Delroy Wilson, Hylton Beckford & Derrick Crooks. © Copyright 1970 Ackee Music Incorporated, USA/Wetwater Music Incorporated. EMI Music Publishing Limited (75%)/Universal/Island Music Limited (25%). All rights in Germany administered by Universal Music Publ. GmbH. All Rights Reserved. International Copyright Secured. Used by permission of Music Sales Limited and EMI Music Publishing.
3. The Harder They Come. Words & Music by Jimmy Cliff. © Copyright 1972 Island Music Limited. Universal/Island Music Limited. All rights in Germany administered by Universal Music Publ. GmbH. All Rights Reserved. International Copyright Secured. Used by permission of Music Sales Limited.

References

Brathwaite, Edward Kamau. (1984). *History of the Voice: The Development of Nation Language in Anglophone Caribbean Poetry*. London: New Beacon.

Clarke, Colin. (2006). *Decolonizing the Colonial City: Urbanization and Stratification in Kingston, Jamaica*. Oxford: Oxford University Press.

Cliff, Jimmy. (1986). The Harder They Come. *The Penguin Book of Caribbean Verse in English*, Paula Burnett (ed.), Harmondsworth: Penguin.

Coke's capture welcome, but ... *The Gleaner*, 24 June 2010. Available at http://jamaica-gleaner.com/gleaner/20100624/cleisure/cleisure1.html [accessed March 2011].

Collins, Loretta. (2003). *The Harder They Come*: Rougher Version. *Small Axe*, 13(7:1), 46–71.

Cooper, Carolyn. (1993). *Noises in the Blood: Orality, Gender and the 'Vulgar' Body of Jamaican Popular Culture*. London: Macmillan.

Dawes, Kwame. (1999). *Natural Mysticism: Towards a New Reggae Aesthetic*. Leeds: Peepal Tree.

Ellis, Garfield. (2005). *For Nothing at All*. Oxford: Macmillan.

Eyre, L. Alan. (1979). Quasi-urban melange settlement: Cases from St. Catherine and St James, Jamaica. *Geographical Review*, 69(1), 95–100.

Frayling, Christopher. (2006[1981]). *Spaghetti Westerns: Cowboys and Europeans from Karl May to Sergio Leone*. New York: Palgrave Macmillan.

Fulani, Ifeona. (2005). Representations of the Body of the New Nation in *The Harder They Come* and *Rockers*. *Anthurium*, 3(1). Available at http://anthurium. miami.edu/home.htm [accessed March 2011].

Fumagalli, Maria Cristina. (2008). 'You ti'nk hero can dead – til de las' reel?': Perry Henzell's *The Harder They Come* and Sergio Corbucci's *Django*. In Kathleen Gyssels and Bénédicte Ledent (eds), *The Caribbean Writer as Warrior of the Imaginary*. Amsterdam: Rodopi.

Gaztambide-Fernández, Rubén A. (2002). Reggae, ganja, and black bodies: Power, meaning, and the markings of postcolonial Jamaica in Perry Henzell's *The Harder They Come*. *Review of Education, Pedagogy, and Cultural Studies*, 24(4), 353–76.

Gilroy, Paul. (1992[1987]). *There Ain't no Black in the Union Jack: The Cultural Politics of Race and Nation*. London: Routledge.

Gray, Obika. (2004). *Demeaned but Empowered: The Social Power of the Urban Poor in Jamaica*. Kingston: University of the West Indies Press.

Harriott, Anthony. (2008). *Organized Crime and Politics in Jamaica: Breaking the Nexus*. Kingston: Canoe Press.

Henzell, Perry (dir.). (1972). *The Harder They Come*. Kingston: Island Films.

Hope, Donna P. (2006). *Inna di Dancehall: Popular Culture and the Politics of Identity in Jamaica*. Kingston: University of the West Indies Press.

Is Jamaica's most wanted man like Robin Hood? *AOL News*, 24 May 2010. Available at http://www.aolnews.com/2010/05/24/is-christopher-dudus-coke-a-jamaican-robin-hood/ [accessed March 2011].

Jaffe, Rivke. (forthcoming). The popular culture of illegality: Crime and the politics of aesthetics in urban Jamaica. *Anthropological Quarterly*.

Jamaica security forces storm 'drugs lord' stronghold. *BBC News*, 25 May 2010. Available at http://www.bbc.co.uk/news/mobile/10148973 [accessed March 2011].

Meeks, Brian. (2007). *Envisioning Caribbean Futures: Jamaican Perspectives*. Kingston: University of the West Indies Press.

Oxford English Dictionary. 2nd edn. (1989). (eds J. A. Simpson and E. S. C. Weiner), Additions 1993–97 (eds John Simpson and Edmund Weiner; Michael Proffitt) and 3rd edn (in progress) Mar. 2000– (ed. John Simpson). OED Online. Oxford University Press. http://oed.com [accessed May 2011].

Roberts, John W. (1989). *From Trickster to Badman: The Black Folk Hero in Slavery and Freedom*. Philadelphia: University of Pennsylvania Press.

Rohlehr, Gordon. (1973). An award winning film about Jamaica today ... in the language of Kingston's streets. *Tapia*, 17 June, 6–9.

Sives, Amanda. (2010). *Elections, Violence and the Democratic Process in Jamaica, 1944–2007*. Kingston: Ian Randle.

Thelwell, Michael. (1992). *The Harder They Come*: From film to novel. In Mdbye B. Cham (ed.), *Ex-Iles: Essays on Caribbean Cinema*. Trenton, NJ: Africa World Press.

This is not Somalia, we hope. *Jamaica Gleaner*, 6 September 2009. Available at http://jamaica-gleaner.com/gleaner/20090906/cleisure/cleisure1.html [accessed May 2011].

Thomas, Deborah A. (2005). *Modern Blackness: Nationalism, Globalization, and the Politics of Culture in Jamaica*. Durham, NC: Duke University Press.

Toll from Jamaica violence climbs to 73. *Reuters*, 27 May 2010. Available at http://www.reuters.com/article/2010/05/27/us-jamaica-emergency-idUSTRE 64Q6BP20100527 [accessed March 2011].

Warner, Keith Q. (2000). *On Location: Cinema and Film in the Anglophone Caribbean*. London: Macmillan.

Younger, Prakash. (2005). Historical experience in *The Harder They Come*. *Social Text*, 82(23:1), 43–63.

3.4

Neurotecs: Detectives, Disability and Cognitive Exceptionality in Contemporary Fiction

Stuart Murray

The rise of disability studies as a noted feature of criticism within the humanities is a process dating from the mid-1990s. The foundations of critical approaches contained within this emerging subject area come from attitudes inherited from social science perspectives, notably a commitment to political action: Davis (1997:1) has stated that 'The exciting thing about disability studies is that it is both an academic field of inquiry and an area of political activity'. Aligned with this is a desire not to see disability in the traditional categories with which it is often associated, namely absence, lack or loss. These categories constitute the predominant manner through which disability is usually played out in fictional texts, particularly as a metaphor that nearly always relates to ableist concerns and paradigms, or as a prosthetic narrative device in which non-disabled concerns are propped up and relativised by the use of disabled characters. In their seminal work on cultural representations of the disabled, Mitchell and Snyder (2000:127) note not only that disability is seen to function as 'the master trope of human disqualification in modernity', but also that, used in such a tropic fashion, 'disability pervades literary narrative, first as a stock feature of characterization and, second, as an opportunistic metaphorical device' (Mitchell and Snyder 2000:47). Such opportunism is common in narratives of all forms and contributes to a view of the disabled that is uninformed and prejudiced. As we shall see, this takes a particular form in relation to detective narratives, where stock characters with disabilities are frequently integral to the techniques of crime storytelling.

At the same time, however, critical disability studies also operate to conceive of disability as a mode of *difference*, and often productive difference, that counters the prejudices that come with the bulk of standard disability representation. This chapter stems from this kind of affirmatist stance towards representation, one that emphasises human diversity and a notion of the exceptional individual as opposed to the rigid categories of 'abled' and 'disabled'. In particular, it seeks to recognise an idea of *neurodiversity* in contemporary detective fiction by illustrating, through the use of two novels – Jonathan Lethem's 1999 *Motherless Brooklyn* and Mark Haddon's 2003 *The Curious Incident of the Dog in the Night-Time* – how a productive sense of cognitive difference engages with a number of the classic tropes of detective writing. Both texts offer storytelling methods that not only revise the notion of the detective hero, but also create spaces for complex understandings of disabled difference.

A vital context for this discussion comes with the recognition that the years since the start of the twenty-first century have seen the notable appearance of what we might term 'neuronovels', texts that increasingly explore questions of the individual, and of individual agency in particular, in terms of the brain rather than the mind, and offer a move from an interest in *psychology* to one in *neurology* to explain motive and action. Roth (2009) has characterised this move as being a 'shift away from environmental and relational theories of personality back to the study of brains themselves, as the source of who we are'. To do this, the fictions in question frequently concentrate on neurobehavioural conditions or syndromes, often those that have come to prominence in the last 20 years or so, and now occupy a place in our social imaginaries unthinkable just a few decades ago. Recent examples of such fictions include Ian McEwan's 1997 novel *Enduring Love*, which discusses de Clérambault's syndrome or erotomania, and his later novel *Saturday*, published in 2005, which portrays Huntington's disease as well as having a neurologist as its central character. In American writing, the tendency is even more apparent. Benjamin Kunkel's *Indecision* (2005) revolves around Abulia, sometimes known as Blocq's disease, which is a diminished motivation disorder, while both Richard Powers's *The Echo Maker* (2006) and Rivka Galchen's *Atmospheric Disturbances* (2008) are centred around Capgras syndrome, in which an individual believes that a loved one has been replaced by a double. Joshua Ferris's *The Unnamed* (2010) even provocatively invents the condition of 'benign idiopathic perambulation' in its representation of a central character forced, against his will, to walk without stopping. It is possible to extend this idea of the neuronovel further and see a range of post 9/11 novels from America – including Don DeLillo's *Falling Man* (2007) and Jonathan Safran Foer's *Extremely Loud and Incredibly Close* (2005) – as being texts dominated by forms of post-traumatic stress disorder. Here, narratives use neurobehavioural syndromes in order to offer ways into the analysis of contemporary trauma.

The novels by Lethem and Haddon could also have joined this list: the former with a narrator – Lionel Essrog – who has Tourette's syndrome; and the latter where Christopher Boone, the 15-year-old narrator, has a neurobehavioural condition that is never actually mentioned in the text, but is clearly a form of high-functioning autism or Asperger's syndrome. In terms of a linkage to detective fiction, both texts declare themselves to be crime novels: at a pivotal point in Lethem's novel (examined in detail later), his narrator Lionel Essrog declares that '[i]t seemed possible that I was a detective on a case' (Lethem 1999:132), while Christopher firmly declares on the fifth page of that book that '[t]his is a murder mystery novel' (Haddon 2003:3). In addition, the centrality of the detective genre to both novels is underscored by the fact that the title for Haddon's text is taken from Arthur Conan Doyle's 1894 Sherlock Holmes story 'Silver Blaze' and is a line from Holmes that proves pivotal to the solving of the case depicted there, while Lethem's book was the winner of the 2000 Gold Dagger award, given annually by the Crime Writer's Association for the best crime novel.

In truth, though, if we expand the idea of 'the detective', then a number of the other neuronovels mentioned above could fall into the category of 'detection' and 'crime'. This would be especially true of Foer's *Extremely Loud and Incredibly Close*, in which protagonist Oskar searches New York for the meaning to a key that he believes will help him understand the death of his father in 9/11, or Powers's and Galchen's books, in which – because of Capgras syndrome – the central characters believe that a crime has been committed and seek to understand why a loved one has been taken from them. In the loosest of all possible characterisations of 'the detective', we could even see something like Kunkel's *Indecision* being relevant here, as protagonist Dwight Wilmerding undertakes a search for himself in the midst of his indecisiveness. With Lethem and Haddon, however, we are squarely in the realm of detective fiction and, especially in the case of Haddon, not simply fiction that details the solving of a mystery (the initial puzzle of who kills a local neighbour's dog turns into the more meaningful question of where Christopher's mother has gone), but also writing that relies on the idea of the *forms and structures* of detective fiction to support that central plot device.

Traditionally, the place of disabled or impaired characters in crime narratives is either that of the silent or constrained witness, unable to communicate vital evidence, or of the 'differently abled' detective, granted a particular type of insight precisely because of a disability.

Examples of the former range from 'Jeff' Jeffries (James Stewart) in Alfred Hitchcock's US 1954 *Rear Window* (a role reprised by a disabled Christopher Reed in a television remake released in 1998) to Bruce Beresford's US 1994 film *Silent Fall*, in which an autistic boy (Ben Faulkner) has witnessed the murder of his parents but, seemingly 'locked in' by his condition, is prevented from communicating it. In the latter category, we might think of Sherlock Holmes himself, increasingly seen in terms of Asperger's syndrome since the popularisation of that term from the mid-1990s onwards, or television detectives such as the central protagonists of *Ironside* (1967–75) or *Monk* (2002–09), in which a specific disabled difference – here wheelchair use and OCD respectively – becomes an asset in detection. Similarly, the quadriplegic Lincoln Rhyme, the hero in the series of books by American author Jeffrey Deaver, is a figure whom Jakubowitz and Meekosha (2004) have labelled a 'crime scene savant [...] a man without a body [who] becomes a brain unmoved by passions outside his craft'. Added to this, the representation of protagonists in this latter category usually stresses some form of individual 'heroic' post-traumatic struggle in which the character wrestles with the event or circumstance that led to the disablement and the estrangement that ensues. As is often the case in disability narratives more widely, the idea of 'overcoming' the disability is central to the depiction.

Whether these figures are viewed 'negatively' or 'positively' in terms of disability representation, they arguably all conform to the prosthetic idea of characterisation and metaphor outlined earlier with reference to the work of Mitchell and Snyder. The silent witness character promotes a fascination with disabled difference that renders disability a spectacle and enacts a form of voyeurism, in which it is always assumed that the consumer spectator or reader is non-disabled; while the 'special powers' of the differently abled detective function in terms of a 'compensation' narrative through which, as in the Lincoln Rhyme example with its stress on mental ability and savantism, the loss of one faculty allows for the development of another, more distinctive ability. Both negative and positive depictions ultimately speak of a non-disabled *desire* on the part of a reader or viewer to give in to the impulse to view disability as a wonder. As Garland-Thomson (2002:57) has observed, such a process 'creates disability as a state of absolute difference rather than simply one more variation in human form'. Here, the disabled detective or witness is simply one more element in the ongoing acts of fictional narrativisation that, in the complex set of ideologies that surround disability, invite sympathy, pity or amazement, all reductive encounters when seen in the frame of the politics of disability representation.

In the novels by Lethem and Haddon, by way of contrast, the central generic spaces of the crime narrative become locations for ideas of disability that refute the reductive, and rather outline the cognitively disabled as a complex space of human subjectivity. Certainly the *idea* of being a detective, and a writer of detective stories, is a vital one in *The Curious Incident of the Dog in the Night-Time*. The novel starts with Christopher's discovery of a dead dog 'lying on the grass in the middle of the lawn' (Haddon 2003:1) outside a neighbour's house. As he observes:

> Its eyes were closed. It looked as if it were running on its side, the way dogs run when they think they are chasing a cat in a dream. But the dog was not running or asleep. The dog was dead. There was a garden fork sticking out of the dog. (Haddon 2003:1)

This is the original crime for which Christopher attempts to find an answer, that which turns him into both a detective and a writer of that detection. As he says:

> [i]n a murder mystery novel someone has to work out who the murderer is and then catch them. It is a puzzle. If it is a good puzzle you can sometimes work out the answer before the end of the book. (Haddon 2003:5)

When assessing the workings of other kinds of fiction, he instead notes: 'I don't like proper novels, because they are lies about things which didn't happen and they make me feel shaky and scared' (Haddon 2003:25).

Picking up on Christopher's need for structure, Gilbert, in a 2005 article in the journal *Children's Literature in Education*, observes that 'Detective fiction offers Christopher a way to understand and frame his own story' and that such fiction also 'supports [his] desire for a highly delineated existence. In writing his detective story he attempts to read and shape the apparent random nature of the world around him' (Gilbert 2005:243, 244). Underlying Gilbert's reasoning here is, of course, the foundational idea of *logic*, specifically in this instance the argument that Christopher's autism allows him to see detection as a series of logical puzzles. Gilbert (2005:245) also concentrates on what she terms Christopher's 'emotional dislocation', a trope that she aligns with Peter Hühn's (1987, cited in Gilbert 2005:243) classic idea that the seminal detective hero is defined by what he terms a 'cold detachment from all human concerns'. From within this reading, Haddon's novel allows for any number of knowing comparisons with Sherlock Holmes as it progresses.

Gilbert's analysis reveals some of the ways in which the novel works, but it is fundamentally a limited approach that itself is a kind of critical prosthesis. Haddon's novel uses Christopher's cognitive difference, and his detecting ability, to produce a more subtle and nuanced version of agency than her commentary is able to see. Crucially, Gilbert's reading reinforces the various stereotypes of autism (emotionally detached, only interested in logic and puzzles, highly inflexible, always resistant to change, alien, inhuman and so on) that proliferate in the fascination our contemporary culture has with cognitive difference in general and autism in particular. Haddon does use such character tropes in his representation of Christopher, but he does so, crucially, in order to subvert their power as disability stereotypes and to stress the wider concept of human neurological variation. In ways that Gilbert does not spot, Christopher also subtly revises what might be the commonly assumed conclusions regarding the manner in which Arthur Conan Doyle's hero, and his texts, are seen to operate. In a conversation with Siobhan, his support assistant at the school he attends, Christopher talks of his preference for reading Sherlock Holmes stories and, in response to her point that 'readers cared more about people than dogs' and that it was people, and not dogs, who were the victims in *The Hound of the Baskervilles*, he simply notes that 'two dogs were killed' in the story: 'the hound itself and James Mortimer's spaniel' (Haddon 2003:6). This kind of detailed revision is, in the careful hands of Haddon, less a point about Christopher's use of logic, and more an illustration of the alternative viewpoint that stems from a neurodiverse perspective. It is, in an almost unobtrusive way, a small act of disability studies criticism, one in which the normality of a disabled outlook allows for fresh insight into the workings of the world of the non-disabled majority.

Equally, though Christopher's use of logic is clear from just about every page of the narrative, the assertion that it entirely governs not only his actions but his feelings and capacities to engage with others is a misreading. A central theory revolving around autism, as outlined by psychologist Baron-Cohen (1995), is that those with the condition are 'mindblind' or lack a 'theory of mind', and as such are incapable of understanding or theorising the thoughts or emotions of others. Yet, as we saw in the above description of the dead dog taken from the novel's first paragraph, Christopher has no problems with such cognitive processing and is fully able to imagine the dog's processes of dreaming. This kind of empathising is, in fact, something that Christopher practises a number of times in the novel, especially in relation to thinking about his father's feelings. It is clear evidence that Christopher is not some kind of automaton directed by logic alone.

The mystery of the dead dog transforms into that of the missing mother, and comes to revolve around Christopher's journey to London to find the mother his father told him was dead. Here too, this act may have the outward appearance of being structured by logic, but it is clearly at heart an *emotional* process. Coming to London, he tells his mother, was 'really frightening' and was a process prompted by his belief that 'Father killed Wellington [the dog] with a garden fork and I'm frightened of him' (Haddon 2003:234). Christopher's fear is clearly an understandable emotional outcome that follows his earlier discovery of his mother's existence through a hidden hoard of letters that she has written to him but he has never seen, something that left him 'sick' and 'curled up in a ball' (Haddon 2003:142, 141) on his bed, positions resonant of an emotional reaction that he may not understand, but that is clear to any reader.

In addition, it is precisely because the whole of *The Curious Incident of the Dog in the Night-Time* is narrated by Christopher that observations like those above about fear and emotion pertain to a subjective position that is normative and natural, and not wondrous or spectacular. Having the whole of the novel in Christopher's voice means that his difference becomes normalised; as Osteen (2008:39) notes: 'his autism is an essential part of his nature, and his decisions and developments emerge through, and not in spite of, his condition'. Making Christopher not only the central protagonist (a position, as we have seen, not unusual with respect to disabled detectives) but also the *source* of all the information that we as readers receive about his quest creates a dynamic by which, as a disabled character, he is not made metaphorical or prosthetic.

Motherless Brooklyn reinforces this point about a productive view of a neurobehavioural difference, and does so in similar terms. In Lethem's novel, as mentioned before, the narrator, Lionel Essrog, has Tourette's; in the tough working-class districts of Brooklyn in which the narrative is set, his condition inevitably marks him out as an individual open to persecution. The location of the novel is a place characterised by a 'jumble of stuff at the clotted entrance to the ancient, battered borough', somewhere officially 'Nowhere, a place strenuously ignored in passing through to Somewhere Else' and populated by boys 'in their morose thuggish glory' (Lethem 1999:37, 36). When his friend and mentor Frank Minna, the leader of the local group of youths affectionately known as the 'Minna Men', is killed, Lionel (nicknamed 'freakshow' throughout because of his tics and verbal outbursts) becomes the main agent in tracking down the murderer. In the following scene, approximately halfway through the novel, Lionel's Tourette's is conflated with his new, central role as detective:

> There are days when I get up in the morning and stagger into the bathroom and begin running water and then I look up and I don't even recognize my own toothbrush in the mirror. I mean, the object looks strange, oddly particular in its design, strange tapered handle and slotted miter-cut bristles, and I wonder if I've ever looked at it closely before or whether someone snuck in overnight and substituted this new toothbrush for my old one. I have this relationship to objects in general – they will sometimes become uncontrollably new and vivid to me, and I don't know whether this is a symptom of Tourette's or not. I've never seen it described in the literature. Here's the strangeness of having a Tourette's brain then: no control in my personal experiment of self. What might be only strangeness must always be auditioned to the domain of symptom, just as symptoms always push into other domains, demanding the chance to audition for their moment of acuity or relevance, their brief shot – coulda been a contender! – at centrality. Personalityness. There's a lot of traffic in my head, and it's two-way.
>
> This morning's strangeness was refreshing though. More than refreshing – revelatory. I woke early, having failed to draw my curtains. The wall above my bed and the table with melted candle, tumbler quarter full of melted ice, and sandwich crumbs from my ritual snack now caught in a blaze of white sunlight, like the glare of a projector's bulb before the film is threaded. It seemed possible I was the first awake in the world, possible the world was new. I dressed in my best suit, donned Minna's watch instead of my own, and clipped his beeper to my hip. Then I made myself coffee and toast, scooped the long-shadowed crumbs off the table, sat and savored breakfast, marveling at the richness of existence with each step. The radiator whined and sneezed and I imitated its sounds out of sheer joy, rather than helplessness. Perhaps I'd been expecting that Minna's absence would snuff the world, or at least Brooklyn, out of existence. That a sympathetic dimming would occur. Instead I'd woken into the realization that I was Minna's successor and avenger, that the city shone with clues.
>
> It seemed possible I was a detective on a case. (Lethem 1999:131–2)

As Lionel literally takes up Minna's position as central protagonist, his 'Tourettic brain' produces his daily 'strangeness' as 'refreshing' and 'revelatory' and has him imitating the noises from his radiator as an act of stress-free pleasure. What is indisputable is that, with half the novel remaining, Lethem visibly moves Lionel centre stage – the freak becomes the hero, and in doing so his Tourette's becomes anything but peripheral. On one level, the fact that his condition is seminal to the methods by which he will solve the crime of Frank's murder is an extension of the foundational idea about the detective's 'special powers', but there are subtle differences here. Lionel's linkage of his Tourette's to his capacity to solve the murder is no way a form of compensation, as the above example of pleasure makes clear, nor does it provide any kind of spectacle to the reader, a remarkable achieve-ment given the explosive and public nature of Tourette's itself; indeed, the novel contains a carefully presented critique of such processes of spectacle and misunderstanding. The lead police detective in the case ignores Lionel, assuming that, because of his disability, he can have no productive part to play in the investigation, while one character observes to Lionel that 'because you were crazy everyone thought you were stupid' (Lethem 1999:300). Since Lionel is frequently seen, by those characters who do not know him well, as a spectacle and a freak *within* the novel – he is, as he says of himself, 'a carnival barker, an auctioneer, a downtown performance artist, a speaker in tongues, a senator drunk on filibuster. *I've got Tourette's*. My mouth won't quit' (Lethem 1999:1, italics in original) – he enables the deconstruction of that process of voyeurism in the reading act. As with Christopher, he comes to own his trajectory as an agent of detection, and crucially functions as the arbiter of what that agency means. 'It's a Tourette's thing' he says at one point, speaking to the reader, 'you wouldn't understand' (Lethem 1999:283).

In addition, the novel makes a series of productive metaphorical associations between disability and place in a manner that develops and strengthens this seminal point about individual agency. New York is, Lethem asserts, a Tourettic city: its lights, sounds and activities all mirror the kind of 'bubbling' of language that Lionel feels within himself. As he says about Court Street in Brooklyn: 'my verbal Tourette's [was] flowering at last. Like Court Street, I seethed behind the scenes with languages and conspiracies, inversions of logic, sudden jerks and jabs of insults' (Lethem 1999:57). This is an environment in which Tourette's not only makes sense, but is a condition both natural and suited to its surroundings. In a similar vein, Lionel's description of the Papaya Czar restaurant, in Manhattan's Upper East Side, emphasises its sense of place *through* the logic of what we can call Tourettic association:

> The Papaya Czar on Eighty-sixth Street and Third Avenue is my kind of place – bright orange and yellow signs pasted on every available surface screaming, PAPAYA IS GOD'S GREATEST GIFT TO MAN'S HEALTH! OUR FRANKFURTERS ARE THE WORKING MAN'S FILET MIGNON! WE'RE POLITE NEW YORKERS, WE SUPPORT MAYOR GIULIANI! And so on. Papaya Czar's walls are so layered with language that I find myself immediately calmed inside their doors, as though I've stepped into a model interior of my own skull. (Lethem 1999:160)

The fabric of the city mirrors the *normality* of Tourettic difference, especially in the manner in which it is 'calming'. Representing the experience of New York from within a disability perspective, the inside of Lionel's 'skull' creates an environment that is not full of barriers that are to be overcome (a common narrative even for detectives with special powers, and a standard disability trope). Rather, the sensory stimuli as described here create for Lionel an efficacious location in which to operate, for all that it might be a different version of belonging than for those at other points on the neurological spectrum.

It is noticeable that this location, and the voice of disabled difference that defines it, produces a productive version of Lionel as detective. Throughout the novel, he is continually self-aware about his Tourette's and the benefits it might bring. As he says:

> Tourette's teaches you what people will ignore and forget, teaches you to see the reality-knitting mechanism people employ to tuck away the intolerable, the incongruous, the disruptive – it teaches you this because you're the one lobbing the intolerable, incongruous and disruptive their way. (Lethem 1999:43)

As such, Lionel makes a case for the ways in which his ability to concentrate and focus on language, for example, make him particularly good on stake-outs and wire taps. In the end, the solving of the case hinges on a verbal clue that Minna passes on to Lionel as he is dying, knowing that Lionel will work to decipher it. 'Crazy', freakish, Tourettic Lionel is, then, a productive detective because of, not in spite of, his disability (to echo Osteen's comments about Christopher and his agency).

To move back to Christopher with the example of Lionel in mind, it is clear that *his* detecting abilities in *The Curious Incident of the Dog in the*

Night-Time come because of the centrality of his autism to his method and not, as Gilbert suggests, through his use of detective fiction as a prop to offset the worst aspects of his condition. In his discussion of his own name, for example, Christopher is aware of the ways in which he is frequently related to other meanings, and other narratives, through association: 'My name is a metaphor', he observes, 'It means *carrying Christ* and [...] it was the name given to St Christopher because he carried Jesus Christ across a river' (Haddon 2003:20, italics in original). However, as he goes on:

> Mother used to say that it meant Christopher was a nice name because it was a story about being kind and helpful, but I do not want my name to mean a story about being kind and helpful. I want my name to mean me. (Haddon 2003:20)

In wanting his name to correspond to himself, in asserting this kind of autonomy, Christopher also outlines the parameters of the kind of detective he is. As he says at the end of the novel, in a formulation that carries a clear sense of disabled pride: 'I solved the mystery of Who Killed Wellington? and I found my mother and I was brave and I wrote a book and that means I can do anything' (Haddon 2003:268). Like Lionel, Christopher is a certain kind of presence in this particular detective novel, one that revises the very ideas of what a central detecting figure might be. Roth (2009) talks of the neuronovel in terms of a 'specter' that is 'haunting the contemporary novel', a terminology of particular interest given that Lennard J. Davis has spoken of disability in exactly such terms of the 'spectral'. For Davis, 'the spectre' is the presence of the disabled person that cannot be denied. Such spectres, he writes, 'may be crippled, deaf, blind, spasming or chronically ill', but they are 'clearly no longer willing to be relegated to the fringes of culture and academic study' (Davis 2002:34). With its notion of the 'haunting' disability figure, such a claim offers a challenge both to the wide readership for crime fiction that might simply skip over the disabled character, assuming that it has only secondary significance, and those who work critically in crime writing, who might equally fail to see disability in terms other than those of metaphor or wonder.

Haddon and Lethem's novels mark the centrality of cognitive difference to their narratives of detection but, in doing so, they not only redress the balance in a genre that has, in the past, all too often seen the disabled character in such stories as being only a prosthetic device. They also stress an emerging pattern of human diversity and autonomy that comes with spectrum conditions such as Tourette's and autism. If those with such conditions often lack autonomy in the political sense of being recognised by others, they nevertheless, as Francis observes, practise agency in the sense of

> being able to value, being able to reason, being able to resist impulses, being able to manage and order one's life, being able to put one's plans into practice [and] being able to participate in moral deliberation. (Francis 2009:202)

This is true of both Christopher and Lionel, and if they partake in the increasing fascination with neurology that marks the very contemporary era, they do so on terms that they themselves create. The investigation of psychological depth and motive has traditionally been one way to tell the detective story, but there is no doubt that neurological *range* is now providing another. When Hercule Poirot talked of his 'little grey cells' in outlining his detective powers, he was maybe on to more than we first thought.

References

Baron-Cohen, Simon. (1995). *Mindblindness: An Essay on Autism and Theory of Mind*. Cambridge, MA: MIT Press.

Davis, Lennard J. (1997). Introduction. In Lennard J. Davis (ed.), *The Disability Studies Reader*. New York: Routledge.

Davis, Lennard J. (2002). *Bending Over Backwards: Disability, Dismodernism, and Other Difficult Positions*. New York: New York University Press.

DeLillo, Don. (2008). *Falling Man*. London: Picador.

Ferris, Joshua. (2010). *The Unnamed*. London: Viking.

Foer, Jonathan Safran. (2006). *Extremely Loud and Incredibly Close*. London: Penguin.

Francis, Leslie P. (2009). Understanding autonomy in the light of intellectual disability. In Kimberley Brownlee and Adam Cureton (eds), *Disability and Disadvantage*. Oxford: Oxford University Press.

Galchen, Rivka. (2009). *Atmospheric Disturbances*. London: HarperPerennial.

Garland-Thomson, Rosemarie. (2002). The politics of staring: Visual rhetorics of disability in popular photography. In Sharon L. Snyder, Brenda Jo Brueggemann and Rosemarie Garland-Thomson (eds), *Disability Studies: Enabling the Humanities*. New York. Modern Language Association.

Gilbert, Ruth. (2005). Watching the detectives: Mark Haddon's *The Curious Incident of the Dog in the Night-Time* and Kevin Brooks' *Martyn Pig*. *Children's Literature in Education*, 36(3), 241–53.

Haddon, Mark. (2003). *The Curious Incident of the Dog in the Night-Time*. London: Jonathan Cape.

Hühn, Peter. (1987). The detective as reader: Narrativity and reading concepts in detective fiction. *Modern Fiction Studies*, 33, 451–66.

Jakubowitz, Andrew and Helen Meekosha. (2004). Detecting disability: Moving beyond metaphor in the crime fiction of Jeffrey Deaver. *Disability Studies Quarterly*, 24(2). Available at www.dsq-sds.org/article/view/482/659 [accessed March 2011].

Kunkel, Benjamin. (2006). *Indecision*. London: Picador.

Lethem, Jonathan. (1999). *Motherless Brooklyn*. London: Faber and Faber.

McEwan, Ian. (1998). *Enduring Love*. London: Vintage.

McEwan, Ian. (2005). *Saturday*. London: Jonathan Cape.

Mitchell, David and Sharon Snyder. (2000). *Narrative Prosthesis: Disability and the Dependencies of Discourse*. Ann Arbor: University of Michigan Press.

Osteen, Mark. (2008). Autism and representation: A comprehensive introduction. In Mark Osteen (ed.), *Autism and Representation*. New York: Routledge.

Powers, Richard. (2008). *The Echo Maker*. London: Vintage.

Roth, Marco. (2009). The rise of the neuronovel. *n+1*, 8, 14 September 2009. Available at www.nplusonemag.com/rise-neuronovel [accessed March 2010].

Snyder, Sharon and David Mitchell. (2006). *Cultural Locations of Disability*. Chicago: University of Chicago Press.

4
Constructing Gendered Crime

4.0
Introduction and Rationale

Narratives of crime often bring to light taboos, stereotypes and schemata that relate to gender and sexuality, which is why engaging with such narratives can allow us to question gendered expectations suggested to us as readers. Kate Watson looks at a narrative that deconstructs genre as well as gender-related 'rules', McDermid's *The Mermaids Singing*, all while employing useful metaphors with which the novel can be read. Charlotte Beyer considers feminist crime writers' recent memoirs and journalism, exploring political and sociocultural elements embedded in them, and arguing that such writers identify their writing as 'deviant' itself, while offering positions that are themselves 'marginalised'. Finally, Mandy Koolen also examines gender and touches on images of femininity and sexuality through challenging heteronormativity. She explores sexological beliefs about lesbianism depicted through film, and argues that Jenkin's filmic Wuornos in *Monster* reinforces, among others, an association between lesbianism, deviance and violent criminality. She recommends that the character is instead read in all its contradictions and roundness, very much non-simplistically and non-stereotypically.

4.1

Engendering Violence: Textual and Sexual Torture in Val McDermid's *The Mermaids Singing*

Kate Watson

Val McDermid places *The Mermaids Singing* (1995) and its characters both within and against a prior conception and tradition of crime fiction. *The Mermaids Singing* purposefully contests the classic detective story, which Porter (1981:220) defines as 'a literature of reassurance and conformism'. As McDermid herself comments with reference to this award-winning novel:

> [w]hen I wrote my first serial killer novel [...] it was partly as a reaction against a slew of novels coming out of the US in which hideous violence was meted out to female victims whose only role in the books was to be raped, mutilated, dismembered and strewn across the landscape. Those books were all written by men. I wanted to do things differently, so I chose to write about victims who had a hinterland, who had personalities and who were men. And yes, I wrote clearly about the violence done to them because I believed it was necessary in the context of this book. (McDermid 2009)

The Mermaids Singing embodies the way in which the physical human body and the literary corpus of crime fiction have evolved.

McDermid's novel introduces the characters who, in later novels in the series, will become her recurring investigators: Tony Hill, a clinical psychologist and profiler, and Detective Inspector Carol Jordan. They are brought together to investigate the grotesque mutilation and murder of men in the northern city of Bradfield, with Carol acting as liaison officer between Tony/the Home Office and the police force. The dead bodies are discarded in deliberately misleading places: either in the gay trade district, Temple Fields, or in a notorious pick-up area, Carlton Park. These localities lead Detective Superintendent Tom Cross – who is initially in charge of the murder enquiries and is later taken off the case for misconduct – to presume that the killings are perpetrated by 'a bunch of homicidal poofters' (McDermid 2000[1995]:37). However, Tony and Carol are more intuitive and posit alternative scenarios based on analysis of the bodies and the crime scenes.

The narrative finally reveals that the killer is a male-to-female transsexual named 'Angelica'. In representing such a murderer, I suggest that *The Mermaids Singing* challenges the traditional grand narrative of crime fiction that defines the male as killer and the female as victim. As Skrapec (1993:365) has written, '[o]ur collective sense of security is particularly threatened by the notion of female serial murderers'. Knight (1991:154–5) has described how 'police fiction, with its male violence and its women who are sexually subjugated, either by rape or by knife or often both, is a potent means of normalizing violence'. This more normative equation is scrutinised both by McDermid's novel as a whole and through Angelica's actions. Angelica writes her thoughts and details each murder in a diary, which she hopes will be published posthumously, celebrating what she perceives as her clever actions. Her diary is written in italics, and this first-person, non-gender-specific narrative is interspersed throughout *The Mermaids Singing*.

Angelica's murderous deeds are generated by a complex scenario, in which she uses her job as a phone company's computer systems manager to facilitate, as she states in her diary, '*the task of finding a worthy man to share my life*' (McDermid 2000[1995]:355). Angelica extracts the residential numbers of men who had regularly called sex chat lines in the past year and then cross-references this information against the electoral roll to find which men live alone. She then stalks them and initiates contact via sex phone calls; she takes these disembodied sexual interactions as proof that these men are falling in love with her. However, once the men find a female partner, Angelica perceives this as perfidy requiring draconian punishment (which she video records and finds sexually arousing). Katz (1988:30), in his study of the seductive appeal of crime, defines this reaction as 'the emotional process through which humiliation leads to righteous slaughter'. Skrapec (1993:266), in her discussion of the evolution of the female serial killer, comments that 'this emerging female is "misandropic", decidedly hateful of men. She will seek to punish them for being men, the symbol of her oppressed sense of self.' To some extent, Angelica's murderous rationale correlates with this evolution; I argue that both the gendered-composite Angelica and her creator McDermid attempt to open a discursive space for a female (sexual) serial killer.

Crime and detective fiction are traditionally concerned with crimes that arise from motives generated by family, inheritance and identity. Inheritance, crime, property and rights were common and recurring concerns in the fiction of the Victorian period. The Newgate novels of the 1830s and 1840s dealt with this, as in Ainsworth's *Jack Sheppard* (1839). Lytton's *Night and Morning* (1841) was a mystery revolving around inheritance, as was Collins's *The Woman in White* (1860). A majority of Sherlock Holmes's cases were also related to inheritance and property rather than murder. This conflation of the home and crime recurs later; Rowland (2001:viii) has defined the 'Golden Age' genre as the 'English country-house murder'. *The Mermaids Singing* examines issues surrounding family: Tony has a dysfunctional family history, the psychological effects of which physically affect his body. They leave him, he states, a 'sexual and emotional cripple' (McDermid 2000[1995]:106). Tony was raised by his grandparents, did not have a good relationship with his mother and his father left the family. After Angelica has helped Tony achieve 'the first problem-free sex he'd had for years' (McDermid 2000[1995]:307) via the phone, his narrative explains:

> Tonight, with Angelica, for the first time in his life, Tony had felt a protective care that succoured without smothering. His grandmother, he knew intellectually, had loved him and cared for him, but theirs had never been a demonstrative family, and her love had been brusque and practical, meeting her needs rather than his. The women he'd been involved with in the past had, he now realized, been her emotional doppelgangers. Thanks to Angelica, he dared hope the pattern had been broken. It had caused him enough pain over the years. (McDermid 2000[1995]:308)

Gregoriou (2007:59), discussing deviance in contemporary crime fiction, has detailed the commonplace trope of how 'the detective [...] must engage in transference with the criminal or the patient, must identify with the criminal in order to trace the path back to the original trauma, and hence "the criminal becomes the double of the detective"'. While this mirroring is integral to Tony's compilation of the killer's profile (unbeknown to him the killer is in fact Angelica), McDermid cleverly twists this as Angelica, in this instance, performs the role of therapist.

McDermid uses the interaction between Tony and Angelica to invert another dichotomy: the detective as captor/victim. Simpson, considering sex and romance in lesbian detective fiction, defines the lesbian detective's vulnerability:

> While the rape of the lesbian detective successfully extends and subverts the genre, challenging traditional norms of the invincible detective, it can also be argued to reinforce the stereotype of the lesbian as victim, and negate the agency and subversive capacity of the lesbian detective. Given the rape of the detective occurs almost exclusively in lesbian and gay detective fiction, it may reflect gay and lesbian self-perception of their vulnerable position in society. Textually, it represents an enforced and violent form of 'passing' on which the hetero-patriarchy insists. (Simpson 2009:17)

However, in this case it is the transsexual who is both in a position of power and performing the violating act/s (with sexual intent). While Carol is raped in a later McDermid novel (*The Last Temptation*, 2003), in this instance it is Tony, the male investigator, who is naked and in a vulnerable position. He is held in place by the torture device of '*Squassation and strappado*' (McDermid 2000[1995]:313). Consequently, his controlling grasp over the details of the case is temporarily displaced as the 'female' Angelica shackles him, causing a 'bracelet of bruises round his inflamed wrists' (McDermid 2000[1995]:379) and a 'wrenching rip in his shoulders' (McDermid 2000[1995]:335). Tony must comply with those crime fiction conventions that demand the quelling of the threat of the criminal. He uses his hands to 'grab [...] Angelica's head, banging it hard on the stone floor till her body stopped thrashing' (McDermid 2000[1995]:375) and, acting in self-preservation, stabs Angelica in a parody of sexual penetration. McDermid questions gendered preconceptions throughout the novel. In another example, Sergeant Don Merrick, working undercover walking the streets of Temple Fields, receives a sexual comment about his figure from a gay man. His reaction conveys that '[i]n a moment of dreadful clarity, he realized what women meant when they complained of being treated as objects by men' (McDermid 2000[1995]:126). It is these new insights into viewing gender and sexuality that *The Mermaids Singing* presents.

This notion of recognisable frames of reference and their converse, of being 'drawn out in a question' (McDermid 2000[1995]:345), is seen again in a different and more literal context. Tony, as the profiling and investigative male, thinks about Carol 'as if she were a photograph in a casebook' (McDermid 2000[1995]:85), upholding Bordo's (1997:94) notion that 'the rules for femininity have come to be culturally transmitted more and more through standardized visual images'. This fixed gender portrait is disrupted by modern technology; as Carol's brother Michael points out to her:

> you'll plug in a scanner and scan photographs of yourself and anybody else you want in your game. The computer reads that information, and translates it into the screen images. So instead of Conan the Barbarian leading the quest, it's Carol Jordan. (McDermid 2000[1995]:110)

Technology, text and context here permit Carol to play the leading role in the investigation/quest; her figure can overlay those of her detective predecessors, and she is able to frame her own investigation. The splintered casing of body and text is again paralleled in the events: one offers a distorted mirror image of the other. While Tony's profiling mind seeks to develop the portrait of the criminal 'like a photographic print in developer fluid' (McDermid 2000[1995]:164), his 'fate [is] mirrored in the broken bodies' (McDermid 2000[1995]:386) that Angelica meticulously describes in her diary.

But it is not only Tony who is liminally positioned – Carol, on ascertaining that Tony is also not originally from Bradfield, says 'we're both outsiders' (McDermid 2000[1995]:78). The novel introduces the reader to Carol and her background:

> She'd worked her socks off for the best part of nine years, first to get a good degree and then to justify her place on the promotion fast track. She didn't intend her career to hit the buffers just because she'd made the mistake of opting for a force run by Neanderthals. Her mind made up, Carol stepped out of the shower, shoulders straight, a defiant glint in her green eyes. 'Come on, Nelson,' she said [...] scooping up the muscular bundle of black fur. 'Let's hit the red meat, boy.' (McDermid 2000[1995]:11)

It is a male, Merrick, who 'follow[s] her, waiting for the next set of orders' (McDermid 2000[1995]:20). As a leading female in the police force, Carol is precariously 'walking the [...] tightrope' (McDermid 2000[1995]:32). This is evidenced by Superintendent Cross's comment to her: 'You know your trouble, Inspector? [...] You're not as smart as you like to think you are. One step out of line, lady, and I'll have your guts for a jock strap' (McDermid 2000[1995]:41). As the reporter, Penny Burgess, says to Carol: 'I don't have to tell you what it's like. I work in an office full of guys that are running a book on when I'll make my next cock-up' (McDermid 2000[1995]:30). Yet Carol is strong and mitigates such masculine impositions on her police work.

In a further contestation of masculine dominance, Carol's 'tone of voice and the words she'd chosen [are] a calculated challenge' (McDermid 2000[1995]:73) to the male voice that typically silences the female investigator. It is 'Inspector Jordan [who] always had an answer' (McDermid 2000[1995]:251) and who can use her voice to uncover and decipher the clues of the case. Tony is blinkered by the assumption that '[s]exual or lust murder, in which the act of killing is itself eroticized [...] is held [...] to be an exclusively male phenomenon' (Skrapec 1993:246). It is Carol who can step outside the scripted bounds of patriarchy that blind Tony and ask: 'have you considered the possibility of a transvestite?' (McDermid 2000[1995]:264); '[a]nd you're absolutely convinced that it isn't a woman?' (McDermid 2000[1995]:266). She is also correct in her postulation about the killer's frequency of murders, yet she has to reiterate this: 'For the third time, Carol outlined her idea about the killer importing videos and transforming them into supports for his fantasies' (McDermid 2000[1995]:306). While this questioning solves the case, Carol's voice is, to some extent, muted: Tony dismisses her enquiries about the gender of the killer and Carol's voice, in her challenge to phallocentrism, is overridden by the male.

As a result of this dismissal of the female voice, Tony is later captured by the transsexual Angelica and so reworks the linear voice of the 'straight crime novel' (Munt 1994:24). Tony is implicated in this and so can control it to his advantage; he speaks the words Angelica craves, telling Angelica that he loves her and wants to be with her. Unlike her other victims, Tony conveys an understanding of her mind and position within society:

> You knew you were different [...] but you couldn't work out why at first. Then as you grew up, you realized what it was. You weren't the same as the other boys because you weren't a boy at all. You had no interest in girls sexually, but it wasn't because you were gay. No way. It was because you were really a girl yourself. (McDermid 2000[1995]:359)

This empathy and his feigned sexual appreciation of Angelica's body are factors that help him to bide his time. However, ultimately, it is Carol's deductive dexterity that pieces the puzzle together, and her voicing of this realisation to her colleagues that saves Tony at the crucial moment and ensures the closure demanded by the crime fiction plot.

From its inception, crime and detective fiction has recurrently been described in terms of ingredients and a known recipe. For example, *Punch* satirized the Newgate novel in 1841, drawing attention to its stereotypical 'ingredients', which were later reworked in sensation fiction:

> Take a small boy, charity, factory, carpenter's apprentice, or otherwise, as occasion may serve – stew him down in vice – garnish largely with oaths and flash songs – Boil him in a cauldron of crime and improbabilities. Season equally with good and bad qualities ... petty larceny, affection, benevolence, and burglary, honor and housebreaking, amiability and arson ... Stew down a mad mother – a gang of robbers – several pistols – a bloody knife. Serve up with a couple of murders – and season with a hanging-match. (*Punch* 1841:39)

In this instance, however, the reader is presented with a new concoction. These changes are articulated to the reader by Carol; she rejects being 'fed the official line' (McDermid 2000[1995]:210). Conversely, she utilises and appropriates the 'official line' of Shakespeare's literature to explain the postmodern lines that Angelica is cutting into the victims' bodies. As Carol says to Tony with reference to the frequency of the killings: 'Shakespeare said it. "As if increase of appetite had grown by what it fed on." Am I right?' (McDermid 2000[1995]:268). While Carol is right in her commanding and questioning of food and the new indeterminate sexual body that it feeds, there is still a gendered hierarchy in place dictating that:

> it was acceptable for young male officers to throw up when they were confronted with victims of violent death. They even got sympathy. But in spite of the fact that women were supposed to lack bottle anyway, when female officers chucked up on the margins of crime scenes they instantly lost any respect they'd ever won and became objects of contempt. (McDermid 2000[1995]:18)

The male can throw up and reject meaning, just as Tony discards Carol's question and placement of the killer's sexually fed actions, while the female is bound to contain elements of bodily unease. There is an emptying of the contents of the gendered body, the detecting body and the crime fiction form, as they are perversely filled with vacuity.

This de-familiarisation of criminographic meaning is further unpicked when actual stitching is considered. Thomas Harris's *The Silence of the Lambs* (1988) famously presented the killer Buffalo Bill, who constructed a female skin suit from his victims' skin after being denied sexual readjustment surgery. McDermid extends this concept of a grotesque patchwork and challenges the notion of clothing 'making the man'. Angelica '*cannibalize*[s] *an old-fashioned clothes wringer*' (McDermid 2000[1995]:27) to make an instrument of torture in which to unmake Adam's body. For a later victim, Paul, she explains how to construct a Judas chair by deconstructing the implements of clothing production:

> For the spike, I'd used one of the large cones that cotton yarn used to be wound round on industrial looms. [...] I'd covered it with a thin, flexible sheet of copper, and fastened thin strands of razor wire in a spiral round the outside. (McDermid 2000[1995]:179)

The mechanics of tailoring are literally inside Paul's body, and wrapped with razor wire. A later victim, Gareth, has his cheek '*cut* [...] *to ribbons*' (McDermid 2000[1995]:258). Just as Angelica tailors the victims' bodies to fit her desires, so the text and, implicitly, the crime fiction body of language perform this suture.

Correspondingly, new types of cuts and markings appear. Tony tells his colleagues, and the readers of the text, that Angelica's victims 'all died from having their throats cut' (McDermid 2000[1995]:34). The cut, however, becomes deeper and increases in savagery in response to the escalating aggression of the killer: Damien's death wound is posthumously described as a 'deep slash to the throat [that] had virtually decapitated the man' (McDermid 2000[1995]:34). His body and throat serve as a synecdoche for the bodies of crime fiction, gender and language, all of which are attached to but simultaneously detached from their previous connections. The continuity of crime fiction and its accommodation of cultural change are located in the Thomas De Quincey epigraphs (taken from 'On murder considered as one of the fine arts' 1827) in the novel: 'The fact was, I "fancied" him, and resolved to commence business upon his throat' (McDermid 2000[1995]:70). De Quincey's epigraph vocalises the seemingly well-established transaction of throat cutting between murderer and victim; it is depicted as a smooth-running business and locates McDermid's text as the descendant of a long line of crime fiction forebears. This lineage is partially disjointed by McDermid: she is suggesting that everything changes and yet nothing does.

The consumability and essence of the crime fiction text are, in a world of 'un-knowability of essences or identities' (Garber 1997[1991]:187), transmogrified into a strong taste of fear that the reader – and contemporary culture – is unable to digest completely. As Probyn (2000:63) remarks, food 'moves about all the time. It constantly shifts registers; from the sacred to the everyday, from metaphor to materiality; it is the most common and elusive of matters.' Connolly's dead body embodies this: '[l]ogic screamed that a body so broken should be an island in a lake of gore, like an ice cube in a Bloody Mary' (McDermid 2000[1995]:33). The body of the victim, instead of being an ingredient in a familiar cocktail of crime fiction, is so broken that it can hardly be read. Damien's corpse, in a society that has an 'obsession with healthy eating' (McDermid 2000[1995]:165), is clean and devoid of blood. Angelica's reconfiguring of him is indefinable: 'His penis had been severed and thrust into his mouth. His torso was branded from chest to groin in a bizarre, random pattering of starburst burns' (McDermid 2000[1995]:87). The attachments for a cake-icing kit have here been utilised to 'decorate' Damien's body. The desire to eat in order to satisfy hunger is transposed onto the need to destroy in order to sate sexual desire. As Freud (1991[1921]:121) writes regarding the Oedipus complex, identity and the concurrent admiration and wish to remove the father, '[i]t behaves like a derivative of the first, *oral* phase of the organization of the libido, in which the object that we long for and prize is assimilated by eating and is in that way annihilated as such'. This is similar in the sense that Angelica admires her victims but then has to remove them once they inadvertently threaten and rebuff her sense of female identity. Angelica's actions on her male victims challenge the more typical construction of women as meat, seen in Angela Carter's (1979) *The Bloody Chamber* and Carol J. Adams's (1990) *The Sexual Politics of Meat*.

Damien's identity, gender and sexual body are questioned, but on a dangerous and unpalatable scale: he is fed his own penis. This grotesque parody of oral sex expounds how, as Plain (2001:232) writes, 'flesh becomes meat and sex mutates into butchery'. The deeply entrenched, gendered textual assumption in *The Mermaids Singing* that in medieval culture '*it was OK to use implements of torture on women*' (McDermid 2000[1995]:178) is, in the social world of the text, denaturalised and reversed as 'Suck marks. Like love bites' (McDermid 2000[1995]:83) appear on the masculine body. In this instance, it is the male victim who is tortured and brutally consumed by a different type of desire that is incited by '*[t]he taste of betrayal*' (McDermid 2000[1995]:67).

In McDermid's text, there are different voices using and fracturing the transcripts of crime fiction. Angelica – the abject transsexual killer – creates narrative rupture by interpolating her italicised writing and thought processes within the purportedly hegemonic text of the police procedural crime novel. This contests Todorov's (1977:44) narratological delineation that '[t]he first story, that of the crime, ends before the second begins'. While the murderer/unreliable narrator's thoughts and perspective were employed by Charles Brockden Brown, James Hogg, Edgar Allan Poe and Wilkie Collins in the eighteenth and nineteenth centuries, and by Agatha Christie's narrator/killer Dr. Sheppard in *The Murder of Roger Ackroyd* (1926), this *topos* is further manipulated by McDermid. Angelica flaunts what Allan defines as the role of textuality and criminality:

> Any reader familiar with detective fiction will recognize that the primary concern of the criminal is to remove all signifiers of the crime. Thus the story of the criminal is dominated by a desire to repress the textuality at its very center. It is, furthermore, exactly this repressed material that the detective seeks to reveal. (Allan 2006:49)

Angelica, however, is the antithesis of repression and vividly expresses her desires and crimes via her rhetoric. The separation of Angelica's italicised language from the main, regulated text is not as holistic as first presented; as the text accelerates towards its climax between Tony and Angelica, there are not disparate chapters separating Angelica's thoughts and writing from the discourse of the law. It is only on page 358, when Angelica has captured Tony, that the narratives coalesce. In fact, this criminal discourse is valorised and the first 'Angelica' section, 'From 3½" Disc Labelled: Backup.007; File Love.001' (McDermid 2000[1995]:1), is on the first page of the novel and precedes 'Chapter One', which introduces Tony Hill.

Angelica's discourse imitates the events written in the policed sections of the novel; she reads books on serial killers and both uses and subverts the police form in her stalking surveillance of her victims. Assisted by a piping-hot icing set, Angelica tells her fourth victim, a police officer, Damien, that *'I'm going to question you the way you question your suspects'* (McDermid 2000[1995]:297). Consequently, the divided textual sections of the criminal and police in the novel equally disturb and jar each other. This increasingly textual bodily inability to touch on the meanings is most explicit in the Christmas card to the newspaper that Angelica writes with Gareth's blood:

> *Inside one, with a fountain pen, a stencil set and Gareth's blood, I'd written in block capitals, '[...] YOUR EXCLUSIVE CHRISTMAS GIFT IS WAITING IN THE SHRUBBERY OF CARLTON PARK [...] COMPLIMENTS*

OF THE SEASON FROM SANTA CLAWS.' It wasn't easy to write with the blood; it kept congealing on the nib, which I had to clean every few letters.
(McDermid 2000[1995]:256)

This grotesque lettering usurps 'clean', readable, precut and '*stencilled*' discursive meanings. It can be read as an extension and requisition of the cryptic crossword employed in Golden Age crime fiction, that 'consists of complicated wordplay [...] with completion of the puzzle involving a battle of wits between clue-setter and solver' (Horsley 2005:14). Examining transgender characters in detective fiction, Betz (2009:23) comments that '[t]he investigation's resolution can only be achieved when the proper identifications have been made. The transgender character calls into question not only the outcome but the process of the investigation as well.' Yet there is a resistance to closure, as Tony's last words, and the final line of the narrative, are: 'You've won, haven't you, Angelica? [...] You wanted me and now you've got me' (McDermid 2000[1995]:387). The text ends on an open note, and the dead transsexual killer maintains his/her elusive control over text and protagonist as her psychological marks and a copy of her diary (found after her house is searched) haunt him.

The digested 'demonstrative family' (McDermid 2000[1995]:308) of images and contents of the crime fiction and the gendered corpus are here ripped apart by the bastardised offspring of prior forms. Mailer's (1967:13) gendered placing of the novel within the literary family as '"the Great Bitch"; writing is fucking and mastering her, good writing is "making her squeal"' is reversed in McDermid's text; McDermid and the murderer are both 'fucking' with and rewriting and reconfiguring purportedly 'normative' masculine and patriarchal codes. The maternal milieu is destabilised as Angelica uses the stereotypical Golden Age country house and turns the cellar '*into a dungeon*' (McDermid 2000[1995]:26). This subterranean dungeon/cellar is also symptomatic of a Freudian unconscious body, since it is a place where Angelica can enact her deepest desires. Foucault (1990:3) has summarised sexual policing and its regulation via society: 'Sexuality was carefully confined; it moved into the home. The conjugal family took custody of it and absorbed it into the serious function of reproduction.' However, in this instance 'reproduction' and sexuality can be viewed through a new lens: Angelica uses her home to import recorded videos of her murders into her computer via expensive and specialised editing software in order to '*relive and rebuild my encounter* [...] *till it more closely resembled my deepest fantasies*' (McDermid 2000[1995]:137). She explains that '*Plenty of people would pay a lot of money to watch Paul fuck me in his death spasms on the Judas chair. And as for what I've done with Adam … Let's just say that no-one's ever seen sixty-nine like it'* (McDermid 2000[1995]:203). Katz (1988:8) has remarked that 'as unattractive morally as crime may be, we must appreciate that there is a genuine creativity in it'. Against the background of criminographic 'art' is the postmodern art that Angelica creates, redrawing, reframing and remaking the human body.

Angelica's own family situation is a dysfunctional and emotionally abusive one. Angelica's father left the family and, as with Jamie Gumb/Buffalo Bill in *The Silence of the Lambs*, Angelica's mother was an alcoholic prostitute. This conforms to what Cameron (1996:25) defines as the more usual 'pathologising [of] the mother', illustrated earlier by Norman Bates in Alfred Hitchcock's *Psycho* (1960). Correspondingly, Angelica murdered her mother, masking it as a *'tragic accidental overdose of drink and pills'* (McDermid 2000[1995]:355). Angelica explains that Merrick has previously arrested her a couple of times after she was caught selling her transitioning body to sailors in the area of Seaford, Yorkshire to fund her sex-change surgery. The traditional and comforting matrimony of the body with sexuality and gender are further scrutinised by Angelica's body; she takes this family of seemingly definite meaning and amalgamates the binary elements into incomprehensible being and meaning. Merrick articulates this strange amalgam when he says: 'Christopher Thorpe isn't *married* to Angelica Thorpe, he *is* Angelica Thorpe' (McDermid 2000[1995]:357). Angelica's body literally marries together gendered and sexual ambiguity.

Such equivocation of meaning is again evident in the mixture of the gendered clothing that Angelica wears. Describing her childhood years, Angelica writes that *'I spent more time locked in the cupboard than most people's coats do'* (McDermid 2000[1995]:353). The intermixed and questioning position of Angelica's identity and her placement within and without language as 'She, he, it' (McDermid 2000[1995]:380) are fused in her attire. Tony sees her

> Clothes first. Beige mac, cut continental style, just like Carol's, swinging open to reveal a white shirt, enough buttons undone to reveal the swell of full breasts and a deep cleavage. Jeans, trainers. Trainers. They were the same make and model as his own. (McDermid 2000[1995]:338)

Angelica's clothing here personifies both the postmodern clothed and written action, which is to *'cut from* one category *into* another'

(De Monchy 1995:28). Not only does Angelica metaphorically cut from each separate gendered and sexual category so that she can stitch her own persona, but she is also, as a result of this, cutting across the rigid realist and crime fiction binaries. She comprises equal masculine and feminine components and is envisaged as a disconcerting combination of both Tony and Carol.

Angelica's feminine style and clothing, which contribute towards her assertion that '*I keep myself in shape*' (McDermid 2000[1995]:48), can, however, not escape the 'shape' allocated to her at birth: her 'full breasts' do not fully complement the masculine shoe size that is clear in her requisition of trainers just like Tony's. The ambiguous position of the murderer and contestation of '[i]dentity as natural, inevitable or desirable' (Jordan and Weedon 1995:48) is shown by Angelica's stylistically feminine stiletto shoes: 'She moved well in the heels, her stride measured and feminine. It was interesting, since she had obviously reverted to more masculine movements under the stress of kidnapping and killing' (McDermid 2000[1995]:343). To 'measure' the 'female' body by her clothing and accessories, as the previous texts did, is 'stressed' here; Angelica's movements and clothing are, for the majority of the novel, a conglomerate of immeasurable and undetectable female and male elements. Young, in her interrogation of masculine and, specifically, feminine body comportment and style of movement, has explained how

> [t]he female person who enacts the existence of women in patriarchal society must therefore live a contradiction: as human she is a free subject who participates in transcendence, but her situation as a woman denies her that subjectivity and transcendence. My suggestion is that the modalities of feminine bodily comportment, motility, and spatiality exhibit this same tension between transcendence and immanence, between subjectivity and being a mere object. (Young 1990:31–2)

Angelica's composite body also enacts this tension, yet her previous masculinity enables her to move outside the bounds. As Worthington (2000:17) writes, 'Angelica [...] is a step towards a lady killer in fiction: the text briefly makes possible the concept in the reader's mind even as the closure of the narrative simultaneously seems to close down that possibility.' The crime fiction bounds of genre and gender still hold, but Angelica, as a transsexual, symbolises fluidity.

McDermid's novel affords openings into discussions about the coherence of the body, textual and generic, about violence and its function and limits, and about constructions of gender and sexuality. Angelica's recreated and unconventional figure is formed from recognisable male and female 'norms', and she can still only work within the constraints of the choreography of crime fiction: the narrative conventions of the genre are simultaneously broken and remade, like the bodies of Angelica's victims.

References

Adams, Carol J. (1990). *The Sexual Politics of Meat: A Feminist-Vegetarian Critical Theory*. London: Continuum.

Ainsworth, William Harrison. (1839). *Jack Sheppard*. London: Bentley.

Allan, Janice M. (2006). A lock without a key: Language and detection in Collins's *The Law and the Lady*. *Clues: A Journal of Detection*, 25, 45–57.

Betz, Phyllis M. (2009). Re-covered bodies: The detective novel and transgendered characters. *Clues: A Journal of Detection*, 27, 21–32.

Bordo, Susan. (1997). The body and the reproduction of femininity. In Katie Conboy, Nadia Medina and Sarah Stanbury (eds), *Writing on the Body: Female Embodiment and Feminist Theory*. New York: Columbia University Press.

Cameron, Deborah. (1996). Wanted: The female serial killer. *Trouble & Strife*, 33, 21–8.

Carter, Angela. (1979). *The Bloody Chamber and Other Stories*. London: Gollancz.

Christie, Agatha. (1926). *The Murder of Roger Ackroyd*. London: William Collins & Sons.

Collins, Wilkie. (1994[1860]). *The Woman in White*. London: Penguin.

De Monchy, Marike Finlay. (1995). The horrified position: An ethics grounded in the affective interest in the unitary body as psyche/soma. In Mike Featherstone and Bryan S. Turner (eds), *Body and Society* 1. London: Sage.

De Quincey, Thomas. (1827). On murder considered as one of the fine arts. *Blackwood's Edinburgh Magazine*.

Foucault, Michel. (1990). *The History of Sexuality. Vol. One: The Will to Knowledge*, trans. Robert Hurley. Harmondsworth: Penguin.

Freud, Sigmund. (1991[1921]). Group psychology and the analysis of the ego. In Albert Dickson (ed.), *The Penguin Freud Library. Vol. 12*. Harmondsworth: Penguin.

Garber, Marjorie. (1997[1991]). *Vested Interests: Cross-Dressing and Cultural Anxiety*. New York: Routledge.

Gregoriou, Christiana. (2007). *Deviance in Contemporary Crime Fiction*. Basingstoke: Palgrave Macmillan.

Harris, Thomas. (1988). *The Silence of the Lambs*. New York: St. Martin's Press.

Hitchcock, Alfred. (1960). *Psycho*. Shamley Productions. 25 August.

Horsley, Lee. (2005). *Twentieth-Century Crime Fiction*. Oxford: Oxford University Press.

Jordan, Glenn and Chris Weedon. (1995). *Cultural Politics: Class, Gender, Race and the Postmodern World*. Oxford: Blackwell.

Katz, Jack. (1988). *Seductions of Crime: Moral and Sensual Attractions in Doing Evil*. New York: Basic Books.

Knight, Stephen. (1991). The knife beneath the skin: Crime writing, masculinity and sadism. *Arena*, 97, 145–56.

Lytton, Bulwer. (1841). *Night and Morning*. New York: Harper & Brothers.

Mailer, Norman. (1967). *Cannibals and Christians*. London: Andre Deutsch.

McDermid, Val. (2000[1995]). *The Mermaids Singing*. London: HarperCollins.

McDermid, Val. (2009). Complaints about women writing misogynist crime fiction are a red herring. *The Guardian*, 29 October. Available at http://www. guardian.co.uk/books/booksblog/2009/oct/29/misogynist-crime-fiction-val-mcdermid [accessed November 2009].

Munt, Sally R. (1994). *Murder by the Book? Feminism and the Crime Novel*. London: Routledge.

Plain, Gill. (2001). *Twentieth-Century Crime Fiction: Gender, Sexuality and the Body*. Edinburgh: Edinburgh University Press.

Porter, Dennis. (1981). *The Pursuit of Crime: Art and Ideology in Detective Fiction*. New Haven, CT: Yale University Press.

Probyn, Elspeth. (2000). *Carnal Appetites: FoodSexIdentities*. London: Routledge.

Punch, 7 August 1841, 39.

Rowland, Susan. (2001). *From Agatha Christie to Ruth Rendell*. Hampshire: Palgrave.

Simpson, Inga. (2009). Torn between two genres: Sex and romance in lesbian detective fiction. *Clues: A Journal of Detection*, 27, 9–20.

Skrapec, Candice. (1993). The female serial killer: An evolving criminality. In Helen Birch (ed.), *Moving Targets: Women, Murder and Representation*. London: Virago.

Todorov, Tzvetan. (1977). *The Poetics of Prose*, trans. Richard Howard. Ithaca: Cornell University Press.

Worthington, Heather. (2000). Looking for a lady killer: Val McDermid's *The Mermaids Singing*. Unpublished paper. Cardiff University.

Young, Iris Marion. (1990). *On Female Body Experience: 'Throwing like a Girl' and Other Essays in Feminist Philosophy and Social Theory*. Bloomington: Indiana University Press.

4.2
Life of Crime: Feminist Crime/Life Writing in Sara Paretsky, *Writing in an Age of Silence*, P. D. James, *Time to Be in Earnest: A Fragment of Autobiography* and Val McDermid, *A Suitable Job for a Woman: Inside the World of Women Private Eyes*

Charlotte Beyer

'Untangle the puzzles that strew our lives'[1]

This chapter presents a comparative discussion of life writing by three contemporary female crime writers: one American, Sara Paretsky; one British, P. D. James; and one Scottish, Val McDermid. All three women are established crime writers; yet, compared with their crime fiction, their life writing has received less critical and scholarly attention. However, this chapter demonstrates that the life writing of Paretsky, James and McDermid is central to a fuller understanding of their crime fictions, and forms the basis for understanding their aesthetic and creative developments and their feminist engagements with the politics of language and writing. Their books – *Writing in an Age of Silence*; *Time to Be in Earnest: A Fragment of Autobiography*; and *A Suitable Job for a Woman: Inside the World of Women Private Eyes* – are classed as life writing. This genre until recently found itself consigned to enthusiasts' shelves in bookshops and libraries and was 'seldom taken seriously as a focus of study before the seventies, was not deemed appropriately "complex" for academic dissertations, criticism, or the literary canon' (Smith and Watson 1998:4). However, in exploring connections between female crime writers' life writing and their crime fictions, this chapter demonstrates how James, Paretsky and McDermid's 'life writing includes more than just life stories, and it has the potential to cross genre boundaries and disciplines' (Kadar 1992:152). Therefore, this chapter proposes the term 'crime/life writing' to describe this 'crossing of genre boundaries and disciplines' and employs this term to evaluate these works' respective merits, arguing that crime/life writing is instrumental to an emerging picture of feminist literary identities and crime fiction criticism. The examination of these issues focuses on two main areas of enquiry. The first part of the chapter examines how James, McDermid and Paretsky use life writing strategies to explore the personal, subjective, cultural, sexual and political contexts of their crime fiction. The second part discusses the creative tensions, which these life writings foreground, between feminine non-conformity and 'deviance', and the links between women writers' creative responses, their lived experience and their representations of female detective figures.

'Their stories are as varied and interesting as the women themselves': Feminist crime/life writing

Commonly, autobiography has been perceived as 'the self-reporting of "the great deeds of great men". By this definition, no woman could ever compose a "life"' (Mairs 1994:107). However, according to Buss, women's life writing not only refutes this notion, but demonstrates that 'the personal is political', an idea that 'has always been at the heart of all feminisms' (Buss 2002:3). The connection between personal and political realms (Beyer 2010a:214) is reflected in the crime/life writing discussed here, illustrating that 'it was crucial for women writers to tell the stories of their lives' (Miller and Rosner 2006). This chapter not only shares that assertion, but explores and further extends it, through its subject matter and investigative methods. In her groundbreaking work on women's autobiography, *Writing a Woman's Life*, the American feminist academic and crime writer Carolyn Heilbrun discusses strategies for feminist life writing. She calls 'for women to take the risk of telling stories that went beyond the conventional boundaries of feminine experience' (Miller and Rosner 2006) and stresses the importance for women of exploring their creativity to the full. Heilbrun herself was among the first second-wave feminist crime writers, well known for her detective fictions featuring the academic scholar/detective Kate Fansler (Marchino 1995:155). Her creation of a female academic detective was a risky creative move, which had the potential to upset generic conventions and patriarchal expectations. Therefore she assumed an 'other' writing identity, nom de plume Amanda Cross, under which she published her crime fiction, 'an alter ego [...] another possibility of female destiny' (Heilbrun 1988:110), a fact that reflects the pressure that women writers feel to conform.

Heilbrun asserts that, when a woman writer tells her life story, her 'unnarrated' life, it represents such a radical break from convention that a fresh approach is required to re-imagine both the tradition and the telling:

> there still exists little organised sense of what a woman's biography or autobiography should look like. Where should it begin? With her birth, and the disappointment, or reason for no disappointment that she was not a boy? [...] None of these questions has been probed within the context of women's as yet unnarrated lives, lives precisely *not* those that convention, romance, literature, and drama have, for the most part, given us. (Heilbrun 1988:27–8)

Mairs (1994:80) echoes this point: 'The task may be more than complicated, it may be impossible, for the female autobiographer, who has been entitled – historically, culturally, linguistically, critically, that is, politically – to neither authority nor subjectivity.' Following Heilbrun's line of enquiry ('where should it begin?'), when we examine the openings of Paretsky, James and McDermid's life writings, these reveal much about individual approaches to life writing, and their aesthetical decisions reflect precisely those challenges to tradition about which Heilbrun spoke. In questioning, or even rejecting, linear narratives in favour of episodic storytelling or interviews, Paretsky, James and McDermid's life writing echoes Heilbrun's scepticism of conventional autobiographical approaches. Furthermore, their books also tackle the problem that women writers experience in 'seizing the word', which Mairs described, by challenging patriarchal notions that women have no entitlement to articulate their authority or assert their selfhood in life and literature.

In her discussion of women's life writing, Buss (2002:172) comments on its blurring of generic boundaries; the 'ability of the essayistic memoir to allow the writer to move in her text, in a continuing and integrated manner, between personal life and public activities'. We observe this movement in Paretsky, James and McDermid's crime/life writing, where introspective passages alternate with self-reflexive discussions of the crime genre, social and cultural issues, the detective figure and the gender politics of representation. Thereby, their texts draw attention to issues of authority and identity in relation to 'writing the self' and to writing crime fiction. Furthermore, all three texts are products of their specific historical moments and foreground this relationship to history to varying degrees. In Paretsky, the 'age of silence' in her book's title is the aftermath of the 9/11 terrorist attack, whereas in James, the calendar year 1997–98 forms the time frame for her diary. In both cases, those times were characterised by experiences of national trauma, but also by a sense of change. For Paretsky, 2007, the year when *Writing in an Age of Silence* was first published, became the year when the American nation's 'post-9/11 traumatic stress disorder' threatened to develop into a stifling of public debate. For James, in Britain, 1997 was marked by the extraordinary public scenes of grief surrounding the death of Princess Diana, and by the Labour party coming into government. McDermid's book was published in 1995, when feminist literary detective figures were starting to proliferate and Judith Butler's groundbreaking work *Gender Trouble* (1990) influenced debates around sexuality and gender in both the academe and popular culture. All three writers thus utilise public events and contemporary cultural developments to contextualise their narratives of private lives and art and make them relevant to the reader.

McDermid (1995:85) uses a different approach, by employing her background in investigative journalism to examine the social and cultural obstacles that present themselves to real-life female detectives, such as institutionalised sexism and professional and private marginalisation. She opens her book with a reaffirmation of the link between writing and detecting:

> By the time I read my first woman private eye novel, I was an investigative reporter on a national newspaper. We had a lot in common, it seemed to me. We were both driven by the urge for truth and some kind of justice that wasn't supplied by the official system. We both used unorthodox means to reach our goals. (McDermid 1995:1)

Narrating the life stories of female private detectives, using a mixture of interviews, anecdotes and reflective material, McDermid's text reflects the fluidity of life writing and its parameters: 'Life writing [...] is a less exclusive genre of personal kinds of writing that includes both biography and autobiography, but also the less "objective", or more "personal", genres such as letters and diaries' (Kadar 1992:4). This innovation echoes her achievements within crime fiction: 'Val McDermid is a remarkable writer who has moved the detective genre in several new directions' (Hadley 2002:8).

McDermid's crime/life writing demonstrates that truth and justice are not necessarily located within official discourses, and that non-conformity presents a viable alternative for women. Her book is unique among the life writings examined here. For a start, its approach differs from Paretsky and James's more conventional memoirs. Demonstrating the fluidity of life writing as a genre, McDermid's text presents an exploration of other women's life stories and detective work, alongside the author's reflections on her own writing. By thus incorporating the concept and practice of sisterhood into its narrative fabric and structure, McDermid's crime/life writing is based on a sense of solidarity with other women, and on recognition of the commonality of female experience across the boundaries of class, ethnicity/race and sexuality. The intertextual reference in the title plays on James's *An Unsuitable Job for a Woman* (1972), but it is the smartly phrased subtitle, *Inside the World of Women Private Eyes*, which promises the reader 'the real deal' about women detectives and the challenges they face: 'I couldn't resist picking up my old trade in a bid to discover if the real Kinsey Millhone or Kate Brannigan exists. This is the story of that quest' (McDermid 1995:2). McDermid (1995:276) does not discover the 'real' Brannigan, but what she does find is 'a group of women far more varied than their fictional counterparts'.

P. D. James' non-chronological approach upsets temporal linearity, instead allowing the narrative to dip in and out of time. The title of her book, with its emphasis on the word 'fragment' and its anecdotal structure, further emphasises the partial and subjective. She opens her autobiographical narrative with a reflection on the process of writing a diary and describes her motivations for writing about her personal life: 'A diary, if intended for publication (and how many written by a novelist are not?) is the most egotistical form of writing' (James 1999:xi). James (1999:xi) refers to her life writing as 'a partial autobiography and a defence', designed to keep biographers wishing to write about her at a distance. However, she reveals her vision of altruistic intergenerational sharing as the real impetus: 'My motive is now to record just one year that might otherwise be lost, not only to children and grandchildren who might have an interest but, with the advance of age [...] lost also to me' (James 1999:xi).

James' crime/life writing highlights a specifically British tension between private and public, in its portrayal of her public appearances and roles, interspersed with her private reflections, which do not always concur with her public persona. Commenting on her determination to keep the two spheres distinct, James (1999:184) notes that she 'had decided not to write much about politics in what is essentially a record of [her] personal year'. 'Her method allows her to move freely between present events, the publication of *A Certain Justice*, for instance, and all the obligatory publicity connected with it, the musings on her past and the development of her writing life' (Thomas 2000). James's preoccupation with privacy should be seen in light of the fact that she spent many years as the breadwinner, her husband having become mentally unstable through war trauma. Her oblique references to family problems and sorrow foreground Mairs's (1994:126) observation that 'the person set apart from ordinary human intercourse by temporary or permanent misfortune has little enough time and even less energy for snivelling. Illness and death, whether one's own or beloved's, take *work*.'

'Unapologetic about her own chosen form' (Maitzen 2008), James's observations on crime writing reveal her motivation as one of moral and ethical obligation, reflected in the intensity of her emotional and intellectual response to the 'real-life' crimes that she describes (James 1999:182–3). James's faith and conservative middle-class background chime with her description of 'Empire Day' celebrations at school (James 1999:24) when, during her primary school years in the 1920s, the classroom featured the map of the world with red splashes denoting Britain's imperial domains. Her British reserve reflects a sensibility of detachment and a tension between public and private spheres: 'Even as a child I had the sense that I was two people; the one who experienced the trauma, the pain, the happiness, and the other who stood aside and watched with a disinterested ironic eye' (James 1999:67). Yet James also insists on the relevance of personal experience for women writers, because 'our own pains and joys [...] remembered and relived, sometimes with discomfort, and filtered through the imagination become the raw stuff of fiction' (James 1999:116). Such internal tensions in her text remain unresolved, thereby adding complexity and intrigue to her crime/life writing.

In contrast to McDermid and James, Paretsky begins her memoirs in a more conventional chronological fashion, with an 'earliest memory' recollection tracing her development as a crime writer back to childhood influences, and knowingly drawing attention to writing and the power of knowledge: 'among my earliest memories [...] are books, words, the smell of new books, which to me still heralds the excitement of the first day at school' (Paretsky 2007:xi). Her autobiographical narrative is constructed as a feminist journey, from silence to finding a voice, situating this process within a specific historical-cultural setting and acknowledging its difficulties and struggles (Paretsky 2007:xiii). She says: 'It was feminism that triggered my wish to write a private eye novel, and it shaped the character of my detective, V.I. Warshawski' (Paretsky 2007:xvi). Paretsky's crime/life writing represents a rejection of silence, and a reminder to America of its enduring sensibility of resistance and rebellion (Beyer 2010b:214), which, coupled with the myth of individualism, are important aspects of Paretsky's re-imagining of the crime genre and American identity. Her memoirs also provide a timely critique of a post–9/11 America, which she considers to be suffering from a loss of direction and a malfunctioning moral compass.

The generic descriptor of crime/life writing thus acknowledges the fact that the books examined in this chapter are just as much about crime writing as they are about life writing. In exploring lives, these texts examine the processes of constructing crime, and constructing the woman crime writer's practice and position within society and the literary tradition. In their interrogating the meanings of 'self' and 'identity', Paretsky, James and McDermid's texts problematise the idea of 'truth' and the quest for accuracy associated with traditional life writing. Their creative uses of crime/life writing remind us of the mutability of literary genres and their ability to encompass change and lend themselves to feminist revision – in Kadar's (1992:153) words: 'Like water, genres assume the shape of the vessel that contains them.'

'The violent, the unstable and the angry': Deviance and detectives

Paretsky, James and McDermid use the crime fiction format to interrogate social and cultural values in relation to gender politics. Their crime/life writings expose such issues as violence against women, rape, murder, child abuse, political corruption, modern-day slavery and other contemporary mores. Whether narrating their own lives or those of other women, the project of their crime/life writing is intrinsically linked to the construction of non-conformist, or 'deviant', feminist writing identities, in contra-distinction to the conventional patriarchal norms of femininity. As Smith (1987:5) puts it: 'Those in power determine whose version of reality prevails, whose ways of speaking and behaving will be seen as normal, and whose ways deviant.' Since 'the fundamental structure of patriarchy is binary: me/not me, active/passive, culture/ nature, normal/deviant' (Romaine 1999:10), the woman writer's act of documenting her life and art renders her 'deviant', because she transgresses patriarchal expectations of feminine behaviour. Commenting on the marginalisation of women and other subordinated groups by the dominant literary culture, Romaine (1999:10) explains: 'they have been persistently seen as Others [and] their ways of communicating and behaving are seen as deviant and illogical'. Paretsky, James and

McDermid expose binarisms and the 'othering' of women writers, both in their crime/life writing and in their female detective characters. They maintain that a woman writer is '[n]ot angel, not monster, just human' (Paretsky 2007:51).

The perception that a woman's anger is 'other', and constitutes a threat to the patriarchal status quo, is at the heart of the construction of a 'deviant' identity in these three texts. Heilbrun (1988:13) argues that, to the patriarchal literary establishment, the idea of female anger is one of the most transgressive factors about women's writing: 'And, above all other prohibitions, what has been forbidden to women is anger, together with the open admission of the desire for power and control over one's life.' In a recent interview, McDermid discusses the essentialist gender bias behind the 'notion that women should not write violent fiction' (Bindel 2007). In a genre that regularly portrays violent and criminal activities, and uses linguistic effects to enhance representations of transgression, this prohibition can prove problematic for women crime writers. To James, the crime genre serves a specific function for its female practitioners and readers, as a safe place to articulate taboo: 'Thus psychologically buttressed, we can deal with violent events and emotions with greater security than we could in any other form of fiction' (James 1999:17). Hadley (2002:17) observes that 'James' use of introspective detectives and concern with justice and punishment' underpin her understated use of literary effects in portraying violence, without compromising the acuteness of her social and cultural critique. Thereby, 'the violence that marks the hardboiled tradition undergoes analysis and revision in the feminist series' (Reddy 2003:198).

The gender politics of representation are highlighted in discussions of the use of violence as a literary effect in crime fiction, as part of its generic make-up. As a feminist, Paretsky is acutely aware of her responsibility to avoid reinforcing violent (s)exploitation of female characters when portraying violent crime:

> Serial killers who torture women and children, or rapists who prey on women and children, play an enormous – and enormously titillating, not to mention enormously lucrative – role in today's fiction. I vowed not to use sex to exploit my characters – or readers. (Paretsky 2007:61)

James also criticises the use of gratuitously graphic and sexualised literary language in contemporary crime writing. She sees this troubling development, of 'pimping' the crime plot, in gender terms – as one that is pursued mostly by male crime writers: 'Today the detective story is more realistically about murder, more violent, more sexually explicit, less assured in its affirmation of official law and order' (James 1999:35). Arguing that too many contemporary male crime writers are caught up in a fascination with violence and nihilism, James commends the contrasting linguistic nuance and thematic subtlety of the psychologically focused crime thriller: 'perhaps it is to the women we must look for psychological subtlety and the exploration of moral choice, which for me are at the heart of even the most grittily realistic of crime fiction' (James 1999:20).

With *Writing in an Age of Silence*, *Time to Be in Earnest* and *A Suitable Job for a Woman*, Paretsky, James and McDermid demonstrate that women crime writers continue to engage critically with the politics of language and writing throughout their writing careers, in order to combat sexism in crime fiction and to resist the silencing and marginalisation of women. Their crime/life writings interrogate conventional constructions of feminine identity, a critique that Paretsky makes an explicit part of her book's depiction of 'growing up with "the feminine mystique"' and pitting herself as a woman writer against 'the Angel in the House' (Beyer 2010b:216). Paretsky (2007:9) explains: 'In Kansas during the fifties, in a society where everyone had a defined place, where everyone knew right from wrong [...] girls often saw limited horizons in the future.' Resisting this powerful myth of feminine passivity and conformity is central to Paretsky's fiction and to her creation of an assertive and vocal private eye character, V.I. Warshawski (Beyer 2010b:216).

Similarly, James (1999:123) recalls the limited options available to her and other middle-class girls, for whom university was not an option and whose employment choice was between teaching or secretarial work, or what was referred to as 'the ordinary pursuits of womanhood'. This heavily normative concept of 'ordinary womanhood' underpinned an idea of domesticated femininity that was anathema both to the activity of crime writing and to the creation of female detective figures. Therefore, for a considerable part of her life, James herself strived to conform to conventional norms of femininity, as a 'single mother responsible for two daughters, owing to the mental illness and death, in the early sixties, of her hopelessly war-damaged husband' (Thomas 2000:165). James kept her desire to write secret, as it would have singled her out as 'deviant' and not conforming to patriarchal expectations, and only published her first crime fiction when she was in her forties.

McDermid's crime/life writing is committed to interrogating sexual politics and to mobilising a 'radical departure from the tradition'

(Hadley 2002:77). Like Paretsky's, McDermid's writing 'discusses social ills, especially those linked to urban working-class backgrounds' (Hadley 2002:77). McDermid's writing emerges from a sense of the politics of genre and sexuality, and of writing and detection as politicised endeavours for women. Critical of the status quo, her humorous and energetic writing style emulates the tough-talking discourse of investigative journalism meets hard-boiled crime fiction. However, as we have already noted, McDermid's book differs from both Paretsky's and James's, since its focus is less on her own life and experience as a crime writer, and more on 'real-life' female detective figures and how these have informed her fiction and its portrayal of female detective characters. McDermid's choice of focus foregrounds the tension between reality and fiction, in 'the gap [...] between the creatures of my imagination and the real-life women private eyes who take on the cases that make real differences in people's lives' (McDermid 1995:2). The title of her book's final chapter, 'Truth is stranger than fiction' (McDermid 1995:271), intelligently underlines this tension, by problematising the idea of language as signifying 'truth', and instead foregrounding the fictional nature of all storytelling, including life writing.

In their crime/life writing, Paretsky, James and McDermid insist that the creation of a feminist detective hero is central to their work and their relationship with the crime genre. Paretsky (2007:60) goes so far as to state: 'As for me, I wanted to create a woman who would turn the table on the dominant views of women in fiction and in society.' However, as McDermid argues, in 'real life' being a private detective is still not considered an occupation 'suitable' for women: '"Have you considered becoming a private detective?" are seven words that have never passed the lips of a careers teacher' (McDermid 1995:4). In *Time to Be in Earnest*, James comments on the evolution of female detective figures in women's writing in relation to social and cultural change. Her female private eye, Cordelia Gray of *An Unsuitable Job for a Woman*, is considered one of the first fictional female detectives of second-wave feminism (Reddy 2003:195). Equally, James explains that she uses her other female detective character, Kate Miskin, to convey feminist issues:

> In the first book in which my woman detective Kate Miskin appears, *A Taste for Death*, I didn't set out to explore the problems of an intelligent, ambitious and underprivileged young woman fighting her way to seniority and success in the machismo world of the police, but the book would not have been realistic if these problems hadn't been dealt with. (James 1999:58–9)

This reveals James's determination to produce realistic portrayals of gender and class issues in her crime fiction, and to foreground her awareness of the problem of institutionalised sexism in the police force that directed her creation of Miskin's character.

In *Writing in an Age of Silence*, Paretsky reflects on the enduring appeal of the individualist 'private eye' figure, and comments on the American specificity of this maverick character: 'The private eye is America's unique contribution to the crime novel. It comes out of our fascination with the loner heroes of the old West' (Paretsky 2007:xvi). She proposes her female detective figure as an antidote against postfeminist torpor and 'defends her own sexually liberated fictional characters, positing their stories as a counter-discourse against what she perceives as an increasingly woman-hostile climate in America in the 1990s and 2000s' (Beyer 2010b:216). McDermid's book also emphasises the personal integrity and mental strength required in a female detective, who needs to be able to take risks and must possess an 'urge for truth and some kind of justice that wasn't supplied by the official system' (McDermid 1995:1). Echoing Chandler's famous 'mean streets' phrase, McDermid highlights the feminist non-conformism, and courage to go against establishment norms, which forms an integral part of female detective experience: 'I realised there was another strand that bound me as a journalist to the women who really pounded the mean streets searching for answers' (McDermid 1995:1). While subscribing to the individualist 'mean streets' sensibility of the private eye, McDermid's feminist detective stories are nevertheless firmly rooted in a sense of solidarity with other women. As Reddy (2003:198) points out: 'Unlike the male detectives, the solitariness of the female detectives is not presented as a badge of honour but as a condition dictated by prevailing gender definitions.' For Paretsky, too, her feminist detective is embedded in community and social relationships. Perceiving female identity as constructed relationally rather than individually, Paretsky (2007:101) argues: 'My detective couldn't survive with so much loneliness. On the personal, micro level, she needs friends, dogs, lovers – she needs continuity and connection.' The importance of the community of sisterhood that other women provide is underscored in Mairs's (1994:120) observations regarding 'the feminist autobiographer, writing out of a sense of connectedness'.

In *Time to Be in Earnest*, James (1999:142), on the one hand, reflects on her personal experiences of conformity, to class expectations, to expectations of conventional femininity, and describes herself as a 'bureaucrat'. However, she also emphasises the ways in which women crime writers 'deviate' from traditional feminine expectations. James reflects on the construction and function of crime fiction, and on her own position as a woman crime writer, throughout *Time to Be in Earnest*, thus highlighting these processes of questioning and self-reflexivity as intrinsic elements of her crime/life writing. As she interrogates the function of the crime genre, and the role and ethical position of the crime writer, she asks: 'Who wants to become a crime novelist and why?' (James 1999:212). In response, James poses a number of speculative and rhetorical questions, which provoke the reader into reflecting both on the nature of crime writing and on the ongoing process of 'writing the self' staged in autobiography:

> To give the illusion that we live in a moral and comprehensible universe? [...] To provide a structure within which writer and reader can safely confront terror, violence, death? To show that to some things at least there is an answer? (James 1999:212)

Such moments of self-reflexivity and introspective analysis demonstrate how these three writers' crime/life writing engages with the politics of feminist crime writing practice.

James may mock her own teenage conformity and distinct lack of 'deviance' – 'We were well-behaved by conditioning, not by nature' (James 1999:46) – but she also admits that this youthful conformism was a social and cultural requirement, rather than a natural essence. Writing from the vantage point of old age in *Time to Be in Earnest*, James suggests that her own non-conformity now may lie in her position as an ageing woman writer, in a society that marginalises and shuns old age: 'I inhabit a different body, but I can reach back over nearly seventy years and recognise her as myself' (James 1999:238–9). Furthermore, her recognition of the value of learning and studying for its own sake shows that, in her professional work as well as in her personal life, James is determined to challenge expectations: 'I have my work. I shall continue to write detective stories as long as I can write well and I hope I shall recognise when it is time to stop' (James 1999: 238).

Paretsky's autobiography interrogates the meanings of marginalisation and explores the lived experience of non-conformity: '*Writing in an Age of Silence*, with its emphasis on the importance of "voice", should also be seen in the context of post-9/11 fuelled American anxieties' (Beyer 2010b:215). This is the political and cultural context within which, Paretsky (2007:111) insists, writers 'must be intensely private and interior in order to find a voice and a vision – and we must bring their work to an outside world where the market, or public outrage, or even government censorship can destroy our voice'. The link between fictional representations and cultural, social and national realities is thus reaffirmed: 'the writer's art of rendering history [is] a felt process through their engagement with a personal development, and with their political and creative "journey"' (Beyer 2010b:214). Fusing crime and life writing, Paretsky, James and McDermid's work signals their commitment to their personal and political values, which inform their lived experience and private existence.

'The truth is certainly tougher than fiction': Conclusion

This chapter has utilised Heilbrun's feminist discussion of the specificity of women's life writing as a starting point for exploring the aesthetics and politics that inform Paretsky, James and McDermid's texts. Heilbrun (1988:18) says of the importance of linking thought, writing and action: 'Power is the ability to take one's place in whatever discourse is essential to action and the right to have one's part matter.' Clearly, this translates into the crime/life writing discussed in this chapter, which has demonstrated how, to all three writers, the personal is inextricably linked to the political realm. Feminist crime/life writing connects with real historical and cultural events and questions. Paretsky (2007:78) comments on the significance of American working-class women's identifications with her feminist detective, and the appeal of V.I. to that readership. McDermid (1995:60) describes the marginalisation felt by female detectives and their quest for an authentic community: 'the library was education, meeting-place, refuge and treasure trove'.

Compared to the openings discussed in the beginning of this chapter, how, then, does women's crime/life writing achieve closure, if at all? On the final pages of her book *Writing a Woman's Life*, Heilbrun (1988:130) refutes closure as a negative ideological construction underpinning female passivity and dependency: 'We women have lived too much with closure. [It] is the delusion of a passive life.' Instead, she urges women to 'make use of our security, our seniority, to take risks, to make noise, to be courageous, to become unpopular' (Heilbrun 1988:131). Certainly, all three writers considered in this chapter have taken such creative risks in their life writing narratives. James ends her diary narrative with 'unfinished business', emphasising its subjective and partial nature, and by describing her life writing as 'incomplete, with more omitted than has been recorded' (James 1999:238). In contrast, at the end of *Writing in an Age of Silence*, Paretsky's rhetorical flourish invokes the names of Anna Akhmatova, the poet Sappho and the nineteenth-century black

American feminist Sojourner Truth, among others, to raise consciousness and bring hope of change (Paretsky 2007:137). McDermid closes her book with a tribute to those self-reliant female detectives who have peopled her text, and with an acknowledgement of the detective work they do: 'Smart, strong and sure of themselves, they walk the mean streets to their own beat' (McDermid 1995:278). Indeed, this could be said for all three writers discussed in this chapter. As they determinedly 'write beyond the ending' (Blau DuPlessis 1985), James, Paretsky and McDermid's crime/life writing demonstrates how women writers challenge traditional narrative structures and codified patterns. Their questioning, intelligent works acknowledge the ever-increasing relevance of women's crime fiction, and the importance of the woman writer's role in a postmodern age.

Note

1. All section heading quotations are taken from McDermid (1995).

References

Beyer, Charlotte. (2010a). A Life of Crime: Sara Paretsky's *Writing in an Age of Silence*, (2007). In Constructing Crime Conference, University of Leeds, 30 March.

Beyer, Charlotte. (2010b). Sara Paretsky, *Writing in an Age of Silence*, *Journal of American, British and Canadian Studies*, 15, 214–16.

Bindel, Julie. (2007). I start my day in a condition of rage, *The Guardian*, 17 August. Available at http://www.guardian.co.uk/books/2007/aug/17/crime. gender [accessed April 2011].

Blau DuPlessis, Rachel. (1985). *Writing Beyond the Ending: Narrative Strategies of Twentieth-Century Women Writers*. Bloomington, IN: Indiana University Press.

Buss, Helen M. (2002). *Repossessing the World: Reading Memoirs by Contemporary Women*. Toronto: Wilfried Laurier University Press.

Hadley, Mary. (2002). *British Women Mystery Writers: Authors of Detective Fiction with Female Sleuths*. Jefferson, NY: McFarland.

Heilbrun, Carolyn. (1988). *Writing a Woman's Life*. London: Women's Press.

James, Phyllis D. (1999). *Time to Be in Earnest: A Fragment of Autobiography*. London: Faber and Faber.

Kadar, Marlene (ed.). (1992). *Essays of Life Writing: From Genre to Critical Practice*. Toronto: University of Toronto Press.

Kadar, Marlene. (1992). Whose life is it anyway? Out of the bathtub and into the narrative. In Marlene Kadar (ed.), *Essays of Life Writing: From Genre to Critical Practice*. Toronto: University of Toronto Press.

Mairs, Nancy. (1994). *Voice Lessons: On Becoming a (Woman) Writer*. Boston, MA: Beacon Press.

Maitzen, Rohan. (2008). P.D. James, *Time to Be in Earnest*, *Open Letters Monthly: An Art and Literature Review*, 27 February. Available at http://www.open

lettersmonthly.com/novelreadings/p-d-james-time-to-be-in-earnest-2 [accessed April 2011].

Marchino, Lois A. (1995). The professor tells a story: Kate Fansler. In Mary Jean DeMarr (ed.), *In the Beginning: First Novels in Mystery Series*. Madison, WI: Popular Press.

McDermid, Val. (1995). *A Suitable Job for a Woman: Inside the World of Women Private Eyes*. London: HarperCollins.

Miller, Nancy and Victoria Rosner. (2006). Introduction. *Scholar & Feminist Online*, special issue 'Writing a Feminist's Life: The Legacy of Carolyn G. Heilbrun', 4(2). Available at http://www.barnard.edu/sfonline/heilbrun/intro_01.htm [accessed April 2011].

Paretsky, Sara. (2007). *Writing in an Age of Silence*. London: Verso.

Reddy, Maureen. (2003). Women detectives. In Martin Priestman (ed.), *The Cambridge Companion to Crime Fiction*. Cambridge: Cambridge University Press.

Romaine, Suzanne. (1999). *Communicating Gender*. London: Routledge.

Smith, Sidonie. (1987). *A Poetics of Women's Autobiography: Marginality and the Fictions of Self-Representation*. Bloomington, IN: Indiana University Press.

Smith, Sidonie and Julia Watson (eds) (1998). *Women, Autobiography, Theory: A Reader*. Madison, WI: University of Wisconsin Press.

Thomas, Clara. (2000). Time to be in earnest: A fragment of autobiography. *Canadian Woman Studies*, 20(2), 164–5.

4.3
Understanding Aileen Wuornos: Pushing the Limits of Empathy

Mandy Koolen

In his 1896 description of female sexual inversion, Ellis (1925:201) asserts that '[i]nverted women, who may retain their feminine emotionality combined with some degree of infantile impulsiveness and masculine energy, present a favourable soil for the seeds of passional crime'. Ellis, like many other sexologists of the late nineteenth and early twentieth centuries, describes the female invert's propensity to jealousy and crime as an expression of her infantile lack of control, and thus he depicts women who express same-sex desire as overly emotional, irrational and, ultimately, juvenile. Many contemporary popular culture texts, such as the film *Monster* (2003), demonstrate the persistence of depictions of lesbians as violent, criminal, desperate women who cannot control their emotions and actions. Jenkins worked from fact when writing and directing *Monster*, which is based on the life of Aileen Wuornos, a sex worker who was convicted of killing six men. Yet whereas Wuornos asserted that she had every right to fight back against men who harmed or threatened her, *Monster* erases Wuornos's powerful critiques of male dominance and violence by portraying her as an abused victim who is – underneath her tough, masculine persona – a childish, vulnerable and lonely woman who comes to recognise that the murders she commits are immoral, and feels guilty and regretful. *Monster* not only reinforces many reductive beliefs about homosexual women that are seen in early sexological studies, but also sends a strong message about the *types* of women who are worthy of empathy. Jenkins's representation of Wuornos's persona and the murders she commits suggests that women who kill only deserve compassion if they are emotionally fragile victims who snap after years of neglect and mistreatment, and are remorseful after committing their acts of violence.

I have chosen to focus my analysis of sexology on Ellis's writing since he was the first sexologist 'to deal with female homosexuality in a serious manner' (Miller 2006:18). Ellis 'strongly opposed viewing homosexuality as a vice' (Terry 1999:50) and he 'differed from many of his European counterparts in explicitly rejecting the vocabulary of degeneration, insisting that homosexuality should be seen as a harmless physiological variation rather than a neuropathic taint' (Felski 1998:4). Yet the chapter on 'Sexual inversion in women' in Ellis's influential book *Studies in the Psychology of Sex: Sexual Inversion* (1925) establishes a troubling link between female homosexuality and violent criminality. While Hart (1994:11) notes that Ellis would probably have denied that his writing positioned lesbianism as the cause of criminality, nonetheless in 'Sexual inversion in women' he 'effectively displaced the threat of women's aggression onto the figure of the "true" [congenital] lesbian, who has been the site of aggression in some of the most powerful discourses in Western history'. The tension between Ellis's good intent and the troubling messages that are conveyed by his writing highlights the importance of carefully attending to the complexities and contradictions that make sexology such a fascinating, although often frustrating, discipline of study.

Similar to Ellis, who saw his writing as challenging the social and legal persecution of homosexual people, Jenkins has explained that she intended *Monster* to provide an alternative perspective of Wuornos, who is most often represented in the media as 'a man-hating lesbian prostitute who tarnished the reputations of all her victims' (Broomfield, cited in Human 2003). While Jenkins distances herself from charges that she empathised with Wuornos, she states that she wanted her film to 'explain why [...Wuornos was] not [...a] monstrosity' (*Patty Jenkins* 2010).[1] *Monster* provides a context for Wuornos's crimes and thereby invites viewers to take into consideration the underlying reasons for this woman's violence. Yet, while appearing on the surface to give an empathetic portrayal of Wuornos, a close reading of this film shows that it positions her as a pitiable victim of abuse, and both erases and undermines her powerful critiques of the patriarchal naturalisation of male access to female bodies.

Compelling contradictions in sexological discourse

Sexology, 'the sustained theorisation of sex', flourished in '[t]he period between the 1860s and the 1930s' (Bauer 2009:1). During this time, sexologists 'coined many of the analytical terms – homosexuality, heterosexuality, sadism, masochism – still in use today' (Felski 1998:2). The continuity of ideas developed by sexologists is also apparent in contemporary representations of lesbians as criminal and childlike. In 'Sexual inversion in women', Ellis, for instance, associates female congenital inversion with masculinity, criminality, and immaturity.[2] Although Ellis begins this text by outlining the link between female sexual inversion and 'high intellectual ability' and genius (1925:196–200), he follows this analysis by stating that 'a remarkably large proportion of the cases in which homosexuality has led to crimes of violence [...] has been among women' (1925:200–1). Ellis's (1925:201–2) association of female sexual inversion with criminality is apparent in his discussion of inverts who were murderers, such as Alice Mitchell, who cut her lover's throat after they were unable to marry, and Anna Rubinowitch, who shot her lover and then herself after her lover began to respond 'to the advances of a male wooer'. Ellis (1925: 201–3) also recounts two cases in which female inverts killed the men their female lovers left them for and gives examples of female inverts committing suicide when their love was not reciprocated. After linking the female congenital invert to criminality, Ellis 'comment[s] that there was no evidence of insanity in these women. Rather, they were "typical inverts"' (Hart 1994:10). By naturalising violent impulses in female homosexuals, Ellis's commentary 'implicates inverts as inherently criminalistic' (Hart 1994:10).

In Ellis's text, female homosexuals are positioned as a threat not only to their female lovers – which sends women a strong message about the dangers of getting involved in same-sex relationships – but also to men who are positioned as innocent bystanders in these scenarios. Female homosexuals are even a danger to themselves when they are overcome with unrequited desire and take their own lives. As Hart (1994:10) maintains, 'Ellis effectively introduced the invert as criminal, not against nature, but against society.' The fact that the female invert's criminality and suicidal tendencies are linked to her love of women in Ellis's text suggests that same-sex desire is dangerous to everyone who is involved, either directly or indirectly, in homosexual relationships. The representation of female homosexuals as threatening is apparent in various contemporary films and television programmes, including, for instance, the film *Lesbian Vampire Killers* (Clark-Hall 2009), the television programme *Sugar Rush* (Baxendale 2005) and – the focus of this chapter – *Monster*. In the latter, Aileen Wuornos kills men in order to provide for her female partner and these murders eventually lead to her own downfall when she is imprisoned and executed.

Lesbian immaturity and violent criminality

While Jenkins saw *Monster* as providing an alternative view of Wuornos, this film reinforces conventional media depictions of her as a lonely woman who became a lesbian because she was 'desperate for a connection' (*A&E Biography* 2003).[3] Reflecting on her interest in writing this film, Jenkins (cited in Patrizio 2004) explains that she wanted to explore 'how love felt for somebody who hadn't had love in so long and they were going to be desperate enough to fight for it ever after'. In *Monster*, Wuornos's 'desperate' fight for love includes killing 'johns' in order to support her lover Selby, who is depicted as childish and unable or, perhaps more accurately, unwilling to provide for herself. Wuornos is likewise infantilised since her inability to control her emotions leads to irrational outbursts of anger and violence that culminate in the murders she commits.

Jenkins cast Charlize Theron, a Hollywood star who is well known for her beauty and elegance, to play Wuornos, who is referred to as 'Lee' in *Monster*. Reviews of *Monster* and interviews with Jenkins and Theron tend to focus on Theron's physical transformation to become 'leathery', 'stout and jowly' (Blackwelder n.d.) like Wuornos, rather than considering the messages that this film sends about lesbianism and same-sex relationships.[4] While *Monster* complicates understandings of Wuornos as inherently evil by alluding to the hard life she lived and suggesting that she initially killed out of self-defence, this film reinforces the conventional media representation of Wuornos as an unattractive woman who decided to have a same-sex relationship because she was disillusioned with men.

Lee's desperation is introduced early in *Monster* when she reflects on the day that she met her lover Selby, who is loosely based on Wuornos's real-life lover Tyria Moore. In a voiceover, Lee states:

> that day I met Selby I had spent most of the day sitting out in the rain ready to kill myself so you can understand I was flexible. Everybody's got to have faith in something. For me, all I had left was love and I was getting pretty sure I was never going to love a man again, so I was going to do it.

What this 'it' refers to is ambiguous, since Lee is seemingly either referring to suicide or having a relationship with a woman. This ambiguity sends the troubling message that lesbianism is similar to suicide, in that both are last resorts that only miserable and hopeless women would consider. As Lee is not previously depicted as having any interest in women, her relationship with Selby seems to develop because it fulfils a primarily emotional need for Lee, in particular her longing to be seen as beautiful, which the film identifies as her ultimate desire.

By casting Christina Ricci to play Selby, Jenkins transforms Wuornos's real-life lover Tyria Moore – a masculine woman who is quite large in stature – into the character of Selby, a petite, 'cute as a button lesbian' (Doherty 2004:4). As Horeck (2007:155) aptly notes, '[t]he visual contrast between the fictionalised character of Selby and Wuornos's real-life lover could not be more extreme, and given the extraordinary lengths to which Theron was transformed to look like Wuornos, [...this] seems a significant casting decision'. Even if, as Horeck speculates, Jenkins changed Moore's name and chose an actress who was the physical opposite of Moore in order to avoid legal prosecution if Moore were to be offended by how she is represented in the film, the resulting infantilisation of Selby in *Monster* must be critically analysed, since it reinforces the view that lesbians are immature and underdeveloped.

The infantilisation of lesbians is often traced back to the theory of 'arrested development', created by Sigmund Freud, who maintained that 'some individuals remain "stalled" at the homosexual phase of their psychosexual development' (Miller 2006:25). Yet a close reading of Ellis's 'Sexual inversion in women' shows that the link between homosexuality and immaturity was present in early sexology. Ellis describes the underdevelopment of certain body parts in female homosexuals. Reflecting on female congenital or 'true' inverts – that is, masculine women whose same-sex desire is innate – Ellis (1994[1897]:97–8) states that '[n]o masculine character is usually to be found in the sexual organs, which are sometimes underdeveloped'. Although Ellis (1925:258) provides a valuable challenge to the myth that female homosexuals had 'masculine' enlarged clitorises that they used to penetrate their partners, he does so by suggesting that the genitalia of female homosexuals are childlike. He reflects that one of his case studies, Miss M, was 'very small' at birth and may have been born prematurely (Ellis 1994[1897]:88). He observes that '[s]he is small, though her features are rather large. Medical examination shows a small vagina and orifice, though scarcely, perhaps, abnormally so in proportion to her size' (Ellis 1994[1897]:90). Even though Ellis recognises that Miss M's small genitalia may be 'normal' considering her petite stature, by emphasising her smallness he implies that she has not fully developed into a mature woman.

According to Ellis, it is not just 'true' inverts that are infantile, but also women who have 'acquired homosexuality'; that is, those for whom same-sex desire arises due to social circumstance. Ellis (1994[1897]:87) maintains that the latter women are 'not very robust and well-developed, physically or nervously, and [...] are not well adapted for child-bearing, but [...they] still possess many excellent qualities, and they are always womanly'. Ellis stresses that these feminine women are underdeveloped both physically and emotionally. He maintains that '[t]heir sexual impulses are seldom well marked but they are of strongly affectionate nature' (Ellis 1994[1897]:87). Their undeveloped (hetero)sexual impulses make them easy 'prey' for congenital inverts and their affectionate nature means that they are likely to become obsessively attached to their female partners. The 'clinging codependency' (Berardinelli and Ebert 2005:289) that Ellis associates with female homosexuality is apparent in *Monster* when Wuornos kills men to get money so that Selby will not leave her.

By depicting Lee as prone to irrational violent outbursts while Selby is childlike in both appearance and actions, *Monster* shows the pervasiveness of the past sexological association of lesbianism with immaturity. As a result of Selby behaving like a child who whines when she does not get what she wants and giggles uncontrollably when she does, Selby seems much younger than Tyria Moore who, according to *A&E Biography* (2003), was a 24-year-old woman who was working as a cleaner when she met Lee. Unlike Moore, Selby is unemployed and it is safe to assume that she is around 18 years old in the film since, in a phone call with her father, Selby explains that she is not going to return home because 'I'm an adult now'. The six-year age difference between Wuornos and Moore is exaggerated in *Monster* not only because Moore is recast as a teenager, but also due to the make-up that Theron wears to make her look weathered like Wuornos. As a result, Lee appears to be in her late thirties while, in actuality, Wuornos was only 30 when she met Moore. While physically exaggerated, the age difference between them is simultaneously undermined by the fact that they both act like children, which reinforces the idea that lesbians are emotionally immature. Lee's childishness is conveyed mainly through her irrational anger, as is apparent, for instance, when she gets mad at a bartender for closing the bar. Similarly, when a restaurant manager asks her and Selby to stop smoking and reaches to take Selby's cigarette from her hand, Lee hits his hand away and yells: 'Get your fucking hands off her you piece of shit. If she wants to smoke, she's going to smoke, alright. We're paying customers here.' Notably, during this altercation, in which Lee acts like a childhood bully who succeeds in intimidating three men, Selby sits in the background giggling, seemingly enjoying Lee's aggressive behaviour.

'Everything she did, she did for love': Lesbianism as criminal motivation

Monster links lesbianism with criminality by establishing Lee's fear of losing Selby as central to the murders that Lee commits. In her analysis of media depictions of Wuornos, Hart (2002:78) asserts: 'Not surprisingly, the "inseparable" bond that Aileen Wuornos had with her lover, Tyria Moore, the woman for whose sake she confessed to the murders, has been implicated as the "cause" of her criminality.' *Monster* reinforces the link between lesbianism and criminality by depicting Lee clinging on desperately to her relationship with Selby, willing to do anything, even commit murder, in order to keep Selby happy.

Lee first kills while she is performing sex work to make money so that she and Selby can rent a hotel room. The violence that Lee encounters as a sex worker is highlighted in this scene when she is brutally raped and beaten by a misogynistic 'john' who intends to kill her. Once she is able to free her bound hands, she screams, reaches for the gun in her bag, shoots the man who has just raped her and proceeds to hit him repeatedly with her gun, saying 'Fuck you. Fuck you, you fucking piece of shit'. Whereas Lee's anger is often shown to be irrational in *Monster*, in this scene her anger and violence are justified, as they are her only means of protecting herself when being sexually tortured and threatened with death.

After this attack, Lee tries, and fails, to find another form of employment. She finally explains to Selby why she quit 'hooking' stating:

> I was raped and beat to fuck and was going to be killed but [...] I didn't want to lose you and all I could think is how for the rest of your life you'd think I stood you up and how you'd never know that I fucking meant to be there. I didn't want to die thinking that maybe, that maybe you could have loved me so I killed him.

Although Lee first kills a man while fighting for her life, her blossoming relationship with Selby is provided as the underlying rationale for her violence. Lee fights back because she knows that Selby is emotionally fragile and lonely and does not want to hurt her by not showing up for their date. This rationale highlights that Lee and Selby are both desperate women who need each other in order to survive.

The association of lesbianism with murder in *Monster* becomes more and more disturbing as the film progresses, since Lee keeps killing in order to satisfy the financial demands of Selby, who tells Lee that she is 'starving'. Doherty (2004:5) maintains that Lee's second killing 'is entrepreneurial: she needs money for Selby, her passive-aggressive co-conspirator. "Why did you quit hooking?", Selby whines forcing lovesick Aileen – the breadwinner in the relationship – back out on the streets.' Selby is not an innocent bystander in regard to these murders; rather, in this film she uses her childlike appearance and behaviour to make Lee feel responsible for doing whatever is necessary in order to take care of her. Selby is thereby implicated in the murders that Lee commits and thus she, too, is positioned as a criminal lesbian.

It becomes clear when Lee returns to sex work and kills for the second time that she is still traumatised by the earlier rape. She seemingly ends up killing the second man because his actions and his request that she call him 'daddy' trigger memories of not only this recent rape but also childhood sexual abuse. By emphasising Lee's trauma, Jenkins complicates media depictions of Wuornos as a heartless killer. Furthermore, Lee chooses not to kill the next john she meets, a nervous man who has never had sex before, which suggests that Wuornos did not kill randomly or see all men as abusers who deserved to die.

Yet, as the film continues, Lee is increasingly depicted as a cold-hearted murderer, since she starts to kill men who do not threaten or abuse her. Lee creates stories in her head about these men in order to justify their deaths. She says to the third john she kills: 'So, um, you're married right? I don't get that fucking strange shit. You know come out here, do dirty things to them [prostitutes] instead of fucking your wife. Why, man, so you can rape them?' Lee's use of the term 'them' to refer to prostitutes in the above statement suggests that, after she commits her second murder, she quits being a sex worker; rather, she only poses as one in order to lure men into the woods where she can kill them and take their money and cars. Jenkins's choice to depict Lee as giving up sex work in favour of becoming a robbing murderess provides a powerful statement on the difficulties of being a prostitute by suggesting that killing people is a more appealing line of work.

After killing her third john, Lee discovers that this man was a retired police officer who had a disabled wife. Lee is exhausted and frightened when she returns to Selby, who is waiting for her to get them a car so that they can leave town before they are caught by the police. Lee explains that she killed a police officer and could not take his car because it had a tracking device on it. Selby demands that Lee find another car so that they can still leave as planned. Lee, who is lying on the bed dejected and exhausted, says, 'Selby, please.' This moment when Lee essentially asks Selby to take mercy on her emphasises Selby's ability to exert control over Lee by acting like a child who needs to be provided for and protected. By ordering Lee to get another car, Selby is indirectly telling her to kill once again. Yet Selby refuses to take any responsibility for Lee's actions, asserting: 'Lee, this isn't my plan. This is your deal, okay [...] You have to go get us a car and we're leaving now. Get up.' This scene highlights not only that Selby is implicated in Lee's killing spree, but also that it is Lee's destructive lesbian love for Selby that causes her to keep killing.

The next man Lee kills is a highly empathetic figure. He does not want to have sex with Lee but, rather, wants to help her to improve her life. He offers her a place to stay in his home, stating: 'Our son's room is empty if you want it and I'm sure my wife wouldn't mind a bit.' Although Lee does not want to kill this man, her gun falls out of her purse while she is trying to get out of his car and she ends up shooting him because she is afraid that he would otherwise report her to the police. He begs for mercy right before she kills him, saying: 'Oh god, my wife, my wife. My daughter is having a baby.' Lee's decision to kill this man indicates that she values her own life of crime and her relationship with Selby more than the life of this apparently selfless and caring family man. This scene thereby sends a powerful message about the disturbing and destructive nature of lesbian love.

The link between the title of this film and lesbian criminality becomes apparent when Lee, in a voiceover, talks about a Ferris wheel that she rode on as a child that was called 'The Monster'. Although Lee was fascinated with 'The Monster', she explains: 'when I finally got my chance [to ride it], I got so scared and nauseous that I threw up all over myself before it even made one full turn.' Lee's description of this ride as both alluring and dangerous reflects her relationship with Selby. Later on in the film, Lee ends up riding a Ferris wheel with Selby even though she is visibly averse to doing so. Although Lee looks like she is going to be sick while on the ride, she smiles when Selby looks at her. This film thus implies that this lesbian relationship creates a monster, since it inspires Lee to do things that she otherwise would not do and to pretend that she is not troubled by the crimes that she commits.

Risking empathy

Jenkins depicts Wuornos as a victim of circumstance by highlighting the role that trauma and same-sex love play in the murders she commits. Instead of encouraging viewers to empathetically identify with a strong, unrepentant female killer who fights back against male violence,

Monster suggests that women who commit violent crimes, especially masculine lesbian sex workers, can only be sympathetic subjects if they are shown to be, in reality, emotionally fragile, traumatised women.[5] Jenkins's depiction of Lee as a pathetic and desperate victim who is willing to do anything for (lesbian) love encourages viewers to pity her, and works to negate Wuornos's powerful critiques of misogyny and violence against women.

Whereas Wuornos asserted that she was helping to protect all women from abuse by killing aggressive johns, Jenkins depoliticises Lee's murderous acts by individualising and romanticising Lee's role as protector: Lee is invested in protecting only one woman, the woman she loves. This representation of Wuornos erases her strong commentaries on male dominance, as, for instance, is seen in her assertion:

> Those men are out of control, I'm sick and tired of those men out there thinking they can control us and do whatever they damn well please with our bodies and think they can get away with it [...Thinking] we're going to treat you the way we want to. Abuse you, treat you, destroy you – it don't matter to us, because we can get away with doing that. (cited in Hart 2002:68)

Wuornos maintains that she took the law into her own hands because she was tired of the legal system letting men 'get away with' harming women, especially those who are socially marginalised. Her description of these violent men as being 'out of control' positions her own actions as a rational response to confronting sexual aggression, and thereby counters portrayals of her as a hysterical woman who killed because she was unable to control her rage.

In *Monster*, Lee only once justifies her murders on the basis of resistance to male violence when she tells Selby:

> people kill each other every day and for what, huh? For politics, for religion and they're heroes. No, there's a lot of shit I can't do any more but killings [sic] not one of them. And letting those fucking bastards out there go and rape somebody else isn't either.

Here Lee, like Wuornos, implies that by murdering, she is protecting not just herself but also other women by ridding the world of (potential) rapists and misogynist murderers. Yet the separation of the statements that she cannot stop killing and that she cannot let men get away with raping other women undermines her assertion that she murders repeatedly *in order to* protect women and, rather, suggests that there is something compulsive about this violence.

Lee is remorseful at the end of *Monster*. When saying goodbye to Selby, Lee confesses: 'maybe I fucked up a little bit you know. I know I did. I did fuck up [...] You can help me [...] if you can forgive me.' Cause I don't know if I can forgive myself.' Unlike the repentant Lee in *Monster*, during her testimony Wuornos maintained: 'I killed them all because they got violent with me and I decided to defend myself ... I'm sure if after the fightin' they found I had a weapon, they would've shot me. So I just shot them' (cited in Hart 2002:61). Wuornos challenges the usual understanding of what constitutes self-defence by suggesting that these acts may be proactive as well as reactive. Furthermore, she counters descriptions of her as a serial killer by asserting: 'they say it's the number. Self-defense is self-defense, I don't care how many times it is' (cited in Hart 2002:81).[6] This description of self-defence allows for the fact that women – especially women like prostitutes who perform dangerous work – may have to defend themselves multiple times against male violence.

The significant rewriting of Wuornos's personality in *Monster* reflects the silencing not just of women who commit crimes but also of those who develop powerful critiques of violence against women. Doherty (2004:4) argues that *Monster* sends the message that 'Aileen is not a monster; she is a misunderstood girl, abused at home and on the streets, a pathetic misfit seeking love in all the wrong places'. Instead of pushing the limits of viewers' empathy by inviting identifications with a woman who survived abuse by fighting back – as Wuornos claimed was the case – Jenkins depicts Lee as a pathetic victim of circumstance and thereby encourages viewers to feel sorry for her, and look down on her. Risking empathy with Wuornos would mean closely attending to what she had to say about the murders she committed. It would also entail trying to imagine what it would be like to live through her experiences while remaining aware that this act of empathetic identification may be a 'useful fantasy but it remains a fantasy or illusion' (Jones 2007:22), since we can never know what it is like to live through another person's experiences. In order to empathise with Wuornos, it is not necessary to accept her version of events as truth or to agree with her actions, but it is important to recognise the valuable critiques of oppression and violence against women that she developed because of her lived experiences.

Monster shows that well-meaning texts that attempt to foster sympathy for people who are socially marginalised and oppressed, such as lesbian sex workers, do not necessarily convey queer-positive messages; rather, they may promote homophobic views and further silence queer people. While *Monster* complicates depictions of Wuornos as a man-hating lesbian who killed simply for the thrill of it and, unlike most media sources, shows Wuornos to have some positive, even admirable, character traits, this film also portrays her as being compelled to murder largely because of the pressures of her lesbian relationship. Although Jenkins offers an alternative perspective on this relationship by celebrating Lee's altruistic love for Selby, she follows usual media portrayals by reinscribing the view that lesbianism – which is shown as the underlying cause of Lee's killing spree – leads women to behave in horrific ways. The trailer to *Monster*, which is 'accompanied by the following captions on screen: Every Chance. Every Risk. Everything She Did. She Did For Love' (Horeck 2007:156), makes it clear that Lee commits these murders because of the 'excessive demands of queer love' (Horeck 2007:158). In doing so, *Monster* shows that the link between criminality and lesbianism that can be traced back to early sexology is, unfortunately, alive and well. Recognising that lesbians in contemporary popular culture are often depicted as threatening and predatory indicates that fear of same-sex desire continues to inform the struggles that shape the lives of lesbians in the present.

Notes

1. Patrizio (2004) notes that Jenkins has been 'accused [...] of being sympathetic toward Wuornos'. While Steele (2004), for instance, asserts that Jenkins was 'determined to humanize Aileen', Jenkins (cited in Blackwelder n.d.) maintains: 'I'm not sympathizing with her actions. I'm not saying that [... the men that she killed] were horrible men and they deserved what they got.'
2. While this chapter has focused on the link between the infantilisation of lesbians and their supposed criminal impulses, Hart (1994:14) provides an in-depth discussion of lesbian masculinity and criminality in *Fatal Women*.
3. The *A&E Biography* (2003) sends the message that Wuornos believed 'that any relationship with a man was not going to last [...T]hey were going to [...] dump her'.
4. For examples of interviews and reviews that discuss Theron's appearance in *Monster*, see, for instance, Berardinelli and Ebert (2005), Patrizio (2005) and Blackwelder (n.d.).
5. Reflecting on Hart's (1994) analysis of Wuornos, Horeck (2007:156) notes that Wuornos was 'reluctant to conform to the theory that she was a victim of past childhood trauma'.
6. There is much debate regarding whether Wuornos should be considered a serial killer. As Hart (2002:62) notes, '[t]he media and FBI have called her the first female serial killer'. Yet Wuornos does not fit the 'legal and psychological profile' of a serial killer because she killed 'heterosexual, white, middle-class, males, not members of powerless groups' (Hart 2002:63).

References

A&E Biography Aileen Wuornos. (2003). Available at http://www.youtube.com/watch?v=eFelaUkvNwI [accessed November 2009].

Bauer, Heike. (2009). *English Literary Sexology: Translations of Inversion, 1860–1930.* New York: Palgrave Macmillan.

Baxendale, Katie (Writer) and Sean Grundy (Director). (2005). Season 1, Episode 3 [television series episode]. In Johnny Capps (Producer), *Sugar Rush.* London: Channel 4.

Berardinelli, James and Roger Ebert. (2005). *Reel Views 2: The Ultimate Guide to the Best 1,000 Modern Movies on DVD and Video.* Boston, MA: Charles Justin.

Blackwelder, Rob. (n.d). An Interview with Patty Jenkins. *SPLICEDwire.* Available at http://splicedwire.com/03features/pjenkins.html [accessed May 2009].

Clark-Hall, Steve (Producer) and Phil Claydon (Director). (2009). *Lesbian Vampire Killers* [motion picture]. England: Momentum Pictures.

Crime and Investigation Network. (n.d.). Aileen Wuornos. Available at http://www.crimeandinvestigation.co.uk/crime-files/aileen-wuornos/biography.html [accessed March 2011].

Doherty, Thomas. (2004). Aileen Wuornos superstar. *Cineaste,* 29(3), 3–5.

Ellis, Havelock. (1925). *Studies in the Psychology of Sex: Sexual Inversion.* Philadelphia: F. A. Davis.

Ellis, Havelock and John Addington Symonds. (1994[1897]). *Sexual Inversion.* Manchester, NH: Ayer Company.

Felski, Rita. (1998). Introduction. In Lucy Bland and Laura Doan (eds), *Sexology in Culture: Labelling Bodies and Desires.* Chicago: University of Chicago Press.

Hart, Lynda. (1994). *Fatal Women: Lesbian Sexuality and the Mark of Aggression.* London: Routledge.

Hart, Lynda. (2002). Surpassing the word: Aileen Wuornos. *Women & Performance: A Journal of Feminist Theory,* 13(1), 61–88.

Horeck, Tanya. (2007). From documentary to drama: Capturing Aileen Wuornos. *Screen,* 48(2), 141–59.

Human, Jo (Producer) and Nick Broomfield and Joan Churchill (Directors). (2003). *Aileen:Life and Death of a Serial Killer* [motion picture]. United States: Lafayette Film.

Jones, Norman. (2007). *Gay and Lesbian Historical Fiction: Sexual Mystery and Post-Secular Narrative.* New York: Palgrave Macmillan.

Miller, Neil. (2006). *Out of the Past: Gay and Lesbian History from 1869 to the Present.* New York: Alyson Books.

Patrizio, Andy. (2004). An interview with Patty Jenkins: She makes a monster of a directorial debut. *IGN,* March. Available at http://dvd.ign.com/articles/519/519636p1.html [accessed June 2008].

Patty Jenkins on Befriending a 'Monster' (2010). Available at http://www.youtube.com/watch?v=MJ7GWiXaVuM [accessed March 2011].

Steele, Bruce. (2004). The making of a monster. *The Advocate,* March. Available at http://www.highbeam.com/doc/1G1-113759705.html [accessed March 2011].

Terry, Jennifer. (1999). *An American Obsession: Science, Medicine and Homosexuality in Modern Society.* Chicago: University of Chicago Press.

Theron, Charlize, Mark Damon, Clark Peterson, Donald Kushner and Brad Wyman (Producers) and Patty Jenkins (Director). (2003). *Monster* [motion picture]. New York: Newmarket Films.

Williams, Phillip. (2007). Killer movie, killer moviemaking: Writer-director Patty Jenkins on *Monster*. *MovieMaker*, February. Available at http://www.moviemaker. com/directing/article/killer_movie_killer_moviemaking_262[accessed March 2011].

Index